## ABOUT THE AUTHOR

MICHAEL GRUBER began freelance writing while working in Washington, D.C., in the Carter White House in the Office of Science and Technology Policy, and he later served as a policy analyst and speechwriter for the Environmental Protection Agency. Since 1988, he has been a full-time writer. His novels include *The Book of Air and Shadows*, *Night of the Jaguar*, *Tropic of Night*, and *Valley of Bones*. Married, with three grown children and an extremely large dog, he lives in Seattle.

www.michaelgruberbooks.com

## Books by Michael Gruber

*The Forgery of Venus*
*The Book of Air and Shadows*
*Night of the Jaguar*
*Valley of Bones*
*Tropic of Night*

# MICHAEL GRUBER

# NIGHT OF THE JAGUAR

HARPER

NEW YORK • LONDON • TORONTO • SYDNEY

**For
E.W.N.**

HARPER

This is a work of fiction. Names, characters, places, and incidents are products of the author's imagination or are used fictitiously and are not to be construed as real. Any resemblance to actual events, locales, organizations, or persons, living or dead, is entirely coincidental.

Grateful acknowledgment is made to reprint lyrics from "Brain Damage." Words and music by George Roger Waters, © 1973 by Roger Waters Music Overseas Ltd. Warner/ Chappell Artemis Music Ltd.

A hardcover edition of this book was published in 2006 by William Morrow, an imprint of HarperCollins Publishers.

HarperCollins books may be purchased for educational, business, or sales promotional use. For information please write: Special Markets Department, HarperCollins Publishers, 10 East 53rd Street, New York, NY 10022.

FIRST HARPER paperback published 2007; reissued 2009.

Library of Congress Cataloging-in-Publication Data is available upon request.

ISBN 978-0-06-165072-7

09  10  11  12  13      OV/RRD      10  9  8  7  6  5  4  3  2  1

*Credibilium tria sunt genera. Alia sunt quae semper creduntur et numquam intelleguntur: sicut est omnis historia, temporalia et humana gesta percurrens. Alia quae mox, ut creduntur, intelleguntur: sicut sunt omnes rationes humanae, vel de numeris, vel de quibuslibet disciplinis. Tertium, quae primo creduntur, et postea intelleguntur: qualia sunt ea, quae de divinis rebus non possunt intelligi, nisi ab his qui mundo sunt corde.*

There are three kinds of credible things: those that are always believed and never understood: such is all history, such are all temporal things and human actions. Those that are understood as soon as they are believed: such are all human reasonings, concerning numbers or any other discipline. Third, those that are believed first and understood afterward: such are those concerning divine things, which can only be comprehended by the clean of heart.

—St. Augustine, *Of Various Questions, LXXXIII, 48*

# One

*Jimmy Paz sits up in his bed, folding from the waist like a jackknife with his heart thumping so hard he can almost hear it over the whine of the air-conditioning. A moment of disorientation here: the dream has been so vivid. But he looks about him and accepts that he is in his bedroom in his house in South Miami, Florida; he can make out the familiar shapes in the real glow from the digital clock and the paler beams of moonlight slipping through the blinds, and he can feel the warm loom of his wife's body beside him. The clock tells him it is three-ten in the morning.*

*Paz has not had a dream like this in seven years, but back then he used to have them all the time. There are families that take dreams seriously, that discuss them around the breakfast table, but the Paz family is not one of them, although the mother of the family is a psychiatrist in training. Paz lies back on his pillow and considers the dream he has just had, which was the sort in which the dreamer has God-like perspective, floating over some scene and watching the players perform. He recalls something about a murder, someone has been shot in the middle of a village somewhere, and Paz and . . . Someone, some vast presence next to him, God or some powerful figure, is watching as the men who have shot the . . . Paz can't recall, but it is someone of significance . . . as the killers escape into a forest of tall trees, and these men, to ease their passage through the forest are . . .* exploding *the trees, touching them and making them disappear into red dust. The area through which they have passed is reduced to a rusty desert, and the dream carries a feeling of deep sadness and outrage about all this.*

*The killers are fleeing from a single man dressed in rough animal skins, like John the Baptist. He shoots at them with a bow and arrow, and they fall one by one, but it also seems as if their numbers do not decrease. Paz asks the Someone what this all means and in the dream gets an answer, but now he can't recall what it was. There's a sense of a vast intelligence there, both ferocious and calm . . .*

*Paz shakes his head violently, as if to make the scraps of dream-life go away, and at this motion his wife murmurs and stirs. He makes himself relax. This is not supposed to happen to him anymore, meaningful dreams. He has devoted the past seven years to expunging the memory of his previous life, when he was a police detective, during which career certain things happened to him that could not have happened in a rational world, and he has nearly convinced himself that they did not in fact occur, that* in fact *there are no saints or demons playing incomprehensible games in the unseen world, but that if such games did exist, as many believe, they would not involve Jimmy Paz as a player. Or pawn.*

*Now the dream is fading; he encourages this, he wills forgetfulness. He has already forgotten that the skin-clad man with the bow had his own brown face. He has forgotten the part about his daughter, Amelia. He has forgotten the cat.*

They shot the priest on a Sunday in the plaza of San Pedro Casivare just after mass, which he had just said because the regular priest was ill and because he volunteered to do it. He had not said mass for a congregation of believers in a long time, years. The priest lay there for some minutes; none of the townspeople wanted to touch him, because of the trouble he'd made and because the gunmen were still there leaning against their car, watching the people with interest and smoking cigars. The people stood in silent groups; above, on the rooftops, hopeful black vultures flapped and shoved. The day was hot and there was no breeze, so a few minutes before noon, the gunmen mounted their vehicle and drove away for some shade and a drink. As soon as they left, a group of Indians, six or seven of them, appeared as if from nowhere and carried him off in a blue blanket, down the street to the riverside, the path they took traced by drops of blood in the pale dust. At the edge of the wide brown water they laid him tenderly in a long dugout canoe, and paddled away, upriver toward the Puxto.

He didn't learn of the shooting until two days later, although he dreamed of white birds and so knew that someone's death was at hand. And he had seen the death of someone walking through the night, toward the river, and he knew from the look of it that it was not the death of a Speaker of Language, a Runiya, but of a *wai'ichura*. So he knew who the person was, for there was only one of these in the village. The man was alone in his little compound, lying in his hammock, inhabiting the light trance that was his usual state of being, when he heard the rattles sound. Slowly, and not without reluctance, he gathered the scattered fingers of his being back into his body, back into the daily, leaving the timeless life of the plants and animals, becoming again a human person, Moie.

Standing now, he washed his face at a clay basin and carefully spilled the water on the ground outside the house, stirring the mud with his toe, so that no enemy could seize on the dregs of his reflected face to do him harm. He took a drink of cool chicha beer from the clay pot, using a gourd. The rattlings continued.

He stepped outside into the dull dawn and saw that two terrified boys were shaking the rattle made of armadillo scales that the people used to summon Moie and also to frighten away any unpleasant spirits. He shouted out to stop the noise, that he had heard them and would be along in a short time. He went back into his house and ate some dried potatoes and meat. Then he rolled and lit a cigar, and while he smoked he hummed the usual prayer to the sun, thanking him for rising another day, and gathered the equipment he thought he would need into a finely woven net bag. He put on his headdress and his toucan-feather cape, and last of all he took the otter-skin bundle in which he kept his dreams and tied it securely around his middle. He could feel the dreams clicking a little as he walked out of his house, a comforting sound. The day was overcast, the air thick and thickening into mist among the taller trees. The mist muffled the forest sounds, the monkeys' shouts and the birds' cries; but Moie didn't need sounds to know what was going on in the forest. He strode down the path, followed at a careful interval by the two boys.

The village was not distant, just far enough to be somewhat safe from the magical wars that raged around Moie's compound, and far enough from the river to avoid the spirits of the drowned people and the water witches. A dozen or so clan longhouses were laid out along rough streets leading out from a central plaza around the father tree, and among these stood some smaller structures for the holy societies to meet in, and pens for the chickens and pigs. The father tree was what they called a *ry'uulu*, a big-leaf mahogany, towering 150 feet into the clouds; it took eight men clutching hands to surround its buttressed base. Moie greeted the father tree politely, using the holy language, and the tree answered that he was welcome to come into the village. Then, in everyday language, Moie asked the boys where the priest was. In the dead-singing house, they replied. The "church," he corrected, using the Spanish word. In his youth, Moie had gone downriver to where the *wai'ichuranan* came from, and lived among the dead people for several years, and still recalled their language. It was what he used to talk with the priest.

Moie entered the church, just an ordinary pole-built, palm-thatched longhouse, most of which was used for services. The priest was good with his hands and had built the altar of purpleheart wood and of the same wood had made a large crucifix to hang above it. Nailed to it with real nails was an image of the man the people called Jan'ichupitaolik, or "the person who is alive and dead at the same time." Father Perrin had made him look like a man of the Runiya, with the bowl haircut shaved high on the sides and the facial and body tattooing. Moie bowed politely. Technically he was a Christian, having been baptized with the name Juan Bautista many years ago, but like many such, he did not practice the religion, nor did he believe in its creed. He loved the priest and had allowed the water to be poured on his head and on those of the others in the village as a courtesy. In return he had initiated the priest with the *ayahuasca* and the other sacraments of the Runiya.

Father Perrin was lying in his hammock in the little space behind a matting curtain he called the rectory, always with a smile. Moie didn't understand this joke, but he always smiled, too. The priest had worn his *wai'ichura* clothes to the town, which he never did anymore at Home. He had explained that no one would talk to him there unless he wore these clothes, especially the white collar around his neck, although it was no longer quite white, was gray-green with mold. And Moie had understood that very well, he himself always wore special clothing when he talked to important persons in his own work. The women had removed these clothes, however, and the priest lay naked in his hammock, looking more like a corpse than he usually did. He had three bullet wounds in his chest and belly, now neatly bound with poultices of holy plants. Moie placed his hand on these and felt the vegetable spirits murmuring as they worked, murmuring unhappily because it was past their time to work.

The people stood back silently while Moie made his examination, so he gestured for Xlane to come forward. Xlane was the vegetable spirit doctor of the village as Moie was the animal spirit doctor. They discussed the patient in low voices. Xlane said, "He was nearly dead when they brought him in. That's why I had them call you. Also, since he's a *wai'ichura*, I wasn't sure what to do. I thought his death might be different from ours. Can you see it, Moie Amaura?"

Moie cocked his head and looked around the little cell in the sideways, squinting fashion he had been taught long ago. He saw them, the *achauritan* of the people, hovering behind their left shoulders, vague and clouded in the young ones, more solid in those who would die sooner. The priest's *achaurit* was standing just behind the man's head, as solid as flesh itself, partially obscured by the woman who was fanning the wounded man's face with a palm leaf. Moie told that woman to stop and then told her and the rest of the people to leave the room. When they were gone, he lowered himself to the mat and brought out from his net bag a small stoppered clay flask and a tiny drum. He tapped a tune on the drum and sang his name song, so that the guards who kept the passes into the spirit lands would know him, that he was *amaura*, an initiate, wise and strong, and also that he meant no harm and that he was not a witch set on capturing any of the spirits they guarded. When he was done with that, he inserted a narrow reed into the clay flask and breathed the *yana* into his nostrils, one long shuddering breath for each nostril.

After some time he saw that the colors were draining out of the ordinary things in the room. The hammock with its dying man, the roof beams, the thatch hanging down, the plants outside, and the few possessions of the priest all became gray and semitransparent like smoke, and all the color in the room was concentrated in the figure of the death and in his own body, which glowed ruddy as hot coals. This was as usual, but Moie was surprised that there were no glowing green and red threads connecting the death to the man it owned. He cleared his throat and addressed the bright figure in the holy language.

"*Achaurit* of Father Perrin, this harmless person sees that the threads have been broken. Why are you still here and not flying to the moon to join the other dead? Is it because Father Perrin is a *wai'ichura*?"

"So it appears," said the death. "The *wai'ichuranan* hold their deaths inside them and are dead all the time, but I seem to be different. It may be because he has spent so much time with you speaking people, or for some other reason. In any case, I can't fly away, even though the threads are cut. I'm afraid I might become a ghost."

Moie felt the cold sweat spring up and run down his flanks and face. There hadn't been a ghost in Home for a long time. The last one was a murdered man, whose murderer had fled down the river and so could not pay the murder fee to the clan of the dead man. The furious ghost had killed dozens of people through disease and a variety of physical catastrophes—fires, drowning, the arrows of other tribes, the ravenings of animals. The Runiya have no word for *accident*. It had taken Moie weeks of spirit travel to find the culprit and force him to make the world correct again. He sincerely hoped he would not have to do it again.

"Do I have to find the people who shot him and make them pay the fee?" he asked. "And how will I find Father Perrin's clan in the lands of the dead people?"

"No, it has nothing to do with fees and clans. This is a *wai'ichura* and they are not like you. He wants to tell you something, and until he does, I can't leave for the places you know." This was a polite expression for the dwelling of the dead high above the world. "Now, hear what he has to say, and then I will leave you. It's much too warm for me in this world."

With that, the *achaurit* breathed himself into the nostrils of the dying man, who coughed twice, opened his eyes, and raised his head.

"What happened?" he said in Spanish when he saw Moie. "I was talking with my mother and she said, 'Oh, Timmy, you always were one for forgetting things. You have to go back for a while.' "

Moie was happy to see the man revived but uncomfortable with what he was saying. There were good reasons why Rain and Earth had decreed a barrier between the world of people and the world of the dead when the two of them had first coupled and brought forth Jaguar and then the first human children. The priest sat up in the hammock and looked at Moie and at his own body, feeling the wounds, touching his pale flesh. He was a spare little man, not much larger than Moie, darkened on arms and head by the sun. He had a nose like a parrot, though, and a short beard, the two things that marked him as a stranger. The women called him *vaitih,* which sounded enough like "father" to pass as courtesy but was actually the name of a small green parrot. Moie did not approve of this, but one could do nothing with women and their jokes. Moie always called him Tim, which sounded like a word the Runiya used for a clumsy but endearing baby.

"It's hard to explain," said Moie. "The words for it are not in this language, you know? But you are dead and your death can't go away where it belongs before you tell me something. So now I'm talking to you."

"I see," said the priest after a long pause. "Well, this wasn't what I expected. What do I do now?"

"Your death said you had something to say to us. Please say it and then go."

"Yes, we have the same tradition." Father Perrin let out a dry chuckle, and Moie shivered a little. The laughter of the dead is uncongenial. "My final confession, and . . . hm, this is very strange, I find I don't care about my horrible secrets anymore."

"No," said Moie, "the dead always tell the truth. Go ahead, please."

Another chuckle. "All right, then. Bless me, Father, for I have sinned. It has been twenty-two years and I don't know how many days since my last confession. Do you remember the day I came here, Moie?"

"Yes. We were going to kill you like we always kill *wai'ichuranan,* but you started to fish in a strange way and we wanted to see that."

Both men looked up at the priest's fly rod where it hung from the ceiling.

"Yes, I was using an old Greenwell's Glory on an eight-pound longbelly line and I got a strike in two minutes. It was a peacock bass, a *tucunaré*."

"I remember. We were amazed. And afterward you caught the biggest *pacu* we had ever seen. Then you cleaned and cooked them and invited everyone to eat, and we laughed when you ate the flesh hot."

"Yes, I didn't know that fish was a cold animal and had to be eaten cold. And that's why you didn't shoot me full of poisoned darts. I wondered about that at the time. A little disappointing, really."

"You desired death?"

"Oh, yes. That's how I ended up here."

"I thought it was the fishing."

"I lied about that and about wanting to save your souls. A complete fraud, really. A parody of a failed priest. No, really, I was seeking death and an end to shame. Now this is the truth. I was working in the countryside outside Cali, where the drug lords and the *latifundistas* were cheating people out of the land they were supposed to have under the agricultural reform and I spoke up for them, I organized meetings. Pathetic little Christian acts, and I was told to keep my mouth shut and say mass and comfort the widows and orphans when the thugs murdered the men. But I didn't shut up. I suppose I had romantic ideas about martyrdom, and first they shot at me but missed, and then they shot at me again and missed, there was a boy on a motorbike who did it, but his tire hit a nail or something and blew out and he was killed, God rest his wretched soul, and then they tried to bomb my truck, but something went wrong with the bomb and so the assassin was killed instead. This gave me my little reputation and I think the men who were trying to kill me became frightened, because they're all superstitious heathens just like you, my dear friend, but lucky for them they needn't have bothered because I ruined myself with Judy. Do you know that expression Punch and Judy? No, of course you don't. Punch and Judy is the name of a . . . a kind of dance for children, but Punch is also a kind of pisco and Judy is a woman's name in my land, and these are the two main reasons for priests to fail—drinking and women. Boys, too, I suppose, but that's not in the expression yet. And strangely enough she really *was* named Judy, Judy Ralston. She was a nurse, from Braintree, Massachusetts. She was a short person and she had a big bush of black hair and light green eyes and she was always angry, angry at the government, the police, the health officials in Cali, and the church. A lapsed Catholic, I should add. Tell me, do you know what *lonely* means, my friend?"

"I do. We have no word for this, as you know, but when I was down the river as a boy, I learned this word and I felt the feeling twisting in my heart."

"Yes, well, it comes with the territory, but I never realized what it would mean. No one to talk to, no books, no sound of your native tongue in your ears. I didn't realize how much I was suffering until she arrived with her jeep and her bags of medicines and her American voice."

"You took her in your hammock."

"No, she took me in *her* hammock: yes I know, it's very *siwix* to do so, but we were depraved. She only had to ask me once, this was after the car bombing, and we were shaking in terror as we removed our clothes. She knew everything and I knew nothing and so we continued in love until she conceived a child. Tell me, if I say *abortion,* do you know what I'm saying?"

"No, what does it mean?"

"A child that is unwanted and the woman gets rid of it?"

Moie's face lit with comprehension. "Ah, yes, you mean *hninxa,* a girl baby is given to Jaguar." Moie knew that the priest did not approve of this practice, but he also knew that the dead are beyond anger.

"Yes, I suppose it is similar, but in our case the baby was given to the Cali Water and Sewer Authority. Ah, now I see that while the dead can't lie, they can still feel shame. I told myself that this baby would be the ruin of important work, if this should be discovered, I was a famous figure in the region, a symbol of those who wished to defy the land thieves and *drogeros,* and this was more important than just one baby. So she came back, and we continued, but after that it wasn't the same. Still we clung to it, hating and loving at the same time; and you have no idea what I am talking about. But later, of course, someone told the bishop, and there was an investigation, by the police, no less. A thousand murders a year in Cali and hardly one of them solved, but they had time for my abortion. So they sent me back to America, or they tried to, but when I was at the airport I could not bear the thought of going back and being thrown out, I feared the contempt and the pain I would cause more than I feared the prospect of damnation and so at the last moment I changed my ticket and took a different plane, not to Bogotá and Los Angeles but the one to San José del Guaviare, and from there I walked south, into the forest. I meant to walk along the river and fish, until God took me, but instead I found you. It seems, however, that I was always meant to be shot by a thug, and so despite my wretchedness and dishonor I have been given the grace of being allowed to die for the people. Blessed are the ways of the Lord."

"So this is what you wanted to tell me? About how you came here?"

"Not at all, that was nothing. What I had to tell you is that you and all your people are in great danger. The dead people plan to build a road and bridge your river and come into the Puxto and destroy it."

"But how can they do this? The Puxto is ours forever. It is a native reserve. Or so you have always said."

"Oh, yes, it is a reserve, the whole mesa is protected by law. But greed will find a way. There is a company that wants your trees. The Puxto has one of the last great stands of virgin tropical hardwoods in Colombia. Bribes have been paid. You don't understand what I am saying, do you?"

Moie made the upward chin-tilt that the Runiya use to indicate bafflement.

"All right," said the priest. "You know what money is, yes?"

"Of course! I have lived with the dead people and am not an ignorant man. It is leaves with the faces of people or animals on them. You work and they give them, and then you give them and get things. A dead man gives some money to another dead man and he gives him a machete, and another gives and he gets a bottle of pisco."

"Very good, Moie, you're practically an economist. So let's say one of those leaves you saw is a thousand-peso note. Three of those leaves are the same as one of the leaves from my part of the land of the dead, which we call a dollar."

"Yes, I have heard that word."

"I'll bet. There's no escape from it. Now a one-thousand-peso note buys a bottle of pisco, and ten of them buys a machete. And a piece of *ry'uulu* wood, what they call big-leaf mahogany, just so big"—here the priest sketched a cubic meter in the air—"is worth fifteen hundred dollars." The priest translated this sum into pisco and machetes, so many hands of each, hands of hands of hands of machetes and bottles of cane liquor, and the living man laughed. "That is insane," he said. "No one could ever wear out that many machetes, and ten hands of people could not drink that much pisco in their whole lives."

It was hard to stop giggling, although he knew it was impolite to laugh in the presence of the dead, but he couldn't stop thinking of all those *wai'ichuranan* reeling drunk and waving clusters of machetes in both hands.

When he sputtered into silence, the priest continued. "Yes, insane, but also the truth. They want the *ry'uuluan* and the other big hardwoods and they will come up to the Puxto on their road and cut every tree they find, rip the forest down to bare red earth, and when the government comes and tells them they have done wrong they will say, oh, we're sorry, and pay a fine—thirty dollars a tree and they will take the dead trees away, laughing. That is how it's done. And if you try to stop them they will shoot you all, as they have shot me."

Moie let these words into his ears but they had no grip on

his mind, for to say that the Puxto could be destroyed was like saying the sky could be brought down or the air turned into water. The dead man seemed to read his mind (nor did this surprise him) and said, "Yes, they surely can, they have machines that cut like many hands of men at once and they will do it unless they are stopped. This is why I went to San Pedro and this is why they killed me."

"I will go to San Pedro, too," said Moie, "and I, too, will tell them to stop this. Perhaps they will not kill me as easily."

"I believe they would have some trouble killing you, but even so, it will do no good. I was a fool to think it. No, the men in San Pedro are only little twigs of the thing. Even those in Bogotá are only the branches. To stop it one must go to Miami in America, my homeland, where the great trunk and roots of the thing are, and let everyone there know what is happening in the Puxto. But I am dead now and there is no one else to go."

"I will go."

"Oh, my friend, you don't know how far it is, and you can't speak their language . . ."

"I can. I speak the language of the *wai'ichuranan* very well."

"No, you speak Spanish very badly, with many words in Quechua and your own language, and it is good enough to speak with me, but they would only laugh at you at the Con-suela office."

"What is this Consuela office?" Moie was upset by these words. It had been a long, long time since anyone had laughed at him.

"It is . . . it is like a hunting band of the *wai'ichuranan,* and they hunt for dollars, and hunt and hunt and as much as they get they are never satisfied, they never say we have enough, let us sing and eat until it is all gone, as you alive people do."

"Because they are dead."

"Indeed. Because they are dead. Now let me tell you one more thing. Who knows, some miracle may still happen, someone from outside will take notice and will come here to help. I will say the names of the men who are in control of Consuela Holdings LLC. It is not a thing well known because such men are like anacondas, they hide in the shadows and take their prey by stealth, they grab and then they strangle. So you must remember. Can you do this?"

In answer, Moie plucked a fiber from the floor mat and held it up, and said, "Say their names!" The priest said four names, and as each one fell into the air, Moie knotted it into the fiber. When the last had passed the dead lips, a change came over Father Perrin. His eyes opened wide and he stared, as if something wonderful was about to arrive, the look of a child given a piece of salt to lick. Then he fell back into the hammock, and Moie saw his death depart in good order and felt greatly relieved.

After this, Moie had to wait for an interval before he was in a state to talk to live people again, and he passed the time in thinking about the late Father Perrin and Jaguar and *cosmology*. That was one of the words he had learned in his conversations with the priest. He had not known that there even *was* a language to talk about such things, for the ordinary speech of his people was *inside* their lives; they told the stories of how the world came to be, and for those things that could not be uttered there was music and dancing. Moie and his fellow *jampirinan* had the holy speech, yes, but that was used only to intercede with the spirit world and influence it to help the people. As far as Moie knew, no Runiya had ever stood with his mind outside of everything that there was and looked at it whole, like a woman looks at a yam. It was frightening, but exhilarating as well.

Moie had heard that in other villages, the first thing the *wai'ichura* missionaries did was to tell the people that everything they believed was false, and that only the story they told of Jan'ichupitaolik was true, and they gave food and things to the people so that they would see that the missionaries were right and that Jan'ichupitaolik didn't like to see people without clothes, and also hated the things that people had always done to keep harmony with the spirit world. Father Perrin was not a missionary of that kind, not a missionary at all, as he often said, and he thought that the Runiya were mostly fine as they were. He said that Jaguar was nearly the same as Jan'ichupitaolik and that Earth was nearly the same as the Father and that Rain was nearly the same as the Holy Spirit, but that Jaguar didn't want the Runiya to give him little girls to eat anymore, that was the one thing that made him angry. When Jaguar ate a girl, Father Perrin would take his rod and go fishing, sometimes for days, and not talk to Moie at all. Afterward, he would forgive Moie and make him promise not to do it anymore, and Moie would try to explain that he was not the master of Jaguar, that Jaguar came when he would and that nothing could stop him. Father Tim refused to accept this. It was a *theological* difference (another useful word).

Forgiveness also confused Moie, as did Father Perrin's idea that love rather than power was the ruling force of the world. One had enemies, and the duty of a man was to destroy them if he could and to appease them if he could not. The idea that one should love enemies seemed insane to him and not *ryuxit*. Father Perrin said that the *wai'ichuranan* didn't have that word, but only words for little pieces of it, like *harmony, beauty, peace,* and *bliss.* Moie knew that the world was ruled by *ryuxit,* the harmony of the different children of Jaguar, tree rock snake fish bird all together with humans. What was not *ryuxit* was *siwix,* those things that were disharmonious and therefore forbidden. One might love that which was *ryuxit,* as one loved a woman, but one could not love *siwix* things, that was a contradiction. A *paradox.* Father Perrin had taught him that word, too, meaning things that could be true and not true at the same time, like something being wet *and* dry or light *and* dark. Father Perrin said that Rain, Earth, and Jaguar were all separate but at the same time one and the same. I will make you a theologian before I die, he used to say; that was what the dead people called their *jampirinan.* Moie was not so sure about this, for such thoughts made his head ache, but still the idea plucked at his mind, and he could see that there was something in it beyond his power to express. According to Father Perrin, Jan'ichupitaolik could love *siwix,* and by loving it, he changed it into *ryuxit,* and not only that, but a better *ryuxit* than had been before.

Moie would have certainly dismissed all of this as dead people's nonsense, if he had not visited Father Perrin's spirit in a dream shortly after the priest had arrived at Home. There he found not the shriveled sad soul characteristic of the *wai'ichuranan,* but something immense and powerful, *ryuxit* beyond *ryuxit.* So he had let the man live in Home and set up his church and had taught him as much as he thought proper about the ways of the Runiya and of *axa'jampirin,* the path of the spirits, and he had learned much about the *ax-a'jampirin* of the dead people.

Now Tim was dead, and with Jaguar above the moon, or in heaven with his God, and perhaps this was really the same thing, as Father Perrin had often suggested. Moie sighed and rose and looked at the corpse. The flies and cockroaches had found the body already, they were busy laying their eggs in eyes and mouth and nibbling in dark squirming clots at the torn flesh around the three wounds. He called out and men came in and they took the body down to the river. There Moie made the ritual cuts and filled the body cavity with six large round white stones and drilled a hole into the brain to prevent a witch from reanimating it, and then they sang the funeral songs, as they would have for one of their own, and gave the body to Rain through her child, the River.

The church was sealed up, both physically with mats and ropes and against spirit invasion by Moie, using secret means. No human person would loot there, nor would any mischievous spirit come to feed on the spiritual detritus of the former inhabitant. There was the usual party that night, with food, chicha, and dancing, for Father Perrin was well liked in Home and also the moon was full, which was always propitious. A person who died at the full of the moon was a friend of Jaguar and so to be especially honored. Moie drank less than usual at the wake, and left while the dancing was still going on. He went on trails his feet knew well, although the moonlight barely penetrated the heavy canopy of foliage and it was dark enough that he could see little floating bright specks, as if his eyes were shut. After a while the ground beneath his feet grew harder, more rocky, and the trees grew shrubbier, and then he was on the limestone escarpment that rose above the rain forest in the center of Puxto mesa. From here he had an unobstructed view of the night sky and this was by design, for the people had always kept this small area clear of growth, as it was sacred to Jaguar and served the Runiya as both a cathedral and an observatory, although with a congregation or astronomical staff of only one.

In the center of this space was a long, low white boulder, almost the shape of a crouched cat, upon which, soon after the creation of the universe, First Man had carved an image of his maker. First Man had made the head and ears, made the mouth open, and placed two large natural emeralds in the eye sockets. He had incised the rosettes all over it as well, and these had grown dark moss in them, so that the effect was startlingly lifelike at night.

Moie sat on a low stone before this image and took two nostrils of *yana* and sang his name song in a loud clear voice, asking permission to speak to his god. Jaguar was hiding now behind clouds that blew past him like palm fronds in a storm. He peeked out, for a moment, then again, and now a long cloud tore away and he shone clear against the black sky, the two deep eyes, the muzzle and its curving mouth, the spotted face and net of whiskers. In the holy language, Moie prayed for aid for himself and his people, and after some time had passed Jaguar swelled and grew brighter and descended from the heavens to his image below.

The god listened while Moie told his tale, of the priest and his death and the danger he had foretold. Then the Lord Jaguar spoke, the voice seeming to emerge from the stone jaws. He said, Moie, you must go into the land of the dead and tell the dead people that this is forbidden to them. Say that the Puxto is for me and the speakers of language, the Runiya, and not for the dead.

At this Moie trembled with fear and spoke, "*Tayit,* how can one human do this? The dead people are so many, and I don't speak their language very well. They will laugh at me and turn me away from their village."

Jaguar answered, I will provide you with allies from the dead people who will speak my words for you. And if the lords of the dead people do not do as I demand, I will slay them and feed on their livers. Now drive the fear from your own heart, Moie, for I will go with you and my strength will be yours. And the Lord Jaguar told him other things that would help him on this journey. Then Jaguar sent a part of himself leaping from the stone mouth and it entered Moie through his nostrils and Moie fell senseless on the ground.

When he came to himself again it was dawn, dull and overcast with a chilling mist. Moie rose and walked back down to the village, slapping his arms and chest to restore feeling. Fear was throbbing deep in his belly, but it didn't rise to his heart, because Jaguar was there. The village was asleep, silent but for the sounds of the animals, the clucking of the chickens and the grunts of the pigs oddly muffled by the mist. He thought briefly about what the people would say when they found him gone. Some other *jampiri* would no doubt try to take his place and the people would either accept him or not, or there might be a struggle between two *jampirinan* and some Runiya might be harmed. In any case he might have died on any day, not that there was much difference between dying and what he was about to do. He would have liked to turn his profession over to an apprentice, but he had none. Jaguar had not marked any boys for that in a long time.

Arriving at the church, he tore down the matting and went in. There was a cloth suitcase in the room where the man had died. Moie took it and the priest's clothing and fishing tackle and went back to his compound. Pucu, the younger of the two women, was already awake. "Where are you going?" she asked.

"Away. Put some food in a basket." As she did so, he gathered the materials of his profession into a net bag, and also took his blowgun and darts and a water skin of peccary with the fur still on it.

"When will you be back?" she asked. He looked at her and made his expression stern, although he ached to think that this sweet young face was the last face of his people he would ever look upon. He roped his burden into a convenient pack and said, "When you see me return you will know," and strode off.

At the river, he selected a new one-man fishing canoe, loaded his things into its prow, selected a paddle and a spare and a gourd for bailing, and without a backward look pushed off into the black river, which was called Paluto by the dead people. The rain continued to fall, sometimes a drizzle, more often in sheets that beat at his naked back. By late afternoon he was past San Pedro Casivare, shielded by the downpour from the eyes of the *wai'ichuranan.*

He paddled for days upon days, hands of days, sleeping fitfully, eating the dried food he had brought until it was gone and afterward subsisting on fish he caught with the priest's rod and reel, eaten raw, and an occasional piece of fruit he found floating on the river or hanging over it from a tree. He chewed on coca leaves to fight hunger and exhaustion. Once he shot a monkey with the blowgun, but it sank before he could get to it. He rode the Paluto as it debouched into the Meta, a much wider stream. Moie didn't know its name, nor did he know that the even vaster river the Meta joined was called the Orinoco by the dead people. There was a substantial town at the junction of the two rivers, and now there were large boats in the channel, things that towered over his craft like hills. He also passed swift white vessels full of *wai'ichuranan,* males and females, dressed in bright clothing like parrots, and like parrots they screamed and clucked at him and pointed black sticks and silver gourds at him as he paddled by, but he was not harmed. Now he traveled only when the rain was heavy or very early in the morning. His spirits fell, and Jaguar sent unpleasant dreams of the dead people and their endless villages, the streets of stone and the cliff houses made from stone and glass like shining solid air and rolling things that stank and the dead people thronging around, more than hands could calculate, as many as the leaves in a forest.

In the sky, Jaguar left to visit his mother, Rain. He shrank to emptiness. Then he grew tired of his mother's advice, as all men do, and he returned to shine down round and bright on the endless waters, and left again, and returned again and left. In places Moie encountered boiling rapids and whirlpools, but he had spent much of his life navigating the white waters of the upper Paluto and these proved no worse. After the rapids came calm brown waters so wide that in the early-morning mists he could not see either shore. The rains slowed and ceased and the country around the Orinoco changed from rain forest to drier palm lands. He passed a large city at night, looking like the city in his dream, with bright dots of light streaming from its cliff houses, like captured stars. A roaring thing crossed the air above the river and disappeared. He had heard that the dead people had metal canoes that flew like birds and he saw it was true. Moie himself flew through the air silently using a different method.

After more days, there was another great city and then the palm lands turned to swamp and the river divided itself into narrower streams. He let Jaguar guide his direction and one day he dipped his hand into the river and drank and found the water was salt. He had heard from Father Perrin that the sea was salt, and had not really believed it, but now he knew it was so.

He passed mangrove forests and mud flats and ahead lay a flat sheet of water and in the far horizon a brown smudge that he thought must be Miami America. He tied his canoe to a mangrove root and, taking his blowgun, he waded along the edge of the sea. Before long he came to a shallow bay full of feeding flamingos and other seabirds. He shot two flamingos. On the beach he built a big fire and dismembered the birds and scorched their feathers off and then wrapped the meat in palm leaves and mud and buried them in the hot coals. He ate the stringy flesh and drank water from his skin. Then he headed his canoe out into the gently rolling waves.

It took him all day to cross the ocean, and when he got to the other shore, he was mildly surprised to see that America looked very much like San Pedro Casivare. Father Perrin had told him many stories about his home and it was not like this: only a shambling wooden dock, some low shacks among the palm and pepper trees, and black-skinned people going about their business. He dragged his canoe to the sands and went ashore, properly dressed in his feathered shoulder cape and quetzal-feather hat, for he wanted these people to know he was a *jampiri* and so to be respected. There were some black people standing and sitting in front of a small building and he went up to them and in Spanish said, "Pardon, sirs and madams, is this Miami America?"

They gaped at him. He asked the question again, but they just chattered in a strange tongue and their children surrounded him, staring. A woman ran off down the street and returned with an old yellowish man. This person spoke Spanish. He asked Moie where he came from. From Home, said Moie, and I want to know, is this Miami America, for I have crossed the sea after traveling on many rivers and I have heard it is on the other side of the sea.

The man said, no, it was not Miami, it was the town of Fernandino on the island of Trinidad, and he also said you have not crossed the sea at all, but only the Gulf of Paria. He explained that the sea was much, much bigger and that one could not cross it in a canoe. And would the gentleman like something to drink?

So they sat on chairs in the shade and drank a kind of chicha from bottles, which Moie had not done since he was a boy, and the man, Ezra, told him that he had at one time traveled the whole world, working on the white man's ships, which were canoes as large as hills, and he knew both Spanish and English, the language they spoke in America, although in Miami they spoke Spanish, too. And he said that if the gentleman wanted to go to Miami, he should go to Port of Spain, north of here, and find a ship and get aboard it secretly at night and hide and it would carry him to Miami. Ezra told him many things about how to do this, and the many dangers involved, for in the old days when he was a sailor he had in this way helped many people go to America, to become rich, as he had become rich working for the ships.

Then Ezra called out, and a woman brought a thing, and Ezra put another shining thing on his face that made his eyes look like a fish's eyes and studied the thing the woman had brought, which was white as a cloud and rustled like leaves and was covered with little black marks, like dead ants. Moie had seen Father Perrin do the same with the thing he called Bible, which was how he spoke to the dead of his people. Moie waited respectfully while Ezra spoke to the dead and then Ezra smiled and said that the freighter *Guyana Castle* would leave for Miami in two days with a load of sawn timber. He knew this ship and described it, so that Moie would know it, even at night. Moie thanked him, and Ezra said that it was he that should be grateful, for Moie was the most interesting thing that had happened in Fernandino since the last hurricane. He also said, when you get to Miami, you should get you some clothes, because they would arrest you looking like that. And he explained what *arrest* was.

Two nights later, Moie was in his canoe looking up at the rusting black hull of the *Guyana Castle*. The ship was tied to a long street that went out into the water, and this street was lit with *wai'ichura* lights that were brighter than the moon at the full, and there were men there standing in front of a small street that led upward into the ship. But Moie was on the other side, on the black, oily water, nearly invisible in the shade of the ship itself. Five lengths of men above him there was a low place on the ship's side, where he had to climb. No man could climb up that sheer wall, so Moie mixed some powders together from small skin sacks he took from his net bag, and sucked the powders through a tube into his nostrils, and began a low chant. While he chanted he wrapped everything he wanted to take with him in a rope and placed the end of the rope in his mouth. Now his senses changed, expanded, while the part of him that was Moie shrank away. He smelled and heard things humans could not sense. Through different eyes he stared up at the rail far above. A tension built in his hind limbs. There was a fading sensation of rising through the air before he quite vanished to himself.

When he discovered he was Moie once more, he was in darkness deep in the belly of the ship, surrounded by the stink of oil and steam and the more familiar smell of cut wood. Hard shapes pressed against his back and the ship was no longer docked, but moving, her engines a constant throb in his ears and through his whole body. He was exhausted as he always was by such experiences, but he remembered to keep well hidden, and he had the suitcase and his other possessions at hand. After drinking some water from his water skin, he made himself as comfortable as he could amid the pallets of lumber and ate the herbs and started the ritual that would slow his body's functions down to a level near to death, although he knew his spirit would keep lively enough in a different world.

Silence awakened him, and the absence of motion. He opened his eyes to dim light. They had broken open the hatches at the bow of the ship, and shafts of sunlight made bright pillars there. Moie moved farther astern and lower down, so that the stacked boards were like a dark cliff above him. Machinery clanked and groaned and Moie waited for the night, as Ezra had advised. He was extremely hungry.

The sunlight faded, the noises of unloading ceased, and the only sounds he heard were the fugitive rumbles and clankings of *wai'ichura* machines. Moie prised a two-by-twelve mahogany plank from its pallet and dragged it behind him as he climbed a ladder. His case was secured to his body with the rope. There was no one on deck. As in Trinidad, the ship was tied lengthwise to a dock, and the way off led past a guard. Moie moved silently to the other side, dropped the plank, and followed it into the warm water. He slid belly-first onto the plank and paddled away toward the lights of the city to the west.

The night was perfectly clear and only a light sea breeze

ruffled the surface of the bay. Above in the cloudless black sky Jaguar was waxing, returning from his voyage to Rain. Moie studied the sky and felt his heart seize in his breast. The friendly stars of his home were all gone. The Old Woman, the Otter, the Dolphin, the Snake, all vanished and replaced by a meaningless jumble. It was only with difficulty and the help of Jaguar that he suppressed his panic. The machines of the *wai'ichuranan* must be mighty indeed if they could rearrange the stars. Still, Jaguar ruled the night, even here, and that was something. He calmed himself and paddled to shore, heading for what looked like a small piece of forest embedded in the great cliff houses of the dead.

Muddy sand beneath his feet, he left the plank and walked onto the shore. There were trees here, some strange but others familiar, this great fig, for example. He paused and sniffed the night air. It stank of strange gases, like the ship, but he could also detect the lives of animals, some strange to him, others almost familiar. He began to feel a little better. At least he would not starve.

# Two

Jennifer Simpson awoke early to birdsong, a mockingbird trilling in the garden and the finches in their wickerwork cage on the patio of the big house. The mockingbird finished a long phrase and then began to imitate the finches. She slipped from the bed and stood naked in the doorway of her cottage, a rangy, high-breasted girl with a mass of thick red-gold hair down to the small of her back, and covered from head to toe with pale freckles. Her face was oval, finely featured, with pale blue eyes as blank and open as a child's. (An observer, and there was one, thought "Botticelli," not for the first time.) The air was as cool as it would get today, and every surface of leaf and stem in the garden was covered with glistening dew. It was her favorite time of day, because although she didn't mind communal living, she harbored a lust for privacy. She took a mask and snorkel from a hook on the porch post, retrieved a rolled-up waxed paper bag from a niche in the rough stone wall, slipped her feet into rubber flip-flops, and started down the coral-gravel path. After a few yards she encountered an enormous spiderweb laid across it, occupied by one of those spiders with a spiky body that looked like it was made of highly colored plastic. She reached for the name of it and came up empty. Scotty was always telling her the names of things, but it was hard to keep them all in her mind. Nature Boy, Kevin called him, but privately, and also The Hobbit.

From the terrace of the house Shirley let out a scream and then yelled *"Come and get it!"* three times. Jenny stopped and looked back over her shoulder, waiting to see if the noise had roused Kevin. No, and she was glad of it, because although she loved him and all, he had a way of hovering, and she wanted this time to herself. She knelt and eased herself under the web, shuddering a little when it caught on her back. The rule was nothing was killed in the garden, everything lived in balance, no pesticides, no fertilizers, the way nature intended. Jenny was down with that, and Scotty seemed to make it work.

The pool had been dug out of living coral rock, and the spoil from the dig had been used to build a little hill on which grew dozens of different kinds of bromeliads and orchids. From near its crest a good-size waterfall, driven by a solar pump, burbled merrily down into the pool. The water was clear as air. Scotty had arranged for it to feed the garden sprinklers, from which it seeped back through the porous soil to return to its source, just as nature intended water to do. The rain made up for any loss. She spat into the mask, rinsed it out, slipped it on, and lay down upon the rippling surface.

It had been designed to imitate a natural pond in Amazonia, and it was big, a half-acre of surface and forty feet deep at the deepest. Rupert, the owner, had been to Amazonia a number of times and had built the pool with that in mind, although he had never got it to balance right until he found Scotty. Scotty was a genius at practical ecology, so said Rupert. Everyone had a genius, that was Rupert's idea, and given the right social conditions, it would flourish. Jenny had not until now received any evidence of her own genius, but Rupert said she was only nineteen and should give it a chance. When Jenny was seven, one of her foster parents had taken her to a dentist in Sioux Falls, and in the waiting room there had been a large tank full of tropical fish, brilliant, darting things full of light and life, and there was a tiny statue of a mermaid in it that seemed to open a little pirate chest at intervals, when a mass of bubbles would emerge and go glittering to the surface. Jenny had been transfixed and had thought at the time that no heavenly joy promised by the Disciples of Christ Sunday school could match actually *being* that little mermaid, spending the hours opening the pirate chest, surrounded by brilliant fish. And now here she was.

She took a breath, jackknifed her long body, and plunged downward into the deep. The fish scattered before her, hundreds of fish, she had no idea how many. Scotty knew; he kept careful records of birth, growth, and death, part of the ecological balance. Jenny had little interest in that part of it, although she knew the names of the main kinds: discus, like enameled dinner plates, a dozen varieties of cichlids with bright flowing fins, clusters of solemn angelfish, headstanders streaked with crimson, clouds of tiny jewel-like killifish, golden dorados, the jagged metal flash of hatchetfish: and also, swimming slowly in a tight group, looking like thugs outside a candy store, a substantial school of red-bellied piranhas. These were Rupert's special pets, which Jenny thought was a little weird. They were also the only beings in the compound that got red meat, for Rupert would go out at dusk every day when he was in residence and fling bits of dripping offal to them from the crest of the waterfall hill and watch the water boil as they thrashed in their blood frenzy. Scotty said they were perfectly harmless unless you were bleeding or moving in an erratic fashion, although what a piranha would think erratic was something she did not know, nor did she believe that anyone else knew. She tried to avoid them on her swims, for she didn't trust them nor the look in their beady little eyes. She'd known guys with that look.

Still, here she was in the better-than-heaven, the little mermaid in the clear water, far from Iowa, in Miami, with plenty of sex and food and a place to stay where they didn't hassle you, and something important to do in life. The Earthly Paradise: one of Rupert's phrases, and it was true.

The important thing was saving the tropical rain forests, which was why Rupert had gathered them all together in his house, so they could all live in an ecologically sensitive way, giving an example to the world, and forging a political movement. Jenny did not see that they were doing much forging. The community spent a lot of time—the Professor excepted—sitting around naked or half-naked, smoking superior marijuana and discussing what it was okay to eat or use, depending on whether the product was ecological or not, and they spent a lot of time recycling; the total trash produced by the six of them, plus guests, didn't fill a shoe box a week. The forging part was mainly her and Evangelina Vargos, who lived off the property, going out nearly every day in the brightly painted VW bus, setting up a table in some public place, and trying to get people to take folders and sign petitions and contribute to the Forest Planet Alliance.

Jenny's secret was that she snuck food to the fish, disturbing the ecological balance Scotty so diligently (and irritatingly) sought. The fish were allowed to eat only plant and animal matter derived from the garden plot fertilized by water and sludge sucked up by the solar pump. What she fed them was thus beyond un-kosher—bread balls made from toxic loaves purchased on the sly from the Winn-Dixie and secreted in various hidey-holes around the property. Now she hung in the crystal water with her arm extended to a cloud of living jewels that pecked with delicate mouths at her fingers and the dissolving bread. It was so cool, the absolutely coolest thing in her life so far, better than dope, quite often better than sex with Kevin, and she wished very much for someone she could share it with. Then the food was gone except for tiny flecks, each surrounded by a little mob of fish, and then even that was gone and the fish dispersed into their normal flowing patterns.

She surfaced, blowing, and lay on her back, her young breasts bobbing prettily above the water. Her nipples were stiffened from the slight chill of the lower levels, and this produced a pleasant tingling in her groin, and she thought that if Kevin were still in bed she might slide in there and get him to give her a good one, as she often did after these expeditions. Then she spied Rupert walking down the path to the pool, naked, old, and terribly hairy. She sighed. The sight of Rupert Zenger naked always had a peculiar detumescent effect on her, for which she felt a passing shame. He could not after all help being fifty, and the body, of course, was a healthy thing, as he himself often said, but she wished he wouldn't shove it in all their faces so often. He was a solidly built, exceptionally hairy man, with a Brilloesque beard down to his chest and a full head of hair of the same consistency sticking straight out eight or so inches all around his long skull. He had a bony face, ugly in the honest Lincoln style, and large mild brown eyes that reminded Jenny of one of the Amazonian mammals in the Forest Planet brochures, a brocket deer or a tapir. She watched him approach and kicked herself to the shallows. As always her eye was drawn, if briefly, to his crotch. He certainly had a big one, truly the largest she had seen, and it was both funny and a little scary the way it swung like a clock pendulum as he walked. The Tripod, Kevin called him, nor did she appreciate the boyfriend's sly suggestions that she and Scotty's girlfriend, Luna, were angling to get a piece of it, and she always having to tell him that she wasn't interested, and she didn't think Luna was either, and that his was perfectly big enough and fine. Zenger paused and selected a towel from the large plywood box full of them on the pool margin.

She hoisted herself up onto the smoothed coral slab that ran along the near edge of the pool, removed her mask, and wrung the water out of her hair. Zenger came up behind her and said, "Good morning, Jennifer. Had your swim?"

She turned a little, and unfortunately there It was a couple of feet in front of her face. She made herself look up at his face.

"Yeah, it's great. It looks like another nice day."

"Indeed. There are croissants for breakfast. And the Heidi mangoes."

This was his way of giving the order, a little annoying, too, he never actually asked for anything or treated anyone like a servant, but Jenny made breakfast for him and the whole group every morning. The expectation was there, although she could not recall when it had been decided that this was part of her function. Shirley screamed again, which was certainly part of *her* function. Rupert walked slowly down the gentle slope into the water.

Ten minutes later, dressed in a Forest Planet T-shirt and white shorts, with her hair in a damp braid, Jenny stood in the huge, cool, and elaborately equipped kitchen, cutting mangoes into slices and arranging them in parenthetical rows on a blue glazed platter. She had ground the organic shade-grown fair-trade coffee and placed it in the drip machine and had the croissants warming in the oven. No carcinogenic microwaves here. The mangoes done, she set a white camellia at the edge of the plate and brought it out to the patio. The table was set for six with colorful native ceramics from Latin America and the Caribbean and tablecloth and napkins made of hemp fibers by indigenous craftspeople. She went back into the kitchen, poured the coffee into a thermos flask, and used a powerful Oster juicer to extract the juice from a dozen and a half organic oranges. While she was doing this, Scotty came in and, as he did every morning, arranged in a tall crystal vase the flowers he had just picked from the garden: yellow orchids, frangipani, a branch of wildly violet bougainvillea. Jenny looked up from her machine to watch him do it. Scotty said flower arrangement was a high art in Japan, and that samurai had competed to be the best at it. Jenny didn't know if this was more of Scotty's weirdness or really true, but she did see that there was something about the way the flowers looked when Scotty did them that was different, that made them look like they had grown that way, and that she never quite got when she tried it herself with the pickle jar in her cottage.

The Hobbit. As usual when Kevin supplied a name, Jenny felt her mind locked into seeing the person that way. Scotty was quite short, inches shorter than Jenny herself, and built like a barrel, with a head that looked a little big for his body, and he *was* extremely hairy, bearded, and with his dark hair drawn back into a ponytail. But unlike the hobbits in the movies (and Jenny had seen all of them, all more than once), Scotty's face, which was actually pretty handsome in a rough way, she thought, had on it a forbidding expression, almost a scowl, as if life had petulantly refused him something he thought he deserved. His eyes were tired blue, startling against the deep tan of his face. He was only a little over thirty but looked older: Jenny thought of him as an old guy, in the same class as Rupert and the Professor.

He finished his flowers and brought the vase out to the table, all this without a word or a glance at Jenny. She was used to this and not offended. People had their peculiarities, this she had learned early in a series of foster homes, and her position was that you minded your business and they minded theirs and everyone got along. Scotty was a bear in the morning; Rupert wanted things but never asked you up front; Kevin was almost always stoned; Luna was picky and tight-assed in a variety of ways; the Professor never got naked in public and he talked funny, being English. All bearable faults. As for Jenny herself: not the sharpest knife in the drawer, an expression she had overheard Luna using in reference to her in a conversation with Rupert, which she wasn't really hanging out under a window to listen in on, but happened to hear anyway. It had hurt her at the time, but she had after all heard something like it many times before, and anyway so fucking what, there were other things in life besides big brains, and those that had them, in her experience, didn't seem any happier than the rest of the stupid world.

Breakfast at La Casita (for so the house was named, and the name displayed on a hand-painted ceramic plaque affixed to one of the squat coral pillars at the gate) was where the Forest Planet Alliance gathered each morning to discuss the tasks of the day. All other meals were either informal or by invitation. Rupert often dined out or else entertained important people in the large, airy dining room. On those occasions, Jenny found herself serving and busing, while Scotty and Luna cooked, and Kevin washed up. They received no pay for this, for technically they were employees of the Forest Planet Alliance Foundation and were paid to serve the interests of this 501(c) nonprofit corporation rather than soup, but this was what they did, more or less in return for their food and rent-free accommodations. Jenny thought it was the greatest deal she had ever heard about, and Kevin thought it was a rip-off, but she didn't see him doing anything to change it anytime soon.

At breakfast, meanwhile, everyone sat democratically at the same table, which showed, Jenny thought, that they were not servants after all. The table was located in the center of a patio floored with worn, blood-colored tiles, and the house rose around it on four sides, a single story in golden coral stone, roofed in red Spanish tiling, except for the east side, which was two stories and called "the tower." This was where Rupert had his bedroom. The Professor, Nigel Cooksey, had the room below this, but Cooksey had not yet arrived when Kevin drifted in, dressed in cutoff jeans shorts and a blue work shirt with no sleeves, looking angelic and fresh, darling golden dreadlocks and little fringe of beard, sleepy hazel eyes, she always got a little thrill when she saw him first thing in the morning, how lucky she was to have him. When they'd first met, in a squat in Cedar Rapids, he'd had fairly short hair and just one earring and hadn't been on the road that long, so she knew more about how to get by than he had. She thought that was why he'd hit on her, that and the sex, and she figured he'd drift away like the others when he found out about her problem. And she had actually gone to the club behind the rail yard with him, where they had strobes, and sure enough she'd had a full-blown seizure, and come out of it on the sticky floor, with the other people pretending that nothing had happened, and the music blasting, but he had stayed with her, to her immense surprise and gratitude. She still got a little flash of that moment, him looking down at her with a look in his face that was not oh-what-a-freak-show, but human, a concerned-human-being kind of look. And she recalled that moment whenever he acted shitty. Although now he gave her a grin and a little secret squeeze and slurped up a piece of mango, and then went to the little Mexican cart where the coffee carafe was and poured himself a cup.

Then Rupert and Luna came out of the office, which was a big room in the corner of the house, and was where Luna spent most of her time. Luna had on what she always did, a crisp white short-sleeved shirt and baggy khaki shorts. She was a slim hard-bodied woman of around thirty who seemed to be constructed of piano wire and space-age substances, even her hair, which was dark and shiny, short, and held up on one side with an amber barrette; it seemed made of one piece of prestressed plastic, like the fender of a Corvette. She wore round steel-rimmed glasses on her sharp little nose. Jenny would have figured her for a sexless virgin type, but she knew for a fact that Scotty got to her frequently; the property was small enough and so quiet at night that the sex life of each inhabitant was common knowledge, at least in the audio channel. Jenny and Kevin could hear them almost as well as if they were in the same room, and Luna's rising shriek of pleasure, Scotty's satisfied groan, were frequent accompaniments to the mockingbird's evensong. Jenny had not been much of a noisemaker in that regard before arriving at La Casita but now felt compelled to join the night sounds with whoops of her own, often genuine. Kevin seemed to find it amusing.

Shirley screamed from her cage as she always did when she saw Rupert. Luna told her to shut up, and she fell silent. Like the other local denizens, the big hyacinth macaw almost always did what Luna said. Scotty arrived and sat down next to Luna. He had his social face on now, he made light remarks about the weather, about pruning the fruit trees, received the usual compliment from Rupert about the flowers, and the breakfast got under way, with everyone telling everyone else what they were going to do with their day. Rupert and Luna spoke about a mailing, and the purchase of mailing lists from other enviro organizations, and then some computer stuff she couldn't follow. There was an environmentalist letter-writing campaign about the S-9 pumping station up north that was pumping polluted water into the Everglades and killing all the wildlife. Scotty talked about the rototiller being out of whack and other repair and plumbing stuff and then they got into a little argument about what was compostable and wasn't. Jenny let the talk slide past her ears, letting it blend in with the whisper of the light breeze in the slender palms that rose above the courtyard and the sound of the waterfall. She nodded and smiled when Luna addressed her. Ms. Robotica, as Kevin called her, had arranged permission from the Coconut Grove library to set up a display and table on the little plaza in front of their building. Evangelina Vargos would meet her there and Kevin would drive the VW van. Jenny glanced at Kevin, who rolled his eyes.

"Unless you'd like to help Scotty with the rototiller," Luna added pointedly.

"Oh, no, ma'am," Kevin replied, "driving's just fine with me. I always hoped that when I grew up I would get to drive people so they could hand out little brochures. Chopping down trees to make paper to stop people from chopping down other trees. Makes perfect sense to me."

"The brochures are printed on recycled paper," said Luna with her typical exasperated sigh.

"I know it, Luna. And that's good. I'm sure our recycling program throws terror into the hearts of the fucking corporate bastards and the lumber barons that're killing the rain forest. They're shaking in their boots."

"Then what would you like us to do, Kevin?" asked Luna. "Blow up the Panamerica Bancorp Building?"

"That'd be a start," snapped Kevin.

"Oh, for God's sake, Kevin, grow the fuck up!" said Luna.

There was a silence around the table, as there always was when Kevin gave vent, which Rupert broke by saying in his calm, slow voice, "Jennifer, if you'd be so kind: could you check on what's keeping Nigel?"

Jenny rose at once and left, happy to go, disturbed by the friction that had marred the lovely morning and their breakfast. There was something going on that she didn't understand and didn't like, that was not just Kevin being silly. A look had passed between Luna and Kevin, as if even though they were in opposition, there was something going on between them, like they were pumping each other up in some way, each getting some kind of sick energy from the other. This was just a feeling; she could not put it into words.

Nigel Cooksey occupied the whole southeast corner of the house, a small bedroom and bath and the larger room adjoining the Alliance offices that he used as a study-cum-depository. He was a professor and knew everything about the rain forest and had lived down there for many years: this much Jenny knew, and also that Rupert and Scotty treated him with the greatest respect. Kevin called him Professor Stork and thought that all this studying the problem was a waste of time, because what was the point of knowing every goddamn thing about the forest when by the time he got it all down and published, there wouldn't be a tree left standing. Cooksey kept to himself, or spent hours with Rupert discussing Alliance strategy. A couple of old faggots, had been Kevin's take on the two of them when he and Jenny had arrived at the property the year before, but the vibes had been wrong for that, and when she voiced this opinion Kevin had scoffed (oh, you and your vibes!), but she'd been right. Rupert might be a little weird but was perfectly heterosexual, there were a couple of women he entertained regularly in his bedroom in the tower of the house, and clearly, from the sounds floating out of the garden on those nights, he knew well enough how to wield his spectacular unit.

What Cooksey was she had not figured out yet, maybe he *was* gay, but he didn't seem to do anything about it, maybe not all that interested in sex, although when she entertained that idea her mind skidded a little. Sometimes she thought there was something, like, *wrong* with him because he was the only one of the inhabitants who did not bathe nude in the pool, and so no one there had seen his equipment. It was huge, purple, with spikes and blades on it, like they drew on demons in underground comix, so said Kevin, but Jenny thought he was just lonely, and she always made an effort to be nice to him. She liked his voice, too, it was like on the TV, as when she switched it on sometimes and found it was tuned to the public TV channel and before switching to her show she would listen to that accent, those people talking like they never had a care in the world and no one could ever be mean to them.

She knocked on Cooksey's bedroom door and, receiving no response, went to the next room on the hall, his study, where she poked her head in. Cartons, crates, barrels, teetering piles of books on the floor, bookcases almost to the ceiling, stuffed animals and mounted skeletons of animals atop these, a row of filing cabinets of different sizes and vintages, a wicker fan in slow rotation above, light from the windows greened by passage through the mango orchard illuminating the dusty air, and in the center, Nigel Cooksey leaning back in a wooden swivel chair, sandaled feet and thin knotty legs up on the cluttered worktable, arranged carefully among half a dozen soiled tea mugs and a stuffed hoatzin on a stand. The room had a peculiar, penetrant odor compounded of old paper, bachelor, formalin, whiskey, and incompletely preserved organic materials.

Jenny cleared her throat, coughed, said, "Um, Professor . . . ?" At which the legs shot up, the chair crashed against a wooden crate and spun on its axis, its occupant confronting her with a gaping look, like one of the stuffed jungle creatures that decorated the high shelf. A small white object went clattering across the tile. Jenny stooped to retrieve it. It was a plaster cast of an animal's foot. She handed it to him.

"Rupert said he wanted to meet with you?"

"Oh, dear! It can't be nine already!"

There was a wooden clock on a bookcase shelf, whose face was nearly obscured by stacked journal reprints. Jenny moved these and said, "It's half-past. Did you fall asleep?"

"Oh, not at all, no, I was in a kind of brown study."

Well, *yeah,* thought Jenny, with all the smoke. Cooksey was the only smoker (of tobacco) on the property, and the white walls of the workroom had acquired an amber glaze. He was staring at her in a way he often stared, as if she were a creature he was observing from concealment. His eyes were gray, deep-set, and sad. He said, " 'Never shall a young man, thrown into despair by those great honey-colored ramparts at your ear, love you for yourself alone and not your yellow hair.' Yeats."

"Excuse me?"

"Nothing, my dear. Musing is all. Well, I must stir myself." He placed the cast on the desk.

"What is that thing, a foot?"

"Yes. Of a tapir, *Tapirus terrestris.* You can learn a lot about the larger mammals by their footprints. Weight, of course, and sometimes sex and age. This is a male, perhaps two years old."

"How do you know?"

"How? Why, it's written here on the base of the cast." He laughed, a dry chuckle, and after a slight pause, Jenny laughed, too.

"Gosh, and I thought science was hard."

"If it were, I couldn't do it, slug that I am. Seriously: you observe the animals, you see, and then when they've left, you scuttle out and pour plaster into the prints, and then there's a little gadget with a spring that you press into the soil near the print, until it's as deep as the print was, and it gives you the weight, or rather you calculate the weight from the readings. And if you do that for a few years, you get a sense of how the animals grow and survive. Every creature has a unique print."

"Like fingerprints."

"Just so. I have a large collection of them, all the mammalia, of course, and the larger lizards and crocodilia, and the gallinaceous birds." He stood and gestured to the door. He was tall and very thin and dressed always in faded khaki shirts and shorts.

"After you, my dear."

That was one reason she liked the professor. *After you, my dear!* It was like being in an old movie on TV.

K evin was not in that good a mood as they drove up Main Highway to the Grove, and Jenny was all tensed up, waiting to see if he would take it out on her. Sometimes he would shoot questions at her, or talk about things she couldn't follow and then get all sarcastic about it, or else he would get her to talk about stuff that happened to her while she was growing up, school or the foster homes or the strange kids that she'd shared them with or the foster parents. She had quite a few stories saved up, some of them pretty sad, and just when she thought she was sharing stuff that she didn't ordinarily like to share, he would yank his attention away, like Lucy with Charlie Brown's football, and she'd feel like a jerk for going on about old shit. Or he'd actually say, after listening to her talk for half an hour or so, Why do you keep talking about old shit like that? So she felt stupid *again,* and wanted to bawl.

Kevin himself never talked much about his own past. She knew he'd been to a prep school. She was not sure what a prep school was, exactly, although she knew you had to pay money to go, probably a lot more than the $16.83 per month that the state of Iowa had paid her foster parents for her upkeep in the year before she split, and also she had the adjective "preppy," which meant expensive clothes from Abercrombie's in the mall, and she imagined a place with lots of grass and white people in baggy clothes playing around and looking cool. He had been to college, too, but dropped out because of all the bullshit you had to take from the teachers, and how bourgeois it was, and it was better to be a revolutionary, which he was. Being a revolutionary was all about smoking a lot of dope and spray-painting walls and keying expensive cars, or so she imagined from observing Kevin, and this would eventually bring down the capitalist infrastructure that was destroying the planet, although she was not nearly smart enough to see how this would happen.

She was relieved to find that Kevin was not going to get

on her today just yet, but was venting his rage about the fucking Forest Planet Assholes who didn't know how to do anything but bullshit all day, focusing particularly on Luna the stuck-up bitch, who didn't know half the stuff he did and was a complete phony poseur bourgeois besides. Kevin was smoking a fat number right now, which Jenny didn't like much, not that she had any objection to it as such, but not while driving down Main Highway in the van. She was afraid of getting pulled over, although the one time she'd mentioned this Kevin had come down hard on her for being a totally useless scaredy-cat piece of shit, although as far as she knew he had never been inside a jail, while she had (for possession of a controlled substance) in Cedar Rapids and did not want to repeat the experience. He offered the dope to her but she declined, although she was getting quite the buzz from just being in the van.

At least he stashed it when they got to the commercial part of the Grove. Kevin backed the VW into the delivery slot in front of the library, and Jenny saw that Evangelina Vargos was waiting on the library steps reading a book. She was a small, lightly built woman, with a charming mop of blond-streaked brown hair, green eyes, skin smooth as ivory and just that color. She wore white jeans, complicated and expensive-looking white sandals, a FPA T-shirt, and a good deal of glittery gold jewelry. Jenny felt a little lift in her heart when she saw her. Geli Vargos was sort of her best friend at this point, she thought, although having moved around a lot as a child and being a foster kid, she did not have much experience with the actuality of best-friendness. Geli listened sympathetically to her hard-luck stories, and she listened to Geli's, which were all about rich Cubans in her family being mean to one another and to Geli for not getting married to this bozo they wanted her to marry.

Geli saw them, stood up and waved, and then descended to help them unload the display. Greetings: a kiss on the cheek for Jenny, a slightly mocking hail for Kevin, returned with a sarcastic grin. Kevin and Geli did not get along, a phenomenon Jenny had observed in countless television sitcoms (the best friend and the boyfriend trading barbs) and considered normal; in fact, considered it a proof that she was at last living a version of real life. She rejected all advice to stop hanging out with that Cuban bourgeois bitch or dump that phony asshole for a decent guy, and was secretly delighted that someone thought enough of her to try to change her life.

They unloaded a long folding table, three folding chairs, and a large four-panel display frame, together with boxes of Forest Planet literature and a miniature stereo-component sound system. Kevin set up the sound system and started a tape of Andean music, breathy bone flutes, ocarinas, and two-headed drums. The women erected the display frame and hung its panels: SAVE THE RAIN FOREST; the FPA logo, a blue-green ball with trees sticking out from its circumference like cloves in a pomander; and large laminated photographs of rain forest plants and creatures and some indigenes in feathered headdresses. Nigel Cooksey had taken these photos during his many trips to the region. The remainder of the display comprised a group of brief text panels describing the flora and fauna, and telling how endangered the region was. There were also smaller photos of a despoiled area, bulldozers knocking over trees, and maps and charts showing the accelerating rate of forest loss.

Luna had made the display herself, occasionally under Jenny's wondering eye. This was the first time Jenny had ever seen anyone make something original out of nothing before—anything, that is, more complex than fixing a meal, sewing a dress, or pasting pictures in a scrapbook. Luna had thought it up and got the stuff together and used the computer and printer and a laminating machine and ordered the display frame off the Internet and . . . bang! There it was in real life! How did people just *know* stuff like that? Geli knew stuff, too, she was a grad student at the marine lab, was going to be a marine biologist, and knew lots of stories about what fish got up to when they were alone. She was always encouraging Jenny to go back to school and make something of herself, just as if Jenny was as smart as her, which she wasn't, but it was nice to have someone who thought so. You're a good observer, she said, you have a feeling for animals. Jenny was not exactly sure what this meant.

The tables and chairs arranged, the display displayed, the two women sat on the chairs and awaited the suckers, as Kevin called them. It was a fine October morning in Miami, and the center of Coconut Grove was filling up with tourists and young people there to hang out. Geli and Jenny talked to some tourists, with Jenny focusing on the kids. She had always been good with kids, Kevin often observing it was her childlike mind in play. She talked enthusiastically about the various depicted creatures and their interesting lives. Kevin grew bored, as usual, and said he was going to see what was going on in the park. Several police cars and a brown animal-control van from the county were parked at the edge of the grassy area that led down to the bay, and a small crowd had gathered.

Jenny watched him cross the street and disappear into the crowd, feeling faintly sad and worried that Geli would use this opportunity to run Kevin down again. When she looked up again there was the Indian. He was standing in front of the display staring at the charmingly dim face of a sloth. Dressed in a shabby black suit and a white shirt buttoned up to the neck, he had a small string bag slung over his shoulder and a stained and worn cloth suitcase at his feet. He touched the photograph lightly and then brought his fingertip to his nose.

"That's a sloth," Jenny said. "They live in the trees."

At her words, he turned his head and regarded her. She saw the tattoos on his face, three lines on each cheek and two short vertical marks on his forehead, and their eyes met. Involuntarily, her glance moved to a large photograph of some Yanomami tribesmen, and then back to the Indian. He was still staring at her. A small thrill traveled through her body and she felt the hair stand up on her arms, and she had to drop her eyes. She watched the man move down the display, looking at each photograph in turn. He spent a long time in front of each one, and longest before the picture of a jaguar.

"Geli," she said in a hushed voice, "check out that guy in the black outfit. He's just like those guys in our picture."

Geli glanced up from the petition she had just got some tourists to sign. She looked the man over. "God, I think you're right. What the hell's he doing in Miami?"

"You could ask him. I don't think he speaks any English."

But the man had left the display and now approached the two women. He said something to them, and it was a moment before Geli understood that the language he was speaking was her cradle tongue. In Spanish she replied, "Forgive me, sir, I didn't understand you."

The man said, "I have go to Consuela Holdings. To talk to men. I have say, not . . . not . . ." A look of frustration crossed his face, and he went to the display and tapped on the photograph of the logging operation. "Not this in Puxto Reserve."

"You're from the *Puxto*?"

His face brightened and he showed filed teeth. "Yes, Puxto! Consuela not . . . is *siwix* to do like this. Forbid."

"What's he saying?" asked Jenny.

"I'm not sure. He says he's from the Puxto Reserve. It's in Colombia. God, how in *hell* did he get here? He sounds like he wants us to stop someone logging the Puxto."

"Well, then he sure came to the right people," said Jenny confidently.

"Yeah, but, God, this is so weird." In halting Spanish then she interrogated the man. He said his name was Juan Bautista and he lived in a village near a river Geli had never heard of. They had killed Father Perrin but after he was dead Father Perrin had told him that Consuela Holdings was going to cut all the forest on the Puxto so the dead people could buy many machetes and bottles of pisco. So Jaguar said he must go, and he came down the river to a bigger river in his canoe and thence to the sea, where *Guyana Castle* had carried him and Jaguar to Miami America and now the woman must take him to Consuela Holdings because he had the men to talk to tied in a string and would talk and then go back to the Runiya, because being in the land of the dead people was very hard on his *something*.

"I don't understand that word," she said.

"*Ryuxit,*" the Indian repeated. He gestured to the sky, to the earth, and dashed over and tapped on all the pictures of animals and plants, then touched his heart, clenched his fist, and pressed the fist firmly against Jenny's breastbone. "Like those . . . all like that," he said. "Here in Miami not . . ." He made a flowing motion with his hand.

"What? What's he saying?" said Jenny. There was a strange feeling in her chest where he had touched her.

"It's a little vague just now. Wait here for a second, I'm going to check something out."

With that she dashed up the steps and into the library. Jenny smiled at Juan Bautista, who looked sadly after Geli.

"She'll be right back. We really, really want to help you, man." She got up and pointed to the map of Amazonia. "Can you show me where you come from?"

No reaction. Jenny pointed to herself and said, "I'm Jenny. Can you say 'Jenny'?" A blank look, but Jenny was not discouraged. Many of the foster children she had lived with had been retards, and she'd got along just fine with them. You just had to take it real slow. She pointed to one of the pictures. "This is an orchid. Say *oarrr-kidd!*" She gestured to his mouth and made opening and closing motions with her hand. She saw light dawn in his eyes.

"The Little Brother of the Blood," he said in his own language, and continued, "This is a very useful plant. We grind the tubers and soak the mash in cane alcohol and then boil it down into a syrup. We use it to treat arthritis, diarrhea, headache, temperature, cough, digestion diseases, and to help to heal wounds and boils."

"Good," said Jenny with a smile. "And we call it an *orchid.* Now this is a monkey. Can you say *mon-key?*"

He could, and so on through the other pictures. At the jaguar, he said, "You know, that is very dangerous. I don't think Jaguar would like you capturing his soul like that. A bad thing could happen." Jenny smiled and nodded. At least he was talking.

Kevin returned looking hectic. "Hey, they found a coon's head in a tree and blood all around, guts and all. The cops think it was a wild dog pack, that or homeless guys out hunting. Who's this?" pointing at the Indian.

"His name's Juan Bautista. He comes from the Amazon, and we're going to help him keep this company from cutting down his rain forest."

"You're shitting me! Where'd you find him?"

"He just showed up. It's sort of like fate."

"Oh, right, fate. Did you tell him we don't do shit?" He addressed the Indian. "Wrongo outfit, man. We no stoppo no cutto down treeso, only talko talko, hando out brochureso."

"Well, we have a chance, now, Kevin. I don't see why you have to always be so fucking down on everything. This little guy's got the name of the company that's doing it, and he says they're right here in Miami."

Geli Vargos returned, her face alight. "I looked it up and it checks out. There *is* a company called Consuela Holdings in Miami, and they have an office on North Miami Avenue, 540 North Miami. And I looked up the Puxto Reserve on the Net. There's not supposed to be any logging at all there, so it has to be an illegal cut. God, Rupert's going to go crazy over this."

"Yeah, he'll write a letter to the papers, that's how crazy he'll get," Kevin said. "Or maybe if he's really fired up he'll try to get an interview on NPR. Hey, I got an idea. Let's fucking go up there right now. Confront the bastards with what's-his-face here, the evidence of their crimes. We got the address."

"I don't think that's smart—" said Geli.

"Oh, fuck smart!" He turned to the Indian. "Look, man, we go now, right. To Consuela, tell them no choppo my trees, okay? You come with me now, yes? *Pronto*, Consuela, *con me*."

"Consuela, *pronto, sí,*" said the Indian, making a peculiar twisting motion of his head that seemed to mean affirmation.

Kevin began leading the Indian to the VW. Geli said, "Kevin, come on, don't be an asshole. We have all this stuff here. How in hell are we supposed to pack it up if you take the truck? And you can't speak Spanish—you won't know what's going on."

"I had a year of it in school. *Hasta la vista,* baby!" He placed the Indian in the shotgun seat and jumped behind the wheel.

"Kevin, damn it, hold on!" said Jenny. "This is stupid. We should pack this all up and go together, and like plan it out with Rupert and all."

Kevin cranked it up hard, sending clouds of acrid smoke into the air. "Girls, now be sure to get those petitions signed," he crowed, "me and Tonto here gonna whip some ass at the despoilers' headquarters. *¡Viva la revolución!*"

With that he was out in the street and tooling away before they could get out another word.

Moie sits in the van quietly, feeling content. This is the first time he has been in an enclosed motor vehicle, but he is neither frightened nor impressed. He knows the *wai'ichura* machines are strong and quick, but he thinks they don't give the *wai'ichura* much beauty. Jaguar had said he would find allies among the dead people, and allies had been provided. The dead person next to him has his death clasped deep inside him, even though he is very young. Moie senses that he wishes to make each moment dead as well, never still, making monkey noise with his mouth all the time. Now he touches a part of his machine and loud noise fills the inside of it, a painful buzzing with more monkey noises mixed in and also a drum, but the drum isn't speaking any sense, like the drums his people used. He is a little sorry that the woman is not here, the one with the fire-colored hair, not the one who can talk Spanish, although either of them would have been preferable to this monkey. The Firehair Woman is not entirely dead, a little like Father Tim really, he can almost see the shadow of her death behind her in its usual place, and he wonders what she has done to be even that much alive in the land of the dead.

# Three

In the lobby of the office building, Kevin looked at the list of tenants spread under glass before the guard's station and was conscious of the guard looking at him. He found a hopeful line on the board and said to his companion, "You have those guys' names, right?" Blank look. Oh, yeah, Spanish.

"¿Quienes los hombres de Consuela?" More blank. He cursed, and the guard looked at him a little more sharply. "No, ah— ¿Como se llaman los hombres malos, los jefes de la Consuela Holdings?"

The brown face registered comprehension and the Indian took from his bag a piece of knotted fiber. As he untied each knot he said a name: Fuentes, Calderón, Garza, Ibanez. Kevin looked at the board. "Okay, there's an Antonio Fuentes here. Let's go make some trouble, Tonto."

They rode up in the elevator to the twenty-third floor. The Indian was very still. Kevin was dancing on the balls of his feet and making a tuneless breathy whistle. When the car stopped, they got out and walked down the hall, looking at doors until they found one that read CONSUELA HOLDINGS, LLC in raised gilded letters. Inside, Kevin looked around and was disappointed in the amenities. His familiarity with world-bestriding firms was limited to what he'd observed in the movies. This place looked cheesier than his father's office at the bank: a small carpeted area faced by a reception counter. A pretty Cuban secretary with long lavender nails was on the phone when they entered. She looked up and said something into the phone and pressed a button.

"Can I help you?"

"Yeah," said Kevin, "we want to see Fuentes." And then the usual business about appointments, and then some shouting and nasty language from Kevin and the threat to call security, and then Kevin grabbed the Indian and went through a door while the receptionist frantically punched numbers into her phone. There was a little hall and at the end of the corridor another door and behind that a large corner office with a view of Biscayne Bay through windows on two sides and a large mahogany desk, behind which sat a small, dark man with dense silver hair and thick horn-rimmed glasses. Kevin got in this man's face and said what he had come to say, about how they knew what they were doing down in the rain forest, how they were illegally logging the Puxto Reserve, and they were going to let everyone know and make them stop it, and that this man (here he gestured toward the silent Indian) was the proof, he knew all about the illegal logging and they would go to the UN if they had to, they'd boycott, they'd demonstrate. . . .

After three minutes of this, which included a lesson on why people and the fate of the planet were more important than corporate profits, Kevin ran down. The man had not said a word; he just looked at the two of them expressionlessly, his dark eyes showing nothing but a faint ennui, as if he were waiting for a train. Then three big men in blue-gray uniforms came into the office and said they had to leave. Kevin said he wouldn't leave without a written guarantee that all illegal operations on the Puxto would cease as of this moment, at which point one of the guards grabbed his right elbow and wrist and did something that caused Kevin so much pain that he sank to his knees and had to concentrate to keep from wetting himself. None of the guards touched the Indian, who meekly allowed himself to be led away, while just in front of him, Kevin howled and threatened a host of violent retributions, all of which were beyond his power to accomplish.

He drove back to Coconut Grove in a good deal of pain. His wrist ached, and one of the guards had given him a couple of shots to the kidney in the elevator. Still, he felt good in a way he hadn't in a long while. The fascists had shown their true colors at last, he had been met with the violence and brutality he had expected, justifying his own fantasies of violence. He observed his wrist on the steering wheel and was gratified to see it red and swelling slightly; he only regretted that no blood had been shed, as he thought there was nothing like a bashed face to elicit the sympathy he considered the key to real political action. As he drove, his clever mind reassembled the events of the recent past into a pattern more favorable to him. He summoned up fear in the face of Fuentes where there had been only contemptuous boredom. In his mind's ear he heard the man trying to justify his crimes in a whining voice. These Kevin had destroyed in a series of brilliant retorts, which he now composed and polished. The guards had tried to subdue him, but he had used martial arts to send them sprawling; oh, yeah, and the Indian, they had tried to mess with the Indian and *he* had avoided their fascistic grasp by means of strange jungle moves, and they had strolled out of there heads high, like a couple of action heroes. He glanced over at the small man sitting silent next to him. That was a problem, if he brought him back to the property they would talk to him, Luna knew Spanish and so did the Professor, which might screw things up. But why bring him back? Who knew what an Indian would do?

Kevin turned off Bayshore onto McFarlane, and almost as soon as he did so, he saw that the display and the rest of the FPA stuff was gone from in front of the library. Clearly the girls had called Scotty, and he'd come by with the truck. He parked anyway and got out of the van. To the Indian he said, "*Vámanos, tenemos buscar las mujeres.*" He went around and opened the passenger door.

"Come on, man, *vamos,* you go around that side. *Busca allí.*" He gestured so the stupid Indian would know to go around the east side of the library. When he was gone, Kevin went inside the building and looked around for about thirty seconds. Then he got back in the van. Shit, I don't know where he is, he explained to the people in his head, I went back to the library and you guys were gone and we looked and looked and then he was nowhere, man. He just disappeared. Kevin started the truck and drove off.

They all came running out to meet him when he pulled into the property, although his reception was considerably dampened when they discovered he had lost the Indian. Nor were they much impressed by his story. Luna was especially furious, and she had a mouth on her, too, to which she did not ordinarily give full vent when Rupert was around, but now let fly. He was an irresponsible moron, a lazy, lying, hopeless, sub-asshole piece of shit, who had just wasted practically the best piece of luck they had ever had, an actual witness from the rain forest, someone they could have written articles about, someone who could have appeared with them on *television,* for God's sake, a man travels three thousand miles, most of it in a canoe, to save his forest and his people, avoiding untold dangers and who should he run into but the fuckup of the Western world! Thus it went on for what seemed like a long time, with Rupert trying to get a word in edgewise, and Kevin screaming back mindless obscenities, and Scotty looking contemptuous and self-satisfied, and the Professor looking stunned, and the tears running slowly down Jenny's face until he couldn't stand it anymore and threw a flowerpot against the wall. In the stunned silence following this act he stomped back to their cottage cursing. Then the sound of the slammed door.

"He has to go, Rupert," said Luna in the echo of that sound. "I mean it. He's a lazy son of a bitch, he does nothing but lay around and smoke dope, he's a disaster politically, and this last stunt is completely unforgivable. Jesus! We could have learned so much from him, we could have given him shelter. . . ." She raised her eyes to heaven and clenched her fists in frustration, not a pretty sight. To Rupert she said, "So? Can we *please* get rid of him?"

"What about Jen?" This from Scotty, earning a sharp look from Luna, who said quickly, "Oh, Jenny's fine. No one has anything against Jenny."

Jenny snuffled and said sulkily, "I'm not staying here without Kevin."

"Whatever was meant to happen will happen, Luna," said Rupert in his calm, maddening way. "And if the few of us can't live here together peacefully, what hope is there for the world at large? Isn't that right, Nigel?"

After a brief pause, Professor Cooksey said, "Quite," excused himself, and went back to his workroom.

"Well," said Rupert, "let's all take some time to calm down, shall we? Jenny, could you . . . ah . . . deal with that plant?" And they all disappeared to their various lairs, leaving Jenny alone on the patio, staring at the shattered pot and the smear of earth on the bloodred tiles.

———

Night. Moie lies in his hammock high up in a great fig tree in Peacock Park in Coconut Grove. He watches the moon come up from the sea. He sees that Jaguar has nearly returned from his mother, and by this sign he calculates how long it has been since he left Home. He recalls the word *lonely,* feels the feeling it represents, wonders if he will return there, and also wonders a little about the Firehair Woman, and if he will see her again. He has her smell in his nose and can easily find her, he thinks, even in this place of unbearable stench. If it is necessary.

But now he tests the air for another scent, one he acquired earlier in this strange day, that of the man Fuentes. He had not understood what the Monkey Boy had said to Fuentes, but the meaning was perfectly clear, as was the response of Fuentes. He feels Jaguar's anger building in him and feels a faint sadness for the man, as he sometimes did when they gave a little girl to the god. Some things are necessary, however. It is not for him to judge. He chews some more of the paste he has prepared; after a few minutes he feels the god start to take hold of his body. Moie has never discussed this event with anyone. He has never known anyone who carried Jaguar except for his old teacher, who has been dead for years, and even when he was alive it was not something they discussed, any more than they concerned themselves with the circulation of their blood.

Moie feels numbness begin in his hands, his feet; the waves of numbness flow toward his center and meet in a certain spot in his belly. Sounds and smells fade; his vision grows dim, contracts, goes to black. Now he is out of his body and can see again, if dimly. He sees his body there on the tree limb, perfectly inert, its arms and legs hanging down. He regards it with only mild interest, no different from the interest he takes in the bark of the tree, its leaves, the little insects of the night crawling among them, the motion of the moon through the clouds. He is free in nature, indifferent to and perfectly accepting of its benevolence, its horrors. In this state of profound detachment he observes Jaguar unmake nature. First there is a man in a tree, and then there is some kind of *event* (not really, because event implies duration, and this occurs outside of normal time), and then the same place is occupied by a golden cat spotted with black rosettes, a creature with about four times the mass of the man. Inside this being is Moie, held like a memory in the consciousness of the god. He will recall what is about to happen as we recall dreams.

With the waxing moon high in the clear heavens, Jaguar descends from the fig tree. Like a slice of solid moonlight he flows out of the park and goes south, slipping through the sleeping yards, over walls and fences, to a chorus of frantic dog-barks. He encounters finger canals, and either works around them to the west or swims across. He is a good swimmer. There are few people out in these neighborhoods this late at night; they sleep secure behind their alarms and guard services. Jaguar stops at a canal bank and sniffs the air.

\*    \*    \*

Antonio Fuentes is restless in his bed, in his fine house on the canal at Leucedendra. He can't get the *Indio* out of his mind. The screaming American was nothing, but the *Indio* was *not* nothing, should not have been there at all, and the American should not have known about the Puxto cut, and should not have known that Consuela Holdings was behind the Colombian timber operation doing the cutting. There were several dummy corporations designed specifically to cloud that connection, so how could an ignorant *Indio* and a tree-hugging *pendejo* have worked it out? Answer: they could not, and therefore someone was trying to fuck them over, someone with connections down there in Colombia. That was the problem when you dealt with Colombians: there was no law at all, not even corrupt law; you never knew if you had paid off everyone who could screw up your deal, which is why they had a man like Hurtado involved.

He slips out of bed and into a robe and walks to the French windows of his bedroom. His wife stirs but does not wake. They both take sleeping pills, and he hopes he will not need another one tonight. It would make him groggy all morning, which he cannot really afford. He has called a meeting of the other principals of Consuela to discuss the threat represented by the incident in his office. He hopes they can resolve it without bringing the Colombian into it directly. Fuentes has squeezed the law many times during his career, but this is the first time he has ever done business with an actual *narcolista*. Although officially, on paper, there is no connection. He doesn't like it, but the profits are potentially enormous, and it is not like they are actually in the drug business themselves. Probably not actually, but the important thing is, he doesn't have to know anything about it. And to make sure the insulation is still intact, or if not, to repair it. He thinks that the screaming boy should not be hard to find, if it should come to that.

Fuentes opens the French window and steps out onto the little balcony. The air is fresh and scented by night-blooming jasmine and the marine tang of the bay. He is on the second floor here and he can look out at the expanse of water. It is a clear night with a fat moon riding high above a single line of cloud. He can just make out the lights of Key Biscayne and Cape Florida to the east. Sometimes, he has found, a little pacing back and forth on this balcony will tire him enough so that he will sleep.

He takes a few steps and stops short. There is something wrong. What is it? Something he has forgotten to do? He glances back to the bedroom wall: the emerald gleam of the security light is on, the house is sealed. He hears a scratching sound overhead and starts violently, then allows himself a secret, self-deprecating laugh. Raccoons. He will have to have the man out with the traps again. But this whole incident has made him uncharacteristically jumpy. I'm nervous as a cat, he thinks to himself, and begins to pace.

He paces the ten feet, turns, and ten back, and his head while he paces is full of figures. He is the numbers guy in the group. Calderón had the Colombian contacts, Garza generated the seed money, and Ibanez has the machinery to turn the timber into cash, for there are still plenty of people whose hunger for prime mahogany precludes asking any questions about where it came from. It would be good if they had a survey of the area, how many trees they could expect per hectare and so on, to get a clearer picture. Using averages was fine, but they had heard rumors about the incredible density of growth in the Puxto, was it possible it was as high as four trees per? He does some mental calculation on that basis: the mesa was twelve hundred square miles, convert to hectares at 259 per square mile, and say it *was* four trees per, that would be a million trees, figure average radius of a meter and a half, thirty tall, that would be, say, two hundred cubic meters of usable wood from each and . . . and in the midst of these ruminations he hears again that noise above him, a scraping on the tiles.

He raises his eyes to the roof, sees nothing, and resumes his pacing and his thought: two hundred million cubic meters of prime old-growth mahogany, Jesus! Although they'd have to play a little with the market because they wouldn't want the price to drop much below the going fifteen hundred dollars per cube . . . but another sound interrupts his figures, like a cat's purr but much louder.

*Ararah. Ararararh.*

Fuentes looks up again. No, not a raccoon.

———

Jimmy Paz walked into the kitchen of Guantanamera, his restaurant (actually his mother's restaurant), and cast a practiced eye across the room. It was Wednesday, so the specials were seafood salad and *ajiaco criollo,* a beef stew whose recipe had been in his mother's family for generations, and which was famous among local aficionados of down-home Cuban cooking. Cesar, the chef, was accordingly prepping all the marine life-forms that would go into the salad—lobster, stone crab, shrimp, squid—and Rafael, the prep cook, was cutting and peeling the fruits and roots—malanga amarilla, yuca, green plantain, boniato, malanga blanca, calabaza, and ñame yam—that would go into the stew. Also at the prep table, to Paz's surprise, was Amelia, who was carving flowers out of pickled mushrooms and radishes and also slicing lemons in half and giving them a scalloped edge, all for the seafood salad garniture. She was standing on a stool, and the apron she was wearing came down to cover her pink sneakers, as she was only three foot four.

"How come you're not in school?" asked Paz.

"It's a teacher's work day. I told you, Daddy. And we're supposed to go to Matheson after lunch. You forgot."

"I did forget," said Paz. "Do you think I'm the worst daddy in the world?"

The child considered this seriously for a moment. "Not in the *whole* world. But you shouldn't forget stuff. Abuela says you would forget your head if it wasn't tied to your neck." This last phrase was quoted in Cuban Spanish, with the Guantanamero accent Paz knew so well. The child was perfectly bilingual.

"I remember where you're ticklish, and if you didn't have

that knife in your hands I would tickle you *so* much," said Paz, and was rewarded with a giggle. "I'm busy, Daddy," she then said, now imitating the mother, Doctor Mom, an extremely busy person at all times. Paz watched his daughter cut vegetables for a moment. She was slow but accurate, and respected the blade without fearing it. Her grandmother had let her peel carrots at four, and now, nearly three years later, she had many small paring tasks well in hand. The blade she was using was sharp as a scalpel, but Paz didn't worry about it at all, because if she cut herself it would be a clean one, and getting sliced was part of the education of a chef. This was, however, an appraisal he had never put into so many words to the child's mother. He put on his own apron and started cutting up meat for the *ajiaco*: short ribs, flank steak, and *tasajo,* salt-dried beef.

Four hours later, Paz stood in seeming chaos as the lunch rush crested; seeming only, for the three men and the woman who made up the kitchen crew at the restaurant Guantanamera were like trained athletes or soldiers working on the edge of catastrophe amid flashing blades, boiling cauldrons, burners shooting out gouts of flame, pans spitting fat. The waiters shouted, the cooks shouted back, the dishwasher rumbled, and Jimmy Paz worked the grill station within a self-created egg of calm. The dozen or so pieces of expensive protein in front of him—marinated steaks, pork chops, snapper fillets, lobster tails, giant prawns—all cooking at different rates toward different degrees of doneness, on a grill whose temperature varied every couple of inches and that was gradually getting hotter overall as the hours went by—were all present as little clocks and calculations in his head, all perfectly unconscious but crowding any unwanted thoughts from his grateful mind. It was what Paz did instead of religion or meditation. Thus, now, thoughtlessly as a fish swims, Paz produced a meal for a party of four—a lobster, a steak, some pork chops, a handful of tiger prawns, all cooked to perfection and all ready at exactly the same instant. He loaded each entrée onto a warm plate and shoved them down to Yolanda, the line cook, to be garnished, sauced, veggied, and shipped out the service port. And another and another, until, and this was about two-thirty, there was a subtle slackening in the pace, and then the noise faded, there were only two or three things on the grill, and it was over. Paz went to the sink, splashed some water on his face, and drank an icy Hatuey beer down in two long swallows.

"Daddy?"

Paz looked up to see his daughter dressed for the dining room in a floor-length black skirt, a lavishly pleated white blouse (with a name tag that read AMELIA), shiny Mary Janes, and a red hibiscus stuck in her mass of pale brown curls: the world's smallest hostess. This was her *abuela*'s idea and confection, and so cute that people waiting for tables were often brought to their knees through excess of delight. She was very good at it, too, and it took a nasty customer indeed to bitch to this one about seating.

"Uncle Tito says he needs to talk to you," said the child, "table eight." She departed, and after buttoning his tunic and telling Yolanda to mind the grill, so did Paz.

The dining room at Guantanamera was high, cool, white, and gold, with rattan fans moving the air-conditioned air around; many-armed chandeliers cast the bright light characteristic of Cuban restaurants. It was in every respect except size a replica of the dining room at the great tobacco *finca* where Paz's mother had worked as a child before the revolution, and her mother before her, and back to slavery days, all helping to invent the cuisine of Cuba. Paz didn't know how much of this pastiche was irony and how much was clever marketing. The original custom of the place had consisted of exiles nostalgic for the kind of *comidas criollas* that white Cubans believed only black people could authentically produce. That was one of the problems Paz had with his mother's operation. The oldsters were running thin, the tourists were seasonal, and the yuppies did not much fancy sitting down in a room lit like a stadium to a meal rich in carbs and spicy greases. Paz was always trying to darken the room and lighten the menu, hence that seafood salad, but it was hard to tell anything to Margarita Paz.

Tito Morales waved him over. As always when he saw Morales, Paz experienced a stab of regret, tinctured with envy and some resentment. The man was a detective on the Miami PD, as Paz had been, before he discovered that shooting people was an experience he could not ever repeat and had resigned from the force. He himself had put Morales in the detectives, brought him in off patrol as his partner, and although Morales had his own partner now (significantly absent at present), he occasionally came by to have a meal and pick Paz's brain.

Paz sat. "What'd you have?"

"The *ajiaco*."

"How was it?"

"Incredible. I got Mina to make it a time or two at home, but it wasn't anything like yours."

"Just as well. You're getting fat, Morales. You should've gone with the salad."

Morales laughed comfortably. He liked having a man who sold food tell him he was fat. In the seven years Paz had known him, Morales had turned from a baby-faced kid into a solidly built man of thirty, wife-and-two-kids, and a competent, if not particularly brilliant, detective. If he required brilliance, he had Jimmy Paz for the price of a meal.

They bantered for a while about family, sports, the department and its discontents, the latest cop scandal, one of a seemingly infinite series of stupid Miami cop tricks. Then, the reason for the visit, besides Morales's taste for Cuban stewed beef.

"We caught a weird one last night. Tony Fuentes got killed. You heard about it?"

"I saw it in the *Herald*. Struggle with a burglar and he fell off his balcony. The perp got away."

"That's what we're giving out," said Morales darkly.

"And what are you not?"

"The perp ate him. And we doubt it was a burglary."

"That's good police work, Tito. Your average burglar usually goes for the jewels rather than the liver."

An odd look appeared on Morales's face, and Paz thought that this was one reason why the man would never be an absolutely first-class police detective—he was far too transparent; basically, he was a nice, regular guy, unlike Paz. "How did you know it was the liver?" the detective asked.

"It's the tastiest part, if you want to snack off a corpse in a hurry. I speak as a food service professional here. What else did he eat? Or *it* eat?"

"The heart and some thigh muscles. It was quite a scene, my friend. Fuentes was opened up like a can of beans in his garden. Somebody yanked him off his balcony a little past one-thirty this morning. They ripped his throat out first. He was probably dead before he hit the croton bushes. I sure as shit hope so, anyway. The wife got up at seven and found him. Aside from *that,* Mrs. Fuentes, how was your day?"

"You probably don't like the Mrs. for it."

"No, we're stupid, Jimmy, but we're not total morons. No sign of trouble in the family. Business rivals, the usual shit. The only unusual thing that happened to Antonio in the twenty-four hours prior was a couple of guys turned up at his office and yelled at him about how he was ruining some nature preserve down in South America somewhere."

"These were Latino types?"

"No, one was a white-bread gringo. A hippie, the secretary said. Do we still have hippies?"

"He probably thought of himself as an anarchist."

"Whatever. He was the one who yelled. Long blond dreadlock hair, in a black T-shirt with a logo on it, but she couldn't ID it. They had to call security, and the guy was violent, wouldn't leave. We drew a blank with the security guards on the logo, too. I don't understand why nobody ever sees anything."

"They're mainly not trained observers like you, is why. Who was the other guy?"

"He was an Indian. At least that's what they all agreed on. A little Indian."

"Tomahawk or dot-head?"

"Tomahawk, but I got the feeling from the description he wasn't a local type, more like one of those from south of the border. He had these tattoos on his face." Morales drew lines with his finger on his cheeks and chin. "That's what they do down in, like, the Amazon, right?"

"If you say so."

"The other thing is, there was a cat there."

"A cat? You mean at the crime scene?"

"Yeah. Or so it appears. A big one, like a cougar or a leopard. We took casts of the prints, and we're waiting on the zoo guys to ID them. It sounds weird, but from the look of the wounds, the forensic people say that maybe the cat did them, you know? I mean, can you train a cat to kill someone? There was a weird story I remember reading in school about a guy trained an ape to kill for him. . . ."

" 'Murders in the Rue Morgue,' by Poe. He made that up in his head, though."

"So how do you figure this?"

"It's open and shut, in my view. Guy owns a tiger, he's feeding him Friskies tuna out of those little tiny cans, and one day he says, 'Fuck this, why should I keep opening these little tiny cans, two for a dollar twenty-nine, when I can feed Lucille here on Cuban businessmen for free.' And there you have it."

Morales laughed, but briefly. "No, seriously."

"Seriously? You see this outfit I got on? The white color clues you in that I'm in the food service industry and not the weird crime detection industry."

"The Major asked me to ask you, Jimmy," said Morales with an appropriately serious change of mien.

"Oh, the *Major*. Well, let me drop everything, then, and really focus on it." Paz said this as sarcastically as he could manage, and as he did he felt an unpleasant pang of self-contempt. Major Douglas Oliphant had been pretty decent to Paz when Paz had been a detective under him, and did not deserve that. And was Paz getting more bitchy recently? He took a breath, released it. "I don't see what I could do to help," he said in a milder tone. "I mean, you're going to do the obvious, check out the people who own big cats, follow up on the tree hugger and his Indian . . . ."

"Yeah, of course, but what the Major wanted me to ask you about is the possibility that there could be some kind of ritual involved."

"And I'm the expert on cannibalistic ritual?"

"You know more than me," said Morales bluntly.

"Guilty. But I thought we agreed the perp fed him to the pussycat. Where's the ritual?"

"Okay, not ritual, as such." Morales paused, and Paz saw an expression appear on his face that he had often felt appear on his own: that half smile we put on when we are about to say something that will make us appear stupid, something unbelievable or absurd. "So there's no, like, cult that, say, worships animals and feeds people to them?"

"In the movies, maybe. Why go fancy on it? A guy with a trained tiger is bad enough. Or a maniac who for some reason wants the murder to look like it was done by a tiger."

A little pause here before the detective said, "Because there was no guy. The ground was nice and soft, the gardener had been there that morning and spread fresh compost around the plants. There wasn't a single human footprint anywhere on the grounds, and there's an eight-foot wall around the whole property, alarmed, gated, with no sign of forced entry."

"A solo by the cat, then," said Paz. "A wild animal escaped from one of those private zoos you read about, guy's got fourteen half-starved Siberian tigers in a double-wide trailer . . ."

"Which escaped and made its way to Antonio Fuentes's house and lay in wait on his roof until just the moment the man steps onto his balcony and jumps him, even though the area is lousy with dogs and cats and coons. There were peacocks wandering around there, too. It's that kind of neighborhood. You think it just woke up that day and said mm-mm, gonna get me some Cuban entrepreneur tonight?"

A number of wiseass remarks flitted across Paz's brain

then, but he declined them all. Instead, he shrugged and said, "Fine. You got me baffled. What do you want me to say, Tito? It was more magic in Miami?"

"That'd be a start." He paused here and then in a hesitant tone added, "It was a near full moon last night."

"Oh, well, then. Definitely a werewolf. Or were-tiger, in our case."

"Do they *have* were-tigers?"

"Do *they* have . . . ? Tito, for crying out loud, listen to what you're saying!"

Morales laughed nervously and rolled his eyes, to show (falsely) that he knew the comment had been a joke. "Yeah, okay, but seriously, is there, like, any buzz about people using predators ritually, a cult. . . ."

Paz stood up, suddenly tired of the whole line of conversation. "No, Tito, I'm fresh out of cults. I don't fuck with that stuff, I never fucked with that stuff, and I never *want* to fuck with that stuff. What I want to do right now is take my kid to the beach. Sorry. Give my best to the Major."

With that, he returned to the kitchen. Yolanda had served out the last of the lunches, and the grill was void of everything but burnt-on crud. He removed this with degreaser and a steel scraper, using more force than was called for, cursing under his breath. When the grill was clean, he changed into cutoffs, sandals, and a clean mesh T-shirt and went into the tiny office. The girl was sitting in her grandmother's swivel chair drawing with crayons on copy paper. She was already in her red Speedo, shorts, and the pink sneakers.

"Where's your grandmother?"

"In the front. She's yelling at Brenda again. She got the orders mixed up on table two and the man yelled."

"Let's go out the back, then," said Paz.

Matheson Hammock consists of a mangrove forest and a broad muddy beach lapped by tepid wavelets and is nearly the last remnant on Florida's Gold Coast of what the entire coastline of South Florida looked like before white people decided that beach living had status. Amelia liked it because she was frightened of big waves and because the place was literally crawling with littoral creatures—several kinds of crabs, seabirds, jellyfish, and a variety of mollusks. She knew their names and their habits, and tutored Paz about this in a manner absurdly reminiscent of her mother. Not too long ago Jimmy Paz had been something of a Casanova and had not thought much about children before he got this one, but like many such reformed rakes it turned out that he was an excellent husband to a woman not all that easy to live with, and as for fatherhood, each time he looked at his daughter he grew weak with love.

She ran ahead of him on the beach, the lowering sun casting a long shadow ahead of her, causing panic among the herd of fiddler crabs she was chasing. This sun also made of her bouncing curls a golden nimbus about her head; she was golden all over; even her eyes were golden. Technically, as the child of a mulatto (Paz) and a white woman, she was a quadroon, and had she been born in Cuba a century ago she would have gone straight to the brothels of Havana. Now, of course, everything was just dandy for a mixed-race girl, no problems at all coming down the line for the little sweetheart. When Paz brought up his memories of middle school—where as a black half-white Cuban he had enjoyed the unusual honor of being abused by all three of the major races at once—his gut clenched. Naturally, now that the mom was an M.D., the talk was of private schooling in impeccably liberal venues, but Paz knew all about liberals, too. There was no escape.

On the other hand it was a lovely day, the child was healthy and bright, and all that lay in the unknowable future, Paz now demonstrating to himself his remarkable ability to shut down a line of disturbing thought, a skill that had brought him sane through any number of uncanny and terrifying events while on the police force. It was not for nothing that Tito Morales had consulted him on his cat or cannibal murder. No, shut down that line, too.

The child was approaching an area where dunes and beach grass extended toward the bay. She had been told repeatedly not to walk across such areas barefoot, but now did it anyway, despite Paz's shouted warning, and picked up a sand spur in her foot and fell over and got another one in her hand. Shrieks, wails, refusal to let Daddy look at the burrs, hideous hopping about to avoid same; then the frantic capture, the forced removal of the burrs, the child transformed from an intelligent, competent angel into a writhing animal across his lap. Then, the operation complete, exhausted whining, and a demand to be carried back to their blanket.

Which Paz was happy to do, foreseeing an end to the days of carrying, and not wanting to miss a single one. At their blanket, Paz offered her a pink, pilled item, laundered nearly to pulp, that she had needed for sleep during her entire conscious existence, to which came the reply, "I think I'm too mature for a security blanket, Daddy."

"We could use it as a regular blanket, though," replied Paz, and so they did, the girl curled up in the crook of his arm with the spurned item over her and asleep in minutes. Paz tried to read a newsmagazine, but after ten minutes of trying to figure out the latest corporate scandal, he, too, succumbed to nap time.

And awakened in panic: Amelia was not there. He shot to his feet and looked to the shore, and a tide of relief washed over him, because there was the red bathing suit. The beach had filled up a little with people taking a little fun time after work: a couple of families, some teenagers goofing around with a Frisbee, and some kids and a black Labrador dog splashing in the shallows. Amelia seemed to be in conversation with a boy standing in a Styrofoam dinghy bobbing in the small waves close to shore. The Lab was barking insanely at them, without apparent effect. Paz walked toward the water, and as he approached he saw that it wasn't a boy at all, but a very short stocky man, darker than Paz, with straight blue-black hair and some marks on his face. There was something around his neck on a cord. When Paz came within twenty feet of the two of them, the man pushed the dinghy away with the aluminum oar he was holding, and, still standing upright in the stern, propelled the craft rapidly away with an odd swirling motion of its blade.

"Who was that, baby?" Paz asked.

"Just a man. He talked funny."

"Funny English?"

"No, funny Spanish. I could hardly tell what he was saying. He said I had a beautiful chew it. What's a beautiful chew it?"

"I don't know, kid. You know you're not supposed to talk to strangers when Mommy and I aren't there."

"I know, but he was in a little boat," said the child, with the logic of seven years. "And he was sad."

"Why was he sad?"

A shrug. "That's what I couldn't understand. Could we go for ice cream?"

---

Moie paddles on across the shining calm water. That morning he awoke in his tree hammock, with a full belly and a head filled with dreams of killing and the taste of hot flesh between his jaws. He packed his hammock and his black suit into his case, and wearing only his breechclout, he walked down to the edge of the bay. He saw that the wai'ichuranan had left boats floating and tied for anyone to take, just as the Runiya do, so he took one.

Moie's boat is made of what he thinks is some crumbly white wood like balsa, and the paddles are made of metal and a kind of very hard red stuff and are too long. He has to stand and use one of them like a pole.

He goes south, hugging the shore, past Sunrise Point, past Tahiti Beach, past the canal on which stood the house where Jaguar had taken the man Fuentes. He doesn't know why he goes south, only that it is the proper direction to go now. Presently, he comes to a long sand spit extending east into the bay that has many wai'ichuranan on it, although they are not fishing or repairing boats, but just sitting and eating or running around like dogs, and screaming in their monkey talk. He has to pass close to the beach on the course he is traveling, and there he sees the little girl, standing and looking out on the water as if she were waiting for him. She is wrapped in red cloth, as the Runiya do with the little girls who are left for Jaguar, and that attracts his attention. Also, he can see her death quite clearly shining behind her left shoulder. He had noticed already that the *wai'ichuranan* had their deaths showing when they were small children, but then they died, and the deaths went inside of them. By the age that this girl is, they are often all gone, so this was also unusual. Perhaps Jaguar has prepared this one for himself and Moie has to do something with her. But Jaguar is silent in his heart.

Nevertheless, he paddles close to her and says in Spanish, "Little girl, answer me! Are you *hninxa*?"

The girl says, "No, I'm Amelia. What's your name?"

Of course he is not going to tell a little girl his name. "Tell me the truth," he says, "should I take you with me and give you to Jaguar? You can come in the canoe, even though it is wrong for girls and men to be in the same canoe. But it may be that this is *ryuxit* in the land of the dead."

But the girl only stared at him impolitely and said nothing. Then he saw that a brown man was coming toward them, and there was something about the man that Moie didn't like, he did not exactly trail his death like a real person, but there was something *else* accompanying him, something Moie had never seen before. It frightened him. To the little girl, he said, "You have a beautiful *achaurit*," and then he stroked his boat rapidly away from the shore.

# Four

---

Professor Cooksey didn't drive, so Rupert asked Jenny to take him in the Mercedes to Fairchild Tropical Gardens for a science lecture he had to give. Actually Rupert asked Jenny to ask Kevin, who was the group's designated driver, but Kevin had been stoned and in bed with headphones on since the blowup of the day before, and rather than having to pull his cable out and have a fight about it, she decided to do the run herself. She didn't mind this at all because she enjoyed driving the big old car, which was a 1968 model 230, in cream with red leather upholstery, that had belonged to Rupert's mother. It was like being in an old-time movie driving that thing, especially with the Professor next to her talking in his English accent and the churchy music he liked playing on the radio. And, unusually for her, she had a skirt on because the leather got hot beneath her thighs if the car had to stay out in the sun; this, too, added to the effect of being displaced in time.

She didn't know why the Professor didn't drive. Her personal theory was he was too old, but Kevin said he was a drunk and they took his license away. Although she had never seen him drunk, so that might be one of Kevin's stories. When she thought of that, she recalled the story he had made up about the Indian getting lost, which even *she* didn't believe, and when she asked him later why he did it, he was nasty, and that's when he got his headphones on and cranked the music up so loud she could hear the punk squeaking through around the edges, and that was that. Sometimes he got so mad at her she thought he was going to hit her, but he never did, not like some guys she'd been with, so she thought it was mainly a pretty good deal, Kevin and her.

It was not much of a drive from the property to Fairchild, a couple of miles at most, and Jenny could have dropped him off and come back and picked him up later, but she decided instead to hang around the Gardens. There was an atmosphere on the property just now that made her uncomfortable, a miasma of irritability because of Kevin, and also maybe things weren't going so good with the Forest Planet Alliance. Luna was frosty to her at breakfast and spoke to Rupert in whispers, and they had both looked at her in a funny way. Like it was her fault, Kevin being a jerk. She welcomed the chance to get away for a while until it all blew over. And she liked being with the Professor.

"What are you going to talk about?"

"Agaonid wasps."

"I got stung by wasps once," she said. "I was about, I don't know, six or something, and I was chasing a ball. I was living with this farm family, like on a farm? And I stuck my hand into this hole where the ball went, and holy gee, they were all over me! I thought I was going to die."

"Yes, well, these particular wasps don't sting. They fertilize the fruits of fig trees. Each species of fig has its own species of fertilizing wasp."

"Like bees?"

"Exactly. Except that bees are indiscriminate foragers attracted by the color and scent of flowers, and these wasps pollinate only one sort of fig, and are attracted by hormones. The female has to burrow into the unripe synconium, which is a tough pod containing immature blossoms, through a hole so tight that she rips her wings and antennae off."

"Oh, wow! That must really smart. How does she fly out again?"

"She doesn't. She has fulfilled her function and spends

the rest of her short life entombed in the synconium. Her eggs hatch, and her female descendants pollinate other fig trees. A demonstration of the power of instincts driven by chemical stimuli. A great deal of interesting work has been done on plant-insect pheromonic interaction, actually: for example, Kostowitz and Petersen found that trees of the genus . . ."

Once you got Professor Cooksey started on his bugs he went on for a good while, which Jenny didn't mind too much, she was used to tuning stuff out, and with that voice it was like doing ironing with *Masterpiece Theatre* or a nature show on in the background. She had once stayed in a foster home where that was all they would let you watch, educational programs and nothing with sex and violence, not even cartoons. Oddly enough, some of what he told her seemed to stick in her head by accident and would pop out later with her not even knowing it was there. She occasionally wondered what it was like to know a lot and read the kind of books that Professor C. had, with small printing and no pictures, although he had a lot with pictures, too, that he didn't mind her looking at. When she did think about it she felt a heaviness grow behind her eyes, and she felt kind of sorry for those people, like there would be no room for their own selves inside their heads with all that *stuff* pressing down.

She parked the car, and he walked off with his stiff birdish stride to the Garden House Auditorium, and she strolled off toward the lakes. The day was bright, the air mild, and the tall palms swayed in a gentle breeze from the bay. As always the foliage and the precision and artfulness of the plantings had a psychedelic effect, even, as now, when she wasn't chemically stoned. She thought that if there was a heaven and if it was like Fairchild, then death could have no terrors. Although she had been turned off religion at an early age via the never-fail method of enforced churchgoing, she retained an ample capacity to experience awe, and this was now well exercised as she entered a corridor of gigantic royal palms interspersed with dense plantings, many showing their seasonal blossoms—pink trumpet vine, bird-of-paradise, bellflower, ground orchid. She stood before the blooming plants in thoughtless delight, as a peasant might before an ancient Madonna, quite lost to the world. Flowers made her happy, and she stumbled over the vast question of why everyone just couldn't be happy with what simply was. A motion attracted her eye: an anole lizard had run out on a branch of a lignum vitae tree. She moved closer to inspect it. It was vivid green, a traveling exhibit of what green *was,* and in full male mating fig: as she watched, it shot out a vivid red throat pouch three times, advertising this state, and then scuttled away.

A laugh burst from her. "Guys," she said out loud. She often talked aloud to herself while in the Gardens, or to the plants and animals there. It was a habit she had acquired as a child, to keep herself from dying of loneliness. She had lived in places where no one actually spoke to her, except to give an order, for months on end.

She walked around Royal Palm Lake and past the amphitheater and then to the rain forest exhibit. One of her secret shames was that, even though the rain forest was really, really important, and even though she drew her sustenance from an organization dedicated to its salvation, she didn't really like it all that much, even the compressed simulacrum of one presented by the Gardens. She found it dank and gloomy and clammy hot, and she didn't care for the way everything crawled over everything else grasping for light and things to eat. In a strange way it reminded her of winter in an Iowa kitchen, steam and bad odors and the adults looming overhead and the unwanted children on the rough floors clamoring and striving and pushing one another. Still, she visited the place every time she came, hoping that she would get it, and feeling down when she did not.

When she came to the little path that led to the entrance to the great conservatory that housed the more delicate tropical plants, Jenny was passed by three running men in the tan uniforms of Fairchild groundskeepers. They seemed to be searching for something, calling to one another, and pausing at intervals to peer behind branches. Shortly they came back

along the path at a slower pace with a blue-uniformed security guard in tow.

"Did you get him?" one of them asked the others, and was
answered, "No, he must have left over the wall."

Jenny asked, "What's going on?"

One of the groundskeepers, a portly woman with cropped
gray hair and rimless glasses, said, "Some guy stealing
plants. He was just standing there like he was shopping in a
supermarket, taking cuttings with a little knife and sticking
them in a bag."

Another groundskeeper added, "Yeah, they usually come
over the walls at night. What'd he get, Sally?"

"Not a lot, from what I could see. Usually they dig up
plants, but he was just doing snips. Some bark peelings, too."

The security guard spoke. "You say he was a black guy?"

"Not really. I didn't get much of a look at him, but I'd say
he was an Indian of some kind—brownish red skin and
straight black hair. He was wearing some kind of bathing
suit, a bare chest anyway, and boy, could he disappear. I
mean I was ten feet from him and I saw him chopping at the
jatoba, and I yelled, 'Sir, excuse me, you can't do that,' and
then he was just gone."

The guard's radio burbled, he spoke into it, and then said,
"Well, we'll keep an eye out for him, but he's probably back
on the reservation by now."

He left, and the group dispersed. Jenny walked back along
the path into the rain forest exhibit, looking at the plant labels, laboriously sounding out the names on each until she
came to one that read HYMENAEA COURBARIL—JATOBA TREE,
and then some fine print about what all the natives used the
tree for, which she didn't bother to read but looked upward
along the trunk. The groundskeeper had said he'd been cutting on this tree, and Jenny figured he was probably still
around it. At least it was a place to start looking.

It was a gray-barked tree, around forty feet tall, with shiny
thick leaves and dark brown podlike fruit. Its foliage started
about three-quarters of the way up and was tangled in some
thick climbing vine. She stared up into the green gloom and

called out softly, "Hey, Juan! Whatever your name is! Are you there?"

No sound but the breeze whispering among the branches and a lawn mower off in the distance. She continued staring upward, and as her eyes adjusted to the shade, she saw something brown that was not a fruit, or bark, or shadow. At first she thought it was an animal, a coon, or, absurdly, a sloth, but then she saw that it was a man's face, his.

"Hey, you can come down now. They're gone. They think you're out of the Gardens. Come down!" She gestured broadly and wished again that she wasn't so dumb and could speak Spanish. But the Indian appeared to catch her meaning. In what seemed like no time at all he flowed down the trunk like a python and stood in front of her, regarding her gravely. He was wearing nothing but a breechclout and a kind of furry belt, and a thong around his neck with a little bag hanging on it. He had his cloth suitcase secured over one shoulder by a woven band, like a mailman carries his sack.

"Wow, we thought we lost you!" she said. "You shouldn't have gone away when you were with Kevin. Anyway, you could've got arrested. They don't allow cutting plants and stuff here. See, it *looks* like a rain forest, but it really *isn't*."

Blank stare from the Indian.

"Look, man, here in Gardens you no pick! No do like this!" She went to a small bush and looked around to make sure no one official was watching, and plucked a leaf, while shaking her head vigorously. "No do this, see? Not allowed."

He took the leaf from her and examined it. In his own language he replied, "This is *mikur-ka'a*. I use it mainly for skin diseases, but it's also good for headaches. Also, if someone has been cursed by a witch, I have them bathe in a decoction of the leaves, and it usually works pretty well, depending on the witch, and so on. We could try it, if you have that problem."

"That's right," she said encouragingly, "no do. No pick. Get in big trouble."

"Although you don't seem witched to me," he added. "It's hard to tell with dead people."

"Right, but we can't just stand around talking," she said, "we have to get you to the car and out of here. Let me go ahead and check if the coast is clear, and then I'll wave, like this, and you come on. Try to stay off the paths, okay?" She sighed. "Hide in bushes, yes. *Sí*. We go car, *sí*?"

"*Sí*," said the Indian.

She smiled. "Great! Okay, follow me!"

She started off down the path that led from the rain forest area to the parking lot. She waited for a group of tourists to pass and then performed a come-along gesture. The path behind her was empty. "Oh, no!" she cried. "He got lost again!"

But hardly were these words out when the Indian stepped from behind a large cycad three feet behind her. She gaped in amazement. "Wow, that's awesome! How did you do that?" Receiving no answer, she said, "Okay, just follow me, then."

She started out again, without the gesturing now, but stopped every fifty yards or so to assure herself that he was still with her. Each time he appeared among the plantings almost within arm's reach, although she didn't see or hear him move. When they were nearly at the entrance, she led him through some narrow paths to the wall that separated the Gardens from Old Cutler Road.

"Okay, you have to go over the wall here, because you can't just walk out past the guard. I'll get the car and pick you up. You *comprendo*?" She gestured broadly, climbing and staying, repeating them until she was sure he understood. Which he did, apparently, for she drove around and retrieved him without incident. Then she drove the Mercedes back to the lot and parked in the shade of a cocolobo tree.

She turned the radio on and adjusted the dial. "When I'm alone, I listen to country. Kevin hates it. He likes alternative/punk, Limp Bizkit and Maroon 5, like that. I mean, I can handle that kind of music sometimes, but country is more real, if you know what I mean, it's about, you know, love and having hard times, like life is, or maybe I'm just a hick. That's what Kevin says. Of course, compared to you, I'm like totally downtown." She laughed. "God, what an idiot, Jennifer! You don't understand a word I'm saying, do you? But you sort of know what I mean in a funny way. I can sort of feel it. Like a dog does, but better. Maybe I could teach you English. Do you want to learn English? Okay, here goes: I am Jenny." She pointed to herself and repeated the phrase, and then just her name, and then pointed to her mouth. "Jen-ny."

"Jenny," said the Indian.

"Good! Terrific! Now, what's *your* name? Is it Juan? I'm Jenny, you are . . ." She pointed. The Indian made a little chin-raising gesture she had seen earlier and which she now understood was a kind of nod. But now he seemed to hesitate, and he stared at her, into her eyes, for what seemed like a long time, as if trying to make up his mind about something. Finally, he placed his hand flat against his chest and tapped it twice.

"Moie," he said.

She pronounced the name as he had, *Mou-ee-eh*. "Great! You Moie, me Jenny, this"—touching the interior, pointing broadly—"is car. Say *car!*" And so on, with objects and parts of the body. Jenny could not figure out how to show verbs very well, but she had a fine notion of how to teach a dull child, having been on the receiving end for many years, and they made good progress, she thought. After an hour or so of this, she brought out a vacuum bottle of iced tea she had brought along and a crumpled joint. She lit up, turned the music louder, took a hit, and passed the smoldering number to Moie, who placed the coal-end in his mouth and sucked.

She watched, amazed, and after a while said, "You're supposed to give it back, man." This idea having been conveyed, in word and gesture, they filled the interior of the Mercedes with hypnotic fumes, after which Jenny opened the door and rolled down the windows. Moie pointed to the fading smoke. *"Chaikora,"* he said.

"Yeah, we call it pot, or ganja, or marijuana. A lot of names. Dope. This is pretty good dope. We grow it ourselves. You like?" She mimed goodness, rubbing her stomach, smiling broadly, kissing her hand, to which he responded in his own tongue, "You dead people are very strange. You know *chaikora,* but you take it without chanting, and also you don't mix it with its brothers and sisters, so that it can speak to you properly. We say that *assua* is the brother and *uassinai* is the sister of *chaikora.* Together they are one of the small holy families that help you listen to the animal spirits. Now, without the rest of the holy family, we can't hear the animal spirits very well, but only the spirits in our own heads. What's the good of that?"

She giggled. "Yeah, I hear you, man. It's dynamite boo. Oh, wait, this is a great song." She leaned back and closed her eyes and listened to Toby Keith sing "I Love This Bar." Time passed.

The sound of a car door opening. Professor Cooksey slid into the backseat.

"Well, Jennifer, I see you found our friend. You never cease to mystify and amaze me."

"Yeah, he was in the Gardens, stealing pieces of plants. He almost got busted, but I got him out of there. I'm trying to teach him English."

"Are you, indeed? Well, good for you." Jenny saw that the Professor was staring at the Indian in a strange way, really hard, like he was trying to see into his head, and the Indian was staring back, like he was trying to do the same. She had a familiar and sad feeling that stuff was going to happen that she wouldn't be able to understand.

"My dear, could you turn that music down a bit? I'd like to see what this gentleman has to say for himself."

"He can speak Spanish," she said. "Geli was talking to—"

"Yes, but I doubt he speaks it very well," said Cooksey, and then he began to speak in a language she had never heard before, and she was about to feel kind of crummy about being shut out and all until she saw Moie's face light up with sheer pleasure; a flood of the same speech issued from his mouth.

"I'm amazed, *Tayit,* to hear Runisi in the land of the dead. Are you a priest?"

"Not I, but I spent a lot of time in the Jimori country. Do you know them?"

"I have heard of them, of course. They are vile and steal wives and eat babies."

"They say the same about the Runiya people. Also that you kill all foreigners in your country."

"They are liars, then, as well," said Moie, and after a pause, added, "but we do kill foreigners. Or most foreigners. Did you know Father Tim? He was a dead person like yourself."

"Well, you know there are very many of us, too many to allow us to know all the others, as you can. Why do you call us dead people?"

"Because we Runiya are alive in this world. We are inside it, and the plants and animals, stones and sky and stars, sun and moon, are our friends and relatives. That's what it means to be alive. A fish is alive and a bird, too. But you are outside the world, looking in on it as the ghosts do, and making mischief and destruction, like ghosts do. Therefore we say you are dead like they are. Also, when a person is alive, they carry their death behind them, there"—and here the Indian pointed over Cooksey's left shoulder—"and this is one way we tell a live person from a ghost. But you carry your deaths inside you all the time, so you can have the power of death over all things. So we call you dead people."

"I see," said Cooksey, "and very good sense it makes, too. Now tell me this: you came a long way from your home to stop us dead people from killing your forest. So I have heard from my friends. Tell me, how do you think you will stop them?"

So Moie told the story of what he had learned from Father Perrin after he was killed, and as for how he would stop it, he knew he could not. Just one man could not stop such a thing, and he was not a fool to think it. But Jaguar had promised him that if he brought him to the land of the dead, then Jaguar would stop it.

"And how will he do that?"

Moie made a peculiar gesture using his hands and his head that was easily interpretable as a shrug. "We say: we can ask Jaguar what will happen, and ask him what we should do, but we never ask him how he will do what he does. And if he told us we would not understand."

"That's probably wise," said Cooksey, and then they spoke of many things, Cooksey answering many of the questions Moie had about the land of the dead, until, observing an increasingly impatient Jenny, he added in English, "Well, I think the thing to do is return to the property for a bite of lunch, and then we might venture to discuss how we can help our friend here. Drive on, Jennifer."

At about this time, some miles to the north, three men were seated at a white-clothed and silver-set table in a small executive dining room on the thirtieth floor of the Panamerica Bancorp Building. All three were of the same background, Cubans and the sons of the families who had ruled that island for generations before the revolution of 1959. They had left Cuba as young men (and not floating on rafts either) and had prospered in the United States. In purely financial terms, they were vastly richer than their forebears, yet they harbored, along with most of the rest of their class and generation, a sense of grievance. Their American contemporaries, with whom they did business and played golf, were men of power, but they had never owned a country absolutely and owned all the people in it. Their power was not of that sweetest kind. These Cubans had been able, with the acquiescence of America, to transfer much of their culture to South Florida, which they ran as a kind of fief, the unalterable principle of which was that no one could ever become president of the United States who would normalize relations with the Monster across the Straits of Florida. They were confident, sensual, intelligent, unimaginative, industrious gentlemen, and if they shared a fear, it was that they would never get to dance on Fidel's grave.

And now another more instant fear: the man who had called this meeting, Antonio Fuentes, had been murdered the previous night, for they had contacts in the police and knew the truth about the full horror of the crime. Cayo Delgado

Garza, the host of the luncheon meeting, and the chairman of the eponymous Bancorp, had wanted to cancel it, out of respect, but the other two had insisted that it go forward. These were Juan X. Fernandez Calderón, called Yoiyo, the most vigorous of the three, a developer and financier, and Felipe Guerra Ibanez, who owned a large trading concern. They were all dressed in expensive dark-colored suits and quiet ties; Garza and Ibanez had pins of fraternal organizations in their lapels, in place of which Calderón wore an enamel American flag. They all had immaculately trimmed heads of hair, light brown in the case of Calderón, silver on the other two. They had soft manicured hands, on the wrists of which hung inherited gold watches. Garza was paunchy, Ibanez thin, Calderón still trim and athletic. He played tennis and golf frequently and kept a yacht; unlike the others, he had blue eyes.

A silent brown waiter in a white jacket with shiny buttons served drinks and vanished. They drank the liquor in grateful drafts and spoke feelingly of the dead Fuentes. The waiter returned. Another round of drinks and the lunch ordered, and now they turned to business. Garza asked Calderón, "So . . . Yoiyo: what do we make of this?"

An eloquent shrug. "I'm just as baffled as you. Who would kill Tony? As far as I know he didn't have an enemy in the world. And to tear him up like that! It makes no sense."

"It does if someone is trying to frighten us," said Garza quietly. Calderón stared at him for a second and then shot a look at Ibanez, who indicated by the subtlest possible expression that this was something worth considering. It was clear to Calderón that they had discussed the matter without him, and he felt a jab of anger. But the three men had been doing business together profitably for years. They knew one another well, at least in the way of business.

"What, you're suggesting that this had something to do with Consuela?"

"He was the chairman, the public face, to the extent it has

a public face," replied Garza. "And there was that incident the other afternoon, the reason why Tony wanted to meet."

"That's insane, Cayo. Some little bird-watcher is not going to chop up a man to make a point."

"He had a South American Indian with him," said Ibanez.

"So he had an Indian, for which, by the way we only have the evidence of that dumb secretary and the dumber security guards. How many South American Indians have they seen? I mean, think about it for a minute! A man bursts into a business office, yells a lot of propaganda, gets tossed out, and then what? He goes to the businessman's home and murders him and chops him into pieces and tries to make it look like some kind of tiger did it? It's preposterous."

"They knew about Consuela and the Puxto," said Garza. "Maybe that makes it a shade less preposterous."

This appeared to take some of the bluster out of Calderón. He nodded and drank his Laphroaig. "Yes," he said, "that's troubling. They shouldn't have known about the Puxto. But it's still stupid to connect the two events without more information. The two things may be unrelated."

"Do you think that's likely, Yoiyo?" asked Ibanez gently. Calderón looked straight into the seamed turtle face and said, "Why not? Look, what was it, eight or nine years ago? That nigger maniac chopped Teresa Vargas into pieces, and that was connected to nothing at all. Some insane cult, whatever . . . so this could be the same, the cat prints. It's Miami, these things happen. You never think it's going to happen to someone you know, but now it does. It happened to the Vargas girl, and now it happened to Fuentes. That's one possibility. The next possibility is it was political. Tony gave money to the resistance, he was quiet about it but it wasn't a secret. We all do, yes? So maybe it was that."

"You think Fidel sent an agent to kill Antonio Fuentes?" asked Garza, incredulous.

"Of course not. I'm just laying out the logical possibilities. So, next, we have, yes, something connected with the Consuela deal. Something out of Colombia. Why? Everything is arranged at that end and has been for months. So we don't know, and frankly, I'd find it hard to believe. As a matter of fact, it feels like a maniac again to me. Maybe that nigger left disciples, only this time he's going after men and not pregnant girls."

"But you'll check out the Colombian angle, won't you?" said Ibanez. Again Calderón saw that look between the two of them. Consuela had been his deal, and the message here was that if there was any mess associated with it, it was his to clean up. He got a quarter, no, now a third, of the profits but had all the work to do. A certain resentment here, but if things had to be done he would rather do them himself than leave it to this pair of *viejos*. He took, however, a considerable time before responding, to show he was not their errand boy. "Of course," he said then, "I'll be glad to, Felipe."

The rest of the lunch passed pleasantly enough, in discussions of other matters of business, local politics, and their various interests. After lunch, Calderón called his driver on the cell phone and found his white Lincoln waiting for him when he reached the street. He was driven back to his firm's headquarters, housed in a new mirrored glass cube on Andalusia in Coral Gables. His private office was furnished in mahogany, leather, and worn old Persian carpets, all expensive, understated, and chosen by an interior decorator not often employed by Cuban businessmen. Calderón did not want to be associated with that sort of Cuban at all, the people who had run little shops in Havana and were now magnates in America. *Cursilería* was the word for the style of such people, vulgar and ostentatious.

He was efficiently rude to his staff, and after some scurrying and scraping, he conducted a meeting about a golf course and resort condo development he had begun near Naples, on the west coast of the state. It was the largest thing he had ever attempted, and he had financed it with an unstable structure of rolling credit, in addition to nearly all his own liquid capital. The profits would be colossal, but he was now somewhat overextended, which was the main reason why he had organized Consuela Holdings LLC. The timber money should start coming on line just in time to cover the first series of notes on Consuela Coast Resort and Condominiums. Provided everything went off on schedule.

When he was alone again, he dialed a number in Cali, Colombia, and after a few brief conversations in Spanish with underlings, he was connected to a man with a low, quiet voice. Calderón understood that Gabriel Hurtado was what the U.S. media called a drug lord, but he was quite capable of cloaking this knowledge from his ordinary consciousness. He was a man of aristocratic pretension and habit, and the ability to ignore the ultimate sources of one's wealth is a commonplace talent among such men. The Kennedys and the Bronfmans spent bootlegging dollars with clear consciences, and the fortunes of his own family and those of most of his Cuban friends derived at a couple of removes from slave labor. Money washes, as the saying goes, and in any case Hurtado was not a mere thug. He was well connected with the government of his nation and was at least as well insulated from drug cartel massacres as Joe Kennedy had been from the machine guns of Al Capone. There is an immense flood of Latin American money swimming around Miami seeking safe investment, whose provenance does not bear too much inspection, and many such dollars under the control of Hurtado had over the years swum into the projects of JXF Calderón Associates, Inc., to the mutual profit of both men.

They exchanged pleasantries, and then Calderón told him about the events of the last few days, stressing especially the knowledge of the Puxto business shown by the maniac in Antonio Fuentes's office.

"So the reason I'm calling," he went on, "is to check out whether the leak came from your end."

"That's impossible," said Hurtado. "My people know how to keep their mouths shut." This was said with a certainty that could not be doubted, although Calderón's mind did not long settle upon what made for such certainty. He said, "Of course. What I meant is the possibility that someone down there wants to make trouble for us, for you, in some way. A rival. Someone who thinks he didn't get enough of a . . . consideration, a commission, whatever."

A pause on the line. "I'll look into it. There was some crazy priest down there in San Pedro who was threatening to make a stink, but he's out of the picture. Meanwhile, you got some *cabrón* wandering around Miami with information he's not supposed to have. What're we going to do about that, Yoiyo?"

"I'll handle it at this end," said Calderón.

"You may need some help."

"I'm fine, Gabriel. I was just checking with you."

"That's good, but I want you to remember that I have commitments on this thing, to people down here. I'm talking about significant people. So it can't go sour on us. You're clear on that, yes?"

"Yes. Absolutely."

"Fine. Your family okay? Olivia and Victoria and Jonni?"

"Everybody's great," said Calderón.

"Good. You'll keep me informed, yes?" The connection broke before Calderón could respond. It was not really a question anyway. Calderón was now trying to recall whether, in the course of their extensive business relationship, he had ever mentioned his family to Hurtado. It would not be a thing he routinely did. He had the old-fashioned Cubano sense of strict separation between the world of affairs and the interior world of the home. He was, however, absolutely sure that Hurtado had never asked about them by name before. Suddenly he discovered that he wanted to leave the office and have a strong drink of scotch.

---

Moie watches the world float by from the windows of the *wai'ichura* canoe that floats on dry ground. He says the name *car* in his head and is grateful to the Firehair Woman for having given it to him. It is always good to have the names of things. He is happy to have met Cooksey and to have received answers to many of the questions that troubled him. He now understands that the *wai'ichuranan* cannot change the stars in the sky, and also that they didn't know they were dead at all, but thought they were living life. He thinks of the stars again, that they are not always the same in the sky but like trees along a path, and that as you move a long way across the earth they change in the same way. This is a wonder to him and makes him a little sad.

The car turns and enters a compound of several buildings and they dismount from it, all three of them. There are other dead people there, including the Monkey Boy, who looks a curse at Moie, which he averts with some words in the holy tongue. There is an angry woman who speaks too much and too loud and one man with a beard who speaks slowly and is the chief of this place, and another man who has a hairy face but does not speak much. They chatter in their monkey talk but also to him in Spanish, and when he does not understand, Cooksey says in Runisi what they have said.

They sit at a table, and the Firehair Woman brings food that tastes like clay and hot brown water. He is not hungry at all but takes a little so that the gods of this place are not offended. The Angry Woman talks about the death of the man of the Consuela whom the Monkey Boy screamed at the day before in the house the size of a mountain that you go to in a little hut with no windows that hums in a way you can feel in the belly. The Monkey Boy is happy he is dead, but the others are confused. Who has killed him? they wonder. Moie says in his own language that it is Jaguar, and they all look at him strangely. They are silent for a moment. Then Cooksey asks, "Moie, did you kill this man yourself?" And Moie answers, "Perhaps I would have, if he came to my country, but here I have no power. No, it was Jaguar alone who did this. He is angry at the men who want to destroy his country, and if they don't say they will stop, I think he will kill others, too." He sees that they are amazed, but they say nothing more about it at this time.

# Five

The wailing dragged Paz out of the dream, brought him onto his feet stumbling as the dream paralysis passed from his limbs. He struggled into a robe. His wife, now awakened herself, cried, "What is it?"

"Amy's having a nightmare."

"Oh, Christ, not again! What time is it?"

"Four-thirty. Go back to sleep," said Paz, walking quickly from the room. Entering his daughter's bedroom, he saw by the glow of the Tweety Bird night-light that Amelia was sitting up in bed weeping and clutching her old pink blanket to her face. She stretched out her arms to him, and he sat on the side of the bed and held her to his body, cooing and stroking her hair. This was the fourth one in the last couple of weeks.

"What was it, baby, did you have a bad dream? Tell Daddy, what was it? Did you see a monster?"

Gasping, the child said, "It was a aminal."

"An animal, huh? What kind of animal?"

"I don't know. It was yellow and it had big teeth and it was going to eat me all up."

At this, Paz felt a shock of fear shoot through him. It was at this moment that he understood that he had come to the end of the seven years of peace. What he always referred to as "weird shit" had now officially returned. He wanted to join Amelia in tears but instead took a deep steadying breath and asked hopefully, "You mean like a dog?"

"No, it was a little like a dinosaur and a little like a kitty cat."

"Boy, that sounds scary," Paz said, terrified himself. "But it's all gone now. It can't get you, okay? Dreams are just in your head, you know? Animals in dreams can't really bite and scratch you. We talked about this before, you remember."

"Yes, but, Daddy, I waked up . . . I waked up and the aminal was still here. I was all waked up and it was still here."

She had slipped a little back into her baby talk, not a good sign. He said, "I don't know, baby, sometimes it's hard to tell exactly when you're all waked up, especially if you're having a bad nightmare. Anyway, it was just a dream. It wasn't real."

"Abuela says dreams *are* real."

Paz took a deep breath and uttered an inward malediction. "I don't think that's what Abuela meant, baby. I think she meant that sometimes dreams tell us things about ourselves that might be hard to find out otherwise."

"Uh-*uh*! She says *brujos* can send you bad dreams and they can choke you for *real*."

"But the dream you had wasn't like that," said Paz with authority. "It was just a dream. Now, it's the middle of the night and I want you to try to get back to sleep."

"I want to read first."

"Oh, honey, it's the middle of the night . . . ," he whined, but the child had already leaped light as a fairy to her bookcase and brought back a large-format volume called *Animals Everywhere,* and Paz had to leaf from Aardvark through the beasts of field and forest, ocean and stream, one for each letter, reading each caption, and not missing out on a word, for the child had the whole thing nearly by heart.

"That's the animal that was in my bad dream," she declared, pointing her small finger at the page.

"Uh-huh," said Paz nonchalantly. The smart move here was not to get excited and move on quickly to the harmless

Kangaroo. She was out by the Opossum. He shelved the book, tucked her in with a kiss, and left, but not back to bed.

In the kitchen, he found his wife wrapped in a pink chenille robe, in the act of placing a large, blackened, hourglass espresso maker on the burner.

"How is she?"

Paz said, "Fine, just a dream. You're going to stay up." He gestured to the coffeepot and took a seat at the counter.

"Yeah, I have some case notes I have to write up that I fell asleep over last night."

"It's still last night now."

"Yeah, right. And before I forget, speaking about tonight, I mean twelve hours from now, don't forget the food for Bob Zwick and whoever."

"That's tonight?"

"I knew you'd forget."

"I'm a bad husband. Can't I talk you back into bed? We could fool around."

She looked at him, eyebrows up, a half smile on her lips. She was still a handsome woman, he thought, pushing forty and seven years into a pretty good marriage. She'd stopped obsessing about her weight and was a little lusher than she had been, but she carried it well on her substantial frame. A Marilyn type, blond, generously breasted and hipped, although the face did not go with the 1950s pinup body, being sharp-featured and intelligent, sometimes neurotically so. She had been Lorna Wise, Ph.D., when wed, and was now Lola C. Wise Paz, M.D., Ph.D.; like her name, a handful.

"You tempt me, but I really have to get those notes done, or I'll be fucked all day."

"Choosing the figurative over the literal, so to speak."

She laughed. "Guilty."

"That being the case, since you're being so professional, can I have a consult?"

The coffeepot hissed, and she attended to it, pouring herself a large cup of tarry black, offering by gesture the pot to him. He shook his head. "No, I'm going to try to get a couple more hours."

She sat across from him, took a couple of sips. He'd addicted her to this kind of coffee early in their relationship, and it had helped carry her through what she always referred to as medical-motherhood school. "So consult. The doctor is in."

"Okay, just before Amy started yelling I was having a dream, vivid, clear, like I don't usually have anymore. I'm sitting in our living room, but instead of our couch I'm leaning against a kind of fur wall, like a leopard skin fur wall, and I'm waiting for something, I forget what, just a sense of anticipation. And then I realize that the fur is moving in and out, and that it's a living animal. I'm actually leaning against an animal, yellow with those little circular black dots on it, like a leopard. This is all incredibly clear. It's a leopard the size of a horse, huge, maybe bigger than a horse. And I'm not scared or anything, it just seems natural, and then we have this weird conversation. It says something like, 'You know the world is dying,' and I say, 'Oh, right, war, pollution, global warming,' all that shit, and it says, I don't know, 'You could stop it if you wanted to,' and I get all pumped up, I'm like, 'I'll do anything, whatever you say,' and it says, 'You have to let me eat your daughter.'"

"Good God, Jimmy!"

"Yeah, but in the dream it made perfect sense, and what I was thinking about then, was how would I explain it to you, why it made sense, you know? That crazy dream logic? And the leopard gets up and stretches, and it's like something on a flag, you know . . . from mythology? And I want to fall down and worship it, even though it's going to eat Amy. So I hear her crying, and I want to say to her, hey, it's okay, it won't hurt, it's part of what has to happen to save the world, but then it penetrates that she really *is* crying and I wake up."

"That's quite a dream. Try half a milligram of Xanax before retiring."

"But what does it *mean,* Doc?"

"It means there's static in there during REM sleep while your brain transfers material from short-term into long-term memory and your cortex interprets the static into factitious incident. It's like hearing music in the hum of a fan or seeing pictures in clouds. The brain is a pattern-making organ. The patterns don't have to have any meaning."

"I know, that's what you always say, but get this: okay, I go to see what's up with Amy. She tells me she had a nightmare about an animal trying to eat her, the bad kind where you think you woke up but you're still in the dream. So I calm her down a little and she goes for her animal book and makes me read it to her and she picks out the animal. From her dream."

"You're going to say it was a leopard, right?"

"A jaguar. What do you think of that?"

"A coincidence."

"That's your professional medical opinion? A coincidence?"

Lola did a little eye rolling here. "Yes, of course! What else could it be, mind travel?"

"Or something. I always forget you have this weirdness-deficit thing."

"It's called reason, Jimmy. The rational faculty of mankind. What are you doing?"

"Interfering with you. Running my hands inside your pathetic stained chenille bathrobe. Checking to see if it's still there. Oh, yes. What do you think of that, Doctor?"

Lola closed her eyes and sagged against him. She said, "This is so mean of you when I have to work."

"A quickie. Get up on the counter."

"What about Amy?"

"I gave her powerful drugs," he said, "barbiturates, brown heroin," and lifted her onto the Formica.

She said, "This is what I get for marrying a Cuban."

"What, Jews don't fuck on the kitchen counter?"

"I don't know, but I'll ask around," she said as his mouth closed down on hers. For a while she forgot about her pile of work, and he forgot about dreams.

Lola Wise Paz was at this period a resident in neuropsychiatry at South Miami Hospital, a short bicycle ride from her home. She'd owned a doctorate in clinical psychology when she and Jimmy Paz hooked up, and she'd borne the child, and then, in something of a panic about time's wingéd chariot hurrying near, she had decided to go to medical school at age thirty-four. Paz had backed her play in this, and the two of them had worked like cart horses to make a living, clear time for study, and do the endless tasks of parenthood, helped in this last by the mighty Margarita Paz, the Abuela of Doom. Now, as on most mornings, after Lola had pedaled off, Paz got the kid dressed and fed, delivered her to the first grade at Providence Day School, went to the restaurant, prepped lunch, and cooked much of it. Meanwhile, the Abuela picked up Amelia and brought her to the restaurant Guantanamera. Grandmotherly affections, it appeared, proved even stronger than the desire to exert total control over her restaurant during every single minute it was open. When the lunch rush had declined to a trickle of orders, Paz found his offspring trying on a cook's apron that the grandmother had apparently altered to fit her. Paz looked the tiny prep cook over with a professional eye. To his mother he said, "She looks good. Why don't we let her handle the lunch tomorrow? We wouldn't have to pay her because she's just a little kid."

"I do too get paid!" Amelia protested. "Abuela gave me a dollar."

"Okay, but lay off the booze and cigarettes unless you want to be three feet tall your whole life. And ticklish."

After the shrieks had subsided, Paz set her up with a pan of radishes to be carved into roses. When she was settled, he went to talk to his mother. Margarita Paz was a black peasant from Guantánamo and still bore as she closed in on sixty the marks of that origin: strong arms, wide hips, a bosom like a shelf, and a hard, calculating stare. She dressed in bright colors and lipsticks and nail polishes that set off her shiny chocolate skin; a turban was often on her head, as now. Paz had always been a little afraid of her; he knew no one who was not, except his daughter.

"The produce was garbage today," she said when he came into her little box of an office. "Talk to Moreno, and tell him we're definitely going to switch to Torres Brothers if it happens again. Tell him his father never treated us like Americans."

"I'll take care of it, Mamí," said Paz, although the produce was prime as always. Complaining and snapping orders was her way of showing affection. "Look, I wanted to ask you . . . Amelia's been having nightmares, and she wakes up screaming at night, and when I tell her not to worry, that the monsters in the dreams aren't real, what do I get? Abuela says they *are* real. I wish you wouldn't tell her stuff like that, okay?"

"You want me to lie to my granddaughter?"

"It upsets her. She's too young to be worrying about all that."

"And what about you? Are you also too young?"

Paz took a deep breath. "I don't want to start with this now, Mamí. Santería is your thing, we're not going to get involved in it. Not me, and definitely not Amelia."

"What kind of dreams?" asked his mother, ignoring this last, as she did any statement she chose not to hear.

"That's not important. We don't want you telling her stuff like that."

She shot him a sharp look; it was that "we." Mrs. Paz had always imagined that when her son finally brought home a daughter-in-law, she would be a girl amenable to direction, as was only right. Instead, she got an American doctor with insane ideas about child rearing. A doctor! The *man* should be the doctor, and the woman should take care of the children, emphasis on the plural, and listen to her *suegra* with respect, or else how was society to continue? But this daughter-in-law had been so bold as to state, on more than one occasion, that if Margarita insisted on inducting the girl into "your cult" she would have to reconsider letting her spend so much time with her grandmother, and all because a few little charms, an *ide* for her small wrist, the sacrifice of a few birds in order to cast the child's future and protect her from danger . . . absurd, and especially after all she had done for them. It did not occur to her to wonder why her son had chosen a woman precisely as stubborn and hardheaded as his mother.

She sighed dramatically and threw up her hands. "All right! What can I do, I'm just an old woman, it's perfectly all right to ignore me. I never expected after the life I've lived, to end up being despised like this, but let it be! I won't say another word to the child, ever. Take her away!" Here she removed a bright silk hankie from her sleeve and dabbed at her eyes.

"Come on, Mamí, don't make me crazy. It's not like that and you know it. . . ."

"But," she said, and now fixed him with her terrible eye, "but there is something." Here a gesture, hands like birds, conjuring the unseen.

"What something?"

"Something"—darkly—"there is something moving in the *orun,* I don't know what it is, but something very powerful, and it has to do with you, my son, and with her. Yes, you think I'm stupid, but I know what I know."

There seemed to be nothing to say to that, so Paz kissed his mother on the cheek and went out.

"That's a good rose," he said to his daughter, "but you need to slice the petals thinner so they'll flop over and be more like a real flower. Look, watch me." With which he picked up a parer and an icy, crisp radish from the pan and in eight seconds whipped it into a blossom.

Amelia looked coldly at the proffered garnish. "I prefer it the way *I* do it," she said, showing yet again how close to the tree fell the fruit among the tribe of Paz.

S ome hours later, Paz was again sweating over a grill, but now he had taken on a load of his own banana daiquiri and was feeling pretty fine. The grill stood on his own patio, and on it sizzled and smoked several racks of Cuban-style barbecued pork ribs, marinated in lime juice, cumin, oregano, and sherry. Amelia had set the picnic table for five, a seafood and endive salad had been prepped and was now cooling in the refrigerator, in company with two magnums of fairly drinkable Spanish white and a dozen little pots of flan. He had a tape going, *guajira* music, Arsenio Rodriguez, that floated out through the windows of the Florida room and mixed with the sweet smoke from the grill. Paz before marriage had hardly ever cooked at home, and his social life had consisted of presex activities only. Lola had become more social since the M.D. came through, and they had people over almost every week. He didn't mind cooking for these events, nor did he mind Lola's friends. She did not hang out with people apt to patronize him. Before his marriage, Paz had acquired virtually all his knowledge of the intellectual world from pillow talk. He dated bright women only, showed them a good time, provided plenty of athletic sex, and afterward sucked out their brains, for although he was natively bright, he had no patience for sitting in a classroom listening to the professorial drone, or for poring over texts, or for being tested. He had an extraordinarily retentive memory, which was fed only via the audio channel, and could produce, during these dinner parties, remarks that were surprising from the mouth of a high school grad cook and former cop. He was inordinately pleased when this occurred, as was his wife, the intellectual snob. At such times he could see it on her face: look, he's not just a stud.

He heard the clicking of a coasting bicycle, and Lola rolled into view in the driveway. Amelia came shouting up to show off the garland of yellow allamanda blossoms she had constructed and also the dollar earned at the restaurant. Then a kiss for Paz. She looked around, sniffed luxuriously.

"That smells great. You're being the perfect husband again."

"Not perfect. I grabbed Yolanda's butt in the reefer before lunch."

"Oh, I totally understand about that," she said. "I know how men are—you haven't had a piece of ass in what, seven hours?"

"Seven hours and thirty-two minutes," said Paz, "but

who's counting?" She laughed and went off to shower and change her clothes. Paz drank some more daiquiri and painted more sauce on his meat.

**B**ob Zwick was a blocky, confident man with a Jewish Afro of some length and an unrepentant New York accent that in social situations he rarely let rest. He had graduated from MIT at sixteen and thereafter had spent five years working on M-theory with Edward Witten at Princeton. Having plumbed the secrets of subatomic structure as far as he wanted, he had surprised everyone by switching fields to molecular biology, had picked up another Ph.D. (Stanford) in that, and then, feeling the need for a little break, had come down to Miami to work on his tan and get an M.D. at the university. There he had met Lola, had hit on her instantly, as he did on very nearly every woman who crossed his path, been laughingly rejected, and become her friend. Zwick, it had to be said, neither pressed his suit beyond the first no, nor held a grudge. Paz would not have picked him off a menu as a pal, but he got along with him, had even taken him out on the boat to fish a time or two. He found Zwick entertaining in a headachy sort of way, like daiquiris.

Dressed this evening in shorts, sandals, and a T-shirt that said PRINCETON COSMOLOGICAL CO. INC. CUSTOM UNIVERSES, WE DELIVER, he strode in, embraced and kissed the hostess, snatched up Amelia and whirled her around to the giggle point, shook hands with Paz, and introduced his current girl, a leggy blonde with a bony sardonic face. She was wearing a sleeveless top and a long skirt of some nubbly clinging stuff, in lavender. Paz felt a little flutter in his belly, but she didn't bat an eye.

"Beth Morgensen," she said, extending a cool hand. "You must be Jimmy Paz."

"I am," he said and wondered if she had told Zwick, and more important, whether she would let it out this evening.

"What is that, a banana daiquiri?" said Zwick. "I want one. Beth, this guy makes the best banana daiquiris in the galaxy. These are galactic-level daiquiris."

"So I've heard," said Morgensen, who had, in fact, consumed any number of them during the months eight years ago when she had been one of Jimmy Paz's many girlfriends. He produced the drinks, along with a salver of boiled shrimps with small pots of various sauces, and avoided her gaze.

They drank around the picnic table and talked, their shoulders swaying helplessly, their fingers tapping to the music, and Paz rose several times to replenish the blender, helped by Amelia, who liked squeezing limes and breaking bananas into the beaker. On the last of these trips, he ran into Beth Morgensen, coming from the bathroom. Paz sent Amelia out with a full blender. Morgensen watched her trot off.

"Well, Jimmy Paz," she said, looking him over boldly, "all domesticated with a kid and a wife. Who woulda thunk it? I guess I blew my chance."

"I didn't know I was in the running. You were aiming for a full professor, as I recall."

"Silly me, then. How long have you been married?"

"Seven years, around there."

"Oh, the danger period."

"I don't know. I'm pretty happy."

"She must be a kaleidoscope of delight, then." She moved closer, placed her arms on his shoulders, did a little hip grind to the music. "It's hard to believe," she said, "that you're into fidelity. Not the Jimmy Paz I used to know."

"People change, although now that I think of it, you were always a cheap date. A couple of scoops and you were slipping out of your panties."

"True enough. Would you like me to slip out of them now? Only you would know."

Paz gave her a false little smile, a faked laugh, and eased away.

More drinking. The shrimp peels piled up in the bowl. Zwick was holding forth on the mystery of consciousness and how he intended to penetrate what he called "the last great unanswered question in science." Paz said, "I thought that was string theory. I thought it was getting relativity and quantum mechanics to work together, quantum gravity, the Theory of Everything stuff."

Beth screamed in mock horror. "Oh, no! You asked him about string theory! Wake me when it's over."

"Yes, theoretically," said Zwick, and in a Germanic accent, "tee-or-et-ically, but that's all it's ever gonna be, these patzers will be crashing gold nuclei into each other forever, and maybe, *maybe,* they'll get hints of something, and maybe, they'll get something from the telescopes, peek a little at the big bang a zillion light-years away, but they'll never be able to deliver the confirming experiment. Not like the quantum work, not like relativity, where you have fucking *thousands* of confirming experiments." And he went through several of them in detail, a short course in both quantum electrodynamics and general relativity, using shrimps and utensils as particles (or waves) and napkins to model the Calabi-Yau spaces in which the putative seven extra dimensions of space-time were wrapped in the unimaginably small compass of the Planck length. He was a superb teacher, funny and with a consummate grasp of the subject. Even Amelia seemed to be following the spiel before she drifted off to play with the cat.

"Yes, but you haven't said why none of it makes sense, why no one can actually generate our sensory world out of all that craziness," said Morgensen. "Instantaneous action at a distance, time stretching, cats being alive and dead at the same time, all of that. I personally think you guys just made it up."

"Because you're a primitive creature and not a scientist," said Zwick. "A lovely though primitive creature."

"I beg your pardon: I *am* a scientist."

"No, you're a pseudoscientist. Sociology is a pseudoscience, using statistical methodology to massage a set of lies. It's like phrenology. It doesn't matter how accurate you are with the fucking *calipers* or whatever, the underlying theory is crap, as are the data sets. Science is physics: theory, analysis, experiment. Everything else is dogshit."

"And see who gets another crack at my milk-white body," said Morgensen, "probably not Mr. Dogshit here."

"And yet from another perspective," said Zwick instantly, "we see that sociology is actually the *queen* of the sciences, profound, illuminating, un-dogshitlike. . . ."

"But according to you, string-theory physics is dogshit, too," said Lola.

"No," Zwick replied, "it has the shape of real science, it mathematically predicts stuff we know to be true already, but it's really unlikely to be anything but a kind of, I don't know, *theology,* which is why I bailed. It's gotten absolutely medieval, guys spinning out theory that there's no hope of ever confirming because there's not that much energy in the universe, I mean to get down to the strings or the dimensions wrapped up in the Planck length. And the cosmos stuff, yeah, but it's like looking for a cat in a blacked-out room. Dark matter? Dark energy? Please! But biology, especially neuro, is where physics was a hundred years ago. We're generating volumes of new, real information just like Rutherford and all of them. We can look inside the brain now, actually watch it thinking, just like they discovered how to look inside the atom. Magnetic resonance imaging technology and the cyclotron are machines of the same order of importance. Plus, we have genomics now, which means we can trace the genetic switching that creates learning, that creates behavior, down to the molecular level. So psychology is out the window. I mean it was always crap, but now we know it's crap. There's no psych to 'ology' on."

During all this Paz had been quiet, sucking it in along with a lot of Bacardi, and having obsessive thoughts about Beth Morgensen. He hadn't thought about her for three minutes in over eight years, but now she seemed to have moved in and taken a lease on large tracts of his midbrain. What she was like in bed, how different from the Lola, the wife, how light the relationship had been, how much fun, how little like warfare. Although he knew that it was relationships just like that in their many dozens, in their ultimate ennui, that had driven him into matrimony. But still . . .

More to clear his mind of this garbage than because of any real engagement, he said, "Bullshit. There's no way you can know that."

"Well, not now, but we will. The whole field is being systematized, physicalized, which is the characteristic of all real science. We're moving toward a real understanding of the neural code, the way the brain actually *works,* in exactly the way that we really understand how the underlying properties of quarks establish the qualities of elementary particles, which establish the qualities of chemical elements, then molecules, then life, and so on."

"Never," said Paz.

"Why, never? What's your argument?"

Paz stalled by doing a superfluous check on the grilling meat. A woman's face and body floated into his mind, long and white, frizzy brown hair, pointy nose, slanted gray wolf eyes, small hard breasts, Silvie the philosophy major and the theory of logical types.

"The theory of logical types," Paz said, "Alfred North Whitehead."

Both women were delighted to see Zwick brought up short by this. "What the fuck does that have to do with anything?" he demanded.

"Because a set can't be a member of itself," said Paz, drunkenly confident. "Say that total knowledge we have about any given subject is a set, set A. And say all the things science or people, the culture, knows is another set, set B. Any number of set A's will fit into set B, by definition. We know everything possible about how to make flan, about the mass of the particles, about the number of barbers in Cincinnati, right? But the set 'understanding consciousness' is a set of a different type. It's not another set A. It's larger than set B, which is actually made up of all human minds. For the human mind to understand consciousness would be a violation of the theory. That particular A just won't ever fit into the B, ever."

Zwick stared for a moment, rolled his eyes, and said, "That is complete and utter horseshit."

"Plus," said Paz, "the mind is not necessarily a product of the brain. You can't disprove dualism, and if you deny it, it's just another belief. It's not science."

" 'The mind is not a product' . . . what is this, the Middle Ages? There *is* no mind. What we interpret as consciousness is an epiphenomenon of an instantaneous electrochemical state generated by a piece of meat. It's an illusion devised by evolution to organize and coordinate sensory data with actions."

"Then who am I talking to, and why should I believe you any more than you believe in spirits?"

"Hey, the proof is let me go into your skull and make a couple of tiny cuts and there won't be a you anymore. Trust me on this, pal."

"I do trust you, but it don't mean shit. I could go in there and shoot my radio while it's tuned to Radio Mambí. The radio won't make noise anymore; does that mean that Radio Mambí just ceased to exist? Not that that would be a bad thing."

"What, you think that there's a substance called 'mind' that's somehow floating in the ether and our brains just pick it up?"

"Not necessarily, but it's just as logical as saying that mind is determined by the meat. And it would account for demons and dreams and clairvoyance better than your way."

"Jesus! This *is* the Middle Ages. Where to begin? Okay, first of all, any dualism falls before Occam's razor—that is, it adds an unnecessary level of complexity to a phenomenon that can be fully explained—"

"Fuck Occam and fuck his razor," said Paz, and then, "Wait a second, hold that thought!"

A tiny clock had just rung its notional alarm in Paz's nonexistent mind, and he got up and snatched the cover from the grill, revealing racks of glistening, steaming ribs at the precise moment at which they were perfectly done.

"Let's eat," said Paz, and everyone applauded.

During the actual dinner, Lola turned the conversation artfully away from cosmological themes, drawing Beth out about her work, which was a study of the lives of Miami street prostitutes, or girls who let boys kiss them for money, as they explained to Amelia, and herself supplied numerous amusing anecdotes about life as a neuropsych resident in the emergency room, her current duty, and also about going through med school with Zwick, his complete incompetence at any healing task, apparently a man who had never once found a vein on the first try, and often not on the twelfth either. Zwick took this good-naturedly enough, asserting that he'd only become a doctor to be able to do fiendish experiments on human beings and had no guilt about it at all.

They drank nearly half a gallon of the Spanish white, and after they cleared away and served dessert, Paz brought out a bottle of Havana Club añejo rum, and they sipped off that for a while until the child got cranky and had to be dragged off to bed.

"I'm scared to go to sleep, Daddy," she said when he'd got her under the covers at last.

"You're so tired you'll be asleep before you know it."

"Yes, but what if the dream animal comes back?"

"It won't. It's bothering another little girl tonight."

"Who?"

"A naughty girl, probably. Not like you."

"But what if another animal comes?"

"Well, in that case, would you like to borrow my *enkangue*? No dream animals are going to mess with that."

"Uh-huh. Abuela made that for you, didn't she. To protect you from the monsters."

"That's right."

"Mommy says it's just superstition."

"Mommy's entitled to her opinion," said Paz blandly and slipped the charm on its thong over his head. He tied it carefully to the bedpost. "Don't open it, okay?"

"What will happen?"

"It might stop working. Now, good night."

"I want a story." She got one and held out for just three pages of *Charlotte's Web*.

\* \* \*

**B**ack on the patio, Paz slipped an Ibrahim Ferrer CD into the machine and stood listening to the mellow voice singing an old bolero, music from the great age of *son,* the 1940s, his mother's music. It was velvet dark now, insects buzzing in the trees, jasmine floating in the air, the only light coming from citronella candles in yellow glass jars on the table. He put an arm around his wife's shoulders and led her into a close dance. From a distance, from out in the dark yard, he heard the sound of Zwick and Beth having an argument.

"What's all that about?" he asked into her ear.

"She's drunk and belligerent. He doesn't respect her mind enough. He doesn't think people who want to have serious careers should have kids. She was looking at Amy like she wanted to kidnap her. The biological clock is running down on old Beth, and a tenure-track associate professorship doesn't seem to be filling the void, nor do brilliant heartless dudes like Bobby Zwick, the poor bitch."

"You've been there."

"I have. With guys like that, too." She gave him a hard squeeze.

"What I get for being a dummy."

"You're not a dummy, dummy."

"But not as smart as Zwick."

"No, but you're cuter. I'm not sure *anyone* is as smart as Zwick. Although that line about Whitehead threw him a little. You never fail to amaze me."

The sounds of argument faded, succeeded by some weeping, some softer talk; then, the faint creak and rattle of a rope hammock.

"Uh-oh, do you think they're doing it back there, in our hammock?" Paz asked.

"I hope so. They can warm it up for us. God, when was the last time we did it in the yard?"

"Not since Amelia learned about doorknobs."

"Go have children," Lola said.

Zwick wandered back and sat at the table and poured himself a couple of fingers of old rum. Paz and Lola joined him.

"Where's the girlfriend?" Lola asked. "Strangled?"

"Passed out in the hammock. It's all your fault, Paz, you and your daiquiris and your añejo and your ontological speculations. Did you know that physics is a patriarchal conspiracy to promote a dominant worldview? As is medicine."

"Well, when you solve the mystery of consciousness it won't matter," said Paz. "You can recode everyone's brain."

Zwick laughed, a little more elaborately than the comment deserved. "Yeah, and what if that changes physics? Listen, you want me to tell you the secret of the universe?" He mimed a paranoid looking over both shoulders. "Don't tell anyone. Okay, so let's say we have these vast pillars of physics, relativity and quantum electrodynamics, and they're both as elaborately confirmed as anything in the world. Maybe *too* elaborately confirmed, out to a part per billion or more. Now, you're a detective, right? What if I told you that every time there's been a physical breakthrough, we've found a piece of abstract math that's just tailor-made to fit the new concept? Einstein *just happened* to find Riemann geometry to fit general relativity. And the quantum boys *just happened* to find matrix algebra and tensors. And when they first proposed string theory, it *just happened* to fit Euler's beta-function, a two-hundred-year-old piece of math that had never been used for anything before. And Calabi and Yau's canoodling with hyperdimensional geometries *just happened* to describe how the extra dimensions required by string theory are curled up. Not to mention the fact that a whole bunch of universal constants *just happen* to lead to a universe where conscious life evolves, and if one of them was changed even a tiny bit there'd be no stars, no planets, no life. What would you say to a case like that?"

"I'd look for a frame-up. Or it might just be a slam dunk."

"Yes! But *which*? That's the killer question. Now let's say they confirm string theory physically. Let's say it's Hawking's conjecture that black holes radiate outside their event horizons, and we find a black hole small enough to study and string theory predicts that radiation exactly. Then we know it's true, hallelujah! Physics has the theory of everything at last, except . . . except what if we made it all up? Observation is a slender reed when you come right down to it. Thousands of astronomers observed the skies and fit their observations into the Ptolemaic system, making loops and littler loops to save the appearances until the whole thing collapsed, but string theory can't collapse because it's a theory of everything, everything is already accounted for, and confirmed by a zillion observations. But observation itself is a product of consciousness, and *we don't know what that is!*"

"Why you're a doc now."

"Why I'm a doc. So let's say I'm wrong, John Searle and all of them are wrong, consciousness is not a little trick of the brain, let's say it's its own thing, a basic constituent of the universe on a par with space-time and mass, that only occasionally comes to rest in brains but has its own life, maybe down in the Calabi-Yau spaces or out in some connecting universe. That's your substance dualism, yes? You and Descartes. Then you could have your gods and demons, hey? Your miracles."

"But you don't believe that," said Paz. His throat was suddenly dry, and he poured himself a little of the fruit juice they had laid out for the child.

"Nah, this is just drunk talk. But let's say it *is* true we did discover the secret of consciousness, just like we discovered the secret of the physical world, and then there would be these two new pillars of knowledge, the exterior and the interior worlds reaching up to the heavens, and then some Einstein would come along and figure out how they locked together. Then what? We might hear a buzzer, like *ennnnnhk!* And across the sky in humongous letters, GAME OVER. Or we might learn not only how to observe the quantum world but to actually change it. Actually manipulate the intimate fabric of space-time and mass-energy!"

"This is not going to happen soon, is it?" asked Lola. "Because I just dropped off a big load of dry cleaning."

Zwick snatched up a candle and held it under his chin,

and in a horror-movie voice intoned, "We would be like GODS! Mwah-ha-ha-ha-ha!"

And they all laughed, but each was a little uneasy in the laughter, each for a different reason.

# Six

Jenny tossed a broken banana into the blender to keep company with the celery, the beets, the spirulina protein powder, and the psyllium husk extract and goosed the HI button. Through the glass top she watched the smoothie come into being, a pinkish gray vortex. Making the midmorning smoothie for Rupert was one of Jenny's tasks, along with feeding the birds, the cats, the boyfriend, and recently Moie, the Indian; or the Runiya, as she had to remember to call him. But Moie didn't eat, which worried her, although she herself did not think much of the cuisine at FPA. Rupert thought that it was wrong to consume animals raised for food, and thought that they should set a good diet-for-a-small-planet example, and also establish solidarity with the indigenous people of the rain forests. Rupert got Professor Cooksey to question Moie about his diet, and how to prepare it, but Moie didn't know about any foodstuffs but meat (in which he included fish, which in turn included turtles, reptiles, and waterfowl) and seemed somewhat affronted to be asked about "women's things." Meat and women's things were how he divided edible substances.

She was supposed to watch him as well, which was not difficult, much easier than minding a kid, for he was in general docile and gentle. In the mornings, when she did her chores, and during the times, as now, when she had to prep and serve food, she parked him in front of the big TV in the living room. They had cable, and she usually punched up a nature program for him. He seemed to like these, and he would also sit solemnly with her while she took in *One Life to Live,* her favorite show, although here she had to explain what was going on, because it was kind of hard to get into the plot if you hadn't been watching for a long time.

She poured the smoothie into the special smoky green glass that Rupert liked to drink it from, placed it on a serving tray, added Luna's herbal tea and Geli's coffee and Professor Cooksey's regular tea, extra-strong with milk, a plate of chocolate chip cookies and a Sprite for herself, and brought it into the office. They were all talking about Moie and what to do about him now that there was this murder of the old Cuban guy, and she was sort of interested in that, so after she'd placed the tray on the table and everybody had their stuff, she sat down in a chair away from the meeting table and listened. That was cool according to Rupert because she wasn't to think of herself as anything but a full member of the community and not just, like, a maid or anything. Which she mostly thought. She had been an actual maid at one time and so she knew the difference.

Jenny thought that coming into a meeting in the middle of it was a little like coming into the middle of *One Life to Live,* it took a while to figure out what was going on, but you knew the characters, so in a little bit it made sense. Luna was all about using Moie to make a big stink about the people trying to cut down his forest. She had a friend who was a TV producer on Channel Four, and she thought she could get a feature made, and also some of the national enviro groups might pick it up. It was a great story, how this little guy had traveled all that way from South America in a canoe. Geli said, unfortunately he's not a Cuban, and when Luna asked what that meant, Geli said, he's illegal, he's in the country illegally, and if he comes out in public the INS will arrest him and he'll be stuck in Crome Avenue behind a wire with all the Haitians, and then Luna said, oh, shit, I didn't think of that, and then added, Rupert, you should talk to your congressman, because Rupert gave a lot of money to this congressman, Jenny always forgot his name, something like Woolite, and he sometimes got him to do stuff, like make a speech about something the FPA was hot on, in the Congress. But Rupert said, maybe that's not such a good idea at this point until we have clarified about this murder. And he asked Professor Cooksey what he thought, was Moie capable of killing someone that way?

"Well, he says no and I believe him, up to a point," Cooksey answered, after a considered moment. "He says Jaguar killed the man, which gives me pause."

"What do you mean?" asked Luna.

"I mean it sounds like this 'jaguar' is a kind of god to him, so it might be a figure of speech, as we would say when someone of whom we disapproved met with a bad end, 'God punished him.' On the other hand, it could be a case of shape-shifting."

"Which is . . . ?" said Luna.

"It's a form of ritual. I've observed it any number of times in the field. A shaman takes some drug, usually a form of *ayahuasca,* which is an extract of the *Banisteria* vine together with other plant materials, and goes into a trance, during which his animal tutelary spirit takes possession of him and confers special powers. These can be things like superhuman strength, the ability to see in the dark, the ability to travel in spirit form, and so on. It's no longer him, d'you see, but the animal spirit. And in that case, our Moie could possibly have committed a murder and have no real knowledge of the crime."

Jenny noticed that Rupert's face had assumed the dreamy half smile that it wore when he had heard something he didn't want to hear and wished that someone would do something to make it go away. "That's unfortunate, then," he said. "Obviously, that greatly reduces, or rather eliminates, the possibility of him being of any value to us as an organization. In fact, I'm not sure it wouldn't be the best thing, all things considered, for us to inform the police."

Luna's face had become pale under her tan, and her eyes

had become all pinched looking, which Jenny knew was a signal that something bad was going to happen, and so it did.

"The *police*! Rupert, what the *fuck* are you talking about? What the hell have we been fighting against besides the kind of shit that's going down in the Puxto, of which Moie is living evidence? *Living evidence!* And you want to lock him up because some Cuban scumbag got himself killed?"

In his most maddeningly reasonable voice, Rupert replied, "Of course I don't *want* to lock him up, but giving, ah, refuge, to someone who may be a serious felon would compromise the principles of our organization and open us to, ah, the possibilities of criminal prosecution. You can see that, surely?"

That was a big mistake, Jenny thought: when Luna got that pinched look what you wanted to do was either agree with her or get the fuck out of town for, like, three days.

"No," said Luna, "what I see is that, in fact, this organization has no principles at all, except making some rich people feel good about their money. Oh, *I* don't buy tropical hardwoods and *I* use shade-grown fair trade coffee in my three-thousand-dollar espresso machine, give me a fucking good citizen medal! And so let me make it really, really clear. If anyone calls the cops on that man, I personally am off the reservation on it. I will blow the whistle. I will let every enviro in the world know what went down, who he is, and what's happening. I will call every TV station in town. There'll be TV crews in permanent residence outside that gate, and you can explain why the preservation of the rain forest is important but not quite important enough for Rupert Zenger to take any risk at all of even being suspected of doing an illegal act. I don't care if you kick us out, I don't care if me and Scotty have to sleep in our fucking van and live on rice and beans—"

"We could make a tape," said Geli Vargos into the angry speech; Luna stopped her rant, and they all stared at Geli. "We could tape his story, just him talking into the camera, with a voice-over, and then we could add subtitles translating what he said. And send out copies to the media. That would expose the Consuela company and put pressure on the Colombians to stop them from destroying a national park, especially since the Puxto got set up by contributions from enviro organizations in the first place."

Rupert said, "I don't see how that solves our problem. A tape like that is meaningless to the media unless they have confirmation that the man is what and who he says he is. A little brown man with a bowl haircut and tattoos could be anyone. So we would have to identify ourselves in any case, present him for interviews. . . ."

"No, it's a good idea," said Luna. "If we do it right, it'll cause a sensation. He'll be a public figure, and it won't matter if he's an illegal immigrant."

"Why won't it, Luna?" Rupert asked.

"Because if we do it right, a mass mailing of tapes, by the time the INS gets around to it, it'll already have happened. We'll have the interviews already. I could offer Sunny Riddle an exclusive on it, the epic voyage from the Orinoco. And after that, hell, let them take him and stick him in the jail. Let them repatriate him. He doesn't *want* asylum, for God's sake. He just wants his forest intact. And we could get a book out of it, too, we could get a grant, send a team back to Colombia, Moie in his natural habitat. Jesus, it would put this organization on the map!"

"I see we're no longer concerned," offered Professor Cooksey in a dry tone, "that this fellow might be in the habit of carving people up while in a drug-induced trance?"

"Actually," said Rupert, "we have no real evidence of that, do we? It's just, ah, speculation, as you admit yourself. And Geli's right. And Luna. It could be a big breakthrough for us." He turned away from Cooksey and regarded the two women with his benign brown eyes. "Now, how shall we arrange this taping? Perhaps a more anonymous location would be best, away from the property." He took a large bite of chocolate chip cookie and awaited their response. Professor Cooksey turned his head and looked Jenny full in the face, as if he knew just what she was thinking.

*　*　*

Jenny got up and walked out, not bothering to collect the snack tray or ask if anyone wanted anything, as she usually did. She rarely felt anger, because what was the use of getting angry, anyway? But she had not liked what she'd heard. She thought Professor Cooksey could have made an objection, or she could have herself, although she never spoke up when organization business was discussed. The conversation had reminded her unpleasantly of other conversations she had heard, between social workers and foster parents, about her. They always spoke over her head, as if she wasn't there, deciding what to do about her *problem*. Of course, Moie wasn't actually there, but they were treating him the same way, as a hassle and not as a real person who might have something to say about what was going to happen to him. Professor Cooksey was the one who spoke most often to Moie, knowing the language and all, but he mostly talked about plants and the kind of weird stuff he did in his home in the rain forest, and about gods and spirits.

She walked through the courtyard and down a garden path to the pool. There, as she had expected, was Moie, gazing morosely at the waterfall and humming to himself. She squatted down next to him and asked him how he was doing.

He said in Runiya, "When I first came to the land of the dead, I thought you *wai'ichuranan* could move the stars in the sky and I was very afraid. Cooksey says that isn't so. But this is nearly as bad. You make a little world here, as in this pond, as in your garden, but it is all wrong, all *siwix,* and it hurts my belly to see it. The creatures are alive, but the thing is dead. Have you never once listened to what a plant or animal has to say?"

She nodded and smiled. "Yeah. It's pretty cool. See, it's like all natural. The pump runs off solar. The sun, see"—she pointed to the sky—"it makes the water go around. Sun, waterfall, see?"

"You are a most strange being," said Moie. "If I could speak to you properly, I would examine you and find out why you are barren, even though the Monkey Boy drags you into his hammock very often. I should ask Cooksey about this, although perhaps it is part of being dead that you make few children. Also I wonder where your elders are. I have heard some tribes eat their elders and so perhaps you do this as well. Again, I will ask Cooksey."

"Cooksey's having a meeting in the office," she said, recognizing the spoken name. "We can go see him later. You want to come watch my program with me? *One Life to Live?* Jessica and John? And Starr?" She mimed turning on a TV and sketched a screen in the air. She backed away from him making come-hither gestures. A few minutes later they were settled in front of the screen, she in a worn but cozy rattan armchair, he on his haunches leaning against the sofa.

———

Moie watches the stolen ghosts of the dead people in the spirit box. They seem to be living the ordinary lives of dead people, although it is clear to him that the box is ruled by demons. Sometimes the dead people disappear and a demon appears and shouts and makes noises. As now, he sees a demon come out of a bottle and shout at a dead woman, who smiles at it. The demon flies around her hut making everything into metal, like an axe blade, with sun shining from the furnishings, although they are inside the hut and there is no sun. Then the demon returns to the bottle and the woman speaks of how she loves the demon. Her daughters will never have children, Moie knows. Now a dead person tries to poison a demon dog, but it doesn't work. The dead person places poison in two bowls, but the demon dog picks the wrong one, and eats, and doesn't die but instead talks to the man and tells him how foolish he has been—he should have put the poison in both bowls! It's clear that the *wai'ichuranan* are not as clever as the Runiya when it comes to killing demons. Now some flashing that he can't understand, one scene after another so fast he doesn't know what's happening, then come the humming, squeaking sounds that always presage the return of the spirits.

The Firehair Woman is talking, as she always does when

the spirits are showing in the box. Moie thinks this is part of her worship. He himself can catch spirits in a box, if they are causing trouble in the village, for example, or if there is a bad person around, like a witch or murderer, then he would steal the man's spirit and lock it away, so his body could more easily be burnt up. But no Runiya would think of talking to them. Only really stupid or bad people leave their spirits behind when they go above the moon, and what can be learned from talking to these? He wonders if these spirits are her ancestors. That would at least make sense, for the Runiya speak to their ancestors all the time, and for this purpose they keep their ancestors' dried hearts in beautifully decorated pouches hung from the rafters of their longhouses. He wonders if there are dried hearts in this spirit box. Once, the first time she showed him the spirit box, he tried to pry the back of it off with his knife, but she became excited and pulled at his arm. He understood that looking into the spirit box was *siwix* for her, and so he didn't do it.

She is smiling and pointing to the box and talking. She wants him to see something. He looks. In a room of one of the *wai'ichura* longhouses, two spirit *wai'ichuranan* are preparing to do *puwis*. (There is a louder humming, which always comes when something important is going to happen; he has learned that much.) But he has seen this many times before. The dead spirits are always, always, preparing to do *puwis*: they kiss, they rub each other, they take off their stupid clothing, or most of it, and yet they never do any *puwis*. Of course, everyone knows that the spirits cannot do *puwis*, it is only for the living.

So these dead people spirits are lying down on the platform where they sleep, covered with a blanket, and the dead woman spirit is making noises, similar to what this kind of woman would make in life; he has heard this many times now from the Firehair Woman and Monkey Boy when they do *puwis* in their hut. Also Angry Woman and Hairy Face Man do it, but she makes a different sound. Moie knows that the spirits are not doing *puwis*, for the woman is not on her

knees showing the man the dark folds of her *aka* to excite
him.

In any case, he is no longer able to see them. He can only
see a hole in the wall of the longhouse. A *window* is their
word for this hole. The humming increases. Now he sees the
man and woman again, and it is as if he has passed through
this hole. Moie can do this, too, going through the walls, and
so he knows that an *aysiri,* a sorcerer, is somewhere around.
Yes, now he sees the *aysiri,* who has made himself small to
go into the spirit box. The Firehair Woman is talking, talking, and Moie wishes she would stop, because this is interesting, for a change. The *aysiri* has a pouch in his hands, and
Moie knows just what it is, a *layqua,* a spirit catcher, for he
has one himself, although he did not bring it with him to the
land of the dead. His is smaller and has bright feathers on it.

Now the *aysiri*'s head grows large, showing that he is very
powerful, and Moie can see his spirit catcher more closely.
He sees that there is a little spirit box attached to this *layqua,*
in which the sorcerer can see the spirits being captured. He
shakes his head, and thinks that the *wai'ichura* sorcerers
must be stupid to need such a thing, since Moie or any decent Runiya sorcerer would of course *feel* when the spirit he
was aiming for was captured. But he has to admit it is clever
and interesting for the *aysiri* to come right into his spirit box
and show all those watching how he captured the spirits and
demons in it. Moie thinks that it is because there are so
many *wai'ichuranan,* no one can tell who is an *aysiri,* so he
shows his power to those who watch the spirit box, in case
they have troubling spirits they wish to capture, or if they
have an enemy whose spirit they wish to steal and bind in
the box, then they would know whom to consult. He is
pleased with himself for having understood this; he understands so little of the dead people and their ways. Now there
are demons dancing again, and loud unpleasant sounds, and
he turns away.

"Do you understand?" Jenny asked again. "They're going to make a tape of you. Like that private detective was taping Daniel and Lindsay?" She pointed to the TV screen and then mimed a video camera pointing at Moie. "They're going to make a tape of you, so you can tell your story on TV. Maybe you'll get famous and be on *Letterman*! Or *Oprah*!" He looked at her blankly, as he usually did when she had to describe something complicated.

"Oh, God, just wait here a second, okay? I'll show you."

She dashed out of the living room and down the hallway to Professor Cooksey's rooms. To her surprise she found Kevin poking around the office.

"What're you doing?" she asked.

"Looking for you. Want to go out somewhere?"

"Sure, where?" she said, a little startled. In her experience, Kevin was not one to propose amusing trips.

"Oh, I don't know. We could go to the zoo. Hang out with Bill Kearney. Play with the animals." When she hesitated, he added, "We could take the little guy along. He's probably never been to a zoo."

Jenny felt a wave of gratitude. That was *so* Kevin, she thought. Just when you were going to give up on him he'd do something real nice. She gave him a hug and said, "Sure, I just have to show him something." With that, she grabbed Cooksey's Panasonic camcorder from its shelf and checked the tape and battery.

"That's a fancy unit," Kevin said. "You sure you know what you're doing with it?"

"Oh, yeah," said Jenny. "I lived with this foster family once, this guy, Harold Logan, was like totally obsessed with that program *America's Funniest Home Videos*? He would, like, make the kids do stuff, like crash their bikes and fall into pies, dumb shit like that. He was dying to win the grand prize, it was, like, thousands of dollars, and he kept sending tapes to them and never got on the show. Personally I thought it was fixed. Anyway, I was the oldest kid, so he taught me how to use one of these because he thought it would be funnier if he was in the tape. Okay, so he set up this shot with a trampoline they had? He was a big fat dude. The kids were jumping off the porch roof onto the trampoline, climbing out the bedroom window and bouncing off it. That was the setup. Then he comes out of the window and jumps, and the deal was he rigged the trampoline to, like, collapse when he hit it. That was the stupid joke, right? But it didn't collapse, and he comes off of it, boing, and flies through the air and crashes into the barbecue, which he had going for hot dogs and shit, and it goes over with the table he had the charcoal lighter on, and it spills and it catches him on fire. I mean, fuck, his hair and everything and his wife comes running out and tries to put him out with a pitcher of lemonade that she's carrying, but he's still burning, yelling curse words and everything, and finally she put him out with the hose. I got the whole thing on tape."

"Did he win?"

"No, man, he was like all burned up, really ugly, and they would've had to, I don't know, bleep out all the holy shit motherfuckers and all, so it could be on the show. And after that they took all the kids out of there for endangering."

"Yeah, well, that's show business."

"I guess," she said and carried the camcorder back to the living room, Kevin tagging along behind her.

She showed the camcorder to Moie. "See. This is like the one on the TV, except I think this one is better. What I was saying is they're going to make a tape of *you* so you can tell your story on the TV." With that, she pointed the camera at Moie. To her immense surprise, he let out a scream of horror and ran out of the room. Jenny stared after him in dismay.

"What'd I do?"

Kevin laughed and said, "Maybe he has stage fright. What's this about making a tape?"

Jenny explained what she'd heard at the meeting.

"Yeah, it figures," said Kevin dismissively. "More public relations shit."

"Well, do you have any better ideas?"

"Who me? Nah, I'm just a worker bee. So, do you want to go?"

"Sure. Let me put this back."

She had just replaced the machine when Cooksey came into the room and looked at her inquiringly.

"I was just showing Moie what a camcorder was," she explained. "We were watching the TV, and I said he was going to be on TV and I wasn't getting through to him, so I brought it out, and you know what? He looked like I was trying to shoot him or something and he ran away. Shit, maybe he thought it was a gun."

"Oh, I doubt that. I'm sure he knows what a gun is."

"You think? Anyway, me and Kev want to take Moie to the zoo with us. Would that be okay?"

She asked hesitantly because of what had happened the last time Kevin and Moie were out together, but Cooksey seemed delighted with the notion. "What a splendid idea!" he said, smiling. "I'm sure that will be an interesting experience for all."

She found the Indian in the old shed where he had chosen to sling his hammock, crouched on the ground, mumbling to himself and looking unhealthy in the light that streamed through the dirty green corrugated fiberglass roof. It took her a while to convince him to go and to explain what a zoo was. She mimed several types of animals—the monkey, the parrot, the tiger—while he stared. At last he collected the bits of bone and feather he had been fiddling with and replaced them in the woven bag he always carried. She had given him a FPA T-shirt and a pair of old Bermuda shorts she'd found in the house and she made him put these on, and a pair of rubber flip-flops, and then they joined Kevin in the VW van.

The drive to the zoo down in the south county was forty minutes, during which Kevin played a Metallica tape at top volume, while Jenny spoke to Moie. The Indian sat between them on the bench seat like a good child, looking straight ahead. He seemed to be in a trance, although Jenny was sure he was picking up on what she was saying. She kept hoping that somehow, if she talked to him long enough, even chatter, he would somehow acquire the ability to speak English. She had once shared a home with a kid who didn't speak at all and she had done that and after a while he extruded a word or two, and she recalled how good that had made her feel.

Rupert was a big shot at the Zoological Society of Florida, so they had cards that got them in free, and once past the gate, Kevin headed straight for the Metrozoo office, where he found out where his pal Kearney was working.

"He's fixing some pipe near the petting zoo," Kevin reported, and they walked down the path in that direction. It was a fine fall day, sunny with small clouds, and the zoo was pleasantly uncrowded. Jenny explained the concept of a petting zoo to Moie.

"It's where kids get to touch the animals. Pet them." She petted his arm to demonstrate. They passed a food concession and she bought a soda and a corn dog, offering Moie a bite and asking him if he wanted anything to eat. He put his finger on his mouth, which she had learned was the sign for not wanting to eat. She wondered what the opposite sign was. "Jeez, man, you never eat anything," she said. "What's up with that?" Then Kevin spotted Kearney kneeling over a valve box set into the pavement.

Jenny watched the men greet each other and submitted to the usual hug and the usual little grope. She didn't care for Kearney, a small guy with smudged black plastic glasses, pale eyes, and a weaselly look. He had many ornaments pierced through his face and his arms were heavily tattooed, giving him the appearance of a malevolent Christmas tree. Kevin told her to take the little guy to see the animals, him and Kearney were going to talk some business for a minute, which Jenny thought was just a way of going off and getting stoned. She said nothing but felt a little blue because this was not going to be a fun trip after all but probably another of Kevin's stupid deals. She started feeling annoyed at Moie, too, she always had to *mind* stuff, kids and animals and now this dumb Indian who you couldn't even talk to . . . .

She grabbed his arm and led him through the little gate into the petting zoo. There they met a white goat on the path. The goat stopped, stared, did a 180 in the air, and raced away at top speed, scattering families and knocking over a toddler. The herd of sheep raced in a tight mob to the farthest corner of their enclosure, where they packed into a tight pile bleating, their stupid faces occasionally popping up to stare before vanishing in a mate's wool. The rabbits scrabbled and squealed their high-pitched cries; the two burros tried vainly to leap their fence. A zoo employee who had been showing a few children how to feed a calf from a bottle was staggered when the calf tore away and went dashing back to its mother, bawling.

Jenny led Moie through the area, growing increasingly nervous, as it was clear that something was wrong. Every animal was going nuts, and the people were picking up screaming kids in their arms and running out of the place. Jenny saw fancy pigeons battering themselves bloody on the mesh of their cage. A pair of peafowl struggled clumsily into the air and alighted on a low limb of a live oak, the male filling the air with its demonic screams. As they walked, it dawned at last on Jenny that they were the locus of the worst of this animal pandemonium. She looked closely at Moie, but his deep black eyes revealed nothing but mild alertness.

"Okay, so this is a little boring, let's go somewhere else," she said, and then she spotted a sign directing them to Dr. Wilde's World—Wonders of Tropical America exhibit. She read it aloud and exclaimed, "Hey, that's where you're from, Moie. Come on, it'll be like a trip home."

Dr. Wilde's World was housed in a new buff- and aqua-painted building and was extremely high-tech, with voices in the air from the various exhibits and a giant TV screen showing the wonders of the neotropics. They were watching this show when Moie suddenly stiffened, rose from his seat, and walked out. She followed him, a little annoyed because the show was kind of interesting, and she preferred exploring the rain forest in the air-conditioned dimness rather than in the actual sticky-hot thing itself. They passed a restroom sign. Jenny made clear by signs and motions, as to an untalented dog, that she wanted Moie to stay put in this very spot and not move an inch. He was not there when she emerged. Fighting panic, she dashed past the huge tank of Amazonian fishes, past the poison frog display, past the toucans and parrots, and the coatis, and javelinas, until, with a rush of relief, she found him standing rapt in front of a larger glassed-in cage.

"That's a jaguar," she said. "It says here her name's Anita." She read haltingly from the card in front of the cage, but she could tell that the Indian was not listening, and so she stopped and stood silently by Moie, looking.

The animal was stretched out on a broad wooden shelf, seemingly asleep, but as Jenny watched, its nose twitched, its ears sprang erect, and it opened its golden eyes. In an instant it leaped down from its perch and pressed its nose against the thick glass, staring at Moie. It panted; from its open mouth came a low, loud growl. Moie was making noise, too, a rhythmic chant, the same phrase repeated over and over again.

"What're you doing?" she said, and it felt like her ears were stuffed, the sound of the words seemed stuck in her head. Her stomach felt tense, as with fear, but it might have just been the corn dog, she thought that Rupert was right, she shouldn't eat crap like that, and there was something wrong with her eyes, too, a kind of flickering of the light, and she looked up at the ceiling fixture to see if maybe it was that. She had to be careful of flickering lights because bad fluorescents sometimes set off a fit, but these were concealed spots casting a dim rain-forest type of glow against the ceiling, and she realized that it wasn't the lights but really *everything* that was flickering, and the angles of the walls seemed a little off and the glass of the cage was sort of bending like the surface of wind-blown water. She took a deep breath now because she found that she had forgotten to breathe.

She tried to blink away the distortions, but they got worse and there was a low hum that was coming in a weird way from the words that Moie was chanting, and the hum got lower and lower until it was almost a scraping sound. She looked around to see if there was anyone she could ask what was going on, but the lights had somehow dimmed way down, and it was as if she and Moie and the cage were the only things left in the world, the corridors leading out in either direction were full of gray nothing.

When she looked at the cage again, Moie was inside it, squatting on his haunches. The animal was sitting, too, with its face six inches from his. They were motionless in profile, as if carved on the wall of a jungle temple. She touched the glass, and it was just glass, slick and slightly warm. She tapped on it twice with her knuckles, softly, to check if it was still really solid. Slowly, Moie turned his head to face her. She saw that his eyes were no longer their former deep and mild brown but green-gold, with vertical slit pupils. She let out a little cry and then a cool breeze seemed to flow upward through her body, and she tasted the familiar tang of something like sweet ashes, and felt the dread of the epileptic aura.

When she came to, a middle-aged woman with a kind, competent face was wiping her mouth. Jenny was on her side on the hard floor, with something soft stuffed under her head, which throbbed painfully. The good news was that nothing had been jammed into her mouth, and since she'd just gone to the toilet, she hadn't pissed herself. Her vision cleared, and she saw Moie standing with Kevin and a cop, who was talking into his radio and some zookeepers and people cruising by, with the moms telling the kids not to stare while staring themselves. The kind woman helped her to her feet and asked her if she needed anything. Jenny said she was fine, and she said the same to the policeman, to the worried representative of the zoo, and to the paramedics who came dashing up as she was leaving the building, although she was not at all fine. She ached in all her limbs and wanted to go to sleep and not wake up.

In the truck, Kevin said, "I thought you were taking those pills."

"I stopped. They made me sleepy and nauseous."

"Sleepy is better than throwing fits."

"Seizures. They don't call them fits anymore. I don't

know, I guess I was hoping I was cured. Sometimes it goes away when you get older. I only had that one since we hooked up."

"One is too many. Jesus, man, you looked all gray. I thought you were going to croak on me. Why did it happen? You said there had to be strobes to make it start."

"Yeah, but other stuff does it, too."

"Like what?"

"You'll laugh."

"No, I won't. Tell me."

"Moie did . . . something, some kind of chant and everything got crazy and, um, he walked through the glass. He was in the cage with the jaguar."

"In it? How the fuck'd he do that. The access doors are locked."

"I don't know, man, he just *was*. It was like he was talking to the jaguar, and when I tapped on the glass, he turned around and he had, like, jaguar eyes."

Kevin laughed. "Oh, shit, man, are you fucked up!"

"You said you wouldn't laugh. I'm telling you what I saw."

"Oh, fuck, you didn't see shit. You had a fit and then you imagined it."

"I did not," she said uncertainly.

"Yeah, you did," said Kevin, "because stuff like that only happens in horror flicks, or when you're taking acid and shit. You imagined it. Hey, ask him! Moie, *mi hermano,* did you change into a jaguar back there? No? See, you made it up."

This exchange made her even more tired than she usually was after such an episode, and she drifted into sleep, from which she was awakened by a change in the motion of the truck.

She looked out the window. They were driving slowly down a street of luxurious houses in the Spanish style, set deeply in yards full of lush tropical plantings. The street signs were white-painted concrete markers set upon the sidewalks.

"Why are we in the Gables?" she asked.

"Just checking something out. That big job coming up on our right is where Juan Xavier Calderón lives."

"What is he, in a band?"

"No, dummy, he's one of the three Consuela Holdings guys your little man here told us about. There used to be four, ha-ha."

"So why do you want to see his house?"

Kevin ignored the question. "Be nice to live like that, wouldn't it? That's what you get for fucking up the world. I bet he's got a pool back there, and a tennis court and shit."

"Okay, you saw it," she said nervously. "Could we go home now? I got a bad headache."

"There's always some goddamn thing wrong with you, you know that?" said Kevin. He punched up the radio volume and threw the van roughly into gear. They drove away in a cloud of exhaust and heavy metal.

——

Moie wonders why Monkey Boy always makes the car shout at him when he drives. He has noticed that when Firehair Woman drives, the car speaks more softly, with a gentler humming. Perhaps it is to keep him awake, as Monkey Boy's *aryu't* is so shrunken that he is barely human anymore. Firehair Woman is trying to make him human but does not know how. If Moie could speak her language, he could give her some advice on these matters. And there are powders he has that could help. The woman's *aryu't* is rich and thick, but uncultivated, like a yam plant in an abandoned garden. Although he does not speak their language, Moie has the keen ears of a hunter and has heard the name Calderón, which he knows. He will be able to find this house again, and the man who lives in it.

——

Professor Cooksey went for a walk after supper when the weather suited, as now. In the tropical evenings he would wander through the little streets in back of Ingraham Highway, and along the Coral Gables Waterway, inhaling the balmy blossom-scented air and the dank odor of that broad canal, and wondering whether this would be the evening he would throw himself into it and die. A sense of propriety more than the scraps of religious faith he retained kept him always just at the brink of action, although he had many a night stared for a long time past the toes of his sandals down at the slick black skin of the water. He did not think that he was actually depressed, a word that in any case he despised, as he despised the grotesque self-involvement of most Americans, because he did his work, he was alert, he tried to be kind, he took an interest in the world of nature around him. He thought of it as sadness, or melancholy, and it had a reason.

Despite the suicidal thoughts, these late jaunts almost always produced some animal delight: a little parade of raccoons, a night heron fishing under the canal bank, an opossum in a tree, a roosting macaw, a giant African toad; and often the trilling of a mockingbird overhead. At such moments he would occasionally exclaim and call out to his wife, to share the joy, and recall that she was dead. Sometimes he did not recall this quickly enough and heard her voice in his ear. On those evenings he would scuttle home and drink whiskey, courting oblivion.

No such event occurred on this particular evening, which was only memorable for the observation of a green monkey high up in a palm tree, an escapee from some domestic or commercial zoo. He entered his room in a lighter mood than was normal therefore and was not entirely surprised to find Moie waiting there, squatting in a corner, contemplating the skull of just such a monkey.

"Remarkable," Cooksey said in Quechua, "I just saw one of those out on the street."

"Only one?"

"Yes."

"A lonely thing, then."

"Yes. It must have escaped from its cage. Or from a large zoo full of monkeys that used to exist some small distance from here; a hurricane blew the place apart and many escaped. The city is full of them."

Moie placed the skull carefully back in the case from which he had taken it.

"I went to such a place today."

"So I understand. And how did you like it?"

"I didn't like it. It was a dead place, even though the animals seemed to be alive. They moved and ate and drank, but they were not all there . . . it is hard to say what I mean, even in Quechua. It is a *cosmological* difficulty. So Father Tim Perrin always called it."

He had used the English word and Cooksey smiled. "Yes, *cosmological* difficulties are the worst."

"Yes. There was a jaguar they had in a glass box. I spoke with her. She had been born in a box and had never killed, and she didn't even know who she was. It was like a child who has been dropped on its head and afterward can't speak or see. It was very sad. Then I felt Jaguar stirring in me, and he let me . . . the word in Runisi is *jana'tsit*. Do you know this word?"

"I do not."

"No, I've seen that you don't do this. It is a way of going to another place without going on the path that leads to it through this world. In this way I was led to this animal and I spoke to her and told her who she was. But as I was speaking to her, a holy person climbed into the Firehair Woman, and she fell down and shook and white waters flowed from her mouth."

"You mean Jenny?"

"Yes, Jenny. I didn't know that *wai'ichuranan* could carry holy ones in this way, but I knew there was something about her that was not dead, and this shows it well."

Cooksey thought for a moment. "Among us, we say that is a sickness."

"Of course, but you think you are alive as you are, so that means nothing. But she didn't know how to welcome the holy one, so she suffered. Or so it seemed. Did you know there is a plan to steal my spirit and place it with the others, and all the demons, in the spirit box?"

Cooksey suppressed a smile. "Yes, but this is another cosmological difficulty. I will explain. You wish to stop this company from logging your forest, and among the *wai'ichuranan,* who are very many and live in many villages and towns far from Miami, this is how it is done. We have a machine that is like a mirror, but where a mirror holds your reflection only while you are standing in front of it, this machine saves the reflection and can send it through the air to all the spirit boxes, which we call televisions. And it can also remember your speech and say it in your own words to all the *wai'ichuranan.* So you will appear in everyone's television, and the people, or some people, will be angry at what is being done, and perhaps this will make the company stop what it's doing. It has nothing to do with your spirit. The television is not a spirit box at all, but only a machine, like this lamp on my desk. There are no witches involved. What you call demons are pictures made by machines. The people you see behind the glass are real people in faraway places, and not stolen spirits."

"I hear what you say, but it's hard for me to believe it."

"Why is it hard?"

"Because the faces of the people in the spirit box, the *television,* are different from the faces of real people, and even different from the faces of many *wai'ichuranan.* They have no . . . I must use my own language . . . no *aryu't.* Having a real spirit inside you. You have it and Jenny has it, and the Hairy Face Man, too, and even the others a little, but not these behind the glass. We say that when a spirit is torn from a human through sorcery it becomes separated from the world, and because of this it is very hungry all the time. It wishes to fill itself up and suck the spirit from living things. It thinks only of itself, how it can grow greater, until it fills the whole world. And when we see such a spirit in the forest, we know it is one and not a real person because this hunger shows on its face. They can't disguise it, although they can talk in soothing ways. We are not often fooled. And I see the same kinds of faces on the people behind the glass of the *television,* and therefore I say that they are all dead spirits, whatever you say about machines. Tell me, haven't you ever observed this difference yourself?"

"I have," Cooksey admitted. "But, with us it is a kind of mask. Don't you put on masks and paint your faces when you talk to your gods?"

"We do, certainly. But now you say that the television dead people are worshipping gods, where before you said that they were speaking to people far away, as a deer might smear musk on a tree to give a message to other deer. What gods are worshipped in this way?"

"Wealth and fame," said Cooksey. "Our chief gods, and also sometimes the god of fornication."

"Of course; you are dead, so you worship the gods of death. I understand. Nevertheless, I can't go into the spirit box. It would be death for me, and then I would be not Moie, and become happy to live in a zoo, like that poor animal I saw today. I will have to find another way to make the company stop, or, I should say, I will have to wait for Jaguar to find another way."

"What would that be?"

"How should I know? Am I Jaguar? In any case, I might not be allowed to tell anyone. Jaguar doesn't want everyone to know his business."

"I thought you considered us your allies."

"Yes, I do. I think you want to help, but often magical allies are stupid, especially when they are humans, and even more so when they are dead people. I will have to . . . there is no word in this language for it; we say, *iwai'chinix,* to make them live in a different way before they can help, and I'm not even sure I can do it, since I am very weak here. But for now, I believe I must leave this place."

"Yes, I can see where you might wish to. But where will you go? And how will you live?"

"I will find a large tree to live in. I've noticed that the *wai'ichuranan* walk the paths without ever looking up, so no one will disturb me in my tree. As for living, there is water all around, and Jaguar will feed me. What more do I need?

Now, if you would like to help me, you must show me a large tree."

"I believe I know just the tree you require," said Cooksey. They spoke for some minutes longer, Cooksey answering Moie's questions, and asking a few of his own, and then they both slipped out into the night.

# Seven

At the sound Yoiyo Calderón was instantly up on his feet in the dark, scrabbling in a desk drawer for his pistol and at the same time kicking away the light blanket that constrained his feet. He was not in his bed, he had not been in his bed for several nights, not since the dreams had begun; he was sleeping on the long, lush leather of the couch in his den. His nights were now spent here because he did not want to disturb the sleep of his wife, not that he was ever particularly sensitive to her rest or any other aspect of her being, but she asked questions and gossiped and had a wide circle of acquaintances. He did not want it abroad in the Cuban community that J. X. F. Calderón was losing it, was going *loco,* was afraid of bumps in the night.

The sounds were coming from the front of the house, he thought. Thumps and scratchings, like rending wood, and a low coughing growl. He looked briefly at the phone. Call the police? No, not in the house, looking around, asking questions, poking into his affairs. Instead, he slipped into a light robe, and pistol in hand, he walked out of the room and down the stairs in the dark. In the entrance hall he stopped and listened again. It was cool now, the air conditioners were silent for the season, the only noises were the quiet clicking of automatic machinery in the house, a distant vehicle, the ever-present rattle and swish of tropical foliage in the breeze. He looked at the security panel, the little green lights said all locked up, secure, which was far from how he felt, and with a soft curse, he switched the thing off and unlocked the front door.

There was his front walk, his lawn, the peaceful Gables street. He took a step outside, pointing the gun. There was a black lump of something on the path, and when he leaned over to look at it, he cursed again, this time aloud. It was a pile of feces, of a vaguely familiar type. Calderón was hardly an expert on cat shit, coming as he did from a social stratum that employed others to empty cat boxes, but his daughter had always had cats, and he had observed the occasional accident. This was cat, and if its volume was any indication, it had emerged from a beast the size of a man.

A sound behind him made him whirl, gun outstretched, finger closing on the trigger. He saw two things at once. One was his front door, its oak surface torn to ribbons by long scratches. The other was his daughter, Victoria, standing in the doorway, dressed in pink silk pajamas, her mouth gaping in shock. Calderón shoved the pistol into the pocket of his robe. "What's wrong?" she asked.

"Nothing. Go back to bed." He started for the doorway.

"It's not nothing. I heard sounds. That's why I got up. And you were pointing a gun."

"Well, obviously it *was* nothing or I wouldn't be standing here talking to you," said Calderón, raising his voice. He was staring at the soft earth of the flower beds on either side of the walk. With his slippered foot he effaced the pugmarks of a gigantic cat, or at least those he could reach from the walk. "What are you doing?" Victoria asked.

"Nothing! How many times do I have to say it? Now go back to bed or we'll have your mother down here and that's all I need."

He made a shooing motion with his hand, and after a few seconds, she turned and walked away. He followed her into the house, and as he switched on the security system a dissatisfied frown appeared on his face, as it often did when he contemplated his daughter. Calderón was not happy with his children. Juan Jr., the elder, or Jonni, as he called himself, was in New York, attempting to become an actor or singer and living rather prematurely the life of a star on his father's money. This girl had been married off right out of college in a wedding that left little change from a hundred grand, to the Pinero boy, a connection with one of the wealthiest Cuban families in Miami. Who drank, as it turned out, and had peculiar tastes (although this was not discussed among the Calderóns) and who had, three months into the marriage, run his Mercedes off Alligator Alley and into a canal. Victoria returned home, where she would probably remain forever. Not a beauty, unfortunately, but at least she wasn't like some of these girls he saw around town, Cuban girls, from good families, too, with their bodies hanging out of their clothes and up to God-knew-what craziness. His one concession to modernity was to allow her to work, under his eye, naturally, and here, at least, she had proven her father's daughter. He'd started her in the development office at JXF, where she'd shown an excellent eye for property and had, in fact, been the lead on the Consuela Coast deal. He was glad she was competent, but it irked him like an unscratchable itch that it was the girl and not the boy who was in the business.

Calderón returned to the den, where he dozed uncomfortably in front of a stupid movie on the gigantic television, until dawn appeared through the windows. When he heard the servants stirring, he called down and ordered Carmel the maid to clean up the mess on the front walk, and then got his construction manager out of bed and told him that some kids had vandalized his front door and that he wanted it replaced instantly. Some hours later, when he walked out, a crew was already at work on the door. Asked what he wanted done with the old door, Calderón said, "Burn it."

But the door and what it represented was not so easily removed from his mind. All during that morning he found himself drifting away at meetings, brought out of fearful reveries by an unnatural silence, looking up at a table full of worried or too-interested faces, and having to fake some response. This could not be tolerated, for his empire was sustained by an inverted pyramid of deals, each one larger than the last, each one secured by what had gone before. Should the word get around in certain circles that Yoiyo Calderón was losing it, should his Consuela Resort go sour . . . it was not worth thinking about, it wasn't going to happen, he would . . .

What? Like many men of his generation and profession and culture, he had no true friends. He had contacts and associates instead, and he certainly was not going to bring up what had happened last night with Garza and Ibanez. He'd promised to handle any problems with the Puxto timber deal, and that was all they needed to know. His wife was a decoration, his father senile, his son useless, he had no brothers, he could not discuss these things with an employee.

He had a meeting after lunch about Consuela Coast with Gary Rivas, his VP for sales, and Oscar Clemente, his CFO, and some of their junior people. And his daughter. The discussion was about cash flow, as nearly all his meetings seemed to be about recently. Like any big project, the Coast, as the firm called it, got its initial funding from banks, collateralized by the property itself, which money was used for initial planning and the obtaining of permits, then the construction of the first units and the amenities, in this case a country/yacht club, golf course, and marina. The money from the sales of the first units would be used to service the loans and allow construction of the next tranche of units. Actual profits would not kick in until 70 percent of the homes and condos had been sold; until then, the company was running on vapor. This was the nature of the business, and it was not for the faint of heart. This was why Calderón liked it.

They sat, they talked small a little, and then Rivas and Clemente passed out spreadsheets and went into their presentations. Rivas had the bad news, although he did not call it that. He was about Victoria's age, dark-haired, generous of gesture, cap-toothed, and tailored to an almost unnatural degree of perfection, as if injection-molded from plastic, like Barbie's Ken. It seemed that the nineties were over, and condos on the west coast of Florida were not leaping off the shelves at a low end of $1.2 million. He thought he would make his targets off the Europeans and the Asians, and the thankful decline of the dollar, but it would be a near thing. Victoria looked at his projections and thought it would be an impossible one, even if the Coast became the most fashionable buy for every plutocrat from Lisbon to Shanghai, but she remained silent. Her father didn't question the figures either, and they moved on to Clemente.

Uncle Oscar, as he was called among the Calderóns, had a freckled bald dome of a head on which artful swirls of dark-dyed hair reclined. His bright black eyes flicked in disconcerting magnification behind huge thick black-framed lenses. He spoke a thickly accented English, interlarded with frequent spates of Cuban idiom. Clemente was a classic green-eyeshade type, a legacy from the previous generation of Calderóns, who'd won his spurs sneaking Victoria's grandfather's millions out of the island just before Satan took over Havana. According to him, the pyramid of interlocking loans was holding up and would cover the company's burn rate well into the following year, assuming a whole list of good tidings: the prime rate low, labor available and docile, all contractors diligent and smartly on schedule, the banks willing with the usual rollovers, and . . .

Victoria's eyes darted to a set of asterisked entries that seemed to balance out the spreadsheet to create this miracle of financial solidity. She added them up mentally and said, "Wait a second, where does this five point five mill come from? Investment income?"

They all stared at her, and she felt her face flush. "I mean . . . it doesn't appear on the latest financials, and without that it doesn't look like we'll be able to service the major loan from First Florida. Does the bank have this as part of our collateral?"

Oscar looked at Calderón, and it was clear to Victoria that the CFO didn't know the source of the money either. Calderón said, "It's Consuela Holdings money. It's there. Let's move on."

"Consuela? There's no cash flow from Consuela. It's a

speculative outside investment. Why're we claiming it as an asset against which we're proposing to borrow?"

Calderón chuckled. "My little girl's a financial genius now. A year ago she couldn't tell an asset from a baby buggy and now she's running the business for me. Kids, huh?" Everyone around the table had a good laugh at that, and now Calderón stared at her with his special macho gaze until she dropped her eyes and he said, "When I want your advice I'll ask for it, understand? Now, Oscar, let's get this finished."

Calderón observed his daughter shrink into submission, which reaction made him feel somewhat more in control, and after the meeting he retired to his office, having told the secretary to hold calls. He sat behind his desk squeezing a little red ball said to be good for relieving tension and thought about the real problem, the one closely related to the $5.5 million the stupid girl had mentioned. Clearly, someone had killed Fuentes, and this someone was now trying to threaten him by last night's vandalism. Fuentes had been torn by what was supposed to have been a big cat, an obvious scam, and someone had marked his property, as if by a big cat. They were trying to frighten them away from the Puxto, that was clear enough, and therefore it was necessary to find the people who were doing this and stop them or frighten *them* off. He had applied fear before this, including physical fear on occasion, and he understood that once the decision was made, there was no point in holding back. He dialed a number in Colombia, not the one he had used some days ago, but a special one, a cell phone, for emergencies only.

"Yes?" said the quiet voice.

"Hurtado?"

"Yes."

"Calderón. Look, the situation we talked about the other day? I think you need to be involved."

"I'm listening."

"There was an incident at my house last night. It's connected with the death of Fuentes, I think."

"Someone contacted you?"

"No, just some vandalism, a warning. The marks of a big cat, just like there were around Fuentes's body."

A hissing silence; then, "And what is it you expect me to do about it, Yoiyo?"

Calderón took a deep breath. "Well, you know they killed one of us and threatened me. This is not the work of some little environmentalist *cabrón*. This has to come from your end, despite what you said before."

"Really? What about the man and his Indian at Fuentes's office?"

"A distraction. These environment crazies, they climb up and live in trees, they drive spikes, at worst maybe a bomb, and then they're all over the papers with their manifestos. This is different. Forgive me for saying so, but it has a Colombian feel to it."

"A Colombian *feel*?"

"Yes!" Calderón's voice rose. "They tore Antonio to *pieces,* goddamnit! They ripped the heart from his body, his liver . . . Americans don't do things like that."

"No, that's true. But calm yourself, my friend. I'm sure something can be arranged. We need to find who's doing this business and make them stop, this is the important thing, yes?"

"Of course. So, you'll organize this in some way?"

"I will. My people will be in touch with you. And Yoiyo? You'll let me handle this quietly, yes? No publicity, no fuss, and no contact with the authorities. Do we understand each other?"

"Yes, of course."

"Good. My best regards to your family."

The line went dead. Calderón wiped his face with his handkerchief. It was some minutes before he trusted his legs to carry him to the little bar in his office.

**V**ictoria Calderón returned to her much smaller office, where there was no bar. Her body was damp with a nasty fear-sweat. She plucked at her clothes and wished for a shower. She sat behind her desk and tried to work. The words and figures danced wrongly across the page, and she mouthed an unaccustomed curse, and another, and then gave vent to her quite considerable store of Spanish profanity, learned mainly during her brief marriage, but not of course loud enough to be heard through the flimsy walls of her office. Yes, it was still true: he could with a word and a sneer turn her into the brainless ornament of his fancy.

Now, almost without thought, she found her fingers punching the buttons of her phone, and in a moment she was listening to the warm, humorous voice of her favorite person in the world, her mother's crazy sister, Eugenia Arias, who, blessed with a perfect ear for tones of woe suppressed, cut through the attempted small talk with "What's he done to you now?"

After listening to her niece for some time, she said, "Come down to Eskibel's and I'll buy you a drink. Three drinks. Then we'll go to the fronton and make piles of cash, and then maybe we'll both get lucky with a *pelotero.*"

Victoria giggled. "Oh, God, I should! It'd drive him crazy."

"It'd serve him right, the bastard. Oh, come! You can be here in half an hour. We can grab a bite and be in our seats by seven. Yes?"

Victoria actually thought about it for a long moment. Aunt Eugenia, the younger of the two sisters, was a jolly, fleshy woman, as unlike her sib as nature and temperament could arrange. She was unmarried, screwed around with low, beautiful, worthless men, drank copiously, kept an antique Jaguar saloon with a chauffeur to drive it, and made, to the dismay of her family, an excellent living as a professional jai alai gambler. She was tolerated at the larger family gatherings, but Yoiyo Calderón did not approve of her, and so his daughter was strongly discouraged from her society.

Victoria answered, "I don't know . . . I'd have to lie to him, and to my mom, and he'd find out and then I'd be in the doghouse for weeks . . ."

"What, he's going to *ground* you? Vicki, I have news for you: you're an adult. You're twenty-eight. Let him kick you out. You'll move in with me, I'll teach you to bet jai alai. You've got a good head for figures, you'd be a natural at it."

A laugh caught Victoria by surprise, the suggestion was so outrageous, so not her. She changed the subject and they talked on, of family and Eugenia's louche life, and when they ended the conversation, Victoria felt herself again. Which was? She didn't quite know, but it was not as an escapee like Eugenia, she decided as she turned again to the close-ranked numbers, not escape, but victory. Her father's daughter, after all.

There was a plaque at the base of the tree, placed by the South Florida Horticultural Society. This plaque proclaimed it the largest tree in Florida, and informed the interested that it was a *FICUS MACROPHYLLA,* a banyan fig, and had been planted around 1890 by a minister to provide shade for his church. It still provided shade to the large brick-built steepled building that had replaced the tin-roofed original, and also, in the late afternoon, to the low, modern structure that housed the Providence Day School, K through six. The tree covered an area the size of a big-league baseball diamond, a vast ball of dark green elongate shiny leaves suspended over dozens of trunks and subtrunks, smooth and gray as elephants, and in the spooky cloud-stopped light of this afternoon, like elephants these seemed to march with infinite slowness across the lawn that surrounded it. There was a wooden bench established under one of its boughs, slung cleverly between two living buttresses. Upon this sat Miss Milliken, the first-grade teacher, who read to her class from *Tik-Tok of Oz,* a special treat at the end of the day. The parents knew to collect their children there on paradisiacal afternoons such as this, and there was a small circle of adults, almost all well-turned-out local matrons or young nannies, standing around the clump of sitting children, listening while the chapter was read out. The sole listener who was neither matron nor nanny was Jimmy Paz.

The book closed, the children sprang up and began to chatter, the parents moved in. Some grabbed their youngsters and moved off in a determined manner, to tightly scheduled activities meant to build up résumés. The students at Providence Day came from a social stratum that did not believe in wasting the unforgiving minute, whose members believed that it was never too early to sacrifice to the gods of success. Jimmy Paz was not one of these either, nor were several others, who demonstrated by their costumes and vehicles that they were the heirs of the former indigenes of Coconut Grove—the laid-back, the artistic—even if wealthy enough to afford Providence's stiff fees. These gathered around Miss Milliken to chat, to discuss their children briefly, to hang out with one another in the welcome shade of the great tree.

Unconvivial Paz, no former hippie, no artist, followed his daughter's lead into the green center of the ficus. Here he observed a demonstration of tree climbing and was forced to admit that he could not swing upside down from a low limb by his knees. He could, however, still tickle her so that, giggling, she lost her grip and fell into his arms.

"Daddy, do you know there's a monster in this tree?"

"I didn't know that. Is it scary?"

She considered this briefly. "A little scary. Not *very* scary, like *arrrrrgh!*" She demonstrated what scary would be like by physical gestures and a snarling face. "He talks to me," she added. "In Spanish."

"Really. What about?"

"Oh, stuff. He's from a real jungle, and he can talk to animals. I showed him to Britney Riley, but she couldn't see him. She said I was *stupid.* I hate her now."

"I thought she was your best friend."

"Uh-*uh.* She's a total dummy. My new best friend is Adriana Steinfels. Can she come to our house?"

"Not today, honey. Can you show me the monster?"

"Okay," with which she took his hand in hers and led him deeper into the maze of prop-roots. The air there was damp, cool, and filled with the spicy-rotten smell of the leaf and fruit litter below. They came to a gray-green vertical column that looked as big around as a dump truck: the main trunk of the state's largest tree. Amelia pointed upward. "He lives up there," she said, and waited for a moment, listening, then shrugged. "I think he's not there now. Where's Abuela?"

"Something came up. She had to go to her *ilé.*"

"Could we go, too?"

"We could," said Paz, somewhat to his own surprise. It would mean a fight with his wife. Did he want that? Maybe it was time to have the whole thing out. Whether Paz believed in Santería or not, the thing was part of his child's heritage, not to mention his own, and this absolute ban had suddenly become unbearable. Amelia was not a Britney or an Adriana, a white bread . . . the word *gusano,* a maggot, floated into consciousness, and was shoved down again. The kid was a mutt, and seven was not too early for her to learn where she came from. Okay, now they'd have it out. He loved his wife dearly, in parts, but her materialist self-righteousness he did not love, and he'd come to the end of avoiding the issue. So he told himself, and ran a few little testing arguments through his head, as husbands so often do, as he left the bowels of the fig tree and entered the open air, clutching the little warm hand. The monster in the tree, though—also not a good sign. Amelia had gone through a number of imaginary playmates, and Dr. Mom had explained at length that it was perfectly natural at the appropriate age. Was this the appropriate age? Nearly seven? Paz had thought that real friends took over the social impulse about now, and dumping a real friend because of an imaginary one could not be right. Now he was about to take the child to a place where nearly every adult had an imaginary friend who emerged unpredictably from the spirit world and took them over completely—would that be *therapeutic* under the circumstances? He knew what her mother would say to that. Paz told this line of thought to stop and it did but promised to come back *real* soon.

The *ilé,* the Santería congregation, was lodged in the unprepossessing home of Pedro Ortiz, located in the largely Cuban-inhabited area southwest of the original Little Havana on SW Eighth Street, which bore therefore the Spanglish name of Souesera. He had to park the Volvo two blocks away, so great was the number of cars—mostly venerable and including a number of well-used pickup trucks—that crowded the streets nearby and also the small former lawns of the houses, now converted into green-painted asphalt parking lots. It was the feast day of St. Francis of Assisi, an important day in Santería, for when the African slaves first saw statues of that saint, they had conflated the beads of his rosary with the palm-nut chains used in Yoruba divination and so associated the Italian saint with Ifa-Orunmila, the *orisha,* or spirit, of prophecy. It was considered particularly auspicious to get your fortune told on this day, hence the crowd and hence the presence here of Margarita Paz. Paz explained some of this to his daughter as they walked; she took in the information in the perfectly accepting manner of children, and then asked, "Will they tell a fortune for me?"

"I don't know," said Paz honestly. "You could ask Abuela. She knows more about this stuff than me."

"What's in that bag?"

Paz hefted the plastic sack. "Yams."

She wrinkled her nose. "Do we have to eat them?" Not a yam fan, Amelia, despite his best efforts. "No, they're for the *orisha,*" he said. "Ifa *loves* yams."

"Yuck," said Amelia, unimpressed by the tastes of the Lord of Fate.

They went into the house. Paz's nostrils were immediately full of the typical smell of such places—burning wax from scores of candles, the sweet incense sold in *botánicas* throughout the city, the earth smell of piles of yams, the sweetness of coconut and rum, and beneath all, the acrid odor of live fowl. Despite the murmur of the crowd, these could be heard clucking from their pens in a room at the back of the house.

He held tight to Amelia's hand, although the place was full of children running free. Besides these, the people were of all ages, as one would expect at any church, and of all colors, too, although tending to the darker shades indigenous to the Cuban community.

"Look, Abuela!" Amelia cried and tore away to greet her grandmother. Paz liked to see the two of them together, because of the expression that came over his mother's face when she embraced her *nieta*. It was joy unrestrained, an expression he did not recall seeing there during his own youth. Once he had felt a pang of resentment at such times, but no longer. None of that mattered anymore, whether or not his wife the shrink agreed. Some of the joy even carried over to him. Mrs. Paz embraced him, kissed him on both cheeks, smiled, showing the gold teeth.

"You brought her," said Mrs. Paz.

"Sure, why not?"—a question that had a real answer, which they both knew.

"Thank you," she said, and Paz had to keep from gaping. It was the first time his mother had ever thanked him for anything.

The grandmother and the child moved through the crowd, greetings and cooings arising in their wake. Paz followed, bemused, feeling the removal of a weight he had not realized he was carrying. The child was no stranger to praise, but her immediate family was small, and praise was associated with accomplishment. She had not ever received a flood like this, and he saw her shyly blossom. Paz got the feeling that the members of the *ilé* had been prepped for this by grandmotherly boastings. And why not? he thought; she's had a rough life, this is a small enough pleasure to give her. His mother seemed to have transformed herself into an entirely different woman from the stern field marshal of the restaurant and his childhood home. Not for the first time he wondered why she had not raised him in Santería. Apparently age was no barrier, as the many children here proved. Again he suppressed resentment.

They approached the sanctuary, a tent of yellow and green silk partially enclosing a squat cylinder covered with satin brocade in the same colors—the *fundamentos,* or sacred ritual symbols, of Ifa-Orunmila. Dozens of candles in glass holders burned around this shrine, and the floor was covered with layers of yams and coconuts. Amelia was allowed to deposit a yam and then taken to see the cake, a huge wedding-style confection of many tiers, on which was inscribed in icing *Maferefun Orunmila.*

"Is that a birthday cake?"

"Yes, in a way," said Mrs. Paz. "It's the day we celebrate and give thanks to Orunmila. See here, it says 'thanks be to Orunmila,' in Lucumi."

"Could we eat it?"

"Later, dear. First we have to see our *babalawo.* Now, he's a very holy man, so when we meet him, we bow and say '*iboru iboya ibochiche.*'" They practiced this a few times and then pushed through a thicker crowd to where Pedro Ortiz, the *babalawo,* sat on a simple caned chair. Mrs. Paz and Amelia dropped to their knees and said "may Ifa accept the sacrifice" in the modified Yoruba language called Lucumi by Cubans. Mrs. Paz introduced Amelia to the *santero.* Paz watched from a short distance. Ortiz was a slight cordovan-colored man with a thick head of black hair just starting to go gray and large dark eyes that seemed all pupil. He embraced both Mrs. Paz and Amelia and then looked over the heads of his followers directly at Paz, who understood that the *babalawo* knew pretty much what he was thinking. It interested Paz that he had expected this and was untroubled by it. Yes, weird stuff happened, weird stuff would continue to happen. It was a permanent part of his life, and it looked like it would start to be a part of his daughter's life, too. His mother was beckoning him. Ortiz rose and shook hands. No bow was apparently expected from the great quasi-agnostic. Mrs. Paz said, "He has agreed to throw Ifa for Amelia. It's very important, but you're the father, and so you have to agree."

"Um, right. What's going to happen?"

"Just agree, Iago!" she said sharply.

"Okay, Mamí," he said. "Your show. I trust you." As the words came out, he found that he actually did.

Ortiz led the way into a smaller room in the back of the house. In it were vases full of tropical blooms and trays of fruit, and there were depictions of the *orishas* on the walls: Ifa in his guise as St. Francis, Shango as St. Barbara, Babaluaye as St. Lazarus, and the rest. In one corner was a life-size statue of St. Caridad, the patroness of Cuba, and along one wall was a large mahogany cabinet, the *canistillero,* repository of the sacred objects. The only other furnishings were a folding bridge table with a round wooden box in its center, and four straight chairs. Ortiz sat in one of these and waited while the others sat. Ortiz looked into Paz's eyes and said, "We don't usually ask Ifa to tell the future of children, you know. Their future is so little formed that it would be disrespectful to ask. In a way, their little spirits are still held in the hands of their ancestors, such as yourself and Yetunde here." Here Ortiz smiled briefly at Mrs. Paz, who nodded when she heard her name-in-religion. "And of course the child's mother. So, what I will do is throw Ifa for you yourself, asking if there is anything that needs to be done or not done for the child's sake. It's difficult to make such a reading, but I have agreed because of the love and respect I have for Yetunde. So, now I need you to give me five dollars and twenty-five cents."

"Oh-kay," said Paz, "five and a quarter. Here you go." He handed the man a bill and a coin. Ortiz wrapped the coin in the bill using a complex origamilike fold. He opened the box on the table and took from it a chain made of eight curved pieces of tortoiseshell connected by brass links, and an ordinary drugstore notebook and pencil. The word *opele* floated up from memory. Paz had seen one of these before but never in actual use. Ortiz pinched the currency and coin around the center of the *opele* and pressed this to Paz's forehead, breast, hands, and shoulders, and then did the same to Amelia. He placed the money in the box, and after a low humming incantation that proceeded for some minutes he raised the chain and let it fall with a small tinkling clatter on the table.

The *babalawo* studied the line of the shells, observing which had fallen concave side up and which ones concave side down. This, Paz knew, is how Ifa speaks to men. Ortiz made marks on a sheet of paper torn from the notebook, a vertical stroke for concave-up and a circle for concave-down, two columns of four marks. He studied these, frowning, looked sharply at Paz, frowned more deeply, studied Amelia. Finally he uttered a soft grunt and asked Paz if he had a dog.

"A dog? No, we don't. We have a cat."

Ortiz shook his head. "No, it would be a large dog, or . . . something. Are there neighbors with such an animal?"

"There's a poodle down the block. Why are you asking this?"

"Because . . . hm, this is very strange, very strange. I have been doing this for forty years and I don't recall the *orisha* ever sending this. You know, all this was born in Africa and there are some things that happen in Africa that don't happen here. The locusts don't come and eat our crops. We don't give cows in exchange for our wives. Very strange." He stared at the *opele* as if he hoped it would change itself into another shape.

"But it involves a dog?" Paz asked.

"Not really. But what else could it be? Here we have no lions. Lions don't carry off our children here in America. But here it is, 'the oldest child is taken by the lion.' That's how the verse goes."

"You could do it again," Paz suggested after a moment. There was a peculiar cold chill in his belly, and without thinking he reached out and grasped his daughter's hand.

But Ortiz shook his head. "No, we don't mock the *orisha*. What is given is given. But it's certainly a great puzzle. I will have to pray about this, and make a sacrifice, too. Oh, and that is another peculiar thing. There is a sacrifice required."

"You mean an animal, right?"

"No, the oracle speaks about a human sacrifice, but it's not definite. The verse reads 'who is so brave as to sacrifice the dear one?' When such things appear, we always take it to mean a spiritual sacrifice, a purification. But, as I say, in forty years, this has not been told to me. There are very many figures, not only two hundred fifty-six from the one throw, as you see, but changing with the days and the seasons. Not all *babalawo* know this. Come back and see me again, and may Orunmila give us more light then."

The three of them walked out of the room, and an elderly woman passed them going in. A long line of people had formed, like that outside the toilets at a theater, all chattering softly in Spanish, waiting to know the future. Paz felt a ferocious anger displacing the fear from his mind, together with whatever small scraps of credulity he had so carefully assembled. After sending Amelia off to where they were serving cake, he directed it at his mother.

"What was that all about?"

"You're angry."

"Of *course,* I'm angry. Animals eating kids? Human sacrifice? Do you have any idea what it's going to take to get her to bed now? She already has dreams about animals eating her up."

His mother's eyes grew wide. "What! She has dreams like that! Why didn't you tell me?"

"Why? Because they're just dreams, Mother. All kids have nightmares at her age, and this kind of crazy . . . *stuff* doesn't help. Speaking of which, I must have been nuts to bring her here. All of this . . ." He gestured to the room, the devotees in their standing clusters. He couldn't think of any word that was not vile, for all of this.

"You don't understand," she said with uncharacteristic calm. "You should be made to the *santos,* like a man. But you hold back, and this is why Orunmila can't speak to you clearly."

She spoke as to a child, and this made Paz even angrier. His mother wasn't supposed to be calm like this, he wanted a fight. He said, "I'm taking tonight off," a statement normally guaranteed to produce a battle.

But she only nodded and said, "If you like."

"I'll see you later, then," he said and turned away to collect Amelia.

Who was not to be found.

Paz strode through the rooms, pushing past crowds that seemed to have grown thicker, and thicker, too, the odor of the candle and incense, and warmer the rooms. Sweat ran into his eyes and soaked the sides of his shirt. He called her name, he asked strangers if they had seen a little girl (pink shirt and jeans, pink sneakers) and got concerned but unhelpful looks, shakes of the head. With panic rising in him, he ran outside and looked up and down the block. The air felt wonderfully cool against his hot skin, but he plunged back into the heat and the noise, with his stomach lodged in his throat.

And found Amelia sitting peacefully on her grandmother's lap, having bits of smeared yellow and green icing wiped from her mouth. She said, "Daddy, I got a piece with Orunmila's name written on it."

"That's nice," said Paz from an arid mouth. "Where were you? I was looking all over for you."

"I was right here with Abuela all the time."

Paz could not meet his mother's glance. He would have sworn out a federal affidavit that he had been in this very room four times in the past ten minutes, and that it had contained neither Margarita Paz nor her small descendant.

**P**az let Amelia sit in the shotgun seat of the Volvo like the irresponsible daredevil dad he was. The wife always made her sit in the backseat for that extra level of safety, but Paz as a cop had seen a lot more car wrecks than she had, and he thought that safetywise it was a toss-up. Also he liked having her up there with him. He himself had spent what seemed like years in the front seat of an old Ford pickup with a bright stainless catering rig on the bed, sans seat belt in an interior vaunting any number of steel edges capable of piercing young skulls. He had survived this, and such riding with his mother remained among his dearest memories of childhood.

He was now driving in a dreamlike state, more or less southward toward home, but when he reached the turnoff to South Miami he passed it by and headed farther south on Dixie Highway. I could keep going, he thought, down to the Keys, to Key West, the end of the road. He could get a boat and a hose-rig and dive for conch, and Amelia could sit up topside and mind the regulator. He could open a little shack and serve conch fritters to the tourists and drink a lot of rum and let Amelia take care of him. That was a kind of life. He knew guys who had it, and they seemed pretty happy until their livers crumpled or they went boating in their rusty old automobiles. He wanted a beer to go with these stupid thoughts.

He pulled into a truck stop just north of Perrine, at the point where suburban Miami fades into rough and rural. It comprised a squalid array of gas stalls and a low office/grocery made of peeling white concrete, somewhat uglier than it had to be, as if in defiance.

"Can I have a Dove bar?" asked Amelia.

"No, your mother's going to slaughter me as it is. I'll get you a juice box. Don't move and don't touch the car."

"I can drive a car."

"I'm sure, but not today, okay?"

Paz got out and went into the store. The air was cruelly refrigerated and stank of microwaved tacos. He purchased a six-pack of Miller talls and a box of juice. He sat in the car, popped a can, and drank most of its tasteless fizz in one long swallow.

"That lady has clown hair," said Amelia.

Paz looked. The lady, an African American, indeed wore a thick helmet of bright orange hair, also tiny blue satin shorts, high-heeled sandals, and a red tube top that served up her large breasts like puddings. There were several other similarly dressed ladies lounging around, chatting to truck drivers and a car full of what looked like Mexican farmworkers. As they watched, the lady with the clown hair walked off with a stocky man in a feed cap and a long trucker's wallet stuck in his back pocket and fixed to his belt by a chain.

"Is she that man's wife?" asked Amelia.

"I don't know, darling. I think they're just friends."

"He's going to let her ride in his truck. He's a demon."

"Is he. How can you tell?"

"I just can. I can tell demons and witches. Some witches are good witches, did you know that?"

"I didn't. What about monsters? Are there good and bad monsters?"

"Of course. The Credible Hunk is a good monster. Godzilla is a good monster. Shrek is a good monster."

"What about vampires?"

"Daddy, vampires are just make-believe," explained Amelia patiently, "like Barbies. Look, there's that lady who had dinner with us."

Paz looked. Beth Morgensen had just stepped out of a Honda and was talking animatedly with a couple of the road whores. They appeared to be well acquainted.

Paz downed the rest of his beer and started the car, planning on a quick getaway, but the sound of the engine had attracted attention, and Beth walked over, grinning. She gave Paz a fat kiss through the window, holding lip contact a little longer than was strictly required, and then eyed the beers.

"Getting your load on before going home to the wife. How perfectly working-classish of you."

"Ever the sociologist."

"Accompanied by the little darling, I see. How are you, sugar?"

"Fine," said Amelia and sucked loudly on her juice straw. Whatever was happening was grown-up stuff, boring and a little disturbing. More interesting were the funny ladies who now came vamping up to the car, cooing over Amelia in a friendly way. Beth made introductions, as at a garden party. It was all very civilized. One of the whores offered to watch the child while Paz did whatever business he needed to do (laughter). Another offered a lowball price on account of you got such a cute baby. Not that I want another one. More laughter, in which Beth joined. Paz pasted a sickly grin on his face and traded wisecracks until their business called and they drifted away.

"Are you what they call a participant-observer in this study?" Paz asked, with a little edge to it, at which Beth Morgensen chuckled and said, "Oh, no, Jimmy darling, you know I'm a charitable foundation. I just give it away." She drew a business card from her bag, licked it lazily, and stuck it to the visor above his head. "Call anytime. Sociology never sleeps."

On the way back, Paz removed the card from the vinyl, and instead of tossing it, his hand moved as if compelled by a mystic force and slid it into the pocket of his shirt.

# Eight

Jennifer sat on the floor of the fishpond just deep enough to allow her snorkel to clear the surface, with a coral rock on her lap to counter buoyancy. She had never thought about drowning herself before, but now, after what had happened, she let the idea linger in her mind. She wondered whether it would hurt a lot, whether it was fast, and realized that this was one more thing she didn't know. Because she was stupid, *hopelessly stupid,* according to Luna during the tirade she had delivered after the discovery that Moie had vanished yet again. Like she could watch him every single fucking minute! And then Luna had told Rupert, practically ordered him, to get rid of her, and Rupert, instead of his usual mild peacemaking, had looked at Jenny with an expression on his face like that of a spoiled baby who'd just been denied a treat (and Jenny knew that look as well as anything), and he'd said, well, maybe, considering all this, it might be best if you started looking for another living arrangement. But really the worst thing was later when she was alone with Kevin, crying her eyes out, and he'd said, oh well, tough shit, babe, let me know where you end up. And when she said, I thought we were together I thought you loved me, he'd said, oh, yeah, I do, sure, we could still see each other and all. So then she had taken her sleeping bag and moved into Moie's old shed and had slept there last night.

She held out her hand and fed bread filaments to a horde of jewel-like tetras and cichlids. She would miss this at least; maybe the fish would miss her, too. Did fish miss? Yet another bit of knowledge her stupid head did not contain. The bread gone, the tetras dispersed like flung sequins, and Jenny's attention was drawn to a large oscar moving slowly in midwater in an erratic manner, like a plate stood on edge and wobbling. It had hurt itself, a common problem in the pool, for the fish were not accustomed to the razor-sharp edges of the coral rock from which the pool was made, coming as they did from an environment where nearly every solid object was coated with mud or soft algae. This Scotty had told her with some irritation, as it was the one feature of the pond he could not control. They sometimes moved quickly in their various mating rivalries and collided with coral and ripped their scales off. He said they should drain the thing and put in a soft porous liner, but this Rupert was unwilling to do, being a cheap bastard, according to Scotty. The oscar turned clumsily, and she saw that it had a red gash behind its little arm fin. She considered emerging and finding Scotty. He had a forty-gallon hospital tank for such cases, but before she could put this thought into action, the red-bellied piranha struck and ripped a ragged chunk out of the wounded fish, and then in an instant there were ten more piranha writhing in a cloud of blood and tissue. Then the piranha were gone, as was the oscar, except for some tiny specks, the center of a cloud of killifishes and tetras, cleaning up the scant remains.

Jenny was out of the water almost before she knew it, standing on the edge of the pool and shivering, although the sun was out already and warm. She stripped off her mask and wrapped a towel around her body. Well, that was out, no drowning, not in that pool, silly really, because what did you care if you were dead, but on the other hand, maybe they would *know* you were trying to kill yourself, the struggling and all, and what if they decided to eat you while you were still alive? She shuddered, not from the air temperature, and almost ran to the green-roofed shed.

Professor Cooksey was there, rubbing his chin and staring at the ground. Jenny was not pleased to see him. He had offered no support during her condemnation, had looked at her in his usual blank manner, as if she were one of his bugs. But automatically, her gaze followed his to the ground.

"What're you looking for?" she asked.

"Hm? Oh, nothing. But observe that footprint. Doesn't it seem odd to you?"

She looked. The floor of the shed was soft earth, from the fall of years of potting soil and humus, and took prints well. This one was human, of a smallish bare foot, the toe and heel marks well defined. It was the only barefoot print on view, the others being shoe prints, either the lugged soles of Scotty's Merrell shoes, her own cheap flip-flops, or Cooksey's leather sandals.

"It's Moie's probably," she said. "What's wrong with it?"

He looked at her briefly and knelt to point. "Why, don't you see? It's much too deep. It's deeper than Scotty's here and far deeper than yours or mine, although I would have said that you and Moie were of a size. How much do you weigh?"

"I don't know. About one twenty, one twenty-five."

"Hm, and this print is yours, I take it, conveniently close by. Let's see what we can make of this." Cooksey took a small brass ruler from his shirt pocket, measured the depth of both prints, stood up, took a small leather-bound notebook from his pocket, and made some calculations. He frowned, mumbled, "No, no, you idiot, that can't be right!" and resumed his scribbling. After some minutes he sighed and said, "Impossible, but there it is. According to these figures, Moie weighs two hundred and six kilos."

"Is that a lot?"

"I should say so! It's over four hundred and fifty pounds."

Jenny said, "But he could have been carrying something heavy. Wouldn't that make the dirt squash down more?"

Cooksey stared at her, and then a look appeared upon his face that she had never seen bestowed upon her in her life, a look of delight that had nothing whatever to do with her physical appearance. "By God, of course! What an imbecile

I am! That's what comes from doing this just for animals, who rarely haul any baggage. Well, my dear, you have just accomplished an act of scientific reasoning. Good for you!"

Jenny felt herself blushing from her breast to her hairline, smiling hard enough to make her mouth feel funny. Cooksey added, "Still, if we assume he's around your size, and even accounting for the extra upper-body strength of men, that's quite a load, well over three hundred pounds. And what could it have been? A boulder? An anvil? And look here, you can see it's a normal walking footprint, the ball and toes digging into the earth more firmly than the heel. He's not standing here heaving something up like a weight lifter. I ask you, could you or I snatch up three hundred pounds and trot off with it as if it were a parcel from the shop? No, and therein lies the mystery. In any case, you may wish to inquire why I was visiting here in the first place."

"Uh-huh."

"Well, I am, ah, aware of your difficulties—I mean, being asked to leave—and I feel responsible in a way." And here he related Moie's problems with mass media, and what had transpired thereafter. "But if you really wish to stay here, I believe I can arrange something. I require an assistant. My specimens are an absolute brothel, and I barely have room to turn around in, as you may have observed. Um, and there'll be a modest stipend from my grant, of course."

Jenny did not know what a modest stipend was but did not admit it. "Yeah, but what about Rupert and Luna?"

"Jennifer, not to blow my trumpet, but I draw a great deal more water in this organization than our Luna. A word with Rupert and the thing is done. What do you say, then?"

"But . . . I mean, I don't *know* anything."

"Yes. And therefore there is nothing to interfere with learning. I have my little ways, and the average graduate student is ordinarily not disposed to learn them. So—are we agreed?"

Nor are they as decorative, nor as full of fine animal spirits, he thought, but declined to say as she flung her arms around him and pressed her damp and marvelous body to his.

\* \* \*

During the following week Jennifer found to her great surprise that the skills required of a research assistant were very like those she had learned in the succession of Iowa farmhouses and homes where she had been fostered. These included: moving heavy or bulky objects without getting hurt; not spilling things, or if you did by accident, cleaning them up quickly and efficiently; scrubbing walls, floors, and windows; putting things in stacks of the same kind and storing them in places where you could find them again; and doing everything you were told to do in a cheerful manner. Professor Cooksey was a good deal nicer than many of the foster moms and dads she had endured, always patient with her mistakes and never treating her like the retard she was. When the work was done, all the specimen boxes were neatly arranged on shelves (which Jennifer had put together with Scotty's help), the scattered papers were put away in files, the journals were racked in green cardboard journal boxes with neat machine-printed labels on them, and an entire room, a former laundry, once filled with cartons, had been cleared, cleaned, and painted. The place now smelled of furniture polish more than tobacco smoke or formalin, and Jennifer was absurdly proud of it.

One morning when Cooksey was meeting with Rupert on the terrace, and she was mopping the floor, Kevin came and had a look and commented that she had finally found her place in life as a janitor. He meant the remark as one of his casual put-downs, but rather to her surprise Jenny felt no sting. "It's honest work," she said. "You should try it sometime. It might do you good."

She turned away from him and continued mopping, and waited for a nasty comeback, which failed to come. Instead, Kevin said, "So what's the situation, babe? When're you coming back to the cabin?"

"I don't know, Kevin"—still mopping—"do you want me back?"

"Well, shit, yeah! What do you think?"

She stopped her work and faced him. "What do you think I should think? When they kicked me out, you were, like, totally cool with me taking off. So, what, you changed your mind?"

"Hey, I'm sorry, all right? I was wrong, okay? You don't have to get all bitchy about it."

She leaned on her mop and stared at him, as all the good energy she had enjoyed over the past few days seemed to drain out of her. For the first time she noticed something blurry in his face, and she realized that it had to do with all the time she'd been spending with Cooksey. The professor's face was solid in a way, a reflection of what was really going on in his head, while Kevin's was always waiting to see which expression was right for getting him what he wanted, like now, he was giving her the melting, yearning look, slightly hurt, and despite herself it was starting to work. She really did love him, even when he was a total piece of shit, and she knew he really loved her, or would someday if she just kept at him, if she could find a way of making him more like Cooksey. But not just now, just at the moment she had no patience for his tricks. She said, "Well, if I'm bitchy, you don't have to hang around, do you?"

"I didn't mean it like that. Come on, babe, be nice." The fetching smile, and now he took a step onto the freshly mopped floor. "Out!" she said. "I got work to do."

And he slammed out, muttering curses, leaving her shaken and amazed at herself. This argument had proceeded at a peculiar low volume, for Rupert was out on the terrace and Rupert required at least the appearance of harmony. Luna was the only resident allowed to give vent at full voice. Later that day, Jennifer removed the backpack that held all her chattels from the cottage she had shared with Kevin and parked it in the former laundry room, together with her sleeping bag and air mattress. The little room was floored and walled with Mexican tiles, like the kitchen, except for the places where the old sinks had been removed, which were patched with rough concrete. There was a small window and a separate door to the outside. As she surveyed it, she wondered at her own presumption. She seemed to be changing in a way she had never expected.

Cooksey appeared at her elbow. "Moving in, are you?"

"Only if it's all right."

"Not to worry, my dear. You created the space, and may claim it. Although I'd appreciate it if your domestic affairs did not interfere with our work, hm?"

"No. And thanks."

"Good. As to that, work I mean, I believe we are ready to begin."

"I thought I *was* working."

"No, no, I mean *work*. Scientific work. Surely you didn't think I required a mere slavey? A char?"

Jennifer didn't recognize the words but she understood what he meant, and had thought it.

"What kind of work?" she said suspiciously.

"Evolutionary biology. That's what I do, you see. In addition to my work for the Alliance, I have to maintain scientific respectability by doing research and publishing papers, or else no one will take me seriously when I speak out about the destruction of rain forest habitat and so on. Now, the cryptic species of fig-pollinating wasps are an important area of study in evolutionary biology. The trees can't reproduce without the wasps, you see, and the wasps can't live without the trees. Moreover, each species of tree has one and only one species of wasp that can pollinate it, so we have an example of coevolution. We think; the issue of one-to-one specificity is much discussed now in Agaonid circles, and that's what I'm working on. Have I lost you?"

"Uh-huh. Professor, I dropped out of school in seventh grade."

"Yes, quite, but perhaps not entirely a disadvantage. Taxonomy is one of the few scholarly fields in which original contributions can still be made by people with no education whatever. You'll call me Cooksey, by the way, except if we're ever on a campus where I'm actually professing."

He led her over to his desk, now uncluttered, and sat her down in the leather chair he used for reading. He sat behind his desk.

"Now, what do you know about evolution?" he asked.

She thought; a scene from a movie crossed her mind. She said, "Monkeys turned into people?"

"Just so, very good. But a great deal happened before that. In the beginning, God created the heavens and the earth and the earth was without form, and void; and darkness was upon the face of the deep, and the spirit of God moved upon the face of the waters. We have that part down, or at least the scientific version of it, and now after billions of years we observe millions of different sorts of creatures, plant and animal and neither, and how did they all come about is the question, and we think that the answer is that they changed over time. They started out simple and evolved, they changed form. Now look at the two of us. We eat steak, potatoes, and beans, let us say, or tofu, potatoes, and beans as long as we live here, but we remain Nigel and Jennifer: we don't become cows or vegetables or tofu. We take things in, air and water and food, and things come out of us, but we remain identifiable bodies. Why is that?"

Jennifer didn't know and said so. In fact, the question had never vexed her mind.

"I'll tell you, then," he said. "The cells of our body contain a chemical code that causes our bodies to make us and nothing else, out of food and water and air. And we reproduce, don't we? But, of course, not exactly. Nigel and Jennifer, let us say, have a baby, but the baby is neither Nigel nor Jennifer. Reproduction is a shake of the dice, not even considering the little changes that creep in from errors of various sorts during reproduction. Most errors are bad for baby, but some few are good. The baby might be even more beautiful than Nigel, even more brilliant than Jennifer."

A small blush covered Jennifer's cheeks at this. He didn't seem to notice but went on. "Now, it's a fact of nature that there is never enough to go around. Every creature needs a place to live and the means of life, food, and so on, and these are always in short supply; so what may we expect, given any population of creatures?"

It was not a rhetorical question. Jennifer realized he was waiting for her answer, and that a shrug and an "I don't know" were not adequate. It was a kind of game he was playing, in which he really believed that answers would somehow spring into her mind if she thought about them. It was a little frightening, but exciting, too. She reached into what she had always thought was an empty bag and to her surprise came up with "Some of them die? Because I was in this home once, and they were real poor, and the mom, Mrs. McGrath, liked one of the kids the best and fed her the most food, and the others didn't get hardly anything. The state closed her down, though."

"Very good. Mrs. McGrath was practicing artificial selection. Charles Darwin made a similar observation, and that's how he came to invent the whole idea. But in nature there's no state to close her down. So we have both a struggle for existence and small variations among creatures from the same parent, and what follows?"

A shorter pause this time. Jennifer thought about foster-care families, and horrible low-end day care centers, and nasty fights over bits of food. "Some will do okay and some won't, so that after a while there'll be more of the better ones."

"Because . . . ?"

"They'll have more babies, and the babies will be like them. How they changed."

"Very good. A near perfect statement of the theory of evolution by natural selection. But as they say, God is in the details. Or the devil. It's all very well to think great thoughts about the origin of all things, but let's see if we can figure out how tiny pieces of it actually evolve, a test, as it were, of the theory. Here we are fortunate in the fig wasp and the fig. You recall what I told you about the life of the Agaoniids? It was the day you found Moie in the Gardens."

"No," she said.

"Really? I thought I was being perfectly lucid."

She had to look away. "I kind of tuned all that out. I'm sorry."

After a moment, he said brightly, "Well, never mind. I'm sure you'll absorb it, by and by. For the moment we have to get you keying out specimens. That means telling one tiny bug from another one that looks almost the same. She might even *be* the same to the eye but have important differences in her genes. You see, in these little wasps we have the opportunity—the privilege, I should say—of observing the generation of new species. Their mode of life is so tightly constrained, the evolutionary *niche,* as we call it, is so small, that evolution itself is, one might say, squirted out so that we can observe it in a short human life span. Are you game?"

Jennifer nodded. "Uh-huh." He smiled, showing his yellow teeth. "Splendid! If you'll step over here . . ." He left his desk and went to a long wooden table on the other side of the room, where stood a binocular teaching microscope with two sets of eyepieces, along with racks and racks of shallow specimen drawers. From a shelf he reached down a plastic-covered chart, dull with age and use, and set it up before her. They sat on lab stools. "Today we have naming of parts. 'Japonica glistens like coral in all the neighboring gardens, and today we have naming of parts.' "

"Say what?"

"A poem, but never mind that. I meant that you have to learn the parts of the bug before you can use the keys. Now, this long thing is the antenna. The tip is called the radicle. Say it!"

She did.

"Next the pedicle. Say 'pedicle'! Good. Next the annelli."

And so on, she repeating the meaningless words as he proceeded from the antenna to the head itself, the wings, with their diagnostic patterns of veins, to the thorax, the legs and the gaster, ending with the long ovipositor, all the little shields, knobs, and spikes with which taxonomists classify the insect world. This took half an hour. Then Cooksey pointed with the tip of his pencil to the tip of the model's antenna. "What is this, please?" he asked.

She didn't know. The pencil twitched down the hair-thin appendage. Blank. Blank again.

"I can't do it!" she wailed.

"Nonsense! Of course you can. You're resisting because you associate learning with pain. You must relax and let the names flow into you. We are made for memory, my dear, and there is a fruitful plain in your head that just needs some water and some seed."

"I'm too stupid." She was about to break down sobbing, and she bit her lip hard to stop it.

"No, you're not. If you were stupid you'd be dead, or a drug addict, or a prostitute, or have three children. Think about it!"

Jennifer did, and it was true. She had thought it was just dumb luck. Something popped in her head, like snorting a long, long line of cocaine. The world looked different, and she knew that, unlike a drug rush, it was a difference from which she would not come down.

"In any case," Cooksey continued, "some of the stupidest people I know are invertebrate systematists with international reputations. Now, from the beginning. This is the radicle. Say . . ."

"Radicle," she said. "Radicle."

On the evening after Paz brought Amelia to the *ilé,* he and Lola had fought a major fight, and Paz hoped that it had been the main battle and not a mere carpet-bombing prelude to further assaults. Although it was a family principle to settle such things before retiring for the night, Lola had fled the field and locked herself in the bedroom she used as an office, whence he could hear the sound of weeping, of cursing, of small missiles being flung. An overreaction, he thought, and said so through the door, but received no intelligible response. This in itself was unusual and worrying. Lola was not one to avoid discussion about emotional states; to the contrary, she doted upon them, long explorations into their separate and conjoined-in-marriage psyches until sometimes Paz felt like a specimen on a slide. He bore up, however, this being a part of his beloved, and thought himself a better husband for it.

Maybe that was part of the problem, he mused as he sat in the early-morning garden with a cup of Cuban coffee in his hand: maybe he had been a little *too* accommodating. He considered the house itself, their home. Her house originally, a typical Florida ranch house in South Miami, made of white-painted stuccoed concrete block with a gray tile roof and aqua-blue-painted steel hurricane awnings. Charmless as architecture, it was, however, old enough to be surrounded with well-grown foliage: a huge bougainvillea covered one side wall and part of the roof with purple blossoms, and the backyard was shaded by a large mango, beyond which was a good assortment of fruit trees—lime, orange, grapefruit, guava, avocado. Inside she had furnished it with spare Scandinavian wood and leather, fanciful or abstract pictures in mirror-steel frames, and rya rugs. Not his taste; he preferred old stuff, eccentric junk, the *Last Supper* on velvet—no, not really, but that was occasionally implied by the wife. His mother claimed the house looked like a doctor's office.

Yes, the mother—that had come up, too, big-time. Paz reviewed what he could recall of the charges and countercharges while he waited for the coffee to kick in. He had come home drunk, had endangered the life of their precious by driving drunk. How could he? Well, first of all, four beers did not make drunk. Then the lecture from the doctor on alcohol impairment. Okay, guilty, never again, at which point the kid pipes up with guess where we were today, and tells all, the voodoo ceremony, the yams, the stinky smoke, worshipping at false idols, *plus* the visit to the ladies who kiss boys for money and Daddy was talking to that lady who came to dinner. Easily explained, of course, although not the card from Morgensen. Paz had idly tossed it out onto his dresser, and when the wife, that skilled researcher, had discovered it lying there it proved to have on its reverse a set of lips imprinted in red lipstick. That Beth! What a kidder! And so the story of Beth and Jimmy way back when had to be told, or wrenched out, each perfectly honest statement out of Paz's mouth sounding like a philanderer's evasion. Paz was in the peculiar position of having done nothing wrong with Beth Morgensen but also secretly knowing he had wanted to, *still* wanted to, if it came to that, but *wouldn't,* being an honest guy, but *might* if this kind of shit went on much longer, and who could blame him?

Not a profitable line of thought. He was squelching it when Lola emerged from the house, dressed in her usual T-shirt, shorts, and sneakers and carrying a canvas bag with her work clothes in it. She shot him a venomous look and strode on through the patio and out to the shed in the yard where she stored her bike.

"Good morning!" Paz called. No answer. She got the bike and was wheeling it to the driveway when Paz got up and intercepted her.

"Are you ever going to talk to me again?" he asked, grasping the handlebars.

"I'm still too angry. Let go of the bike, please."

"No. Not until we talk."

"I have to get to work," she said, struggling to free the handlebars. "I have patients . . ."

"Let them die," said Paz. "This is more important." At this, she sighed ostentatiously and folded her hands across her breasts. "Okay, have it your way. Talk."

"Okay, we had a fight, I apologized, and now it's over. You forgive me and we move on, just like always."

"It's not as simple as that."

"Explain the complexity."

"I feel totally betrayed. I don't know if I can trust you now."

"What, because I had a couple of beers?"

"Don't be smart! I still can't believe that you took our daughter to a voodoo ceremony, fortune-telling and blood sacrifices and . . . and yams. Without even the courtesy of discussing it with me. Filling her head with frightening toxic nonsense. How could you!"

"It's not voodoo, Lola, as you know. I wish you'd stop calling Santería voodoo. It's insulting."

"It's the same thing."

"Right, like Catholic and Jewish is the same because they both come from Palestine. I explained all this to you last night. It's not a conspiracy. It was spur of the moment. Margarita was there, and Amy asked me, and I didn't see the harm in—"

"It's ridiculous barbaric nonsense. You don't even *believe* in it!"

"Maybe that's true, but my mother does, and I have to respect that. And Amy only has the one grandmother, and they love each other, and I'm not going to stand up and tell her her grandmother is full of shit because she follows the *santos*. It's part of her culture, just like science, just like medicine."

"Except medicine is real. That's a slight difference. Medicine doesn't cause nightmares in little girls."

Something in her tone, a higher pitch, a shake in the voice, made Paz stop and examine his wife more closely. This stridency was not like her at all; a joke, a light mockery, was more in her line when discussing the peculiarities of his culture.

"What's going on, Lola? This can't just be about Santería. We been married seven years, and you never went nuts about it before."

There *was* something wrong. She was not meeting his eye, and Lola was ordinarily a major fan of eye contact. "Maybe," he added lightly, "you should've married a Jewish doctor after all."

"Oh, and a little sneaky anti-Semitism added to the mix now? Look, I absolutely have to leave now or I'll be late for rounds."

Somewhat stunned at this last interchange, Paz lifted his hands. She jumped up on the bike and rolled clicking down the shell driveway.

* * *

Later that morning, Paz was at work in the restaurant, having deposited his daughter at school without incident and without discussion of any bad dreams. She had summoned him (he lying awake alone in the marriage bed) with a shrill cry in the night, and he had arrived at her side to find her still in a sense asleep, but whimpering and shaking, eyes open but unseeing—terrifying. Paz had neglected to mention this episode to the resident psychiatrist: Lola had (mercifully) slept through the whole thing. Nor did he intend to.

Paz was preparing yuca, a tedious task, which he now welcomed. The yuca is a pillar of Cuban cuisine, but it is a tricky tuber, devious like life itself, Paz was now thinking. It has an ugly rough bark, which must be removed, and then the toxic green underskin must be carefully stripped off, without losing too much yuca. It bleeds a white liquid while this is happening. The core must also be removed, as it is inedible. Paz, too, felt stripped and bleeding, and he knew there was something poisonous at his own core. He laughed out loud. *The Yuca Way to Personal Growth,* a book he might write: *A Cuban Line-Cook's Guide to Enlightenment.*

He prepped a bushel of yuca and then ran it through a food processor. The sludge would be the basis of Guantanamera's famous conch 'n' crab fritters and also a new dish Paz was trying out, deep-fried prawns in yuca batter mixed with rum. He made a handful of these, adjusted the flavorings, shared samples with the rest of the kitchen crew, took counsel, and then played with seasonings and the temperature of the deep fryer. By eleven he'd decided it was good enough to serve as a special with a raw jicama salad, and so informed the waitstaff. His mother was absent, so there were no arguments that yuca tempura prawns had not been thought of in Cuba in 1956 and hence were not to be served in her restaurant. But where was she? She'd gone to pick up Amelia at the usual time. A little tick of concern started, which was quickly submerged in the violent amnesia of the lunch rush.

Surfacing around half past two, Paz looked down to see his little girl soliciting his attention. She was dressed in an ankle-length armless sheath of yellow silk patterned with large green tropical leaves, and tiny white strapped sandals with a modest heel. Her hair was braided and arranged in a shining crown around her head set off by a white gardenia behind her ear. Around her neck was a necklace of green and yellow glass beads.

"That's quite an outfit. Been shopping with Abuela?"

"Yes. We went to a special store." She fingered the necklace. "These beads are blessed. It's not just a regular necklace, Daddy."

"I bet. How's the room? Everybody enjoying?"

"Yes. There're millions of Japanese people all dressed the same. Why do they do that?"

"I don't know. It's a custom, I guess."

"Anyway, the reason I came in is there's a man outside who wants to see you. He knew you were my daddy. Table three."

"Thank you. What does he look like?"

She thought for a moment. "Like a football player, but bald, too."

"Right. Tell him I'll be out as soon as I finish these orders."

Police Major Douglas Oliphant did look like a football player and had actually been one in college, a linebacker for Michigan. He was dark brown in color and calm in mien, and Paz liked him as well as any man he had ever worked for. Oliphant ran, among other things, the homicide and domestic violence unit of the Miami Police Department. He looked up from his nearly empty plate and nodded at Paz, indicating the seat opposite.

Paz sat and said, "You had the prawns."

"I did. I'm almost ready to say you're more valuable to humanity and the city cooking this stuff than you are catching murderers. Terrific food, Jimmy."

"Thank you. The answer is still no."

"You don't know the question yet."

"I bet I do. Tito was by the other day. You want me to advise on this big shot who got eaten up by the invisible voodoo tiger."

A tight smile from Oliphant. "That would be nice. It would be a civic gesture and appreciated by all your friends in the Cuban community, especially in light of recent events."

"Such as?"

"Last night the home of a man named Cayo D. Garza, a Cuban-American banker, was vandalized. His front door was clawed to ribbons and deposits of feces were left on his front walk. On examination, these feces proved to be that of a jaguar. According to the zoo. Our crime scene people don't have much expertise with jaguar shit. It's not something that comes up a lot. We took a look around his yard, and we found big-cat paw prints, not unlike the paw prints found at Fuentes's place."

"The partially devoured Fuentes."

"Him. So we're now real interested, and when Tito looks at the known associates of Mr. Garza, what does he find? The late Antonio Fuentes. And upon further investigation of the K.A.s of Fuentes and Garza, we find Felipe Ibanez, an import-export fellow, and guess what? He had exactly the same vandalism two nights ago, although he thought so little of it that he declined to report it to the police. He was having someone replace his door when the Miami Beach cops showed up, and he'd already flushed the jaguar poo-poo, but we found paw prints there, too. They're both out on Fisher Island, big estate-type places. Now, it seems that Fuentes, Garza, and Ibanez were partners in a venture, because when we ran their names through county business records, we found a little d.b.a. they set up last year called Consuela Holdings, LLC. Four equal partners. The fourth guy is Juan X. Calderón. You know him?"

"Why would you think that?"

"Because when I said his name, your face jumped."

Paz shrugged. "He's a mover and shaker in the Cuban community. Yoiyo Calderón. Everyone knows who he is."

"What's he like?"

"Ask Tito. He's Cuban, too."

"I'm asking you."

"I'm the wrong guy. People like Yoiyo don't associate with people like me."

"He never eats here?"

"Never."

"That was a very definite statement. You know what he looks like, then?"

Paz was about to say something angry but checked himself and grinned at his former boss. "Hey, that was pretty good. Interrogated in my own restaurant. Very classy, Major. Maybe we'll put it on the menu."

Oliphant allowed himself a tight grin. "Just a couple of old comrades shooting the shit." He popped a yuca chip into his mouth and crunched. "Come on, Jimmy. Help me out here. These are big shots we're talking about, and I'm getting incredible pressure from the pols on this Fuentes thing. If it's some kind of Cubano vendetta I need to know about it. Especially the weird aspects . . ."

"Uh-uh. What, you suddenly have a dearth of Cubans in the P.D.? I'm the only one you can think of to ask?"

"I did ask. I'm getting mixed messages, shifty looks. Everybody's got a second cousin works for these guys, and I get the feeling the Consuela trio are all informed about the investigation before I am. Which is why I came to see you. And I'm still getting shifty looks."

Paz held up his arm and pulled back the sleeve of his tunic. "Look, man, you see the color of my skin? The kind of Cubans we're talking about only want to see that color in the kitchen, or carrying a plate. They don't hang with me or mine and tell me their secrets."

"But you know Calderón."

"To look at. I wouldn't say I know him."

"But he doesn't eat here. I thought this was the best Cuban restaurant in Miami. What, he doesn't eat out? He only likes Chinese?"

"Him and my mom had business dealings years ago. They had a falling-out. That's the story."

"What kind of dealings?"

"I don't know the details. You could ask her."

"Uh-huh. So what's the book on Mr. Calderón? The reason I'm asking is we got a murder and two acts of what you have to call threatening vandalism against three out of four partners in a venture, of which Calderón is number four. We had someone call at the Calderón place. He claims he had no scratches, no cat prints, no jaguar shit, although his home sports a brand-new front door. I have to think it's connected, a business thing. So . . . Juan Calderón. Good guy, bad guy, maybe capable of violence . . . ?"

"Okay, Major, since you press me: he's a typical *gusano* piece of shit. Him and his father came over with a pile of cash in the first wave and bought into a lot of businesses, and made another shitload putting money out on the street to Cuban entrepreneurs. Then he got into development and made a third shitload, which is what he does now. Capable of violence? Probably, as long as it wasn't traceable back to him, or if he had a bad day he might kick a servant. But if you asked me would he murder his partner and eat a couple of chunks off him, or order it done, I'd say no. It's not their style."

Oliphant opened his mouth to respond, but at that moment Amelia, a sheaf of menus clutched to her chest, came by with a party of four and seated them at a nearby table. After she was done, she stopped in front of Oliphant.

"Is everything all right, sir?" she asked.

"Everything is just fine, miss," said Oliphant, with a beaming expression on his face that Paz could not recall seeing there before.

"Except," said Paz, "I would like a little girl to sit on my lap."

"Daddy, I'm working," she said severely. And to Oliphant, "May I send the waiter by with a dessert menu?"

"No, thank you," said Oliphant. "You know I used to have a little girl who sat on *my* lap. It was better than dessert."

"What happened to her?" asked Amelia.

"She grew up and moved away."

Amelia took this in without comment, said, "I'll bring your check," and departed.

Oliphant laughed and shook his head. "That's not cute or anything."

"She's not bad. I was about that age myself when I started in the business. Probably illegal as hell, but you're not going to tell the cops. Look, Major . . ."

"You need to call me Doug. You don't work for me anymore."

"Doug. I wish I could help, but, honestly, I'm out of the loop with that crowd."

"Okay," said Oliphant. "But if you think of anything, you'll let someone know, okay?" His tone and expression made it perfectly obvious, in a nice way, that he knew Paz was holding something back.

The three surviving partners of the Consuela company lunched in the Bankers' Club that day as they did nearly every Wednesday. People expected to see them there, men in fine suits, and a few women stopped to speak, to smile, to touch hands, but it was difficult to tell whether this was a kind of grooming behavior, acknowledging membership in the pack, or the first probing tugs of the jackal at the belly of a dying animal. A little of both, was Yoiyo Calderón's thought as he smiled back and extended his hand. He did not like the way Ibanez looked: old and tired and frightened. Even Garza, who normally presented the slick and predatory face of a cruising shark to the observing world, appeared pasty, his movements lacking their accustomed vitality. He encouraged them to order a second round of cocktails. The liquor brightened them a little, like a cheap paint job on a clunker car, enough to show the room there was nothing wrong with their affairs. That was sufficient under the circumstances, Calderón thought. In business, especially business in the tightly knit Cuban community, appearance was 90 percent of the battle. The men ordered their usual lunches, too, all large lumps of costly protein, and appeared to eat. The service staff knew how little of it they consumed, but they did not count.

"So when does this start?" Garza asked.

"Today," said Calderón. "Hurtado moves fast when he wants something done. That's a good sign, I think."

"Yes, marvelous," said Ibanez bitterly. "He's a credit to the human race. What will this entail, this protection he's offering?"

"You won't notice a thing. Some cars on the street, is all. The whole point is to move with discretion and remove who-ever's doing this."

"I still can't believe I'm involved in this," said Ibanez, as if recounting a bad dream. "They came to my *home*! The maid found what they'd done when she went to walk the dogs in the morning, the door clawed. . . . She was hysteri-cal, and the stupid bitch went to my wife. Two hysterical women, Jesus Christ, what was I supposed to say?"

"Yes, Felipe, we've heard all about your hysterics," said Calderón. "But let's not turn into women ourselves, hey? A few days and all this will be over. They will make some other stupid move and then"—he snapped his fingers—"gone. The Puxto will come through and we'll be fine."

"How can you be sure it will be days?" asked Garza. "Why not months?"

Calderón had feared this very question. He cleared his throat and said, "Hurtado thinks the pressure is coming from Colombian interests. He's put the word out that we are mov-ing up the schedule for the cut, more crews on the road, ac-celerated delivery of equipment, and so on. They will be, let's say, stimulated to increase the pressure."

"You're using us as *bait*," said Ibanez in an outraged voice, rather higher in volume than was usual in the Bankers' Club. A party at the next table looked over with interest. Calderón kept his own voice moderate, not with-out effort; he could feel the veins at the side of his head throb.

"Felipe, use your head. We're all targets already. We've all been hit. Time is of the essence here, as is secrecy. There is a police investigation going on. Whoever these people are, it's vital that we get them before the police do. Speaking of which, have they learned anything?"

This was directed to Garza, who had a nephew in the Miami P.D. and was their source of information in that quarter. Garza shrugged. "The usual stupidity. They're planning to check out the local environmentalists, if you can imagine. Obviously, they know we're all connected in a business way, and they're curious about why Calderón wasn't hit like we were. You cleaned up the mess too quickly, Yoiyo. You're starting to look like their prime suspect."

Calderón forced himself to laugh at this, and after a moment Garza joined him. Ibanez managed to move his face into a grimace that might have passed for jollity if the look in his eyes were ignored. Calderón felt a little better now. Laughing in the face of danger; it was what was expected of a man, after all. And the show of it had done some good, he thought. A table of Cuban businessmen at their ease and laughing; what could be more normal? They finished their coffee, speaking only of other, less contentious affairs. The waiter brought the check in its leather folder and laid it before Ibanez. Garza, however, reached across for it. "My turn," he said.

But as his sleeve pulled back, Calderón saw to his shock that above his gold Piaget watch he had a thin bracelet of red and white beads. Like every Cuban, Calderón knew what this meant. It signified that the cool and ruthless Cayo Garza had solicited the protection of Shango, *orisha* of rage and war, and also that the man was a lot more frightened than he let on. Calderón wondered now if Garza knew something that he didn't about the source of their troubles. A passing thought, this, serving only to lower his respect for the man and convince him all the more that only he himself was in firm control of the situation.

Now it is night and all these people are asleep: Jennifer and Professor Cooksey, Kevin and Rupert, Paz and his family, the Cuban-American businessmen and their families and friends. Wakeful still is a man named Prudencio Rivera Martínez, together with a number of his colleagues. They wait in vans parked near the houses of the men of the Consuela company. They are from Colombia and are good at this sort of work, patient and relentless. Each van holds three men, one alert, the others dozing on pads in the rear compartment. Prudencio Rivera Martínez is their captain, and he is in a modest rental Taurus, driving from site to site and around the neighborhoods involved, so that he will know them if need arises. At irregular intervals, he checks his men via cell phone, but tonight there are no problems, no disturbances.

Moie is awake as well, in his hammock high in the boughs of the great ficus tree. He has a plastic bottle of water and a small package of Fritos given to him by the little girl. He has never eaten a Frito before but finds them good and finishes the whole package. He likes the salt and the flavor of the corn. When he is a man he enjoys foods other than meat. There is a remarkable amount of meat on the streets of Miami America, he has found, much more than he expected, considering how many dead people there are. If Miami was full of Runiya, they would long ago have eaten all this meat. He believes that the *wai'ichuranan* have forgotten how to hunt. This is because they have machines that make food like a bird makes eggs. He has seen this with his own eyes.

Now he removes a clay jar from his net bag and sucks some powder into his nostrils. When he feels the *yana* arrive, he sings the song that opens the barrier between the worlds. The *yana* slides him free of his body, as a knife slides the fillet from a fish, and he floats into the dream world. But before he drifts entirely away he recalls, as he often does at this moment, what happened when he first gave the *yana* to Father Tim. The priest had laughed and would not stop laughing, and Moie was hard-pressed not to join him, although in all the generations since Jaguar gave *yana* to First Man, it was not recorded in the memory of the

Runiya that anyone had laughed. Usually they were frightened to death the first time.

So later when they returned from the dream world Moie had asked the priest what was so funny, and Father Tim said that the *yana* gives you the eye of God, and to God everything must be amusing, as we find the stumbles and tantrums of small children amusing. They think it is the end of the world, but we just pick them up and give them food and a hug, knowing that their momentary pain will soon pass. And this is when Moie discovered that Father Tim was able to keep himself separate from the god when he traveled the dream world in the *yana* trance. This was a wonder to Moie, and the two men talked often after that about what Father Tim called *ontology.* Long, long ago, said Father Tim, everyone's thoughts were like water, connected to every thing and part of every thing. There was no difference between people's thoughts and the rest of the world and the fathers of the *wai'ichuranan* lived just like the Runiya. Then one of these ancestors had a thought that was made not of water but of iron. And soon many of the *wai'ichuranan* had such thoughts, and with such thoughts they cut themselves away from the world and began to slice it up into tiny parts. Thus they gained their great powers over the world, and thus also they began to be dead.

Then Moie understood the difference between even such a *wai'ichura* as Father Tim and himself. When Moie took the *yana,* he was Jaguar and Jaguar was him and he was part of the life of everything that was—animals, plants, rocks, sky, stars—but Father Tim could only be so in a flickering sort of way, as in some night when the moon was gone and the fire in the hut had died to coals. *Through a glass darkly* is how Father Tim described the sight he had of his Jan'ichupitaolik, and he said that he had to wait until he came to the land of the dead before he could be like Moie was. Were you not a heathen, Moie, he often said, you would be a saint.

So now it is Jaguar-in-Moie who travels like a vapor through the dream world of Miami. Distances in the dream world are not as they are in the world under the sun, so he is easily able to find all the people he needs to visit. He visits his allies and gives them dreams of strength and power, readying them for the struggle. To his enemies he gives dreams of dread. There are screams in the night in expensive districts; lights go on, pills are consumed in numbers, as is liquor. This is how battle is waged in Moie's country.

At last he visits the girl, and the father and the mother. Here he finds something very strange. There is a *tichiri* around the child, and not only that, it is one that he doesn't recognize, an alien entity, but quite powerful. Moie had not realized that the dead people could call *tichiri,* but apparently it is so. He wonders if this is the same as his discovery that there are different animals living in the land of the dead, or if it is like his mistake about the stars. He will ask Cooksey about this. Meanwhile, it is hard to enter the dreams of the father, and nearly impossible to enter the girl's dreams. The mother is no problem at all, so he spends the most time there.

He really has no idea why Jaguar desires that he do this, but the desire is as good as a command. Jaguar does many things Moie cannot understand, and this is far from the strangest. At some point he will be told. Or not.

# Nine

Another one that was wrong! Jenny rubbed her eyes and peered again through the objectives of the binocular microscope. She used the needle to nudge the tiny specimen so that the light struck it at a slightly different angle. She would have said it was a *Pegoscapus gemellus,* except that the pattern of its radial and costal wing veins was more like that of *P. insularis.* Only it couldn't be *insularis* because it lacked the characteristic leg segment proportions and recurved ovipositor that marked that species. The ovipositor was long but almost straight; there was nothing like this combination of features on the key chart. Sighing, she removed the oddball fig wasp from the microscope stage and put her in a vial with half a dozen others that were similarly screwed up. The next one was a good *gemellus,* and she dropped it into a labeled vial and made a notation of its specimen number in the notebook.

She was not pleased when a wrong one turned up, for in the week or so that she had been keying out for the professor she had come to expect that the little wasps would behave themselves and fall properly into either one of the two species they were studying. Finding ringers offended her sense of order, which was as strong as it was recent, perhaps strong *because* recent. Prior to this, Jennifer had not devoted three brain cells to any contemplation of nature's diversity more complex than the one expounded in "Old MacDonald Had a Farm."

Along with her knowledge about the taxonomy of the fig wasps, she had absorbed the faith that *every* living thing had to fit neatly into the immense ragged bush-structure of life—phylum, class, order, superfamily, family, genus, species—all connected by evolution. It boggled her mind; in fact, it was her very first boggle. So every living thing had to go somewhere, and the odd little wasps displeased her for that reason. She understood that her preliminary sorting would be confirmed by mitochondrial sequencing in the lab later on (not that she had any clear idea what that was), but she wanted to get it right, to please Cooksey. That was something new as well. Although she had always tried to please—given her background, she would hardly have survived otherwise—pleasing Cooksey was different. Cooksey did not seem to be pleased because what she did was good for Cooksey as much as because doing something well was good for her and also good for . . . here she was uncertain, because she lacked the concepts, but she sensed that for Cooksey doing things right was a form of worship. God is in the details, my dear, something he said often. It was her very first contact with true parenting, and it went to her head like crank.

On the other hand, she had begun to comprehend the difference between what she was doing and what real biologists did, going into the field and being surrounded by millions of species and figuring out what went where and the pattern of relationship, how the substance of life poured through the depths of time in an unending and ever-varying stream. That kind of understanding would be forever beyond her, she knew, but the mere idea that there were such people (and Cooksey was one of them) made her feel better about herself than she ever had before. It was like being the worst player on a world championship team: still pretty great.

And she had discovered she could lose herself in the microscope as well as she had in the fishpond. As now: therefore, she did not hear Geli Vargos come in, did not register her greeting, did not respond until a hand touched her shoulder, when she yelped and jumped and nearly toppled the stool.

"Wow, you must have been deep in it," said Geli.

"Yeah, I was. Anyway, where've you been? I haven't seen you for I don't know how long."

"Oh, you know, family stuff. My cousin's getting married. My grandfather's going crazy. The usual *Cubano* twenty-four-seven nonsense." This was said in a tone that did not suggest a willingness to go into detail, which Jenny thought a little funny, because Geli was usually delighted to expatiate on the doings of her family, and she had in Jenny, whose own life was void in this area, a devout listener. Geli pointed to the microscope setup. "What're you doing with the mike?"

"I'm keying out species of Agaonidae for Cooksey."

"You're *what?*"

"What I said. It's for his work on the evolution of mutualism and precision of adaptation. He showed me how to do it."

"Uh-huh. Well, this is a step up from making breakfast. How did all this happen?"

"I don't know. They were going to kick me out on account of I lost Moie, and Cooksey said I could work for him and I'm doing it. I'm a research assistant, how about that? And I still make breakfast."

"I'm impressed," said Geli, although Jennifer detected something in her tone that was not pleased, was a little put off, in fact, and she wondered why.

"Can I see what you're doing?"

"Sure," said Jenny, and set her friend up at the other eyepiece while she tweezed a tiny wasp onto the stage and keyed it, and then another, both *P. insularis,* explaining the differences, proudly using the technical terms, like a real person.

"So does Cooksey check on your work?" Geli asked after this demonstration.

"He did when I was starting up, but not anymore. He says I can do it as good as him, almost."

"Well, good." A pause, and then, "I guess this means you won't be going out on runs with me anymore."

"I don't know. You'd have to speak to Luna about that. Kevin and Scotty've been doing it while you were gone and since I started all this."

"Oh, that's an effective team! Scotty mumbling and Kevin fomenting the revolution. What does Kevin think about all this?" She gestured to the microscope and specimen boxes.

"I don't know. I moved out on him after he gave me grief about it. We haven't talked much, since then. He, like, *mopes* at me." She fiddled with the focus knob and swiveled on her stool. "I still sort of love him, though. We were together like a long time, almost two years. And I get lonely at night, you know?"

Geli actually did not know, but she was not about to reveal this to Jennifer. Nor did she comment on the semibreak with Kevin, which Jenny thought was also a little strange, since she used to go on so about it.

"I've got to go talk to Luna," Geli said. "Will I see you at lunch?"

"If you don't, there won't be any," replied Jenny cheerfully, and returned to her specimens.

She worked steadily for the next two hours and was surprised and delighted to discover that she had come to the end of the series, which was a sample of one hatch from trees of two different species of *Ficus*. She put the last vials back in their specimen boxes, and these back on their shelves, all except the vial of wasps she couldn't identify from the key. Then she stretched her stiff back muscles and went into the kitchen to help Scotty make tuna salad for lunch. Tuna salad at La Casita was made with fresh tuna. Jenny had not realized before coming to the Forest Planet Alliance that tuna was an actual fish that you could buy in fish stores and cook. She thought it was a made-up substance that, like Spam, only came in cans. Nor had she understood that mayonnaise could be manufactured in a kitchen out of eggs and oil, instead of being something that was elemental, like gasoline, that you had to buy retail. She made the mayonnaise as she had been taught, and hard-boiled half a dozen eggs while Scotty washed the greens and peeled avocados and then seared the tuna. They worked together almost silently but well, not getting in each other's way. It used to bother her that Scotty never talked to her, but now that she had a little something in her own head, she didn't mind it that much, she was less bothered by the absence of chatter. Also, she had Cooksey.

Talking with Cooksey was different from talking to the rest of them, different indeed from talking to anyone else she had ever met. Geli, for instance, was always willing to tell you stuff, about science and politics, but it was like she was the teacher and you were the pupil and you had to sort of be admiring and oh, wow, I didn't know that, how smart you are! But it never occurred to Cooksey that everyone didn't know everything he did and so he just zoomed on, assuming she would understand, like she'd been to college in England, too, and when he would pause and say "Eh?" to see if she had understood, she would say right out she hadn't. At which a peculiar expression would come over his face, as if she really *did* understand, say, sex allocation theory or whatever and was pretending not to as a joke, and then he would demonstrate, by means of skillful questions, that she really *did* understand the stuff. There is no idea in all science that can't be grasped by the persistent application of the second-rate mind, said Cooksey, quoting Whitehead. He quoted Whitehead a lot, also Yeats, and a bunch of other people Jenny had never heard of. Not, he said on that occasion, that *you* have a second-rate mind, my dear, for since it is almost perfectly empty, we have not had a chance to rate it at all. And you are in any case persistent, as I have often observed.

They had a large colorful platter shaped like a fish, which the household invariably used to serve fish. Rupert liked it so. Scotty piled the creamy smooth salad in it and added chopped scallion, lettuce leaves, capers, radishes, and other

garnishes in such a way that it looked like a Japanese painting of a real fish. Jenny picked up the warmed bread and a
chilled bottle of chardonnay and followed Scotty and the
tuna platter out to the terrace.

Jenny didn't know whether the changes she had observed
recently in the group owed more to her new status or if
something else was going on. She was not, as she told Geli
often, all that good at figuring stuff out, but she was *real*
good at vibing when something was off, and here there was.
She recalled well that before Moie disappeared, Rupert
would usually talk to Luna and Cooksey, and Luna would
talk to Rupert and Scotty, and Scotty would talk to Luna and
Kevin, and Kevin would only occasionally talk to her,
mainly to slip a snide comment sideways under his breath.
When Geli came to lunch, she always sat next to Jennifer
and talked to her and to Luna. Now everything seemed
turned around. Geli and Luna were sitting on either side of
Rupert. Kevin was right up there on the good end of the
table with them, and now the Professor and Scotty were sitting on either side of Jennifer, at what Kevin always used to
call the peasant end of the table. No one commented on
these changes. When she sat down, Jenny told Cooksey that
she had finished the series. "Really? That's wonderful, my
dear. We'll have to find you something else to do." And then
he launched into a discussion of orchid pollinators with
Scotty, pausing every so often to include Jennifer in the conversation, and after a while, Scotty began to do the same.
Normally as silent as a cat, he could talk a blue streak about
plants and fish, although he had never done so with Jennifer
before this. It sort of made up for Kevin treating her like she
was invisible. And what was all this with Kevin and Luna?
They hated each other, but here they were, chatting away
like nobody's business. It was very strange; even stranger,
Jenny didn't mind it one bit.

After lunch, Jenny came back from cleaning up in the
kitchen to find Cooksey perched on a stool near the microscope station checking through the lab notebook.

"Did you record all of them on this page?" he asked. "These columns seem to show different numbers."

"Yeah, but there were some that didn't fit. I must've screwed up some way. Sorry. The ones I couldn't figure out're in here." She held up the vial and Cooksey peered at the indeterminate black mass within. " 'Didn't fit' meaning that you couldn't classify them as either *gemellus* or *insularis*?"

"Yeah. And I couldn't find them in the key, either."

"That's odd. Well, let's have a look, shall we?"

He sat at the microscope and placed a wasp on the stage. He peered for some time and then examined another and a third, muttering to himself. He rose and pulled a reprint file down and studied several reprints. He consulted the key, looked in the microscope, checked another reprint. Mutter, mutter, and then, "Well, I'll be blowed!"

"What? Did I make a mistake?"

He looked her in the face, and she saw that his eyes were shining. He was beaming like a two-year-old with a fresh cookie. "Oh, not at all. Oh, no! I believe you've discovered a new species of *Pegoscapus*."

"Is that good?"

"Good? It's splendid! Epochal! I myself have been studying these little blighters for over twenty years and I've only discovered one new species."

It had never occurred to Jenny, having only recently learned about species and that they each had a name, to imagine that there were animals that didn't have one. It made her feel peculiar, and she asked, "But, um, what do we call it? I mean, in the notebook."

"Whatever we bloody well please!" crowed Cooksey.

"Really? You mean just make something up?"

"Indeed. Of course there are certain traditions. Species are usually named for some aspect of the organism, like its shape or habit, or its native heath, or to honor someone in the trade. In *Pegoscapus* alone, as you know, we find Hoffmeyer and Herre so distinguished. I myself named my *Tetrapus* after my late wife."

At this, something seemed to deflate in Cooksey, the light that had just shone from his eyes dimmed, and he appeared to shrink a little. Jenny observed this and found it dreadful. Into the silence now she blurted, "What was her name?"

"Portia," said Cooksey dully.

"Like the sports car?" asked Jennifer. She was startled to see the look on his face after she'd said this, a stunned expression akin to one following a blow to the base of the skull, and she began to worry that maybe she had said something insulting, because you could never tell with English people, they thought a lot of weird stuff, and now he looked like he was going to have a heart attack, his face going pink and strange sounds issuing from deep in his chest. She was about to say something when the first unmistakable laugh burst forth. This was even more startling because she had never heard such a sound from Cooksey before, a dry chuckle was more his style, and she knew that he was not really laughing at her, so it was all right, if a little strange.

She watched him as the laughter poured out, tears squirted from his eyes, and his knees wobbled. "Oh God Oh Christ," he expostulated at intervals, and after a while she started laughing, too, just to join in and for happiness and delight that her own dumb remark (because, although she had known a girl named Chrysler once, obviously a high-class guy like Cooksey wouldn't have married a girl named after a car) could have caused such a gush of exhilaration.

Cooksey was still in the paroxysm, eyes tight shut and completely out of control now (Oh Christ Oh God); he bounced off the microscope table and would have collapsed on the floor had she not caught him in her arms. She sank down with him under the table, cradling his upper body. He smelled of tobacco and guy. Jennifer's laughter slowed, then stopped, because what was coming out of Cooksey wasn't laughter, or not entirely laughter anymore.

After some time and a few long whooping breaths, he opened his eyes and looked at her. His cheeks were slick with tears. "Oh, God," he said. "How utterly disgraceful. Please forgive me."

"It's cool. I guess it was pretty funny to you. And, like, not just funny."

"No. It was a sort of private joke and it just . . . I suppose it rather unleashed some . . . things. It's hard to explain. I imagine one had to be there." He made no move to rise but continued, "We were at a conference in Bellagio; it's a lovely place in Italy, with a palace they use as a conference center. And one of the participants was a young woman named Maserati. I think she actually might have been related to the famous automobile dynasty, but in any case, she was quite pretty in an Italian way, and she appeared to set her cap for me, I can't imagine why, and of course I was flattered. I'm such a fool at that sort of thing. There's a good deal of naughtiness that goes on at such affairs, and Portia and I hadn't been together all that long. Well, Portia was mad with jealousy and being Portia she made no bones about how she felt and we had a row, and in the midst of it, all I could think of to say was 'How could anyone who has a Portia desire a Maserati,' and it just stopped her cold, and then I said 'and she probably leaks oil as well,' and we both went absolutely mad with laughter. I imagine it was the tension breaking, because it was a very poor sort of joke. Anyway, every time we saw the wretched woman after that, we were positively weak with it, spurting wine through our noses and so on."

A long sigh and a brief silence ensued. "I suppose I've been half dead myself since she died. And then when you said that, it just took me over. I hope I didn't frighten you with that display."

"No, it's totally cool. How did she die?"

He laughed, his usual short bark. "Asks the American girl. You all fly your sorrows like flags, don't you? And expect everyone else to do the same. Perhaps you're right. Keeping it all packed away hasn't done me much good. Well, since you ask, she was bitten by a fer-de-lance."

"What's that?"

"A snake. *Bothrops atrox.* The deadliest reptile in the American tropics. We were in Colombia desperately collecting from a stand of forest scheduled to be clear-cut, a lovely little valley full of the usual richness, and of course since the edge of the cut was advancing, the place was full of refugee creatures, including snakes. We were working too hard at it, exhausted, becoming a trifle careless, which is something one must never do down there, but it was so vital, there might have been dozens, hundreds of species that lived nowhere else and the swine were going to extinguish them to make furniture and to let some peasants grow a few pathetic crops before the soil was exhausted. One evening, far too late, she ran off to check her traps one last time. She failed to return, and I took a torch and went to look for her, and found her lying on a trail a few hundred yards from our camp. It was perfectly clear what had happened. We'd both seen it before. The ants and beetles were already on her. I haven't been back to the forest since."

"Oh, that's awful," Jenny said.

"Yes. She had hair much like yours, that red-gold color, although she wore it short." He curled a loop of her hair around his finger. She thought he was going to kiss her then and wondered what it would be like to be kissed by an old guy, but instead he closed his eyes for a moment and a shudder passed through his long frame. Then he cleared his throat and clambered to his feet and was regular Professor Cooksey again. As if nothing important had happened, he began to fuss with the insects, placing the tiny things carefully back into their vial. "We'll have to publish, of course, and it's up to the international nomenclature people to confirm it, but I don't expect much of a problem. Now, as for the name—I propose *P. jenniferi*. How does that sound?"

"You mean *me*?"

"Of course you! They're your fig wasps. You have achieved immortality, my dear. Your name will live forever, or at least until the last dying twitches of our scientific civilization, and graduate students yet unborn will bear your name on their lips. What do you think of that?"

"Holy shit," said Jennifer.

"A grand sentiment and calls for champagne," said Cooksey. "Let's go see what Rupert has in his extensive cellars, shall we?"

Houses in Florida didn't have cellars, Jenny knew that much, but she waited to see what would happen next on this strange and wonderful day. Cooksey returned shortly with two large bottles and a childlike grin on his face. He had brought a pair of Rupert's fancy crystal glasses, too, that got brought out only for important dinners. Jenny had seen champagne served in movies but had never consumed any. Before she came to the property, her experience of wine had been limited to the cheap fortified swill homeless people used to keep away the cold. Since then, she'd had the opportunity to taste real wine, mainly that left over from Rupert's rich-people parties, swiped from the kitchen by Kevin, but that experience had been flavored by Kevin's pleasure in getting away with something. Kevin discussed wine mainly by mocking the pretensions associated with drinking the good stuff, reading the labels to her with his version of some rich guy's elevated accent. Jenny went along with this, but she liked what the wine did in her mouth. It produced tastes she had not known were possible, sensations she did not have words for. It was one of the things that gave her the notion that regular people had a physical life that tramps like her were missing, and in this it was like listening to conversations among people who used words she didn't understand.

She imagined it was like when the fish swam around her, how she must seem to them, something utterly alien living a life in a different medium, a higher kind of life. These thoughts swam around in her mind at times and made her vaguely discontented, but she did not have any substantial ideas upon which they could settle and become articulate. Kevin divided the world into "rich shitheads in the power structure" and "the people," and she supposed she was in the latter class, but she also thought it couldn't be as simple as that, when she thought about it at all, which was hardly ever. Still, she remained open to physical pleasure—fishpond, flowers, Château Margaux—and understood at some basic level that in this she was different from both Kevin and the dull or bitter Iowa farmwives who had raised her on behalf of the state.

The champagne tasted like a kind of flavored air, hardly a drink at all. Cooksey was pouring it down his throat like water in the desert, however, and keeping her glass full as well. He put a CD into the stereo in his bedroom, and the music drifted out. It wasn't bad, she thought, not like what he usually played, which didn't have any words at all, or else kind of screechy singing in Spanish or some language she couldn't understand. This was a woman singing in English, with just a piano playing, and you could understand the words like you could in country songs, and there weren't any curse words in it.

"Cleo Laine," said Cooksey, although she hadn't asked, and then he filled his glass again and began to talk. Delicious wine, and comparisons with other brands; champagne on other occasions; exploding champagne at his sister's wedding; his home near Cambridge, the countryside, the flora and fauna thereof; his mother's kindness and wit; his father taking him bird and bug watching in Norfolk as a boy; the fens, their similarity to the Everglades, the differences, his affection for low, flat, damp country, the oddness of his spending so much of his life in rain forest; tales of jungle adventure, narrow escapes, strange customs of the natives, stranger customs of fellow biologists; the awesome beauty of the great trees, laden with vines, decked with flowers, coated with scurrying, flying, crawling life. With Portia by his side; not a lot about her directly, but she was in nearly every jungle story, the touchstone of experience, nothing quite real until shared with her.

"Did you ever go to where Moie comes from?" she asked.

He paused before replying. "In a manner of speaking. I've been close to there, to the Puxto, and I knew someone who knew the region very well indeed. Why, we're quite empty. Piggy us!"

Another bottle popped. Now he drew her out, her miserable life, but somehow not miserable told here drinking this wine: the missing father, the teenaged mother dead in a car wreck; no kin, so off to the mercies of the state; the discovery of the epilepsy, so no adopting families for her, the failure in school, the early stupid sex, the abortion, the flight into homeless drifting. She found herself talking easily about things she had not told anyone, even Kevin: the rape, or rapes, if you counted guys she knew already: the scary guys who got her to mule dope for them; arrest and jail.

It was back and forth: he said something, she said something, he took what she said and considered it and added something, an idea, a joke, an anecdote about a similar experience. She was conscious of wanting to say things that she didn't have the language for, and self-conscious about her speech in a way she'd never been. Why did she say *like* every other word, or *you know*? Cooksey didn't. He spoke more like a book, and with that voice of his it was like being on television, but in real life. She voiced this, and he laughed. "Yes, we're having a civilized conversation, oiled by champagne. Why Madame makes the wine." At her puzzled look he picked up the bottle and showed her the label.

"Veeve Clipot?"

He pronounced it correctly and added, "It means the Widow Clicquot. Interesting you read the *q* as a *p*. Do you always do that?"

Embarrassed, she admitted, "Yeah, I don't read all that good."

"And no wonder. You're dyslexic." He explained what that was and added, "You're in good company. Sir Richard Branson is, and any number of other billionaires. Plus Cher, I believe. And my mother, who was a quite well-known anthropologist. It's a bit of a bother but by no means the end of the world. No one's ever told you this before?"

"No. They just thought I was, like, retarded."

"Retarded? Odd word. Well, you were, I suppose. But now you're apparently advancing once more. I'll help you if you like. More wine?"

She held out her glass, speechless, thinking of Cher.

He lifted his glass and held the golden contents up to the fading light from the window. "I always imagine brain cells winking out under the influence of this, like tiny bubbles. Charming. Now, intelligence is rather more complex than people imagine. With us, it's the ability to manipulate abstract symbols. That's what we prize above all else, nearly to the exclusion of all else, with the result that we often put in charge of our civilization people who have absolutely no concrete intelligence at all, who are in fact entirely cut off from real life—economists and such. The greatest virtue of real science, in contrast, is that it constantly throws nature into your face, messy, solid, and complex nature, which often makes a nonsense of all one's airy-fairy abstractions. Obviously, real education would draw out the particular intelligence of every individual, but we don't do that. We think we need abstract symbol manipulators, and so we try to produce them en masse, and fail, and toss the failures into the dustbin. Like you, for example. And of course there are modes of intelligence, broadly defined, of which our culture knows absolutely nothing. My mum was always going on about that, the truly remarkable range of what different peoples choose to do with their brains. I wonder what she would have made of Moie."

"Oh, Moie!" she said. "God, I wonder what happened to him. Do you think he's okay?"

"Perfectly fine, I should think. Aren't you, Moie?" As he said this, he looked over his shoulder into the shadows in the corner of the room by the door. She followed his glance and saw the Indian squatting there. The sight startled her, and she spilled some of her champagne.

"Jesus! Where did *he* come from? I didn't even hear the door open."

"No. Moie is only seen when he wants to be. One example of his particular mode of intelligence, perhaps." In Quechua, Cooksey said, "I'm happy to see you. How are you getting on in your tree?"

"Well. It's a good tree, although no one has spoken to it in a long time. And are you well, and her?"

"We are both exceedingly fine. Would you care for some champagne?" He dangled the bottle, and Moie stood and came closer. "What is this?" he asked, sniffing it.

"It's similar to pisco, but with water added to it, and also air."

"Then thank you, but I must not. Jaguar is back in the sky tonight."

"And can you not take pisco when the moon is full?"

"No. He doesn't like it, and he may need me tonight or the next day or the next. After that I will be happy to drink your pisco with you."

"What will he do with you? If he comes."

"Anything he wishes to do, of course. You shouldn't ask foolish questions, for you are not entirely a fool." He turned his attention to Jenny, who smiled at him and said, "Hey, Moie, what's up?"

He ignored this and said to Cooksey, "The Firehair Girl seems happier than she was before. I see she has drunk a lot of your pisco-with-air, but also there is something else. She's found something she lost, I think."

"Yes, that's a way to say it."

"Yes, and I can see the shadow of her death, almost as if she were a live person. She wishes to do *puwis* with you, Cooksey."

"Surely not!"

"Yes, because I have seen it in her dreams. And also in your dreams. Will you take her into your hammock?"

"It's not our custom, Moie."

"I believe you, for I see the women come to take their children from under my tree, and they all have only one child, or sometimes two. Yet you have so much food. Each should have ten, and all fat ones, too. The *wai'ichuranan* have forgotten how to do it, I think."

"No, it's all they think about. A great deal of *puwis* is done among the *wai'ichuranan,* I can assure you."

"No, I meant they have forgotten how to draw the spirits of children from the sun into the bodies of their women. Anyway, you will pull her into your hammock, or perhaps she will pull you into hers, as I have heard is also done among you. She has broad hips and heavy breasts and will bear many healthy sons for the clan of Cooksey. But I came to ask you if you have heard anything about the Puxto, if they have stopped the cutting and the road."

"They have not stopped, Moie. They will not, I fear."

Moie was silent for a while, then made a peculiar gesture that was like a shrug and also like a despairing slump. "That's too bad," he said in Quechua and then added something in his own language that Cooksey didn't understand. Without another word he went out the door. Cooksey and Jennifer followed him into the garden. Moie had his head back, staring at the full moon, now tangled in the upper boughs of one of the tall casuarinas that edged the property.

"What will you do now, Moie?" Cooksey asked.

"I will go back to my tree and wait," said the Indian, and he turned away to go. But then he paused and addressed Cooksey again. "There is one thing I have discovered. There are *wai'ichuranan* who can call *tichiri*. Did you know that?"

"I don't know what *tichiri* is, Moie."

"I will explain. There is the world below the moon and the world above the moon. Below the moon we men have our lives, and above the moon are the dead ones and the spirits and demons, and so on. We *jampirinan* can travel between these worlds, and also the *aysiri*, the sorcerers, and when you sleep the paths are open, too, and from that comes dreaming. Everyone knows this. But what only a few know is that a guardian can be called, and tied into a *t'naicu*"—here he touched the little bundle that hung from his neck—"so that the dreams of the one who wears it can't be entered, or not entered easily. This guardian is called the *tichiri*."

"And you found one of these guarding one of us?"

"I did. A little girl. We would think it was a waste to guard a little girl so strongly. Who cares what a girl dreams? But this is an unusual girl, I think. Jaguar has her in his mind for some reason. So, tell me, can you call a *tichiri* and make a *t'naicu* in this way?"

"I can't," said Cooksey. "But many parents pray that their children will have sweet dreams. Perhaps that's what you found."

"Pray? You mean to Jan'ichupitaolik? No, this was something else. I will have to think about this more." With that he trotted silently into the shadows.

"What was all *that* about?" Jenny asked.

"Oh, you know, just a chat," said Cooksey lightly.

"It didn't sound like a chat," said Jennifer. The champagne had made her bold. "It sounded serious. Where's he been living since he ran off?"

"In a tree. He seems very content. And yes, it was serious. I think he's going to kill someone tonight."

"Oh, God! Who is he going to?"

"I imagine one of the men he thinks is responsible for cutting down his forest."

"Can't you stop him?"

"Not I. In any case, he doesn't think he's doing it himself. He thinks the man in the moon does it, or Jaguar, as he calls his god." Cooksey looked up at the sky. "I suppose it does look rather like a jaguar, depending on what you bring to it. Some people say it's an old woman with a sack on her back. In some parts of Europe it's a loaded wagon, Charles's Wain, the treasure of Charlemagne."

"But that's just, you know, imaginary. Isn't it?"

"That would depend on what you meant by imaginary. Or imagination, for that matter. You and I were just speaking of intelligence, and there you have a good example. Our imagination works with our particular kind of intelligence to produce televisions and nuclear bombs. His works to allow visits to other people's dreams and the manipulation of mass and energy in entirely different ways to how we do it. You remember his footprint? My mother always swore she'd seen a shaman walk flat-footed up the side of a vertical tree as if he were walking on a street, and she was not, I can assure you, an easy person to fool. Moie imagines, so to speak, that he can turn himself into a jaguar, and perhaps in some strange way he can."

Jennifer felt a sickish laugh bubble out of her throat. "That's wack," she said, and then recalled what had happened at the jaguar cage in the zoo and was silent.

He drained his glass and said, "I think there's a bit more left in the bottle. Would you like some?"

"No, thanks. I'm pretty dizzy as it is."

He nodded. "Well, then, I'll say good night. I'm a bit unsteady myself, and I want to get some reading done before I pass out. I'll leave the workroom light on for you."

When he had gone, Jennifer went down the path to the pool and sat on the low stone bench placed at the foot of the pond. The moon had topped the tree, she saw. It wobbled brightly on the surface of the dark water and turned the little waterfall into a stream of silver. She stared at the moonlit ripples, feeling strange, and it wasn't just the wine. She reached for an explanation and found that she hadn't the words, but . . . it was just that she couldn't simply let go and sink into the thoughtless depths as she had her whole life, there was *stuff* in her head now: that wasp and the business of naming it after her, and Cooksey's whole story and his wife and the idea of a mode of life she had not imagined existed. No, that was wrong: she knew it existed, had seen it all on the TV, but now she had been invited into it in Real Life, and she found herself quaking in the doorway. Flowers and fish were not going to be enough after today, and she found herself racked with longing for what she had been and at the same time with yearning for another and still terrifying life. But I'm too dumb, she thought vainly: her hidey-hole now too small.

She wept then, silently as she had learned to do long ago in strange houses where they didn't like whiny kids, her face distorted into a tragic mask, hugging herself, rocking back and forth on the smooth stone, while from her throat came the tiniest mewling sound, like a kitten lost. It was strange to her to be doing this in the open air, and not in a broom closet, shut up on account of messing herself during a fit, or hiding from taunting children in a girls' room stall at school. She thought this, however, after it was over. A new kind of thought, a reflection on her life. Cooksey had just demonstrated to her how to do that, to look at a life from outside, like it was a movie. But while she wept, she thought nothing at all.

Now she coughed because her throat always hurt after these cries, and her face, too, because of being so scrunched up. She knelt at the edge of the pond and splashed water on her face, and stood and wiped her face with the bottom of her T-shirt. She heard a screen door slam and then steps on gravel, and here was Kevin.

He stopped and looked her over. "Planning a little moonlight swim?" he asked in a stoned drawl. She could smell the marijuana on him. His face was slack with the drug, something she'd never really noticed before.

"No, just sitting."

He handed her his bandanna. After a tiny hesitation she took it and wiped her face.

"Want to go for a drive?"

"Where?"

"Maybe the beach. It's a nice night."

Two weeks ago Kevin being this sweet would have lit up her whole day, but now she saw that he was counting on just that—she actually saw behind the mask of his face to the being within, the empty desperate sadness of that being. She saw also the nature of their deal, that she wanted someone to think for her and take care of her because she was stupid and a spaz, and he wanted someone to admire him and be subject to him because he was a useless piece of shit. This is just like my dream, she thought, and at that moment recalled it to mind, and that she had dreamed it not just last night but for many. She was a child locked in a storm cellar. She'd been bad, and the foster parent was going to do something awful to her, the man would when he got home and she had to get out. There was another child locked in with her, and in a strange dream-way she knew this was Kevin. They were both kids but also themselves. The walls of the cellar were earth, and she started to dig. The substance she dug was not real earth, but soft and slimy like Jell-O and came away in great chunks. She tried to get Kevin to dig, but he wouldn't. Instead, he was taking the chunks of Jell-O and arranging them neatly against the wall. He said he didn't want to get in trouble with the parents. She was torn now, desperate to get free but also fascinated by the construct Kevin was building from the quaking blocks. There was a yellow cat there, too, she recalled, and it ran into the shaft she had dug and disappeared and she knew it had found the way out and she yearned to follow it. Please, Kevin, please, she called to the dream boy . . .

"Please what?" said Kevin.

"Nothing," she said and realized she had spoken aloud. She felt so sorry for him now. He had nothing, really, but his stupid revolution, and sex, and his attitude. She felt a wave of compassion and understood at some level below words that this was what Professor Cooksey felt for her. She had learned it from him. And maybe if she stayed with Kevin she could work the same sort of transformation. Maybe she owed it to him, because for sure she never would have ended up in this place had it not been for Kevin dragging her into it. She rose and faced him and put on a smile, only half faked. "So," she said, "if we're going, let's go."

# Ten

"This isn't the way to the beach," Jenny said.

"Yeah, I know, I just want to cruise by this place in the Gables for a second."

She didn't ask why, nor was she hurt or disappointed, as she might have been a few weeks ago. Kevin always had something else going on when he was with her, and whereas before she had taken this as a personal slight, now she saw it as a taxonomic indicator of the genus *Kevin,* as:

> always has another deal going on when
>   with girlfriend..........................*Kevin sp.*
> never has another deal going on when with
>   girlfriend................................see 14

Jennifer had never got to that part of the taxonomic key but thought it would be nice to find one of those someday, a true 14, or whatever. She knew they existed, because Cooksey was one. Out of habit, she half blamed herself. Had she been more interesting, she might have occasioned more interest. She looked out past Kevin at the house he seemed to be more interested in than in her. It looked vaguely familiar, a big two-story Gables mansion, glowing pale pink in the moonlight, but she was not inspired to ask what was so special about it. Instead she was thinking about Cooksey and

Cooksey's dead wife, about what his conversation had suggested regarding the nature of their relationship. She wondered if it were true, that people could love each other that much, or if it was just a fantasy that Cooksey had concocted, like the fantasies of love on TV or in the movies. She had certainly never seen such a love in real life, and she now understood that what she thought she'd felt for Kevin was as unsubstantial as the images on a flickering screen. How strange to have thoughts like this, she thought, wrenching and horrible in a way but also how totally cool, almost like she was in charge of her own life, like it had a steering wheel.

Prudencio Rivera Martínez is parked in a Dodge Voyager with two of his men at the end of the street. He is half asleep but rouses whenever a car drives by. This is not a frequent occurrence, for Cortillo Avenue in the Gables is short and untraveled, except by those who live in the great homes that line it and those who had business there: guests, servants, contractors. None of the other houses on the street were guarded like the Calderón house. Instead, they had ridiculous little signs warning that if anyone did anything bad, someone would call the police. Martínez understood that things were run differently in America than in Cali, where he came from. In Cali, homes like this would have three-meter walls around them topped with razor wire or broken glass, and each would have a crew of guards on duty and there would be armored limousines and outriders whenever the family emerged.

He was not a thoughtful man as a rule, but he couldn't help wondering what a couple of gangs of Colombians could do to such a street. It would be like scooping up a plate of beans, that easy. For this reason, he didn't think he would have much trouble if this little problem of Hurtado's was being caused by Americans. He personally agreed with his boss that it was a Colombian operation. He had seen the police photographs of Fuentes, supplied by Mr. Calderón from a source within the Miami cops, and he thought it looked like something a Colombian would do: an odd kind of patriotic pride. He himself knew people who liked to spray blood around like that. The eating part he wasn't so sure about, although he had heard rumors from the south, where a civil war had been going on for half a century, about guys in the jungle who ate enemies. He himself was a more fastidious killer, specializing most recently in car bombs. He had people he used when wetter things were required, and he had brought several along on this job, in case of need.

Now the sound of a vehicle again brings Martínez up out of his doze to full alertness. A brightly painted van passes slowly by his window. The glass in his van is heavily tinted, but even so he can make out leaves, parrots, monkeys in the design, and some words in English he doesn't quite get. But he can see the license plate as it rolls by and he records it in a little notebook. That is something he does on jobs like this, writing down license numbers. Obviously, if anyone is going to try something, especially if Colombian, they will use false plates, but still it is a good practice. The painted van slows to a stop before the Calderón house, pauses for a moment, and then moves slowly on. Martínez punches a button on his cell phone. It is answered immediately and he says, "Find out who that is."

"Pick them up?" asks the voice in the phone.

"No, just follow them. I want to know who they are and where they come from." He disconnects the circuit. At the far end of the street, another Dodge van with dark windows moves away from the curb and follows the painted VW around the corner.

―――

Kevin and Jennifer drove across Rickenbacker Causeway to Virginia Beach, a relatively undeveloped strip of public land north of Bear Cut. Kevin took a terry cloth blanket and half of a bottle of Rupert's wine out of the car, and they both walked out of the little parking lot away from the causeway down toward where the mangroves started. Kevin spread the blanket in a little sandy cove covered with the needles of the overhanging Australian pines. It was dark here, the strong moonlight blocked by the overhanging boughs, and cool. It had been a cool day, and the biting insects were hardly active. Jennifer knew why Kevin had chosen a dark spot. She walked on crunching hard sand toward the water.

"Where're you going?" he called.

"To the water. I want a moon bath."

This girl she once knew, Rosalind, had told her that the rays of the moon were healthy for women, that they strengthened the subtle energies and prevented menstrual cramps. Jenny recalled a tiny little straw-haired girl with lots of face piercings and dark bracelet tattoos, into crystals and astrology, too. She had done a horoscope for Jenny on a piece of notebook paper, sun and moon in Cancer, Scorpio rising, and Rosalind had explained what it all meant, you are probably attracted to the sea. Your home environment is very important to you, and you like to make it cozy. You may be very touchy emotionally, and need to hide in your shell sometimes. You are a strong defender of family and tradition. Although your temperament is changeable, people will come to you readily for nurturing and care. You look to your mother for protection and nurturing. That last part was a little off, also the touchy emotionally, but maybe what she was feeling now was some of that kicking in. Or maybe it was all bullshit, like Kevin said.

She slid out of her sandals and waded into the water. It was warmer than the air and had the feel of light oil. The creamy moon rode high, silvering every wavelet. She stood immersed to her knees and let the rays sink into her skin, and wished greatly that it was not all bullshit. She heard the squeak of steps in the sand. Kevin, coming for a little of her famous and astrally correct nurturing and care. "Hey . . . ," he said.

Without thinking, Jenny stepped back on the sand and in an instant was free of her T-shirt and shorts; then she dived into the reflected moon. The water was shallow here, less than five feet. She shot down to the sand and coasted just above the bottom. It was perfectly black, disappointing be-

cause she wanted it to be moonlit under the water, magical
and strange, and she wondered briefly why it was not. She
would ask Cooksey. She could hold her breath for a long
time now because of all her practice in the fish pool, and she
did, suspended in the utter dark.

There was a splash, heard faintly, and a disturbance in the
water, a pressure of something moving. Did sharks come at
night? she wondered, and felt a little tug of fear and self-
contempt. Yet another thing she didn't know. She kicked off
from the sand and shot to the surface. But it was only Kevin,
sputtering and thrashing a dozen yards away.

"God, Jenny, I thought something happened to you!"

"I'm fine. Were you going to rescue me?"

"Yeah, right," he said, laughing, "my action-hero phase."
He drifted over and embraced her, squeezing her breasts
against his chest, kissing her neck. This was a little new, she
thought, it wasn't only that he wanted sex. He almost always
wanted sex, and just now, as a matter of fact, so did she. But
even when they had first hooked up, it hadn't had this feel to
it, like he was afraid she was going away and wanted to be
extra loving. If true, if she wasn't just imagining it, then why
did he act so shitty when they were going to make her leave
the property? He had his hand inside the waistband of her
panties now, the longest finger searching downward like a
killifish after a crumb. She thrust away from him and paddled away on her back.

On the dry sand she stripped her clinging panties off and
pulled shorts and T-shirt on, and found her sandals. She trotted to the blanket and used it to dry her face and hair. Kevin
came trailing along, with a confused look on his face, which
he was trying to hide behind his usual lopsided smile. She
folded the blanket. "Let's go in the van," she said.

In the mangrove thicket, Santiago Iglesias put down his
eight-by-ten night glasses and said to his companion, Dario
Rascon, "Looks like the show is over. Let's go back to the
van."

Rascon said, "That's some piece of ass. I'd like to fuck
that bitch. I'd like to fuck that bitch right up her white ass.

You know something? I never fucked a redhead pussy before. How about that? I just thought of that when I was watching her flash her cunt at us. Not a real one, anyway. You want to know what I think? We should toss the little *maricón* in the woods and fuck her into the ground." Here he made a sucking noise with his mouth and manipulated his genitals, indicating a high level of sexual interest.

"He told us to see where they go," said Iglesias. "You want to explain to him why you thought a piece of ass was more important than doing what the man said, go ahead. I wish you the best of luck."

"*¡No me friegues, pendejo!* Give me ten minutes with that cunt and we'll know not only where she comes from but what she had for breakfast last Tuesday."

"That's a good plan, and I can see you understand the situation a lot better than Prudencio does."

"He just wants the information, man. I bring it in, he won't do shit to me."

"If not, could I have your boots?" Instinctively Rascon looked down at his boots, which were crocodile, elaborately tooled, and tipped with silver caps. Then he snarled, "*¡Chingate!*" and stomped away, followed by the softly giggling Iglesias.

They sat in their van. Rascon wanted to turn the radio on and roll up the windows against the occasional mosquito, but Iglesias said no, partly to annoy the other man and show who was in charge, and partly because he wanted to see what the Americans were going to do. He had a good idea of what, but he wanted to observe it. The two Americans entered the van via the side door. Iglesias saw the van settle on its springs. After a few minutes the body of the VW began to rock rhythmically. Its windows were all open, and shortly thereafter the slight breeze brought to the two watchers the sound of heavy breathing and then a series of short cries, like that of a small bird, rising in register, and then a distinctively male groan.

"She's getting it now, the little whore," said Rascon sourly. "I'm getting sore balls listening to that shit." He massaged these.

"If you're going to jerk off, go outside," said Iglesias.

"*¡Pela las nalgas!*"

"When we get back, you can ask Torres for a piece of his fine white ass."

"*¡Cállate, cabrón!*" snapped Rascon. "You'll see, I'm going to fuck that girl before we're done here."

"Again I wish you the best of luck, my friend," said Iglesias. "In the meanwhile . . . *¡Ay, coño!* Listen, they're going at it again!"

Prudencio Martínez thinks for a moment and then reaches into the backseat and shoves the man sleeping there into wakefulness.

"What's up?" says the man in the backseat. His name is Rafael Alonzo Torres. He is slim and young, the youngest of the men Martínez has brought with him, a hungry and aggressive kid from the Cali slaughterhouse district, blessed with a mild-looking angel face. He reminds Martínez of himself twenty years ago. Martínez says, "You slept enough. Go into the house. Sit in the chair I showed you. And stay awake."

The youth yawns and stretches. He says, "What about Garcia and Ochoa?"

"Garcia's in the kitchen and Ochoa's watching the back. I want you on the bedroom floor."

"Did something happen?"

"No, it's quiet, but we had a car drive by I didn't like."

"A car?"

Martínez gives him a look. "Hey, *cabrón,* just go! And Raphael: make sure your phone is on."

Torres leaves the van and goes to the back of the house. He taps on the door, and Benigno Garcia lets him in. They exchange a few words. Garcia goes back to watching the maid's television in the kitchen. Torres walks through the hallway to the main foyer and up the stairs to the second floor. There are four bedrooms on this floor, each with a bath, and there is also the room at the rear of the house that

Mr. Calderón uses as a study or home office. Torres sits in a chair between the door to this room and the one to the master bedroom. The chair is uncomfortable, and he curses softly as he sits in it, but he doesn't really mind. This is a very easy job compared to some he has been on. And he can sleep anywhere.

Unlike his client. Yoiyo Calderón is sleepless tonight, as he has been for more nights than he can remember. Weeks at least, maybe months. No, he thinks, it started around the time Fuentes died, or maybe a little after, when the Puxto deal began to go sour. He attributes this insomnia to stress, although he is scrupulous about following all the stress-reduction hints in the business and fitness magazines he reads. These helpful sources do not discuss nightmares, however. Successful take-charge American businessmen do not mention their dreams, or even acknowledge that they have dreams, except in the figurative sense of projecting a scheme for increasing material wealth.

Calderón is an educated man, and he is familiar with the ideas underlying Freudian psychotherapy. Dreams, especially repetitive dreams, have some deep meaning, are the signals indicating the repression of an unacceptable desire. He has looked into this on his own, for his daughter has all those how-to-feel-good-about-yourself books, and he has sneaked looks, but they seem like a lot of crap to him. He has never had the slightest problem feeling good about himself. He considered that the Yoiyo Calderón who existed up until a month or so ago was as fine a man as could be found anywhere in Miami—good-looking, decisive, sexually potent, rich, getting richer, a decent husband and father, generous to his various mistresses, a man of his word when dealing with equals, philanthropic to a fault, well respected in the community—and not about to see a goddamned headshrinker either, that was out, although he had asked his family doctor for some Xanax as a stress reliever. Half a milligram before retiring is the dose recommended on the vial, but tonight he has loaded himself with three milligrams in the hope that this will stop the dream.

It is always the same one. In it, he is somewhere in the tropics, dressed in explorer garb. It's hot and dark and he's at a table. A line of natives in fancy regalia stretches out into the dark, and one by one they sell him all their ornaments, which he pays for with bits of paper he tears off a pad and writes banal phrases on, like those found in fortune cookies. New friends will help you. You are greatly admired. He is happy to be getting rich in this way and has convinced himself, in the logic of dreams, that the natives are better off with his scraps of paper than they are with their gold jewelry and plumes. As he works, he becomes conscious of a noise, soft at first, but growing louder, like something breathing, in and out, like the purring of an immense cat, a cat the size of a hill. Then there are no more natives and he is alone with the noise. And now the fear starts, and he feels an urgent need to get away. He shoves his swag into a sack and leaves the hut. He is on a muddy jungle trail in the dark. All around him is the sound.

*Ararah. Ararararh.*

Now he can hear the thud of the monstrous paws, close behind him in the dark, getting closer. He runs, clutching his sack. He feels its hot breath on the back of his neck. He can't possibly escape, his limbs are caught in some sticky mud, and now he screams. He is crawling now in the slow paralysis of nightmare. He turns and looks up and sees its golden eyes, its jaws . . .

And he is awake, sweating, cursing; and when he looks at the clock it is always around three in the morning and he can't return to sleep, the night is ruined for him again. But tonight there is no dream of jungles. Tonight he falls into blackness and awakes on the daybed in his study. He has taken to sleeping there to avoid the shame of his nightmares, the screaming and thrashing. The blinds are closed and the room is very dark. The only light comes from the digital clock on his desk, green numbers telling him it is 3:06. It is cool in the room, and at first he thinks someone has switched on the air-conditioning, because there is a rumble in his ears. No, not a mechanical sound.

*Ararah. Ararararh.*

Terrified now, he scrambles up, kicking the quilt away, reaching for the light switch. The light goes on, and there it is, huge and golden, in the room. He thinks he is still dreaming, a new and even more horrible nightmare, until just a few seconds before he dies.

In the hallway, Rafael Torres is awakened by a noise coming from Calderón's den, a hard sound, like a piece of furniture falling over. He walks down the hall to the door of this room and listens. He hears odd liquid noises and a low growling. It is an embarrassing sort of noise, and Torres hesitates. On the other hand, maybe the guy is sick. He taps lightly on the door. He asks in Spanish, "Mr. Calderón—everything okay in there?" No answer. He sees that the light is on inside the room, so what could be wrong? He opens the door.

It takes him a second to understand what he is seeing; it takes him another second to pull out his pistol. Whatever it is that has killed Calderón is already moving toward him, impossibly fast, but he is a tough young man with the reflexes of youth. He manages to get one shot off before he goes down.

In the kitchen, Garcia heard the sound of the shot. With pistol in hand he rushed up the stairs. Victoria Calderón was awakened by the shot, too, but thought at first that it had been part of her dream. Her dreams were of war in a steaming land. Soldiers were attacking a village, and she was trying to gather up the children and take them to shelter among the trees, but the horror of it was that she always missed one or two of them and had to go back, and didn't want to and tried to think up excuses while the people stared at her with dark, accusing eyes. Then she heard heavy steps outside her door, and as she comprehended that this was no dream, her heart started to pound. She threw a robe over her pajamas and ran out of her room. There was a big man standing with his back to her, one of the men her father called "a little security." Victoria had led a somewhat sheltered life, but she was no fool, and she had understood at her first sight of them that these people did not come from Kroll or Wackenhut, that they were thugs of some kind and that her father was therefore in terrible trouble. The big man was talking into a cell phone in his dialect Spanish. She called out, "What happened?"

The man turned and held his palm up like a traffic cop. She stopped automatically, and this gave her time to see what was lying at the man's feet. The floor here was tile, pale green, against which the scarlet blood made a vivid contrast. It was still crawling in little rivulets toward her along the channels of the grout. It took her a few seconds to make her throat work. "Where's my father?" she demanded.

The man put his phone away. Victoria started forward, but the man blocked her path, shaking his head. She heard the front door open and steps on the stairs. The hallway was suddenly full of rough-looking dark men, some of them carrying weapons. One of them stood before her, his broad face grave and angry. She recognized him as Martínez, the one her father had called the head of the security detail.

"I want to see my father," she said.

"That's not a good idea, miss. You should go back to your room now. We'll take care of this."

"Is he hurt?"

"Mr. Calderón is deceased, miss," said Martínez. "You have my profound condolences. Somehow the assassins got through to—"

Victoria Calderón struck him in the mouth. "Moron! Imbecile! How could you—" she began, and then to her immense surprise, Prudencio Martínez slapped her across the face hard enough to bounce her off the wall. Her vision went red and she slid down to a sitting position against the baseboard. She looked up and saw Prudencio Martínez waggling a finger at her, as at a naughty child. The counterblow was instinctive and without malice; he did not belong to a culture where a woman of whatever exalted rank could strike a man with impunity in front of his subordinates. And in any case the man was dead and she was no longer of any consequence. He left her where she lay, and shouted orders at his men.

It had not taken Martínez long to recover from the shock of the attack, not that he cared, or his boss cared, about the life of Yoiyo Calderón: the failure was less in preventing murder than in not apprehending the assassins. Therefore, the correct move was to quickly reinforce the guards at the other houses, in case there should be another attack. The Colombians left the house, carrying their dead comrade wrapped in a blanket.

When they were gone, Victoria struggled to her feet and leaned against the wall. Her head ached, and the side of her face felt hot and swollen. A slight breeze blew through the corridor, carrying with it a butcher shop smell. She felt her stomach heave and made herself take several deep breaths. She could not be sick now, because . . .

"Victoria? Victoria, what's happening?"

Her mother, blinking in the doorway of her bedroom, looking decorative even in the middle of the night, even fuddled with sleep and the three regular scotches and the sleeping pills. Victoria moved toward her mother.

"It's okay, Mom," she said, "everything's all right . . . we had a little break-in but it's okay now. Why don't you go back to bed?"

"A break-in? Oh, my God! Where's your father?"

"It's fine, Mom, everything's fine," Victoria said in the most soothing tone she could manage, but Olivia Calderón, while a stupid woman, was not insensitive to the tone of her daughter's voice, and so she stepped out into the hallway and looked wildly around for some sign of her husband, and saw the blood on the tiles and screamed shrilly and went running down the hallway to the study and there let out a noise that Victoria had never heard emerging from a human throat and fainted, landing facedown in the pool of clotting blood.

I am not, thought Victoria Calderón, going to collapse into hysterics or faint. This is why I can't be sick or have any feelings. My father is dead, my mother is useless, my brother is an idiot and is in any case far away. I am in charge of this situation and I will do what's necessary. That piece-of-shit thug punched me because he thought I was not a significant player, which means that if I don't make the right moves in the next few days, we will lose everything my family has. She actually voiced these words under her breath, a habit she had acquired as a child when it had become clear to her that her best efforts were never going to make her either a boy or beautiful, and that she was thus fated to disappoint her father and her mother, respectively. It was her way of staying sane; if no one would really talk to her, she could at least talk to herself, and talk sense at that.

But that's for tomorrow, she continued, right now the first thing I have to do is to call the police, and she did, calling 911 from the phone in her bedroom. She reported it as a homicide, although she had not yet seen her father's body. She was going to take the word of Martínez for that. She also reported that her mother had fainted and asked the dispatcher to send an ambulance.

She hung up the phone and walked back to where her mother was lying. She noticed that there were footprints in the pools of blood and decided that these might be of interest to the police. She did manage to turn her mother onto her back, however, so that her mouth was clear of the blood. She wet a washcloth in the bathroom and wiped as much blood as she could off her mother's face and hair. Then she stepped carefully over the puddles and into her father's study.

She made herself look at the thing on the floor. It's peculiar, she thought, that I don't feel much. I'm nauseated by the sight and the smell, but I would be the same at a traffic accident or an explosion, if I were a survivor. Maybe it's because it's not recognizable, the way the head is all squashed, it could be anyone, even though I *know* it's him. I always thought I loved my father and I should be devastated by this, but I'm not. I feel like my life is starting over by this death. I must, she thought, be the cold monster my family always claimed I was, why they said I could never hold a man, I wasn't a real woman and so on. All right, I saw it, he's dead, and now I have to—

A scream from the hallway. Victoria stepped out of the room, carefully again, and saw that it was Carmel, the maid, standing there in a pink robe and furry slippers with her hands theatrically at her mouth. Her wiry hair seemed actually to be standing up, but whether this was from fright, as in the movies, or a product of recent sleep, Victoria did not know. In any case, she went to the woman and shook her, as much to stop the mumbling prayers as to rally her to action.

"Oh, my God, is the señora dead?"

"No, the señor is dead. My mother has fainted from the shock. You have to help me move her."

This was said in a tone that the maid had never heard before from the Little Señora, as she was known in the kitchen, a tone of command more familiar from her father's mouth, and her training overcame her natural repugnance. Together the two women carried Mrs. Calderón to her bathroom, where they stripped off the blood-sodden nightgown, sponged her off as best they could, dressed her in a fresh nightgown, and placed her on her bed, all without a murmur from the woman, who almost seemed to have already joined her husband in death.

The downstairs bell sounded. Victoria went down and let in the Coral Gables policeman, a man several years her junior. She told him that her father had been murdered. He asked to see the body. She took him up to the study. On seeing what was in the room he uttered an unprofessional oath and turned nearly as green as the tiles. Murders of this kind, of any kind actually, are rare in the City Beautiful, as Coral Gables likes to call itself, and the chief duty of any CG cop who discovers one is to call the county police department, which this man now did.

Then sirens announced the arrival of the ambulance. The paramedics determined that Mr. Calderón was beyond help and removed the unconscious Mrs. Calderón to Mercy Hospital. After they left, Victoria went back to her bedroom to make some calls. The first was to her Aunt Eugenia.

"This better not be a wrong number," said the voice that answered after twenty rings.

"Aunt Genia, it's me. Look, there's been a disaster here. You have to go to Mercy and take care of Mom."

"Oh, Christ! Oh, Jesus, what happened?"

"We're not really sure. Some kind of accident, an, an explosion. The police are here and I have to stay and answer questions. Mom's not really hurt, but she got knocked out. Could you please get over there? I don't want her to be alone when she comes out of it. And could you get in touch with Dr. Reynaldo, too?"

"Where's your father, Victoria?"

The obvious question. "He's, uh, he was killed. He died, in the, uh, in the thing . . . oh, no, please, Aunt Genia, if you start crying now I'm going to lose it and I can't afford to. I'll talk to you later and tell you all about it, but could you just . . . go?"

The distressing noises on the other end of the line faded. "Okay, good. Christ in heaven! Jesus, let me pull myself together here. All right, I'm on my way. Have you called Jonni yet?"

"Next on my list. Thanks for this, Aunt G., I'll never forget it. I'll call you later."

She broke the connection and dialed a New York number. After four rings, she heard music and her brother's light, pleasant voice singing a line from a hip-hop song she didn't recognize, which faded and then the same voice said, "You've almost got Jonni Calderón. I can't come to the phone right now, but leave a message and I'll be right back at ya." She disconnected and did the same again six times. On the last of these she heard her brother snarl, "What?"

"It's Victoria, Jonni."

"What's wrong?" with a little quaver of fear. She told him, a truncated version, but with the central fact revealed.

He said he'd be on the first plane down, and after very little further conversation, they hung up. They were not close.

The detectives from the county arrived a few minutes later. They showed her their ID and identified themselves as Detectives Finnegan and Ramirez of the Metro Dade Police. She said, "I don't understand. We're in Coral Gables," and they, or rather Ramirez, had to explain to her, as he had so often before, that the metropolitan county government provided a variety of services to the smaller cities of the county, among which was the investigation of homicides. "You'd been in Miami, ma'am, they have their own homicide unit, but being in the Gables you have us." He smiled sympathetically; he was a medium-size Cuban-American of about forty with clear aviator glasses and a brush mustache. Finnegan was much taller, and a little older, with thinning salt-and-pepper hair and the reserved and respectful mien of a quality mortician. They were both dressed in cheap, simple clothes, sports jackets and polyester slacks, and Ramirez had on a shirt of a particularly repellent green. They both wore ugly, thick-soled black shoes. Neither of them, Victoria reflected, looked like the cops of the media who, even if craggy-faced character actors, projected some kind of personality from the large or small screen. Like most people, she experienced this as disappointment: these guys were clerks, post office types.

Finnegan asked, "Could you show us where the body is, Miss Calderón."

They all ascended. Victoria noted that the blood pool had dried on the edges now and clotted into small jellied islands. The detectives snapped on rubber gloves and slipped white booties over their shoes. They entered the study. Shortly thereafter, they were joined by crime scene technicians in white Tyvek coveralls. Victoria waited in her room, lying flat on her back in bed, and thought about the things she had to do the next day. In the midst of these thoughts, making lists, generating strategies, her mind decided to turn itself off.

She snapped awake to the sound of tapping, to find Detective Ramirez regarding her from the doorway. She was on her feet in a second, woozy, trying to shake herself into full functionality without appearing to need to. Her face truly ached now where the thug had slapped her, and she wished for a chance to fix herself up in a mirror. I should have put ice on it, she mused, and felt shame at this thought.

"We'd like to talk to you now," said the detective.

They sat at the long mahogany table in the dining room downstairs. The tall clock in the corner said 4:45, which meant, hard as it was for her to believe it, that less than two hours had passed since that pistol shot had roused her into this horror.

The questioning, unlike the appearance of the two detectives, was apparently something that Hollywood got more or less right. The questions were the obvious ones, and she told the story without prevarication, but also without any of the background.

"So this guard hit you?" asked Finnegan after she'd described the events following the shot.

"Yes. I was so upset that I guess I went crazy. I hit him. I was hysterical and I guess he thought slapping me would calm things down."

"From the look of your face that was a heck of a punch. Who were these guys?"

"I have no idea. The one who hit me, the one in charge, was called Martínez. I don't know the names of the others. My father hired them. I don't know where. Is it important?"

"Well, yeah!" said Finnegan. "According to you, they removed a victim of a crime from a crime scene, and as far as I know they've failed to report any of this to the police. We'd definitely like to talk to these fellows. I assume your father will have records, payments, contracts with the security firm, and so on."

"As I say, I have no idea."

"Fine. Then what happened?"

Victoria described the scene with her mother, the call to 911, the ambulance, and the calls to the relatives.

And now the classic question, from Ramirez: "Ms. Calderón, do you know of anyone who might have wanted to hurt your father?"

"Nearly everyone who knew him at one time or another, myself included. He wasn't an easy man. He had some business rivalries that got pretty intense, but that kind of thing gets settled by lawyers, or by screaming over the phone, not by . . . not, you know, by someone breaking into a man's home and chopping him up with an ax."

"You think the killer used an ax?" asked Finnegan. "Why is that?"

She shrugged. "I didn't, I mean, I couldn't look at the body, I mean, examine it, but it was just smashed and torn up so much, I guess . . . you know the phrase 'ax murder' just came into my mind. And that kid they took away, the guard. I saw him pretty well. His face and his neck were just shredded."

"All right," said Finnegan, "but maybe when you've had a chance to think, you might put together a list of, as you say, 'rivals,' people your dad had a beef with. There must have been someone on his mind, right? Because he hired guards."

"Oh, that was the vandalism. Someone clawed up our front door about—what's today, the twenty-fourth?—oh, maybe three weeks ago. And left, um, some fecal matter on our walk."

"Fecal matter," said Finnegan with a quick look at his partner. "What kind of fecal matter?"

"I don't know, Detective. I'm not an expert on fecal matter. We disposed of it and replaced the door."

"And you didn't call the police about this."

"No, my father likes . . . liked his privacy. He wanted to take care it himself, so he hired guards."

Now the follow-up questions, as the detectives tried to reconstruct the events of the victim's last day on earth.

Finnegan let Ramirez lead on this, listening and watching the woman. He knew there was something deeper going on here; the crazy story of the so-called guards, and the dead man they had dragged away, went to demonstrate that, and the blow to the woman's face, also out of line. In Finnegan's experience, security guards did not strike their clients, and he was beginning to put together in his head a story he liked better. The vic was in with some mob and this was a hit, and one of the bad guys had got shot or killed, too. They'd slapped the woman around as a warning. All this could be checked out, and he intended to do so, should he be allowed to proceed along those lines. The Metro Dade PD was in general a cleaner outfit than the Miami PD, but murders involving high-end Cubans were subject to strenuous review from the upper levels of the department, especially if they might have political or organized-crime coloration. So however it fell out, this one was going to be a pain in the ass, and . . .

His thoughts here were interrupted by a man in the doorway, gesturing urgently. Finnegan left Ramirez to his work and went out with the man, whose name was Wyman, and who was the head of the crime scene crew. Crime scene crews had become somewhat more importunate of late, a result of the fame of their fictional counterparts on television. In former times, a CS tech would never have interrupted a witness interview. Finnegan had even noticed some of them doing the work of detectives, actually talking to live people at crime scenes, just like on TV. He did not approve.

So he was a little gruff with Wyman in the hallway.

"What is it, Wyman? I'm in the middle of an interview here."

"We found a bullet in the study, a nine millimeter, in the couch back. It's in real good shape. So the story about the shot is true, at least."

"This is what you came in there for, a fucking bullet?"

"No, Finnegan, not the bullet. It's something out in the

back." With that, the technician turned away and went out through the living room and a large semi-enclosed, tile-floored room with many plants and miniature orange trees in pots, through French windows to the patio. There was the usual swimming pool, covered now, and extensive plantings of ornamental shrubs. There were lights and epiphytes in the three large live-oak trees and the whole yard was surrounded by a hibiscus hedge ten feet high and precisely trimmed into a square-topped vertical wall.

"Look up there," said Wyman, pointing to the rear wall of the house. "That's where we think the perp entered."

Finnegan saw what he meant. They were directly under the study window, a tall casement, and both wings of the window were standing straight out from the wall.

"It was open at the time of entry. I guess the victim felt pretty secure because there was a guard in that Florida room we just passed through. We found cigar butts and coffee cups."

"Yeah, that's what the maid said." Finnegan looked up at the window. The lower edge was at least fifteen feet from the ground. A little less than halfway up this wall was a rolled awning. He said, "He could've moved the table and climbed onto that awning."

"He could've," said Wyman, "but what he actually did was, he jumped right up to the window from the ground there and grabbed the wall and the window frame with his claws."

Finnegan looked at the man to see if he was joking, but Wyman's face was serious, with worry lines creasing his broad forehead. He pulled a flashlight from the pocket of his coveralls and shone it on the wall. "There they are, four parallel gouges times two in the stucco and"—here he shifted the bright beam—"same again in the wood of the window frame."

"It could've been some kind of ladder, with hooks . . . ," Finnegan offered.

"Yeah, that was our thought at first. Until we found these."

Shining the flashlight on the limestone slabs of the patio, he led the detective some twenty-five feet from the house. There in the center of the path were four reddish marks. They were smeared but unmistakably the pad marks of a large cat.

"The floor of the study and the area just outside were soaked with blood. I mean, both victims were almost entirely exsanguinated, that's over two gallons of blood. There are these same pad marks all over the place up there and on the windowsill, too. It jumped from the window and landed here, then a couple of steps and it jumped over that hibiscus hedge and landed in the next yard. Then it, or they, turned the inside key of a wrought iron gate and went down a service alley out to Montoya Avenue. And then they were gone."

"So what're you saying, a guy and some kind of animal?"

"I can't think of any other explanation," said Wyman. "And believe me, I tried. It certainly explains the apparent damage to the victim. The man's skull was crunched up like a piece of tinfoil. His belly was ripped open, and it looks like half the liver is gone. And look over here."

Wyman went to an island of plantings under one of the live oaks. He moved the foliage of a ginger plant aside and directed his flashlight beam to the loose earth below it.

"This is where it set itself before jumping over the hedge. We're going to take casts, of course, but I can already tell you you're dealing with a big animal. If I had to take a wild-ass guess, from the depth of that footprint, I'd say around four hundred pounds."

"Good Lord! What, some kind of lion?"

"A tiger, more probably. Lions aren't much for that kind of jumping. Or the world's largest leopard. Or the jaguar from hell. Or extraterrestrials. This is a strange one, my friend."

Finnegan looked up at the tall, thick, unbroken hedge and then down to the ground. There were no human footprints of any kind visible. "So how did the guy get over the hedge?"

"I don't know, Finnegan," said Wyman. "You figure it out—you're the goddamn detective."

Santiago Iglesias's cell phone went off, snapping him out of his light doze. He looked out the window. The painted VW was still parked there, silent now. Beside him Dario Rascon snored intermittently.

Prudencio Martínez was on the line. "I need you here right now," he said, and gave an address on Fisher Island.

"What's up, boss?"

"The *chingada* got himself killed, and whoever it was took out Torres, too."

"*¡Maldito!* How could that happen?"

"How the hell should I know, *cabrón*? The thing is to stop it from happening again. Get moving!"

"What about the VW here?"

"Forget it. We have plates on them. We can find them when we want to."

After being Jaguar, it is necessary for Moie to wash himself, to submerge fully in running water. At home he would naturally use the river, and although he knows there is a river in Miami, he does not like its smell, so here he uses the water of the bay. He is up to his neck off Peacock Park amid the little skiffs and tenders of the marina, with the bright face of Jaguar shining down on him. He licks his lips and laughs. He is still not used to the fact that salt is present in infinite quantities in the land of the dead. It is the single weirdest thing about being here. Where he comes from, cakes of salt are used to buy brides.

He finishes the ritual chanting and emerges from the water. He brushes the drops from his skin and pulls on the priest's clothes. He feels his belly full of meat, and he both knows and does not know what the meat is. He once tried to explain this mental state to Father Tim (although not discussing the origin of the meat in that case), but it was an unsatisfactory conversation. Another *ontological* confusion, but Father Tim did not seem disturbed by this. He always seemed delighted by things he couldn't understand about the Runiya and their ways. It didn't make his head hurt that way Moie's head hurt when Father Tim talked to him about theology and the ways of the *wai'ichuranan*. So Moie learned a new word at that time: *ineffable*.

# Eleven

**P**az got the news in the morning. He came up out of sleep in a hurry and the sort of mild panic we experience when we become aware that someone is watching us as we sleep. Here it was his wife, the normally earlier riser, and she was sitting at the foot of their bed, with the *Miami Herald* in her hand and a troubled expression on her face, although not exactly the troubled expression she had worn for what Paz felt to be months. Time itself had become funny around the house, it seemed; he thought it might have something to do with having variants of the same dream nearly every night. That could throw your calendar off a little. Lola's look now was not one of interior pain, as before (with "No, I can't talk about it" being the response when asked, "What's wrong?"), but a gentler and more accessible expression, suggesting that the problem was exterior to herself.

"What's wrong?" he asked.

"Bad news. Or maybe you'll think it's good, I don't know."

With that she handed the paper to him. The *Herald* had run it above the fold, on the right margin: Developer Slain in Coral Gables, was the headline, and the subhead read: Second Killing of a Prominent Cuban-American Businessman Strikes Fear. He read it and felt a strange pang, as if he had been clutching something alive to his vitals without knowing it, and it had just died with a sigh.

He felt her watching him. "I'm sorry," she said. "It must be a shock."

"A little," he agreed.

"Any feelings?"

He shrugged. "I guess. Surprising feelings of . . . not loss, because I never had anything from the guy, but . . . something. You know I never think about the bastard from one year to the next, and then a couple of weeks ago Major Oliphant drops by the place and asked me do I know him, and as usual I say no, which is the truth, and now this. The only reason he's my father is because my mother screwed him to get a small-business loan, and we had exactly one conversation my whole life, in which he told me he'd kill me if I ever came around him again. My position was nobody outside the family needs to know any of that shit."

Paz stared at the paper for a while here, until the black letters in the murder story ceased to have any semantic content. He took a deep breath and let it gush out.

"Did I have some little pathetic hope that he was going to have a change of heart and . . . and what, take me to a Dolphins game, introduce me to all his pals? Guys, I want you to meet my nigger bastard son, Jimmy Paz. I don't think so. I don't know, you read these stories about women, refugees or whatever, they're carrying this baby in their arms, ducking bullets, starving, bleeding, and then they arrive at the refugee camp and the doctor takes a look and the baby's been dead for a week. How does she feel? I mean she had to have known it, but she talked herself out of it. And now it hits her. Does that make any sense?"

"Yes, in a strange way. What will you do?"

"I don't know, Lola. You think I should send a wreath?"

At this sarcasm, she started to rise from the bed, her face closing again, but he grabbed her hand and pulled her back down.

"I'm sorry. It's a little hard to take first thing in the morning." He stroked her hand. "More important, when are you going to tell me what's going on?"

"Nothing's going on. I don't know what you're talking about."

"You do. You're nervous and crabby—that fight we had, it wasn't right, it wasn't just a fight. You come back from work and you're all glassy-eyed, like you've been taking dope." He paused and craned his neck elaborately, trying to catch her eye. She dropped her head, refusing this. "*Are* you taking dope?" he asked.

"Of course not! I'm under a lot of strain. Working neuropsych in an ER is no picnic. I take an occasional Valium."

This was a lie. Lola has been stuffing herself with buspirone, alprazolam, chlordiazepoxide, diazepam, and halazepam in varying combinations and dosages for weeks, ever since the dreams started, the same dream every night. She's a psychiatrist, for God's sake, she knew the signs of incipient breakdown. She also knew that there was no shame involved in mental disease; still she *felt* shame at her condition and would not speak about it to her husband. She has mentioned obsessive dreaming to her training therapist. They have talked about it. They have discussed what it means to dream obsessively about your husband giving your child to a jaguar to be carried off and eaten. What does it mean that, in the dream, you wish for it to happen? That your husband is dressed in furry skins and carrying a bow and arrow in one hand, and in the other hand a little model of a jail? You think that he's a savage perhaps, a little unconscious racism here? Or that you feel trapped in the marriage? A little jail? It's a common thing. And what about the woman in blue and white who stands behind the husband: your mother, perhaps? And the seven arrows your husband shoots in the dream, do they hit the daughter or the beast? Ambiguous, a source of anxiety, yes? What would it mean if they hit the beast? What do the arrows symbolize? Why seven? It might be sexual, yes, fears of rivalry with the daughter, sexual aggression by the husband against the daughter feared and repressed? What does the jaguar symbolize?

Nothing, Doctor, they symbolize nothing. That's what she always says, a failure at her own game when it strikes so close to home. Sometimes a jaguar is only a jaguar. What she has not told the doctor is that her husband has also dreamed of great spotted golden beasts and also her daughter, all dreaming of the same thing, which is impossible, it's not happening, mere coincidence. If she told him that, they'd look at her sympathetically and put her on the *other* side of the locked wards. The requirement for absolute materialism is the great unspoken given of her profession; spooks, messages from beyond, visions, are all *symbols* of something else, some repression, some trauma in the meat. Not to believe that *is* to be crazy.

She knew that her husband did not buy into that at some level, believed that the unseen world might be as real as fire hydrants and mangoes. He denied it in public, but it is why he took the child to that ritual. And the mother-in-law, a true believer, and they would turn her girl against her, and she would be alone . . .

"How *occasional* is that, Lo?" asked Paz, and unconsciously, a little of the old cop tone insinuated itself into his voice. He heard it, she heard it: it was how you talked to junkies.

"I *said*, I'm fine!" Lola snapped back, with which she shot up from the bed and went into the bathroom. There she looked into the mirror and made a professional assessment. Patient is a thirty-nine-year-old female Caucasian, well nourished but could drop a few pounds, looks like shit, bags under eyes, dry lips, bitten nails, twitches, dull skin. Reports insomnia, stupid fights with husband, night terrors, reduced sexual energy, recurring dreams. History of hypochondria but nothing recent. Patient is, or was, happy with career and relationships, no prior trauma except one voodoo ceremony, one life-saving miracle by a God in which she does not believe, and a few incidences of murderous violence . . .

She decided to sign up for a CAT scan. Let's rule out the brain tumor, shall we? Meanwhile, she thought, on with the

day. She opened the medicine cabinet and took down a vial
of 5milligram Valium tablets.

In the bedroom, Paz rose and threw on a sweatshirt and
jeans. He would make breakfast for Amelia and take her to
school and then return to shower and smoke a cigar and have
some more coffee, just as if this were an ordinary day. In
fact, by the time he completed these routines it would have
*become* an ordinary day: again his extraordinary ability to
bury unwanted thoughts. Had the drug companies been able
to bottle it, Valium and its sisters would have been driven
from the market.

Nor did the subject arise again that day or in the ensuing
week. Paz watched his wife covertly for more signs of mental distress. He found them in plenty but felt helpless to intervene, having learned over the years how difficult it was to
comment effectively on the mental states of one's wife, if
one's wife was a psychiatrist. He was a patient man, however, patience on the Jobian scale being a requisite for homicide detectives, and so he waited to see what would evolve
and paid a lot of attention to his daughter.

A week and a day after the killing of Yoiyo Calderón, after the elaborate funeral (not attended by Paz) and after the
murder had vacated the front pages of the paper for others
more recent, if less gaudy, Paz was at work at the end of the
lunch rush running a wire brush over his grill and thinking
that he should take his wife and kid on a vacation this year,
take the boat and run down the Inland Waterway to the Keys,
stay in a nice marina, let the sun bake all this shit out of the
three of them. He began to think about what the best time
would be to take this break, maybe have to wait until school
break around Christmas, which would leave his mother
alone on Christmas, no, couldn't do that. After Christmas,
then. Would Lola go for it?

A tug on his apron, and he started and spun around with a
curse in his mouth. He was not wound as tight as his wife
yet, but he'd dropped a lot of calm.

"What!" he said, more harshly than he meant, and he saw

the child blink and draw back. He knelt and gave her a hug. "I'm sorry, baby. I was just thinking, and you startled me."

"What were you thinking about?"

"Something nice. Going out on the boat down to Islamorada with you and Mommy. A vacation."

"Could we take Felix and Louis?"

"I don't think cats like to go on boats. We could send them to the cat vacation hotel, though."

"There's no such thing."

"There is. They can order fried mice from room service and there's a bar where they eat catnip and get crazy. They'll love it."

"Okay, but there's a lady out in the room who wants to talk to you. She didn't order anything but *café con leche* and a guava tart."

Paz thought immediately of Beth Morgensen. What if the woman was getting aggressive and starting to hunt him? It was all he needed just now.

"What does she look like?"

"She has blond hair. I never saw her before, I think. Table ten."

**P**az washed his hands and face and removed his greasy apron. As always when coming into the dining room after a shift, he paused for a moment to adjust to the shock of moving from the zone of controlled chaos and heat to that of calm, luxury, and cool. He'd never seen the woman at table ten either, but she seemed familiar in an odd way, something about her eyes and the set of her jaw. An old flame? No, he was eidetic on those. Someone from the police? Possibly. He observed her from the cover of the philodendron-draped woven screen that separated the service hallway from the dining room. She was indeed blond, the hair fine and well cut in a businesslike neck-length style, and wore a tan linen suit, also well cut, over a pale lavender blouse. Paz had an eye for clothes and color, and he could tell that those particular shades of tan and lavender were not colors available at Target or on the bargain racks. So, a wealthy woman, late twenties or early thirties, smooth tanned skin, not pretty. Her features were heavy, the nose prominent, the mouth too wide for the face, a fairly masculine face, really, one of those women who turn out looking a little too much like Dad. Her large hazel eyes, set a little aslant, catlike, with thick lashes, were, however, quite fine.

And a Cuban. Paz couldn't have said exactly what about her appearance marked her as such, but he was sure of it. A nervous Cuban woman: she shifted in her chair several times as he watched and seemed to be looking for someone, or perhaps concerned that someone was looking at her, although the restaurant had emptied out and there were no people in her immediate vicinity. Her long tan fingers tapped on the table, an irregular rhythm that flashed darts of light from ring and bracelet.

Paz walked into the room and quickly to her table.

"I'm Jimmy Paz. You wanted to see me?"

She gave him an assessing look before speaking. She did not return his formal smile. "Yes. Please sit down. Do you know who I am?"

He sat and looked her full in the face for an interval. "No, sorry," he said at last. "Should I?"

"Not really, I guess. I'm your sister. Half sister, I mean. I'm Victoria Arias Calderón de Pinero." She extended her hand and Paz shook it dumbly, and then of course the odd familiarity of her face was explained. He shaved one very like it every morning.

"Ok-a-a-y," he said after a stunned moment. "What can I do for you, Mrs. Pinero?"

"Not Mrs. Pinero, please! Victoria."

"Oh, that's nice of you, Sis. I guess I should have said sorry for your loss."

"It's your loss, too."

Without responding to this, he said, "I'm surprised you even know I exist. How did you find out about me?"

"My Aunt Eugenia. She eats here all the time. She's kind of the family character, the black sheep . . . "

"Excuse me, I believe I am that."

He saw a little color appear on her cheeks. "Oh, Christ." She sighed. "Please don't make this horrible, although you have every right to, I know. The way my father treated you and your mother was disgraceful. I apologize on behalf of my family."

"You know, I think I saw you once," said Paz, ignoring this last. "I was fourteen or so and I just found out where I came from. I biked over to your place in the Gables, and you and another little kid were in the pool. You must've been like seven or around there. I stood there and watched you for a long time, until your mother noticed me. Then your father came over and took one look and he knew who I was and he dragged me behind some bushes and beat the shit out of me and told me he'd do worse if I bothered him again, that and wreck my mom's business. So I guess I'm not interested in the fucking Calieróns or their apologies. Anyway, if that's all, *Victoria* . . ." He pushed his chair back and was about to get up when she said, "Well, whether you like it or not, you're his son. You have the same sarcastic nastiness, the same brutality and pride. Believe me, I've been the favorite target, so I know."

He stared at her and saw her eyes were brimful of tears, one of which now dripped unregarded down her cheek. *His* eyes, his daughter's, too.

He dropped back in his seat and let out a sigh. "All right. Guilty. There was no call to take my sad story out on you. It was decent of you to come see me. So was that all, the apology, or am I mentioned in the will?"

She ignored the sarcasm. "No, and I wasn't either. Besides a trust to take care of Mom, he left everything to Juan, Jonni we call him."

"Lucky Jonni. Is he going to be stinking rich?"

"That remains to be seen. My . . . our father was something of a gambler. He started this project on the Gulf Coast, way bigger than anything we ever did before, something to bring us into the big leagues. He was an admirer of Trump, if that gives you a clue. Anyway, it's a bet-the-company deal, and everything is mortgaged to the hilt. My brother is a nice kid, but business is not his thing. He just about knows how to sign the back of a check. After the funeral, I managed to convince him to give me an absolute power of attorney in exchange for a substantial increase in his allowance."

"So you're the big boss now."

"On paper. As you can imagine, Dad didn't staff his company with men who enjoy taking orders from a woman." She paused and performed a motion, perhaps unconscious, that Paz had seen innumerable times during his tenure with the cops, a slight flicking of the eyes toward the side, a stiffening of the body, and then a glance in the opposite direction. It meant a dangerous secret was about to emerge.

"There's something else," she said. "Why I came. I realize it's ridiculous, I mean, after everything that's happened, why should you care? But I had to try; honestly, I have nowhere else to go."

"I'm listening."

"All right," she said, and told him the story, some of which he already knew from other sources: the Consuela partnership, the death of Fuentes, the vandalism in the night, the peculiar nature of the guards in her house, and the details of what had happened the night Calderón had died. And the matter of the funny money in JXF Calderón Inc.'s balance sheet.

"That's an interesting story," said Paz when she'd finished.

"Yeah, but the problem is how to interpret it. The police think Dad was involved with gangsters. They think he was borrowing money from them, maybe all of them were, all the Consuela partners. They think it's one of those situations where first they lend money and then they take over the businesses, and if the owners resist, they kill them."

"And you agree with that? You think that's what happened to Fuentes and your father? Sorry, our father. You think dear old dad was mobbed up?"

"Maybe. I know the men at my house weren't Cubans."

"How do you know that?"

"They had foul mouths, cursing all the time, and they didn't use *joder* for *fuck*. They used *tirar*."

"That's Colombian."

"I know. I think they were all Colombians. Detective Finnegan thinks it was either a hit by a rival gang or that the men at my house weren't guarding us from someone else, they were holding us hostage, and for some reason they decided to kill Dad."

"This is Matt Finnegan at MDPD?"

"Yes. Do you know him?"

"Yeah, a little. A good cop. How does he explain the dead guard?"

"Not very well. Either the other gang got him or Dad got him. But Dad's gun was never fired. And there's the giant-cat business."

At this Paz felt the hairs prickle on his arms, on the back of his neck. He suppressed an actual shiver. "The giant cat."

"Yes. There were cat prints in the study where he was killed and on the walk outside. And claw marks on the wall under the window. It's nonsense, of course."

"Of course. I take it you're sticking with the gangster theory."

"I don't know. Yes, I think Dad was connecting with some bad characters, but . . . I saw what they did to him. What was the point of all that . . . carnage? It had to be something more personal, something we're not understanding."

"For example . . ."

"*I don't know!*" This was delivered in a suppressed shriek. Victoria closed her eyes and a shiver ran through her upper body. "I'm sorry. This whole thing . . . I'm hanging on by my fingernails here. But the thing is, if it's a mob killing, then the police aren't going to do anything. Whoever did it is in Colombia by now. And if it's not, if it was personal or, I don't know, some horrible maniac, then they won't find him either, because they're not looking in that direction. I mean, they'll try, God knows, two important Cuban businessmen killed, I imagine they'll pull out all the stops, but, well, I have to spend all my time and energy holding the business together. The idea that JXFC is in with gangsters is going to send all our creditors running. The only thing that will stabilize things is if the killers are found and all this goes away. That's why I came to see you."

These words and their implication struck Paz like a slap on the ear. He stared at her. "Wait, you want *me* to find these guys?"

"Yes."

"Because what, I'm the *son*? I have to avenge my father?"

"Yes. I don't care what he did to you, how he treated you, *un padre es un padre para siempre.*"

"Oh, for God's sake!" cried Paz, who had heard a similar sentiment expressed in the same language many many times, with the substitution of the female parent as subject. "First of all, I'm not a cop anymore. Second of all, what gives you the idea that I'd be any better at it than Matt Finnegan with all the resources of the police behind him?"

"You'll have a personal interest. And you're better than they are. You caught the Voodoo Killer. That's when I found out who you were. I was just a kid, watching the news with my Aunt Eugenia, the story about when you caught him. Every Cuban in town was watching because of what he did to that Vargas girl. I mean, we *knew* them, that whole family. And you came on and said something, and my aunt said, Do you know who that is? And then she told me, and said that I should never let my dad know that I knew. After that I looked up stories about you in the papers in the library. And I was proud that you were my brother."

But not proud enough to look me up until you needed something, thought Paz, but said, "The answer is no. I'm sorry, I'd like to help you out, but I . . . I'm just not set up for something like that. I'm a guy runs a restaurant, for crying out loud. . . . "

He noticed that Victoria was no longer staring at him but at a point beyond his shoulder. He turned and saw his daughter standing there, regarding them both with interest.

Victoria said, "Hi, what's your name?"

Amelia stepped closer and looked down at her silver name tag, holding it a little away from her dress.

"Amelia? That's a pretty name. I'm happy to finally meet you. I'm your Aunt Victoria. Your half aunt."

"Where's the other half?" asked Amelia after some consideration. She was not entirely sure what an aunt was. She had an uncle, her mother's brother, she knew, who lived in New York and who went through aunts at a rapid clip. She had friends who had aunts, though, invariably associated with birthday and Christmas presents ("my Aunt Julie gave me this"), to which Amelia had not until now had any response. A half aunt, she supposed, was better than no aunt at all.

"There's no other half. It's just an expression," said Victoria.

"Uh-huh, but if you gave me a Christmas present it would be the *whole* present, wouldn't it?"

"Amelia, don't hustle," said Paz. "And I think you need to go help Brenda fold napkins."

"Daddy, I will, but I'm talking to my *aunt* now. Would it?"

Victoria said, "Yes, it would. What were you thinking of?"

"I don't know yet, because I just got you. Is that a make-believe diamond bracelet or a really real one?"

"It's really real. Would you like to try it on?"

"Yeah!" Pause. "I mean yes, please."

Some preening occurred, the child lifting the glittering thing up to see it catch and throw back the lights of the room. Paz watched this with confused and painful emotions, thinking about blood and the way it told.

Amelia handed the diamonds back with obvious reluctance. Victoria asked, "How old are you now?"

"Almost seven."

"Well, then, in eight years you will have your *quinceañero,* and I'll give you this bracelet as a gift, how would you like that."

Amelia gaped. "For real?"

"Yes. But now your father and I have grown-up things to talk about, and you have work to do. It was very nice meeting you. Now run along."

To Paz's surprise she did just that.

"She's adorable," said Victoria.

"If you like the type," said Paz. "I hope you were serious about the bracelet. She doesn't forget."

"I was. I should have done this years ago, finding you, but I was shit scared of Dad. Embarrassing, but true. Again, I'm sorry."

"Hey, I knew about you, too, and I didn't make a move, and I didn't even have your excuse."

They regarded each other silently for a moment, a silence she broke with "So, Jimmy, what's the story? Are you going to be a belated big brother and help me out?"

"Can I think about it? It's going to be a major wrench for me, and other people are involved."

"Sure," she said, "I understand." She slipped a card from her purse and handed it over. It was a JXF Calderón Inc. card and it had Victoria A. Calderón listed as CEO.

"CEO, huh? You're a fast worker, Sis."

"I am. I have to be. And not to pressure you, but this, what I asked, has to be quick, too, or there's no point." She rose from her chair, and he rose, and she kissed him on the cheek and walked out of the restaurant.

The mother was waiting for him in the kitchen.

"What did she want?" was the first question.

"Mamí, how do you even know who that was?"

"Don't be stupid, Iago, of course I know who that was. I ask you again, what did she want?"

"She wanted me to find out who killed Yoiyo Calderón. Since you ask."

"And will you?"

Paz threw up his hand dramatically. "Mamí, what are you talking about? I'm running a restaurant here, I got no resources, I'm not a cop anymore . . . it's ridiculous. Not to mention I hated the guy."

"He was your father. You have an obligation."

"An obli . . . this is coming from *you,* after the way he treated us?"

"It doesn't matter what he was or what he did. He gave you life. He's part of you. You should do what you can. And also, my son, I run this restaurant, not you."

"Thank you, Mamí, I almost forgot. And you forgot to say 'a father is always a father.' "

At this the mother fixed him with her famous stare, a psychic bazooka that ordinarily would have stripped thirty years off his age and made him mumble and shuffle away. Not this time. Paz was angry now. He was being manipulated into doing something he didn't want to do, that he didn't really think could be done, that was going to end badly in some way. Worse, he was getting a shot at detective work again, it was being laid in his lap, and he didn't know if he could still do it, without a badge in his pocket and a gun on his belt, and also he knew (now the lid was sliding off) that he still lusted after it, that he was designed by nature to do that kind of work, that he was not *really* content to grill meats rather than suspects forever, that he had talked himself into a life that was in some deep way utterly false. So he met the stare, focusing his anger on his mother, and they locked eyes for what seemed like minutes.

And now Paz was appalled to see a tear, slow and fat as glycerin, roll out of his mother's eye and descend her brown cheek; and then another and a small freshet of them fell. Paz gaped, for he had never in his life seen his mother cry; it was as if she had sprouted a third eye. And her face seemed to have lost its carved-in-mahogany look and become sad and vulnerable. Paz felt a pang of disorienting terror, as he might have in an earthquake, seeing ripples on the solid earth.

"What? What is it?" he asked helplessly, and here she shook her head slowly from side to side, and said in a slow sad voice, creaky with strain, "No, I can't tell you. I can't make you. It's much too late. Here you have to go alone and do what you have to do." She pulled a fresh hand towel from the pile on the counter and wiped her eyes, then behind this scrim re-formed her face into the accustomed mask of command. "You'll let me know. It will take some time to replace you on the early shift." With that she turned and left the kitchen, leaving Paz wondering if he had imagined it all.

But the hand towel was there on the counter where she had flung it. He picked it up and found it was still damp with her tears.

Now Amelia appeared, dressed in her shorts and T-shirt, holding her hostess gown carefully on its hanger. He inspected her with care. "I hope *you're* still the same," he said.

"What?"

"Nothing, sweetie. You about ready to go?"

"Uh-huh, but, Daddy, could we stop at the market and get more little Fritos?"

"More Fritos? I just got you a ten-pack the other day. What're you, feeding the whole school?"

The child rotated her sneaker toe in a tiny circle and looked into the middle distance. "No, but it's nice to share snacks. Miss Milliken says."

"Oh, well," said Paz in delight at constancy. "If Miss *Milliken* says, then Fritos will flow forth in a never-ending stream."

"**I**s all you eat Fritos?" the girl asks. They are high in the tree. It is recess time at Providence Day School. The voices of children at play float up through the rustling leaves.

Moie licks his fingers and impales the little bag on a twig. "No, I eat other things."

"Where, in a restaurant?"

"No, Jaguar gives them," replies Moie. His Spanish is coming back a little, he finds, in these short conversations with the girl, although he does not trust the language to express anything complex. This is disturbing, not to be able to speak to others freely, far more than he thought it would be. Father Perrin had been correct: he could not really speak the language of the *wai'ichuranan,* and Jaguar has sent this child to help him. It was not shameful to make an error before a girl, especially one who would probably not live for much longer. Another reason why Jaguar has sent her.

Or so Moie supposes; it is still unclear. He rummages in his net bag and takes out a clay flask. The girl says, "Are you going to change into a monster now?"

"Not now," says Moie.

"How come?"

"You ask too many questions."

"I do not. How come you live in this tree?"

Moie regards the child with a fierce expression, but she meets his eye without a blink. Over her left shoulder he sees her death hanging, well separated and glowing like a small star. He thinks of the word *interesting,* which he has learned from Father Tim, a word the Runiya lack. It describes a hunger Moie has not known existed, but, like pisco for some men, it is hard to give up once tasted. This girl is interesting, and not only because Jaguar has sent her to him.

"How come?" she asks again.

"I will tell you," says Moie. "First, before anything, there was Sky and Earth. Each was separate from the other and they didn't know each other's language, not at all, so they were very sad. They had no one to talk to! But from their sadness there came Rain, who knew the language of both of them. And they were happy for a while. But then Sky wanted Rain to be his wife, and she agreed. This made Earth jealous, because he also loved Rain and he wanted her to be his wife. So they fought a war. Sky sent lightning to strike Earth, and Earth sent fires and smokes from inside him to choke Sky. Then Rain said Stop, stop, I will marry both of you. First I will be with Sky, then I will drop and be with Earth, then I will rise again to Sky. So they went on and on. Rain had many children. She had Sun and Moon. She had River. She was pleased that there were more things in the world, so she went to her husbands and said, It's good to have many things. You must make things, too. So they did. Sky made stars and birds. Earth made plants and trees, and worms and insects and the swift animals. Earth was proud of these things and he boasted of them to River. River said, If you mate with me, we will make something even greater than these things. Earth said, If we did that, your mother, Rain, would be jealous. But River said she didn't care about that and smiled over her shoulder at Earth. So he mated with her. So in time out of her womb came Caiman."

"What's that?"

Moie makes spectacles of his fingers and gnashes his teeth and writhes his body until she understands he is talking about a crocodile, like the one in *Peter Pan*.

"River told Caiman that he could only eat the creatures that put their feet to the water, but he was a wicked child and would not listen. At that time there were no fishes. He left the water and chased the deer and tapirs and ate them, and ate trees and all plants, and the beetles and ants."

"Crocodiles can't eat trees."

"Things were different in those days. Do you want to hear this story or not?"

"I do, but I mostly want to hear the part about why you live in our tree."

"It will come where it comes in the story—" Moie begins, but he is interrupted by a shout from below: "Amelia Paz, are you up in that tree again?" It is Miss Milliken, sounding upset. Amelia slides from the hammock and stands on a broad, nearly horizontal limb. "I have to go now. Will you tell me the rest of the story later?"

"It may happen that I will," says Moie. She smiles at him and disappears amid the leaves below.

Prudencio Rivera Martínez, on what he had good reason to fear might be his final day on earth, waited outside the security barrier for the arrival of the early direct Delta flight from Dallas–Fort Worth. Gabriel Hurtado never entered the United States via an international flight. Instead, he flew to Mexico City, where his organization picked him up and drove him to the border at Ciudad Juarez. There, with the aid of excellent forged Mexican papers, he crossed the border as a businessman of that nation, untroubled among the thirty thousand vehicles that drove north into El Paso on that day and every day. Hurtado's attitude toward the United States of America was amused contempt, rather like that of a peasant for a particularly stupid, if vitally necessary, burro. The Americans had been trying to catch him for years, and yet he never had any difficulty entering the country in this way, or staying for as long as he pleased. His only complaint about U.S. homeland security was that the border controls were so porous that amateurs were encouraged to enter the drug business in numbers, driving down the price of his product. From El Paso they had taken the highway to Dallas, whence he and his companion had enjoyed a restful first-class flight to Miami.

Martínez saw the men emerge from the gate, Hurtado and a man name Ramon Palacios, although this name was infrequently used. At the sight of this second man, Martínez felt some relief, because his presence meant that Hurtado was taking this crazy business seriously, that he thought their adversary was significant, and that therefore Martínez was not entirely to blame for the Calderón fiasco. The two men were both middle-sized and stocky, perhaps a little smaller than middle-sized, smaller than Martínez anyway, and dressed in similar pale sports jackets, open-collared pastel shirts, dark trousers, and shined slip-on shoes with brass fittings. Both had fat dark mustaches and dark hair combed back, although that of Hurtado was starting to recede. People said that Hurtado kept the man around because they looked alike, so that an assassin might become confused. Martínez thought this was a foolish opinion, since you would necessarily have to kill both of them together. Killing only one would do you no good, and Martínez thought also that if he had one shot at the pair he would hit Palacios before Hurtado, because while Hurtado was a dangerous enemy, you would have to be totally crazy to want El Silencio after you with a grudge.

Hurtado gave him a severe smile and a formal embrace, El Silencio offered an uninterested nod and continued his examination of the surroundings. Because of airport security, he was unarmed and therefore uneasy. They went to baggage claim in silence, and after the usual wait, the bodyguard picked out two small leather bags and an aluminum attaché case, ignoring Martínez's offer of help. At the curb waited a black Lincoln Navigator with tinted windows, bought for cash two days previously. Hurtado always rode in Navigators at home, and Martínez wanted him to be comfortable. They entered the vehicle, the boss and his man in the rear and Martínez in the front seat. Hurtado greeted Santiago Iglesias, who was driving. The man knew the name and face of every man who worked for him and a good deal about their personal lives as well—for example, where their families could be found. It was one of the reasons he had lasted so long in the business, that and El Silencio. As they pulled away from the curb, Martínez heard the click of a lock opening behind him and various other metallic sounds. El Silencio was arming himself.

"What's the situation, Martínez?" Hurtado asked, switching without preamble from his joking with Iglesias. No joking with Martínez; he was not yet entirely off the hook.

"I have two men in each of the two houses, and two vans on the street in front of each one. I also have a man at the ferry terminal in a car. It's an island, and that's the only way on or off."

"No boat?"

"We need a boat?"

"*Pendejo,* of course we need a boat. Both homes were vandalized, and whoever did it didn't come on the ferry. Therefore, they have a boat. Also, we're based on an island, so we need a boat. Get one—no, two—and people to handle them, and make them fast ones. How are the clients?"

"They're shitting themselves since Calderón got it. No trouble there. They're like lambs."

"Police?"

"Thumbs up their ass. They've been around to both the Garza and the Ibanez place. We get tipped off and disappear while they come around. Not a problem."

"Yes, that's what you said before Calderón got it. You know why I'm not more pissed off at you for fucking this up, Martínez?"

Martínez admitted he didn't know.

"Because this saves us some trouble. Calderón would

have had to go in any case. He knew things that the others didn't and was starting to be a pain in the ass. So, if he leaves the scene a little early, it's not a problem for me, and also, as you say, the others are in line. The only one we absolutely need at this point is Ibanez, to handle the logs and so forth. So, as far as JXFC is concerned, I assume the son took over."

"No, the daughter, is what I understand. The son is some kind of *maricón*. He's in New York. The daughter is running the company."

"Good. I'm starting to feel better already. She won't be a problem when the time comes. Now, what about these two *fregados* in the painted van?"

"Not yet. The plates came up empty. There's no such number."

"Fake plates? That's interesting. That suggests a serious organization."

From the front seat, Iglesias said, "They were funny plates. The numbers weren't orange like the ones on this car and there was no palm tree."

"They were out-of-state plates," said Hurtado half to himself. He was not particularly angry. There was no reason that a gang of Cali *chuteros* should know that in America license plates varied from state to state. He explained this to his men.

"And it said *yova* on the top," added Iglesias.

"*Yova?*" said Hurtado. "What does this mean, *yova?*"

"I don't know, boss, that's what it said, in big letters and there were clouds and some buildings on it, too, no palms. I-O-W-A, *yova.*"

"Ah, yes, I see," said Hurtado. "This is the name of a state far away, and obviously it would do no good to run the plates there because it wouldn't give us an address in Miami. I think these people are very clever, for Americans."

"You're sure they're Americans, boss?" asked Martínez.

"They're *using* Americans, and there isn't a sniff at home of anyone working against us in this operation. Or so my friend here assures me."

He meant El Silencio. Martínez thought that if El Silencio had been unleashed on the Colombian underworld with orders to find out if anyone was interested in the Puxto operation or was playing games in Miami, and hadn't found anything, then it was fairly certain that nothing was going on. Using the rearview mirror he stole a look at the man. If half what they said about him was true, he ought to have horns and fangs and a tail, but he looked undistinguished, an ordinary Latin American fellow, except for the heavy scarring on his throat. The legend was that when he was ten someone had been killed in front of the miserable little shop his family ran in Cali and, as usual, the killers had taken out all the potential witnesses, his whole family: mother, brother, three sisters. Or others said that the family had been running some racket and became too greedy and got wiped as a lesson. But without doubt the family had been killed and someone had cut the boy's throat, failing to kill him but damaging his voice box, so that he could only make a croaking whisper, and also without doubt at the age of fifteen he had found the man responsible for the murders and kidnapped him and kept him alive for six days and delivered him back to the place whence he came, still alive, but in a condition that shocked even the criminals of Cali. Thus he was brought to the attention of Gabriel Hurtado.

"What do you think about this cat business?" asked Martínez, to change the subject.

"A tactic to frighten us," said Hurtado dismissively. "They must think we're ignorant peasants frightened by magical animals. This suggests the Russians. Or Haitians. In any case, these *chingadas* are definitely the kind who won't leave it alone, and so they'll try for these other two *pendejos* we have and then we'll have *them*. Isn't that right, Ramon?"

El Silencio nodded, but naturally he said nothing at all.

# Twelve

"Onion sauce!" said Professor Cooksey. "Oh, bother! Oh, blow!"

Jenny looked up from her microscope and blinked. "Excuse me?"

Cooksey glared at her and said "Onion sauce!" again and grasped a handful of the yellow legal pages, reprints, and printouts that covered his desk in drifts, and threw them up at the ceiling. She stared at him.

"I feel like Mr. Mole," he said. "This wretched paper and the atmosphere around this house. It's not to be borne."

Jenny knew what he meant. After the second killing, Rupert had become paranoid, or more paranoid than usual, although he said, often and loud, that they didn't know *for certain* that Moie was involved in any violence and that the Forest Planet Alliance had always been vociferously against any hint of ecoterrorism, and if the police were to become involved, the forces of exploitation would be delighted to smear their good name. Therefore, Jenny saw, in a strange way the recent association with Moie was to be made a nonevent. Rupert had ordered the property scoured to remove any trace that Moie might have left behind and had ordered the elimination of any illegal substances. Scotty's marijuana plants had been uprooted and mulched and carried off the property by dead of night, smoking paraphernalia had been deep-sixed, and the library and computers had been scrubbed of anything that would have offended a troop of Mormon Girl Scouts. Luna had stopped talking to anyone but Scotty, and that only in short angry bursts. Scotty's normally morose mien had entered the outer suburbs of clinical depression, and since he was largely responsible for the physical maintenance of the property, the grounds had lately acquired a seedy look, like a man with a bad haircut and a three-day beard. No one had mentioned calling the police.

"Who's Mr. Mole?" Jenny asked.

"Mr. Mole. In *The Wind in the Willows*?" He observed her blank stare. "You don't mean to tell me you've never read *The Wind in the Willows*?"

"I haven't read *anything,* Cooksey," she replied with an irritated sigh. "I'm illiterate."

"Nonsense! Didn't anyone ever read to you?"

"I don't think so. Places I grew up they mainly stuck us in front of the TV."

"Well, that's a shame. And I intend to repair the lack instantly. This minute."

With which he rose from his chair and darted to a bookshelf, where he took down a thin yellow clothbound volume, much worn.

"Here it is, and we won't read it here, oh no. Tell me, do you like boats?"

"I don't know. I never been in one."

"Never been . . . *never* been in a boat? I call that child abuse. My girl, there is, and I quote, 'there is *nothing*—absolutely nothing—half so much worth doing as simply messing about in boats.' That's in this, too." He waved the little book. "I tell you what, let's utterly abandon our fusty academic labors, and this depressing and toxically earnest milieu, and head for the water. Are you game?"

She gave him one of her frank and shining smiles and a little shrug. "Whatever," she said.

They took the old Mercedes, and a foam cooler full of beer and chips and sandwich stuff, which they sneaked from the silent kitchen like children stealing late-night contraband. Cooksey also brought a large stained rucksack full of various clanking gear, so that, he said, they could consider it a scientific expedition and not mere disgraceful lazing about.

They drove for an hour or so down the narrow road through the Everglades until they arrived in Flamingo. Cooksey knew a man who rented out wood-and-canvas Old Town canoes so that, Cooksey said, they would not have to use an *aluminum* abomination, like paddling a boiler shop, and they did rent a sixteen-footer and carried it down a launch ramp, and Jenny sat in the prow, with all their gear behind her, and Cooksey put a foot in the craft and pushed off gracefully. They paddled across Whitewater Bay, a vast sheet of what looked like ruffled pale gray silk dotted with dark mangrove islands, that showed as the sort of silhouettes used in stage musicals to suggest tropic climes. It was easy paddling, with a stiff breeze behind them.

On the other side of the bay Cooksey steered them to a little beach composed of billions of tiny shells, part of a small island that the state had designated a campsite. This was Wedge Point, he said, and time for lunch. There was a cleared area ringed with cocoloba and poisonwood trees and one large tree bearing green fruit, which Cooksey said was lignum vitae. They spread their blanket in the shade of this tree and ate their sandwiches and drank two beers each. Then Cooksey leaned against the trunk of the lignum vitae tree and gestured for her to sit down next to him. He had the book out and she leaned against the trunk next to him and he read her *The Wind in the Willows*. She listened openmouthed, like a child. At some deep level she understood why he was doing this, that he was giving her something she should have had as a small girl, a simple thing, being out in nature with a man she trusted, having a story read to her, a story about nature and animals. He was curing her, in a way, and also curing himself, she understood that, too. He wasn't being entirely selfless, but she didn't know from what illness he suffered.

At a certain point in the reading, she said, "I don't get this part. Who is this guy with the horns playing the music?"

"The Piper at the Gates of Dawn? Well, I think it's meant to be Pan. He's not dead to the animals, at least in this story. He's their lord."

"Like a god?"

"More like the spirit of nature itself. He's shown in Greek art as a faun with a set of reed pipes and furry legs and hooves. His shout makes us mad. It's where we get the word *panic*. Apparently he plays no more. It was a famous story; Plutarch reports it in his essay about why the ancient oracles failed. A ship was passing the island of Paxos and the pilot heard his name called and then a mighty voice shouted out 'Great Pan is dead.' And then he heard the sound of weeping. It happened just around the time of the Nativity, so the early Christians believed it was a symbol for the end of the pagan world. You have absolutely no idea of what I'm talking about, do you?"

"No."

He laughed, not unkindly, and said, "Then let us return to Rat and Mole." Which they did, but he made her read the last chapter herself, and she found that she could actually do it, with a little help. After that, they went around the little campsite, putting out sticky traps, and Cooksey darted about with his butterfly net grabbing flying creatures from the air. While he did that, he talked about the fall of Rome. Jenny knew Rome only as a type of movie and had believed that it was all made up, like Conan and *Star Wars*. She was fascinated to learn that a civilization could collapse without nukes or robots like in *Terminator* and wanted to know why.

"There are many theories," said Cooksey in response to her question, "and any number of great thick books on the subject. Some blame Christianity for sapping the fighting spirit of the empire. Others say that the riches from the conquests destroyed the small farmers who provided the strength of the legions. The empire started to hire troops from outside the empire to defend it and they weren't as good as the Romans had been. There's even a theory that lead in their water pipes made them stupid and crazy."

"What do *you* think?"

He laughed. "My thoughts are valueless—I'm no historian. But my old dad was a pretty fair amateur, we spent a good deal of time poking around Roman ruins. *He* thought they just got tired. People get tired of life and so do civilizations. They didn't believe in their gods anymore, and their political system was dead, just a gang fight among generals, and thousands of foreigners were pouring through their borders, and they couldn't be bothered to keep them out because they needed them, you see, to protect them from the even worse foreigners. So they pulled the legions back from the frontiers and everything sort of melted away, the schools closed, the books were used to start fires, and people forgot how to read and so on. And the buildings and roads crumbled because no one remembered how to fix them, and there was no money anyway and no trade."

"That's sad," she said.

"Is it? Everything passes, you know. First the gods fail and then the people lose heart and the dark closes in. As now. I'll think you'll agree that the gods we worship are, if anything, less powerful than great Pan."

"You mean like Jesus?"

"Would that we actually worshipped Jesus . . . good Lord, is that a Palmira?" With that, Cooksey brought up his butterfly net and stalked a small white butterfly marked with yellow and brown for several minutes, finally scooping it up in the gauzy folds and holding it up to his face, upon which shone a delighted grin. Jenny thought he looked now about twelve. He transferred the insect, still wrapped in the netting, into a wide-mouthed jar; when its fluttering ceased, he examined it through a hand lens.

"Did you kill it?" asked Jenny.

"Well, yes," said Cooksey, peering. "By God, it *is* a Palmira. It's an Antillean butterfly, almost unknown in these parts. It feeds on beggar-tick. My word, there's another one!" He leaped and snagged this one, too; into the jar it went.

"I wonder if it's breeding here now," he mused.

"Not anymore, since you got here, if those were the only ones."

He looked at her closely. "You don't think I should've

killed them, do you? I quite sympathize, but after all I'm a scientist and therefore a soldier in the legions of death. We kill to understand, and we think it's justified therefore. Pan would not have approved. Do you know, our friend Moie thinks we're all dead people, although he believes you are still a little alive."

She was looking at the bright still shapes in the killing jar. "I don't know . . . I mean, no offense, Cooksey, but I don't think I could, like, do that for a living, kill things. It kind of creeps me out. Why is it important if they're breeding here?"

"Well, because it might be yet another tiny sign that the tropics are moving northward in response to global warming. This is a Cuban butterfly, after all. In any case, we will dedicate the rest of the day to Pan and kill no more and merely observe the life around us. This, too, is science, and a quite venerable sort of science at that."

So they did and spent hours observing the insect, marine, and bird life of the small island through hand lens and binoculars until the sun sank to touch the tops of the tallest trees and Cooksey said it was time they started back, because they would have to paddle into the teeth of the wind. But when they cleared the pass and entered Whitewater Bay again, they found that the wind had died away entirely and that the whole sheet of water was as calm as a millpond. Jenny had that very thought, although she had never seen a millpond. Another alien image, this one from the story she had received from Cooksey's old book, but it was not the only one. Indeed, her head now seemed to contain many more rooms than it had, all decorated with pictures and furniture she could not remember, and connecting hallways that beckoned mysteriously. This was what regular people were like, she thought, all this stuff, because when you knew stuff, like the Roman Empire and fig wasps and global warming and the great god Pan, well, the stuff wanted to connect up with itself and out of that came new thoughts you'd never thought before, thoughts maybe no one had ever thought before. It was disturbing, like being dumped in a new foster home and not knowing what was going to happen; you wanted to sit on the bed they showed you and not move until someone told you what was what.

She didn't want to think about all that just now and found she could still shut it down pretty much and just be, and sink into the easy paddling and the passing scene, the silver water like a tarnished mirror perfectly reflecting the peach-colored wisps of clouds and the orange disk of the setting sun, each stroke of her paddle meeting its twin coming up from below before vanishing in the swirl of the stroke. And above floated the birds, white egrets, gulls, once a flight of brown pelicans, in their peculiar prehistoric-seeming lumbering flight, each of these, too, with its twin below for the instant of passage. And looking back she saw their wake, two long lines extending into the unrecoverable past, and there was something nagging at her she wanted to ask Cooksey, what was it?

"What do *we* worship, Cooksey?"

"Pardon?"

"You said something about dying gods and all. And that we didn't worship Jesus. It was just before you found that butterfly."

"Oh, yes. Well, my mother used to say that when people stopped worshipping God they didn't stop worshipping entirely. She thought the urge to worship was hardwired into humankind, like the urge for procreation. So they worshipped lesser gods, mainly themselves, as being most convenient, but also things like money, fame, and sex. Or youth. And these gods all fail, just like Pan did, being tied to corruptible and earthly things. Of course she was quite a devout Catholic. She was a Howard, you see, a very ancient Catholic family where I come from. Very unusual for an anthropologist to be a believer, they spend so much time picking apart the beliefs of the natives, but when people asked her about it she would laugh and say yes, yes, it's perfectly absurd, but I happen to believe it's all true. She had a deep sense of the weird, and I picked up some of it, which is why I suppose I get along with our Moie. He doesn't think Pan is dead at all. It would shock him most awfully to suggest it."

"How does he know about Pan? I thought that was the Romans a long time ago."

"Oh, he doesn't call him Pan. He calls him Jaguar, but it's the same fellow, you know, although with somewhat sharper teeth. Yes, I suspect Pan is loose again in the kingdom of the dead people, and I'd bet he's more than a little cranky after his long sleep. I imagine we're in for some interesting experiences."

"What will happen?"

"Nothing very nice, I suspect. The earth is becoming a little bored with us dead people. Moie, whatever he is, represents a symptom, a bit like that butterfly from the south. I mean, suppose you had a great mansion and invited some guests because you were a generous and kind lady. And suppose these guests started to behave in a rude and destructive manner . . ."

"Like the weasels in Toad Hall."

"Just so. Smearing the draperies with filth, breaking the crockery, insulting the servants . . . well, however generous you might be, you'd probably decide that it had gone beyond a joke and take steps to make the house somewhat less hospitable. You might turn up the heat, for example, so they swelter. You might stop serving nice meals. You might let the hounds loose in the bedrooms to raven and destroy. And so we have global warming, and sea-level rise, and new diseases, and deserts spreading, and failing water tables, and a kind of desperate madness, because perhaps nature includes the invisible as well as all this." He gestured with his paddle at the surrounding scene.

"My mother certainly believed it and she was no one's fool. As I've said, she would've been delighted to know Moie."

"Do you think he'll, like, kill any more people?" asked Jenny. It was still hard for her to associate the gentle Indian she knew with people being torn apart.

"That would depend. He wants the people who are planning to destroy his forest to stop doing it, and I suppose he'll continue to kill those he thinks responsible until they actually stop. At least he seems to have decided to murder the guilty for a change. He can always depend upon us to slaughter the innocent ourselves, assuming any of us are innocent." After an interval of silence Cooksey broke into song, a rhythmic ditty about rolling down to old Maui that seemed to make the paddling easier. They both dug in more vigorously until the canoe seemed to fly of its own will across the water's smooth and flawless skin.

At the boat livery in Flamingo, Jenny felt the first effects of sunburn. Even through the fabric of her shirt the sun had struck fiercely at her redhead's tender skin. And she had a headache, the sun making its contribution but also perhaps the result of deep and unaccustomed thought.

"Are you all right, dear?" Cooksey asked when he returned to the car.

"I'm sort of wiped out," she replied. "You can drive if you want."

His face clouded. "I don't want," he said. "I really can't."

"You never learned to drive?"

"I did. But I can't. I was in an accident. My nerves won't let me. I'm sorry."

"What kind of accident?"

He stared at her, and she saw the age creep back into his face, and she thought it was like the guy in a mummy movie when the spell is broken and he turns into a skeleton on the screen.

"A fatal accident," he said huskily, and turned and entered the car on the passenger side.

They drove away with Cooksey looking pointedly out the window and sending out powerful vibrations of rejection. Jenny had wide experience of sulky men, men who wouldn't talk about it, men who took whatever was bugging them out on the nearest female, so she withdrew herself and thought about the interesting and exciting things that had filled the day, and here discovered an unsuspected value of knowing stuff: you became a more interesting interior conversationalist and didn't have to fill your mind exclusively with moping about other people being mean to you and the worthlessness of your own sad life.

So she thought and drove, which she had always liked doing, especially in this powerful, fancy car, and she started to
drive more aggressively, downshifting and passing trucks on
the narrow two-lane with canals on either side. Cooksey had
rolled up a towel and seemed to be asleep on it, leaning
against his window.

And then she pulled out to pass a tractor-trailer, and when
she was almost past it she saw that it had been following another big semi, its twin, both loaded with crushed limestone
and she saw the lights of an oncoming truck. She floored the
pedal and leaned on the horn. The old car leaped forward as
if back on its native autobahn. Time slowed to a crawl as
they seemed to inch along the gray flank of the leading semi.
The oncoming truck blared its horn, and then, with scant
yards to spare, she whipped the car back into lane.

Cooksey was wide awake, looking at her in amazement.

"Toad of Toad Hall," she said, and gave a toot on the horn.

His face softened, creased into a small grin. "Your first lit-
erary reference, I believe. What you get for reading books.
And . . ." Here he drew in a deep breath and let it out. "I'm
sorry. I tend to shut out the world when pressed. It's both an
occupational and a national fault. And I'm not used to talking about painful subjects."

"You told me about your wife and the snake. The fer-de-
lance."

"So I did. I wonder why?"

"People tell me stuff. I thought it was because I was a retard, it didn't matter what they told me, you know? Like
talking to a doll. I'm used to it."

"Well, then, suppose I talk to you like a fellow human being instead?"

"That's cool," she said, and he told her about how he'd
come back to England with his wife's body and buried her
and started to drunk a lot afterward, living at his parents'
summer place in Norfolk, and he had a little girl, four,
Jemima, and how one day he'd taken her to a pub for lunch
and had drunk more pints than he ought, and driving back
home a tractor had pulled suddenly into the road and he'd

swerved and struck a tree. He hadn't been going that fast, but it was enough. The child had been unrestrained in the backseat, one moment chattering away, singing her little songs, and the next over the backseat, smack against the windscreen. She hung on for two days and then he'd buried her next to her mother and left England.

"What did you do?"

"Oh, nothing, really. A wandering scholar. There are lots of us, filling in for sabbaticals, staffing a grant. And various other things."

"God. Your wife and then your kid. What a bad year!"

A harsh barking laugh from Cooksey. "Indeed. A bad year. Now we know each other's sad stories. What a pair! We shall have to be friends, like Rat and Mole."

"You're Rat," she said confidently, and smiled. He grinned back at her, showing his long yellow teeth.

**W**hen they arrived back at the property it was deserted, and Cooksey recalled that they had all been scheduled to attend some kind of environmental rally at Miami-Dade College downtown, at which he himself had been expected. Entering his office they found Moie staring at the computer.

"Catching up on your e-mail, are you?" said Cooksey.

Ignoring this, Moie pointed to the keyboard and said, "Each seed of this tray of seeds has a mark, and when I press one, the same mark comes on this shining little wall, except this stick, which makes a ghost mark, and if I do this many times it looks like the marks on the bundle of leaves that Father Tim used when he talked to his god. They are like the marks insects make under the skin of a tree, but smaller. Father Tim could turn them into his voice, and he said many of the dead people could do this. Is this how you talk to your god, Cooksey?"

"In a way. To some of the smaller gods, perhaps, not the same one that Father Tim spoke to with his bundle of leaves. How are you, Moie? It's been many days since we saw you."

"I have fed well," said Moie. "Have you fed well?"

"I have fed well."

"And the Firehair Woman, has she fed well?" Here he glanced at Jenny, who grinned at him and did a silly wave from waist level.

"We have both fed well. Look here, Moie, this can't go on. You can't go about killing people and eating them."

"I have killed no one. It's Jaguar who kills and eats."

"But the *wai'ichuranan* don't believe in Jaguar, Moie. They'll think it was you alone who did these killings."

Moie look startled for an instant and then laughed, a peculiar hissing sound he made with his lips pressed together and his whole upper body shaking. When he recovered he said, "That's a good joke, Cooksey. I will tell you another joke now. The Runiya don't believe in water!"

Cooksey waited until Moie had stopped laughing at this one, and said, "Then you must talk to Jaguar and ask him not to. It is very *siwix* to do so in the land of the dead people. Soon the police will learn what you and Jaguar have done, and then they will arrest you. Do you understand what that means?"

Moie thought of what the man had told him at Fernandino on the island of Trinidad, and he said, "Yes, I know. But they don't see me in my tree and also, when I go among them, I wear the priest's clothing."

"That's not what I mean," said Cooksey. "The clothing is a small thing and killing is a large thing. They will lock you in a house with many bad men for your whole life, or they may even kill you."

Moie didn't seem impressed by these warnings, so Cooksey added, "Father Tim would be angry if he knew you were doing it."

"I am not doing it. I have told you this, but you don't listen. I will say it once again: first we went to see them and the Monkey Boy said they should not cut in the Puxto, but this dead person Fuentes called for men and they threw us out of that house, like women throw peelings and entrails into the river. I didn't understand what was said, but that I understood. And this showed me that the Consuela would not listen and would still kill the Puxto. This is why Jaguar killed him, and later this other one. You say that it is bad to kill them, but Father Tim has said that sometimes a small bad thing must be done so that a greater bad thing does not happen. This is *moral philosophy,* and this is the way of the *jampiri* among the dead people. These men of the Consuela Holdings wish to kill the Puxto and all my people, as they killed Father Tim, so it is better if Jaguar slays them first."

"Yes, but, Moie, there is another way, as I've already told you. Many, many of the *wai'ichuranan* don't want the Puxto to be cut. They have some of the spirit of *aryu't* in them. Although they are dead they wish for life and so wish to stop these men, just as you do."

"You say it, but it is hard to believe. Will *they* kill the Consuela men?"

"No. This is not the way of the *wai'ichuranan* in such matters. They will make noises, and make many marks on leaves and the *wai'ichuranan* will see them and know what the Consuela is doing and that it is *siwix,* and also, as I said to you once before, they will send their spirits into the spirit boxes in the houses of the dead people and there is a kind of witch we have called *journalists* who will go up to the Consuela men and speak rudely to them and drag them into the spirit box, and so the Consuela men will be ashamed and not do evil things on the Puxto. This is our way. But if they find you have been killing these men it will be different. They will not think about the Puxto, but only about the killings. They will call you a *terrorist,* which is another kind of witch we have who delights in killing and fear, and they will arrest you and drag you into the spirit box for a long time and you will not be able to stop it. Then the Puxto will be destroyed, because we believe that if a *terrorist* wishes something to be done or not done, we think it is *ryuxit* to do the opposite."

Moie thought in silence for the better part of a minute, then said, "I will think about this in my belly and ask Jaguar what to do. Now, I have to ask you one thing and tell you one thing, for I didn't come here just to play with seeds in a tray. I ask this. Jaguar wants a child to be *hninxa.* Jaguar says that if this child is given, he will have power in the land of the dead people, not just the power of the flesh but also ghost power. It is hard to say this part because it can be said only in the holy language, which you cannot speak. With such power he can make the *wai'ichuranan* alive again, or some of them, so that they will no longer wish to turn the whole world into pisco and machetes and money things. So I ask, is such a thing *ryuxit* among the *wai'ichuranan?*"

"No!" said Cooksey forcefully. "It is the most *siwix* thing we can think of. Moie, you must not do it."

"But it would be a very large good thing if the *wai'ichuranan* came alive again and stopped ruining the whole world as they do now. Also, Jaguar would not take her unless she wished it."

"It's still not allowed."

"Then I don't understand. Father Tim said that Jan'ichupitaolik gave himself as a sacrifice, so that the dead people could have life beyond the moon, in heaven, which was a great good thing. And Jan'ichupitaolik was a man and the greatest *jampiri* of the dead people, and so he was worth much more than a little girl. So this is *moral philosophy* and not *siwix* at all."

"No, no, you are mistaken," cried Cooksey. "Listen, Moie, for this is most important. Jan'ichupitaolik sacrificed *himself* to save the world. He didn't sacrifice a little girl. And surely Father Tim told you that because he sacrificed himself, no other sacrifices would ever be required ever again, by anyone. And also I tell you Jan'ichupitaolik is chief of all the gods, even of Jaguar, and he will be very angry at you and at Jaguar if you do this thing."

"I hear you," said Moie in a polite but noncommittal way. "I will also consider it in my belly. But let me ask you this: if Jan'ichupitaolik is lord of all, as you say, why doesn't he tell the dead people to stop ruining the world?"

"He does, but his voice is very faint. Other gods have louder voices now."

"Yes, Father Tim has told me the same thing. I think that maybe Jan'ichupitaolik has said to Jaguar, Go and slay, for the world I made should not be destroyed. Do you think this is possible, Cooksey?"

Cooksey slowly shook his head and said in a tired voice, "I don't know, Moie."

"Or Jan'ichupitaolik has died and now Jaguar is the chief of all the gods. In any case, I will surely do as he wishes. Now I must tell you a thing. There are new men in the houses of the Consuela. Jaguar has told me. They are men like those who killed Father Tim. They are the dead of the dead, their spirits have rotted inside them and they are hollow and filled by *chinitxi* instead. I tell you this because I think they will come here."

"Here? Why would they come here?" asked Cooksey.

"Because of the Monkey Boy and the man Fuentes. Because of the *unancha,* the totem sign of this place." Here Moie pressed his hand to his chest. "They have painted it on many shirts. I have seen the Firehair Woman give them to many people for money, and also others in this place do the same, and also it is on the *car*." Here he used the English word and looked briefly at Jenny, who smiled at him encouragingly. "These men, these *chinitxi,* are all hunters, and one of them is a very good hunter, not as good as me, but good enough to follow the *unancha* to this place. I tell you this, Cooksey, because you have been a friend to me, and also because the Firehair Woman is an alive *wai'ichura* and the gods speak to her, although she doesn't hear them. As for the others, I don't care, but you may, if they are of your people. For if they come here, they will kill all, as I have heard they do in villages not far from my home. I will be sorry if they kill you, Cooksey, for it is *interesting* to talk with you. This is a word Father Tim showed me. It is like smelling an animal you never met before and you wish to know if it is good to eat or not. Now I am going."

"Moie, wait . . . !" said Cooksey, but the Indian moved very quickly, across the room and through the door. Cooksey ran to the corridor, but there was no one there, nor were there any sounds of footsteps on the gravel path.

"What was that all about?" asked Jenny when Cooksey returned, looking dejected. "Bad news?"

"You might say that," he replied dully, and recounted what

he had learned from Moie, Jenny asking anxious questions, and Cooksey answering as best he could.

"What are we going to do about this little girl?" she asked.

"Damned if I know," he said. "Damned in any case. Christ! What was I thinking putting him in a tree next to a school? I suppose we'll have to tell Rupert."

"He'll call the cops, right?"

"I rather doubt that. Rupert is a good sort, but as between saving the world and looking after himself, the latter usually wins out. And also, can you imagine him going to the police with this story? Yes, Officer, I'd like to report an Indian from South America who thinks he can turn himself into a jaguar and has killed two prominent Cuban businessmen. Yes, he was staying at my house after he killed the first one, but I didn't report it because I wanted to use him as an environmental poster child. No, Officer, I have no idea where he is now. He's often more or less invisible. Oh, and there are a group of demons in town, disguised as Colombian gangsters, but I have no idea where they are either. And, yes, one other thing, that Indian is preparing to murder a little girl, or rather the jaguar who doesn't exist is going to do it. He's a god, you see. I mean it's beyond absurd. And also . . . I'm not entirely sure the police can successfully intervene here. Moie is perhaps not what he appears to be. Perhaps we're involved in something deeply strange. I speak not as a scientist, of course, but as my mother's son."

"I know what you mean," said Jenny. And after a brief pause she asked, "So you don't have, like, a plan?"

He burst out laughing. "Yes, my immediate plan is to drink a large whiskey." He smiled at her. "Well, you don't seem paralyzed with fear, although I would strongly advise you not to wear any Forest Planet Alliance T-shirts in the near term."

"I'm fine. It all seems too weird to worry about. And I still feel kind of good. I mean about today."

"Yes, that's what messing about in boats will do for you. Saving the news of the apocalypse just now, it *was* a lovely day."

"But the weasels are coming."

"Indeed they are, and the wise thing at this juncture, I believe, is to model ourselves on Rat and Mole, and stick to our cozy burrow, and wait for Mr. Badger to arrive and show us what to do. Perhaps he can save that little girl."

# Thirteen

The restaurant Guantanamera did not collapse when Jimmy Paz announced that he was leaving its kitchen to pursue his father's killer, which discovery made him feel both less guilty and more miserable: an even split, he thought, or maybe a little better than even, since his mother had been telling him since early adulthood that absent his daily help, ruin faced the family Paz. In the event, Mrs. Paz made a few calls and came up with Raul, a steady man of middle age who not only knew how to grill meat but also followed Mrs. Paz's instructions to the last tomato, and was not interested in concocting outlandish dishes that had no place in a traditional Cuban restaurant.

Lola was mildly encouraging. It would do him good to get out from under Mom, was the doctor's opinion, and maybe he'd get used to it. After playing cop for a while, maybe he could think about going back to school. It wasn't too late: just look at her. Indeed, look at her: she went to work, came home, ate briefly, and then went to sleep exhausted. She had a glazed, frightened look and blamed it on various work-related stresses, although she hadn't looked like that in her intern year, when the stresses were far greater, and there had been a lot more kidding and sex back then, too. He had a pretty good idea what was going on by now, he could hear her thumping around the house in the middle of the night and he could tell by the pill bottles in their medicine cabinet that she was taking some fairly serious stuff. He wondered if she was an actual addict yet. It happened to docs a lot, he knew, but he'd never figured Lola for the type. So that was another thing on his list, which he decided to cross off before he left the house. Feeling stupid and disloyal he went into the bedroom and plucked a tuft of blond hair from Lola's hairbrush and in the girl's bedroom plucked a few darker hairs from hers.

Securing these items in separate envelopes, he turned to something he had more confidence in. He settled himself in a comfortable chair with a fresh cup of coffee and called a woman named Doris Taylor at the *Miami Herald*. Taylor had been covering crime for the *Herald* since (according to her) before the invention of gunpowder, and had waxed fat on Jimmy Paz's exploits in pursuit of the infamous Voodoo Killer. She was delighted to hear he was, in a manner of speaking, back on the street and was elaborately forthcoming with what she knew about the Miami Ripper, as she now called him or it, asking only to be leaked when he had something new. Thus prepared, Paz called Tito Morales and had him set up a meeting with Major Oliphant to discuss the Calderón murder and how Jimmy Paz could help with their investigation.

The meeting was set up for that very day. Paz dressed in one of his old detective suits, and polished up a pair of four-hundred-dollar shoes and arrived at police headquarters looking very much as he had when he'd walked off the job seven years ago. Oliphant was all smiles until it turned out that Jimmy Paz did not just want to help with the investigation. He wanted to investigate.

The Major scowled at this and said, "This is because he was your *father*?" He had just learned this interesting fact from Paz's own lips.

"More or less," said Paz. "More, really. My mother and my half sister wanted me to, so here I am."

"You know, it would've been really cool if you'd told me about this family connection the last time we talked."

Paz shrugged. "It wasn't something I was proud of. I kept it pretty close. Tito didn't know either." Morales confirmed this with a sour grunt and a nod.

"And now," said Oliphant, "you want to . . . what, be a freelance cop on this thing?"

"No. I'll work with Tito. Under Tito, really; I mean he's got the badge and the gun. It's nothing unusual. The department hires consultants all the time."

"Not to catch killers, we don't. We like to keep that in the immediate family. So, just for the sake of argument, how do you see this so-called consultancy playing out?"

"Well, the first thing is, I have to see the file on the Fuentes case. Tito can fill me in on whatever he's done since the day of. Then you'll have to call the sheriff and get me into the Calderón file and clear Matt Finnegan to talk with me."

"Oh, I'm really going to enjoy *that* conversation." Oliphant held his hand up to his head in the phone-call gesture. "Say, Frank? I got Calderón's kid here, we'd sort of like you to help him track down his daddy's killer. No, he's not a cop, he's a cook, but we here at the Miami PD always like to help out anyone on a personal vendetta. . . ."

Paz inclined his head and smiled. "I know you'd be more subtle than that, Doug."

"The answer is still no."

"That's funny because the two of you were just a while ago all over my ass asking for help and now I want to go full-time on the thing and what do I get? Stonewall. Whereas, if I can speak without offense, neither of these investigations is going anywhere."

"Who told you that?" asked Oliphant, with a bristle.

"Oh, you know—around. There are plenty of people in this town who make it their business to know what the cops are up to, and back when I was a famous police hero and the savior of the community, I got to know most of them."

"You've been talking to the press," said Oliphant. He made it an accusation, something like molesting a minor.

"Yeah. Look, the fact of the matter is I'm going to do this, and I'd like to work with you guys and not against you. If not, there are other investigative resources in the city. What you don't want and what the sheriff doesn't want is to read all about how I found this guy while you all were standing around looking into the middle distance."

There was the usual staring contest after this remark, which Paz let the Major win. Who then remarked, "You know, I always thought you were a modest kind of guy, Jimmy. Unless being a cook has vastly increased your criminological skills. Or unless you know something you're not telling us, in which case you'd be obstructing an investigation, which you might recall is a felony in this state."

Paz nodded and grinned. "Okay, I threatened you and you threatened me back and we're even, so could we chuck this horseshit and get off the dime here? Am I blowing my trumpet a little? Yeah, guilty. But let's review for a second—you got two rich white Cuban guys ripped to shreds, you got claw marks, you got jaguar tracks, you don't have a lead that's worth a shit, except for some literal shit, and you got cannibalism, or something-ibalism. It adds up to weird and uncanny, and it so happens that when it comes to weird and uncanny in the Greater Miami Metropolitan area, I am The Man. And cross my heart and hope to die, I don't know anything about these cases that every newsie in town doesn't know already. Nothing against Tito here or your guys or Finnegan, but you know and I know that there is such a thing as instinct and flair. There is stuff that I'll catch that other guys won't, not because I'm a great genius or anything, but there isn't a lot of experience around town with off-the-wall cases like these, and I got most of it."

Oliphant fiddled with his coffee cup, seeming to be fascinated by the information on it, which was FOURTH ANNUAL CONFERENCE ON CHILD PORNOGRAPHY, PHILADELPHIA 2001. It was a gesture familiar to Paz. The man was doubtful but he was about to roll right.

"That would be the consultancy, then, expert on weird and uncanny criminal behavior?"

"That's us," said Paz. "No job too small."

Oliphant said, "I'll think of something more bureaucratic

after I take a Gelusil." He turned to Morales. "Detective Morales. Show this guy the files and fill him in. I'll call Sheriff McKay and call in some chips and I'll let you know when it's clear to go over to their shop. Meanwhile, I expect you to stay close to Mr. Paz at all times as he consults. I expect you to cup his scrotum in your hands as he consults. I expect you to be there when he awakes and to tuck him into bed at night. You're off of all other cases. Am I making myself clear?"

"Yes, sir," said Morales, straightening a little in his chair.

"And you're clear, too, Jimmy? Straight pool, use our playbook, and no leaking to your slimeball pals up there by the bay."

"Yes, sir," said Paz. "But could you explain to Detective Morales that the part about my scrotum was just a figure of speech?"

"Get the fuck out of my office, the both of you," said Oliphant in a reasonably friendly manner, considering the circumstances.

The Hurtado organization had rented a whole floor of a condominium on Fisher Island, convenient to the homes of the two surviving Consuelistas. Hurtado and El Silencio had one apartment to themselves and the dozen or so gangsters he had brought along shared the others. They had an adequate number of cars and a couple of fast boats. The only thing they lacked was a target. They watched; nothing happened. Hurtado had limited patience. This operation was important, to be sure, but not important enough to risk being out of Cali for an extended time. Therefore, after some days of stewing, Hurtado sent his enforcer out with Prudencio Martínez and a couple of boys to see what he could find.

Hurtado was enjoying a late-afternoon drink poolside at the condo when the shadow of El Silencio fell across him.

"Anything?" he asked.

"Everything," said El Silencio. He pulled up a lounger and looked at the girl in the thong bikini who was keeping his employer company. The girl went away without a word.

Leaning close so that Hurtado could catch his whisper, he elaborated. "The kid in the painted van is the same kid who was in Fuentes's office. Fuentes's secretary remembered his hair. Also he had a shirt with the same sign that was all over the van. Martínez described it and she said she remembered."

Hurtado said, "It seems a little too easy. You know, Ramon, people remember things that didn't happen sometimes when you talk to them. It's part of your charm."

El Silencio shrugged. "I didn't touch her. She talked to him."

"Fine. So what does that get us? Who are these people and where do we find them?"

In answer, El Silencio passed his boss a small brochure.

"What's this?"

"We joined the Florida Audubon Society. A hundred-dollar contribution, the woman wouldn't shut up. There's a list of local nature clubs on the back. With the logos. I marked the one that the boys spotted on that VW van."

Hurtado flipped the brochure over. "Forest Planet Alliance? What is this, environmentalists?"

"That's what it looks like, but who knows what they really are? There's something else. Look at this." He handed Hurtado a color photograph of a young woman with blond-streaked hair leaving the doorway of Felipe Ibanez's mansion and said, "We've been taking pictures of everyone who goes in and out of both houses. This is Ibanez's granddaughter, a woman named Evangelista Vargos. You see her shirt?"

"That's interesting. Another connection, the girl belongs to the same group. And . . . ?"

"Ibanez wants to knock off his partners. He knows this organization from his granddaughter—maybe he even set it up. The bitch is some kind of spy, say. He figures we'll look into these killings, we'll think maybe someone is trying to get a piece of the Puxto deal, someone from home, but this way he can lay it off on these Americans. The environmentalists are all of a sudden killing people who piss them off."

Hurtado shook his head. "That doesn't explain the Indian,

though. And these American kids, I can't see them doing these kinds of things to Fuentes and Calderón, not to mention getting past our boys and taking out Rafael. And Ibanez or whoever would know we'd never go for the idea that this came out of some nature lover club. No, what I think is that Ibanez brought a bunch of tough *Indios* up from somewhere as muscle and he's just parking them with these American *pendejos*. Americans love the fucking *Indios*, and why should they make a connection? So he gets cover and a team of killers at the same time. That has to be it."

"He must think we're stupid," said the other. "So . . . we take them out? I mean Ibanez and the girl."

"No, there's plenty of time for that. And we need Ibanez to run the timber and transport operations. For the time being. What we need to do is find those *Indios*. Take some people and check out this"—he consulted the card—"Forest Planet Alliance. See what they have, who's associated, and so on. Low-key, Ramon. I don't want blood on the ceiling yet, understand? Speaking of that, did you get that garage we talked about?"

"Yeah. No problem. It's south of here, off the highway, very quiet."

"Good man. And the machinery is there? If we need it."

El Silencio nodded, rose from his chair and started to leave. "And Ramon?" Hurtado added, "Send the girl back."

**H**ere's the file," said Morales, dropping two heavy cardboard folders with a thump on his desk in the homicide squad bay. "Knock yourself out."

"You're pissed at me, right?" said Paz, catching the other man's tone.

"At the prima donna act, yeah. I come to you like a pal, I ask for help, and I get shit, and now you set up this . . . situation, where I got my boss's boss with his nose up my ass, and I got no fucking idea where you're going with this thing. And it would've been nice if I'd fucking *known* about you and Calderón beforehand, instead of looking like a

complete and total asshole in there. I mean, I was your fucking *partner.* . . ."

"Right, and I'm sorry. I apologize. And the reason I
changed my mind is because when Calderón got it, it became a family thing. You don't think I was blindsided, too?
You're a Cuban, you know how it works."

"Right, and if my father got whacked, I would be the absolutely last person allowed on the case. But exceptions get
made for Jimmy Paz."

"That's right, Tito. They do. Meanwhile, I am a fucking
supernumerary mugwump on this case and when it clears,
you and you alone will pick up the glory."

"Assuming it clears," said Morales, trying to keep a grin
from forming. "A supernumerary mugwump, huh? You're a
piece of work, Paz."

"I love you, too," said Paz. "Let me read this shit, okay? It
doesn't look like it'll take that long."

Nor did it. Paz already knew the broad outlines on the
Fuentes killing, but it was useful to study the forensic reports and the actual photographs taken at the scene. And
there were details Morales had not shared when he'd discussed the case in Paz's restaurant the previous month. They
had found claw marks on the wooden railing of the balcony
from which Fuentes had been hurled. They had calculated
the weight of whatever had made the paw marks in Fuentes's
garden—a little over 453 pounds, and this was a puzzle.
There was a report from the Metrozoo, from a Dr. Morita,
attesting that although the cast of the paw print shown to him
was undoubtedly that of *Panthera onca,* it was nearly 50 percent too large, nor had a jaguar of such a size ever been
recorded by science: the largest males rarely topped 300
pounds. Dr. M. expressed keen interest in studying the beast
should they ever secure it. I bet, thought Paz as he read this
and turned to the interviews with the staff at the Consuela
Company offices—Fuentes's secretary, Elvira Tuero, and
the three building security men. The police had constructed
Identi-Kit likenesses of both men. One was a young kid,

good-looking in a wispy way, with a scraggily beard and a nest of blond dreadlocks. The other was the famous Indian.

Paz studied this one rather more closely. Identi-Kit photographs all have a certain sameness about them and serve mainly to ensure that the cops don't pick up someone of a different sex or race from that of the suspect, but this one caused a little chill in Paz's belly. Like many detectives, Paz was extremely good on faces. He could summon up a fair picture of nearly everyone he had ever met, and while at the police academy had spent a good deal of time with the Identi-Kit reproducing faces from brief looks at photos of people on the faculty. He could do movie stars, too, to the amazement of staff and students both. The kit had recorded a man of uncertain age, but no longer young, with the broad mouth, high cheekbones, dark eyes, and bowl hairdo of a Central or South American Indian.

What caused the chill was Paz's certain knowledge that he had seen this particular Central or South American Indian before. It annoyed him exceedingly that he could not immediately determine where, but this he put down to rustiness. One item he had expected was missing. Although the witnesses had all stated that the young white male had been wearing a T-shirt with a logo on it, no one had tried to reconstruct it or find out what it represented.

Morales returned, carrying a couple of paper cups of Cuban coffee, and said, "Oliphant said it's okay to see Finnegan."

"Great. What about this logo on the white kid's shirt?"

"What about it? Kids wear all kinds of shit on their T-shirts—rock bands, concert tours, college teams. . . ."

"True, but according to the secretary, this office invasion they pulled was a political action about the environment. The guy's in an organization, it stands to reason he's going to wear his organization's logo, right? This Tuero woman, the secretary, said he was yelling about something called"— Paz leafed through a report—"the Puxto, whatever that is."

"It's like a game preserve in Colombia. The kid thought Consuela was going to cut it down."

"Are they?"

"Not according to Felipe Ibanez and Cayo Garza. And your father. They got nothing going on down there. They said."

"That's not in the file. Or did I miss something?"

"It's a lead that didn't pan." Morales caught Paz's dark look and said, "I should have put it in the file, I know, I know, but it just didn't figure that some tree hugger would chop a man up for some, I don't know, failure of conservation. It didn't fit."

"You thought it was a coincidence that Fuentes had a screaming fight in his office the day before he got killed?"

"Since Calderón got it, I do," said Morales, somewhat more aggressively. Paz realized that the man did not like being cross-examined by a civilian at his own desk, never mind that the civilian had once been a cop who'd got him into the detectives in the first place. Unfortunately, there was no help for this; if Morales had screwed up, and he had, he would just have to take his lumps.

Paz drank some of his coffee. "This is the Colombian gangster theory?"

"Where did you hear about it?"

"My sister. Finnegan told her, and somebody over in the county must have leaked it because Doris Taylor knew about it, too. What's the basis?"

"Well, it's obvious. Two identical killings of people associated with business in Colombia. When we just had Fuentes, it could have been anything, a cult, a random maniac. Weird and uncanny. With two, there's a connection, plus the vandalization and jaguar shit incidents at all four of the Consuela principals' houses. Someone is saying, you fucked with us and now you're going to die. And the Colombians like to get fancy, it's well known."

"Yeah, I heard. So what I'm picking up here, Tito, is you think this is a lot simpler than what Oliphant thinks, that all the weirdness is like camouflage for a piece of *colombianismo*."

"That's how it's looking. And that's how it's going to look up at the county."

"I assume there's people watching the other two guys, Garza and Ibanez."

"Right. They live in the Beach, so the county's covering that."

"Okay, I'm done here. Let's go over and see what Metro has to say for itself."

They drove over in Morales's unmarked Chevrolet, with Paz in the passenger seat.

"Just like old times," Paz remarked.

"Not really," said Morales, and they drove the rest of the way in morose silence.

Finnegan, as predicted, was not happy to see them, nor was Ramirez, his partner. The four men sat in a windowless interrogation room in the sheriff's headquarters in Doral, northwest of the city of Miami, a large modern building that looked like an airport terminal, except not as cozy. Finnegan dispensed with the small talk, saying, "Let me make a couple of things clear. I've been ordered to cooperate and I'm cooperating." He indicated a pile of folders and a large cardboard carton on the table. "There's the file on the Calderón killing. I understand he was your father."

"That's right," said Paz.

"Well, it's against county policy for an investigator to work on a case where a member of his immediate family is the victim. I don't understand what made the sheriff go along with this horseshit."

"Just covering his ass, I guess," said Paz politely. "I know you're busy and we'll try not to take up a lot of your time."

"I'm sorry for your loss," said Ramirez, not sounding the least bit sorry.

Paz gave him the kind of look you give a farting drunk and turned back to Finnegan. "It'll take me a couple of hours to go through this stuff. I'd like to see both of you after I'm done."

"If we're free," said Finnegan. The two county detectives got up and went out of the room. Ramirez was singing "That Old Black Magic" as he left.

"You read this stuff yet, Tito?"

"No, but Finnegan briefed me on what they had."

"Yeah, the county doesn't love it when we get involved with them on account of they're so professional and we're so corrupt."

"*I'm* so corrupt," Morales corrected.

"My mistake. Why don't you take advantage of this special situation and read this, too. I bet there's all kinds of shit in here he didn't tell you about."

The two men read quietly together after that. Paz wrote notes to himself in a pocket notebook. Morales just read. Paz noted that Morales was a quicker reader, or perhaps just less thorough.

"What do you think?" Paz asked when they were both done.

"It's consistent with the theory that this is a Colombian mob thing."

"Anything is consistent with any theory if you pick and choose your evidence right. But for the sake of argument, let's say you're right. Why the stuff with the jaguar?"

Morales shrugged and made a dismissive gesture. "Hey, we don't know dick about these people. Maybe it's a trademark. Some gangs cut the throat and pull the tongue through the hole, some gangs cut the guy's pecker off and stick it in his mouth. This gang chops them up and takes body parts, makes it look like they've been killed by a jaguar. I mean they're wack-job Colombians, who the fuck can tell why they do anything?"

"Oh, so you think there's no actual jaguar?"

"Not really. They could've made those tracks with a stick and a cast of a jaguar foot."

"And the same with the claw marks."

"Right."

"And the damage to the vics was done with some kind of blade."

"Could have been, but—"

"And the same with jumping up fifteen feet into Calderón's window, and then jumping over a ten-foot hedge after he did the job."

"Maybe the guy's a pro, he's got mountaineer training."

"That's good, Tito, a mountaineering Colombian pseudo-jaguar assassin. Who, armed only with some kind of blade, scales a fifteen-foot blank wall, opens a window catch while hanging on to this blank wall, takes out Calderón, who's armed and expecting trouble, takes out a Colombian *chutero*, who's got a weapon out and gets off at least one shot, escapes from a shitload of other similarly armed *chuteros*, and nobody catches sight of him, because there was no more gunplay that night, even though your usual person of that type is inclined to expend many rounds with small provocation. Sounds like more of a ninja mountaineering Colombian pseudo-jaguar assassin, if you ask me. On the other hand, we do know two important things about him."

"What?"

"Well, one, he leaves fingerprints. The county picked up a nice set off the iron gate at the house next door, where the guy escaped. No matches with anyone they could find, but never mind that. The guy pulls off the caper of the year but forgets about wearing gloves. Thus a *sloppy* ninja mountaineering Colombian pseudo-jaguar assassin."

"Okay, so what's *your* theory?"

"You're not going to ask me what the other thing is?"

Morales took a deep breath. "You know, Jimmy, until just now I don't think I ever got why every fucking detective in the Miami PD hated your guts."

"And now you can join the crowd," said Paz coolly. But he had to reflect on his recent observation that he had spent over two hours in a squad bay among men he had worked with for over ten years and not one had acknowledged his presence with a word or even a friendly nod. So he added, "I'm sorry, Tito. I'm a wiseass. I admit it. But those two bozos just now browned me off and I'm taking it out on you."

"You're forgiven," said Morales, "and now I'm going to play the sucker: what was the other thing?"

"It was that the county lab did the same analysis on their paw print that you all did on the one at the Fuentes scene, to calculate the weight of whatever made it. And they got a figure within a pound of the first one, four hundred fifty-three point two pounds. That speaks seriously against your model-paw-on-a-stick theory."

"Why? They could've had two guys stepping on a plate or something."

"Oh, now it's two guys, two huge fucking guys that nobody saw? I know, they *threw* the sloppy ninja pseudo-jaguar assassin through the window and over the hedge and then they just melted away."

"So what're you saying, we're back to the trained cat?"

"No, I'm baffled, too."

Morales raised his eyes to heaven and crossed himself. "Oh, thank you, Jesus, I'm not a total moron."

"Fuck!" said Paz. "I hate this shit!"

"What?"

"There's other stuff, Tito, and I'm going to tell you and I want it to stay between the two of us. Agreed?"

"Sure. What is it?"

"Okay, starting about a month ago, me and Amelia have been having dreams almost every night about a big spotted cat, starting about the time of the Fuentes murder, but before you came to see me. I think Lola's been having the same kind of dreams, but she won't say anything about it to me. But she's a wreck, not sleeping, popping all kinds of pills. Also, I went to my mother's santero and he threw Ifa for Amelia. You know what that is?"

"Sure, Santería fortune-telling."

"Right, and he got all upset and said Amelia was in danger from some kind of beast, a carnivore like a lion. And then I gave her my *enkangue* and her dreams stopped, but mine haven't and Lola's probably. . . ." and then Paz stopped talking and stared at nothing for a long moment, and then banged his hand down hard on the table.

"Damn!" he cried and grabbed a file folder, riffling through it until he found the county's sketch of the mysterious Indian. "I've seen this guy. I took Amelia to Matheson and he was standing in a little Styrofoam skiff talking to her. He couldn't've been more than ten feet away, and when he saw me, he scooted off in a big hurry."

Morales was staring at him with a disbelieving, sickly grin on his face. "Jimmy, ah, what's your daughter and dreams got to do with two murders and a bunch of Colombians?"

"I don't know. Look, Tito, bear with me here. You weren't on the force when the Voodoo Killer thing went down, but believe me, it wasn't what you think. We covered up a lot of it, or I did, I concocted a plausible story about drugs and cults, but it wasn't like that. It was deeply weird. Mind-bendingly weird. And this is another one."

"Uh-huh. And we're going to go in there and explain this to Finnegan?"

"No, forget Finnegan. He's fucking around with us, anyway. This file's not complete."

"It's not?"

"No. They've got a surveillance going on Garza and Ibanez, right? But there's nothing here on any such surveillance, no telephoto shots, no phone taps, which means they think they've got something hot and they're not going to share it with us. I expect both houses are crawling with suspicious-looking Latin-American gentlemen."

"But you said it wasn't Colombians . . ."

"No, I said the killings weren't mob hits. The Consuela people are in deep with some kind of Colombian mob. Victoria Calderón told me that much. But these guys are trying to *protect* the Cubans. They got nothing to do with killing them. And the idea that there's a *rival* gang doing it is just stupid: it puts us back with our sloppy ninja pseudo-jaguar, who can't exist. No, it's connected with this Indian. And our one lead to this Indian is through Mr. Dreadlocks here, and our one lead to him is through his T-shirt. We need to go see this secretary again."

They left the sheriff, after smearing a thin coat of bullshit on Finnegan and Ramirez, and while they were in the car, Paz called Victoria Calderón, and learned that the Consuela

Holdings office was temporarily closed. Ms. Tuero, the secretary, was on leave at home until the surviving principals could decide how to proceed with this aspect of their affairs.

"How're you doing so far?" asked Victoria after conveying this information, as well as the woman's address and phone number.

"Pretty good. Just going through the police files. Like you said, they're thinking Colombians."

"And what're you thinking, Jimmy?"

"Not Colombians. Or not only. And not on the phone. How do you like being the big boss?"

"I'd like it better if I knew what was really going on. Dad kept a lot of stuff in his head, and what wasn't in his head was in Clemente's."

"Who is . . . ?"

"Oh, Uncle Oscar, the old family retainer. I'm going to have to get rid of him or ease him out, and it's going to make a mess, but he still treats me like he did when he was sneaking me candy, age six. The books make no sense. Money coming in and out with no paper attached, purchase invoices for stuff I never heard of, I mean big expenditures: three Daewoo grapplers for twenty-two grand a pop, thirty grand for a Hydro Ax feller-buncher, all kinds of other timber industry machines . . ."

"You're in the timber business."

"So it seems, but we're not in the timber business as far as I know. We buy a lot of construction equipment, obviously, but all this other stuff is stuck in among the legitimate purchases. I mean, what's a boring machine?"

"The opposite of an interesting machine?"

She laughed, a little harder than the remark warranted. "Oh, Christ, Jimmy, am I glad I found you! Do you realize I have no one I can talk to about this stuff?"

"Hey, what's family for?"

"You laugh, but I mean it. Why did we buy a fifty-grand machine for making lots of holes in wood? I mean, it's a furniture plant item. We're all of a sudden in the furniture business, too? Also, it's not just the crazy expenditures I worry about, it's the income. There are huge payments, I mean seven-figure entries, without any invoicing to show what we got paid for."

"Another topic not to discuss on the phone," said Paz.

Elvira Tuero lived in a modest apartment in a Souesera duplex, on a street familiar to Paz. It was just around the block from his mother's ilé, which he took to be a good omen. They had called beforehand, and she had agreed to see them, somewhat reluctantly, it seemed to Paz. There was something frightened in her voice.

And in her face, too. Ms. Tuero was highly decorative, or had been: fashionable shoulder-length blond curls, helped out by chemicals, an attractive oval face, nicely plucked eyebrows over large dark eyes. She was wearing a loose white shirt, tight toreador pants (pink), and toeless gold slippers. Paz noted that her red nail polish needed fixing on both fingers and toes, and that there were unbecoming smudges under her eyes. She took them to the living room and sat them on a dark blue velvet couch, taking for herself an armchair covered in the same stuff, across from a coffee table in which beer coasters from many lands sat under glass.

"I don't know what I can tell you," she said. "I told the cops everything I could remember just after Mr. Fuentes died."

"Yes, but memory is funny," said Paz. "Sometimes we remember things after a while that we forgot right after the event. That's why the police sometimes reinterview after some time has gone by."

"Yeah, that's what those guys said."

"What guys?"

"A couple of men, day before yesterday. They said they were from the security firm working for Mr. Garza. They wanted to know about those people who came in the day before the, you know . . ."

"The murder, yes," said Paz. "And what did you tell them?"

"Well, one of them mostly wanted to know about the shirt the white guy was wearing, the logo on it."

"And did you recall what it was?"

"Not really, but then he started asking me was it this, was it that, and it kind of came back to me. To tell you the truth, I kind of wanted to get rid of him."

"Oh? Why was that?"

"He was creepy, you know. Like if I didn't answer right he would do something, or he wanted to do something mean. He sat too close, and stared, like I was lying. This was just one of them. The other guy asked the questions."

"These were regular American-type people?"

"No. We spoke in Spanish, but they weren't Cubans. Some kind of South American accent, but not Argentinean. I used to have a boyfriend from Buenos Aires. Not Mexican either. Venezuela, Colombia, like that."

"I see. And what did you recall about this logo?"

"No, like I said, the guy *knew* about the logo, he described it to me and he just wanted me to say if I saw it in the office that day. It was a black T-shirt, with a big globe on it, the earth like they show you from space, the blue marble. And around the rim of it were some kind of teeth, like a gear in a watch, but green. And three letters in white on the globe and some writing below it. But he didn't know what the letters were and neither did I. I hope this is the last time I have to go through this."

"I'm pretty sure it will be," said Paz. "Thank you for your time."

"Because I won't be in town. I'm going to stay with my sister up in Vero Beach. I don't want anything more to do with this stuff. Those guys, ever since they came by I've been having nightmares."

"**W**hat do you make of that, señor?" asked Paz when they were in the car again.

"Our Colombians are doing the same stuff we're doing."

"Not just that. They had another source for that logo, maybe something directly associated with the killings. They want whoever's doing the jaguar act to stop, and they're just figuring that the same organization that sent those guys to yell at Fuentes might have had something to do with killing him and Calderón. Very thorough, and it means they have information we don't. Also, and this doesn't go anywhere else, I just found out from my half sister that old Dad was running what looks to be a money Laundromat out of his construction business."

"The plot thickens," said Morales. "These guys were skimming, and the Colombians whacked them."

Paz shook his head vigorously. "No, no, try to follow me here, Tito, because it's important. The Colombians are involved, but not in the two murders. It's the Indian who's doing the murders. The Colombians are trying to nail the Indian."

"How can you know that?"

"I don't *know* it, Tito. It's my operating theory. It's part of my flair, why you guys wanted me involved. The Indian is part of the structure of weirdness, and Colombian mobsters are not. They're probably as confused as Finnegan."

"What? Jimmy, give me a break! You tossed out my ninja assassin, and now you tell me some little guy with a Three Stooges haircut got in there and did all that damage? How do you figure that?"

"If I tell you, you'll say I'm nuts."

"Tell me anyway."

"The little guy knows how to turn himself into a four-hundred-pound jaguar and back again."

Morales stared at Paz, laughed out loud, stared again when Paz didn't join in the laugh, saw something in Paz's eyes he had not seen before, something deeply disturbing, and said, "That's nuts."

"See? I told you you'd say that," said Paz with a laugh. "Relax, I'm just jerking your chain. But I had you for a second there, didn't I?"

"Fuck you, Paz," said Morales glumly. "So why are the bad guys after the Indian? And how did he do the murders? Or was that a joke, too?"

"I don't know how he did it yet, but that's the way it has to be. Tito, I have seen, with my own two eyes, a man with a certain kind of training walk away from a whole SWAT team and out of a locked police car containing two veteran police officers, me being one of them. This Indian could be that kind of guy, you understand what I'm telling you?"

"Deeply weird," said Morales.

"You got it, and the truth will emerge in its own good time. Meanwhile, we need to do two things right away. You have to go by the Florida Defenders of the Environment and find out what local group uses a logo like that and get whatever information they have on it, personnel, activities, location. And you have to drop me off at my mom's place. I need to talk to her."

"We're supposed to stick together, Jimmy."

"Yeah, but I'm with my mother," Paz replied. "How much trouble can I get into? Come on, Tito, we got to play catch-up. Those *chuteros* could wipe out that whole organization and then we'll never find the Indian."

Grumbling, Morales put the car in gear and headed toward Eighth Street and the restaurant. "They could take out the Indian, too," he said. "Then we could all go home."

"I don't think so, man. I don't think it's going to be so easy to take out the Indian, not for them and not for us. That's what I need to talk to my mom about."

# Fourteen

**O**n Sunday night Nigel Cooksey told Rupert Zenger that there were Colombian gangsters in town with an interest in the Forest Planet Alliance. By Monday afternoon Rupert was gone, off to an important conference in Bhutan about the mountain forests of that nation, taking Luna Ehrenhaft with him and leaving Scotty in charge of the property, and the name of his attorney with Cooksey.

"Gosh, that was fast, just like you said," observed Jenny at the gate of La Casita as the airport limo pulled away. "How come he took Luna?"

"Oh, Rupert needs a little entourage. And Luna, despite her bravado, has nearly as strong a sense of self-preservation as Rupert."

"You're kidding! Poor Scotty! No wonder he's been moping."

"Yes, but moping has always been part of Scotty's demeanor. I think Luna was growing tired of it. She has something of an instinct for the alpha male." He drew the gate closed and barred it. "He asked me to come as well, you know."

"Really? Why didn't you?"

"I prefer it here. Bhutan is utterly fascinating I'm sure, but I feel obliged to stay with my collections and . . . things. Nor am I particularly fearful of gangsters."

"Do you really think they'll come?"

"Oh, they're here already."

Jenny couldn't help a quick scan of the surroundings. "What do you mean, 'here already'?"

"Well, as you must know, Rupert's tower provides the only view of the road over all our foliage, and while I was up there last night discussing this and that with him I happened to notice a large black van cruising by, more slowly than the empty road would require, and then it came by again and stopped briefly. We're fortunate that there's no road verge wide enough to park such a machine on Ingraham across from this house, but in any case, the van returned about an hour ago and is now parked just beyond the curve of the road."

"Are you going to call the cops?"

"I think not. After all, what would we tell them? That an illegal alien bush Indian suspect in two murders intimated that, via mystic powers, he has sensed danger from a group of men innocently parked by the side of a public road? No, I believe we're on our own for the present. However, they're likely to wait until nightfall before making any attempt to interfere with us, and we are not without resources."

They walked back to Cooksey's rooms. Jenny felt somewhat stunned by these developments and silently wondered why Cooksey seemed so cheerful. Then she thought of something. "Oh, God, we should call Geli Vargos. They might go after her."

"I'm sure Miss Vargos knows more about it than we do."

"What do you mean, she knows?"

"I mean that your friend is the granddaughter of Felipe Ibanez, one of the principals of Consuela Holdings. Rupert told me last night."

"I don't understand. She was, like, *spying* on us?"

"Not at all. Rupert thinks it was something like guilt, a subject on which I believe he is by way of being an expert. Wealthy people who have grown rich from various forms of exploitation often have the urge to recover their self-respect through good works. Rupert, who as you may know was in

public relations for a large oil company, is one such, and
Geli Vargos seems to be another, although in her case it was
the family fortune that bore the curse."

"So she's still on our side."

"In a manner of speaking. I'm sure she still wishes us
well, but now that there is real danger afoot, I doubt if she'll
go out of her way to help us if it's to the detriment of her
family. Or so Rupert believes."

"He *knew* about this all along?"

"Oh, yes. He was quite upset when we all found out about
the Consuela company's plans for the Puxto from our little
friend. Geli gave quite a lot of money to the organization,
you know."

"But the point for all of us was to *save* the rain forest,"
Jenny cried. "How could he take money that came from cutting it down?"

"You'd have to ask Rupert that, and I'm sure you'd get a
good temporizing answer. In any case, we have little time
and we have to prepare this property to resist intrusion."

"How? By throwing grapefruits?"

"Not quite. Scotty has a shotgun and a full box of shells. I
think we can prepare some surprises for anyone creeping
about in the dark. We're in Scotty's workroom if you'd like
to join us."

"Yeah, but first I got to tell Kevin about all this," said
Jenny, and she hurried off.

Kevin was lying in bed with the headphones on. The stink
in the room made it clear that he had ignored Rupert's
clean-up-dope command. She obtained his attention by
yanking his cable and, after the usual snarling from him,
told her story, which he thought was hilarious, and he got in
some zingers about how he'd been right all along about that
Cuban bitch. She let this pass. When she told him about
Cooksey's plans and Scotty's shotgun he said, "Big deal. I
got a gun, too."

"No you don't."

He reached quickly under the mattress, yanked out a big

blued semiautomatic pistol, and waved it in her face. "Then what the fuck do you think this is? A pamphlet?"

"Where did you get it? And don't wave it around like that."

"Never mind where I got it. And fuck this pissy little operation anyway. I got something major going on." He hopped out of bed and struck action-hero poses with the gun, crouching, whirling, pointing it clutched in both hands. She stared at his antics and with a part of her mind registered that he had obviously never had a pistol in his hands before. Jenny herself had been raised among a population rich in guns of all kinds.

"What do you mean, major?"

"You'll read about it in the papers. Oh, I forgot, you can't read the papers."

She let this slide by. In fact, although she didn't read the papers, her reading had improved a good deal over the past months. "Kevin, you're so full of shit. Did you ever even shoot a gun like that?"

"Fuck you, yes! And you know, the best thing about pulling this thing off is after tonight I am gone from here, baby, and I won't have to listen to you putting me down anymore."

"What thing, Kevin? What are you pulling off?"

He grinned and stuck the pistol in the waistband of his cutoff jeans. "A disciplined revolutionary never discusses operations with outsiders."

"And probably doesn't smoke dope all the time either. What's the operation? This is something that skank Kearney thought up, isn't it?"

"He's not a skank," said Kevin, "and Kearney's not his real name."

"Kevin, I don't care what his name is. He's nuts. And besides, you can't go out anywhere now. Cooksey said there's a bunch of gangsters watching the place."

"Fuck Cooksey and fuck you. He's an old lady anyway. I'm going."

Jenny had another and stronger line of invective in her mouth, when she suddenly realized that she was not Kevin's mother, and that scenes like this had undoubtedly played out while he was at home, with no good outcome. So she walked out of the cottage without another word and started for the tin-roofed shed where Scotty kept his workshop. Halfway there she stopped, turned on her heel, and walked back to the little parking area, where she opened the engine compartment of the VW van and deftly removed and pocketed the distributor rotor. As she walked past the pond, she saw that the surface was dotted with leaf-fall. Scotty hadn't been skimming them lately. Nor, she recalled, had Rupert been keeping up with feeding offal to his piranhas. She paused to throw in a scoop of fish food from the big can placed there and watched the water boil as the population attacked the morsels. The piranha would have to wait. In fact, she found she didn't much care about them; let the sneaky bastards starve, she unecologically thought.

In the work shed she saw that Scotty was at his pipe cutter dropping short pieces from a length of two-inch irrigation pipe. Cooksey was mixing something in a washtub, a pink jellylike substance with a sweet stink.

She wrinkled her nose and asked, "What is that stuff?"

"A kind of napalm. Soap flakes and gasoline and a little diesel. Would you like to help?"

She nodded. Under his direction she began to disassemble twelve-gauge shotgun shells, placing the shot and the gunpowder into different containers and snipping out the primers with an aviation shears. Cooksey poured his mixture into bottles, which he stopped with rags. Then he began to construct small objects out of lawn mower throttle springs, strips of sheet metal, epoxy glue, and small nails. After she finished with the shells, she watched him work. It was obvious from the way his long brown fingers moved over the materials that he had done this kind of work before.

"What're you making?" she asked.

"Booby traps. Scotty, have you one of your pipes ready yet?"

Scotty handed him without comment a length of capped pipe with a small hole drilled through the center of the cap. Cooksey unscrewed the cap and glued a shotgun shell primer into the opening with quick-drying epoxy, and then, using the same adhesive, attached one of his springed constructs to the side of the pipe. He replaced the cap and locked the pipe into a table vise. He attached a long piece of flower wire to the device and handed the free end to Jenny. "Go over there and pull on this," he ordered.

She pulled, the catch snapped, and a nail came down on the primer, producing a satisfying small pop.

"Splendid," cried the Professor. "I see it's like riding a bicycle."

"Where did you learn how to do this kind of stuff?" she asked.

"Ah, as a youth I ran off to join the Royal Marines, over my mother's strenuous objection, I might add. I ended up in the Special Boat Service."

"Simply messing about in boats?"

"Yes, but at a very elevated level. They teach one how to mess about with this sort of thing as well. As I will now teach you."

Margarita Paz lived in a low-rise condo near Marti Park, a building old for Miami, and inhabited by respectable, elderly Cubans. She had once owned a house near her restaurant but had sold it a few years ago and moved here. This was vaguely attributed to Paz's lax progenitive abilities. Who needed a house when it was clear it would never be filled with grandchildren? Her condo was on the top floor, with a nice view of the park, and she had purchased it for cash, because it was the kind of building that no savings and loan in Miami would have financed for a black woman. Literal cash: she had seen the ad, determined over the phone (in Spanish) that it was still available, and had within the hour walked into the real estate office with a small suitcase from which she had extracted neat bricks of one hundred $100 bills, thirty-one in all. The white Cuban person behind the desk had grown somewhat whiter at this display; if a comic-book thought balloon had appeared over her head at the time, it would have contained the word *narcolista*. The papers got signed without delay.

Paz directed Morales into the small parking lot, observed that his mother's pale blue '95 Coupe de Ville was in its stall, and bid farewell to his supervisor-companion. He rang at the outer door. No answer. He used his key. At her apartment door he rang again with the same result, and after a brief wait, he let himself into the small foyer. He called out, "Mamí, it's me." Nothing. Now a little prickle of concern.

In the foyer, on a small wooden stand was a half-life-size clothed statue of a black woman holding a paler infant. The woman wore an elaborate silver crown, and there were silvered metal rays emanating from behind her gown of blue brocade, which was covered with silver embroidery depicting shells, fish, and other marine life. Below her feet tossed plaster sea waves, from which emerged a miniature steel anchor. When Paz was a little boy, this image had been a cheap framed poster; later, that had been replaced by a plaster statue, and then another more elaborate one, and finally this one, probably the most luxurious available image of La Virgen de Regla, aka Yemaya, the *orisha* of maternity and of the sea, to whom his mother was dedicated in Santería. As a little boy he'd imagined it was a representation of Mom and himself.

The living room, which he now entered, was furnished in pale pink velvet and mahogany, heavy, expensive pieces—a tall breakfront, a long couch, armchairs, a coffee table inlaid with a marine scene in pale woods. The lamps on the side table were plaster sculptures, whose pale silken shades were protected by clear plastic. Mrs. Paz, in a flowered blue robe, was lying on the couch like a corpse, one arm and one foot resting on the floor, a copy of *People en Español* fallen from her slack hand, reading glasses dangling from one ear. Her breath came in snorts and hisses.

Paz had not seen his mother asleep all that often, despite having lived in her house for eighteen years. In his mind she was always up and pushing, often pushing Paz as well, full of angry energy focused on never, ever, falling back into the nothing from which she had finally emerged. Here was the consequence: utter exhaustion. Paz was struck by a tender compassion and was wondering whether to tiptoe out and leave the poor woman in peace when she suddenly awoke. A lightning flash of fear appeared on her face when she knew that she was not alone, and then, when she observed who her visitor was, she quickly reassembled her normal stern mask. She made her glasses vanish, sat up, and said, "What?"

"What do you mean, 'what?' I'm your son, I'm visiting you on your day off."

"Do you bring Amelia?"

"No, she's still at school. Look, Mamí, the reason I came is I need your help."

"Money?"

"No, money's fine. This is a spiritual thing."

Eyebrows climbed on her dark face. "I'll make coffee," she said and left for the kitchen.

They sat there at the old, chipped enamel-topped table he recalled from their days of poverty, drinking her bitter brew, and he told her about the dreams, his and Amelia's, of the spotted beast, and about what he thought was happening to his wife, and how he had given the child the charm, the *enkangue* he had received from her years ago.

"That wasn't wise," she said when she heard that. "*Enkangue* are made for one person."

"I know that, but she was scared and anyway it seemed to have worked. She hasn't had hardly any nightmares since I gave it to her."

"You should have come to me."

"I *am* coming to you, Mamí. I need a set for the whole family. I thought, these dreams, and after that reading Amelia got . . . and now I'm looking at my . . . you know, Calderón's death, and there's some kind of big cat involved in that, too."

"Your father," she corrected.

"Honestly, I can't think of him that way. I mean he treated us like garbage his whole life."

"You he did. But not me, never."

"What do you mean? I thought he, you know . . . when you needed money for our first catering truck, he took advantage of you."

She fixed him with a glare. "Is that what you think, son of mine? That your mother is a whore to buy a catering truck?"

Paz felt blood rush to his cheeks, but he met her stare. "You had no choice," he said.

"You know nothing about it."

"Then *tell* me, for God's sake!"

She took a sip of coffee. "Ah, finally he asks, after nearly thirty years. All right, since you ask. Juan Calderón loved me and I loved him. He was a bad man and he loved in the manner of bad men, not like you love, but it was love all the same. He wanted me all the time, and I wanted him. Of course, it was impossible that it should go any further, but this we had, for seven months. You understand, it was something that was common in Cuba, the rich white man takes a black mistress to learn about passion before he marries whatever cold little white girl the parents have arranged. So I became pregnant, and therefore you must never think, my son, that you were not made in love, even in the love of a bad man. When I told him, he wanted to fly me to Puerto Rico so I could kill you, but I said no, and then he said, I will put you in a little apartment, you'll be available. This is how it's done, or was done where we both came from, a few years of comfort, he buys you some nice things, and then he finds another girl, a younger girl, and you go to work as a maid somewhere, and take care of your little *cabrón*. But I said no, I said I wanted a loan from him to start a business, and we fought, because always he wanted to control me. But in the end I was stronger and he gave me the money, and said he would never see me again and if I ever made a claim on him, or you did, he would make something bad happen to the both of us. So I didn't tell you about him, I made up a story, so you wouldn't approach him. But you did anyway. The *santos* made it part of your life. And that's also the reason I didn't raise you in Santería, may it not be held against me. I wanted you to be an American boy. I thought I could protect you with my prayers to the *santos,* and you would have a different kind of life, that you would escape from all this . . . the dark things. But Ifa has drawn out the thread of your fate in a different direction than I planned. And you know this, too, which is why you had Ifa cast for my grand-child and why you come to me now, although for your whole life you've thought that all of this was nonsense."

"I'm still not sure I buy the whole thing—" he began, but she made a dismissive gesture of her hand and interrupted, "Yes, yes, you believe in your heart, because the *orishas* have shown you things, things not even I have seen."

She drained her coffee down to the dregs, and swirled these around in the cup, a habit of hers. Sometimes things were re-vealed there, but apparently not now. She rose from the table. "I'll get dressed and we'll go see Julia at the *botánica*."

Paz just sat there mute, as if he had taken a blow to the head. She paused at the door and added, "I'm sorry, Iago. I was wrong. I tried to control things instead of handing everything over to the *santos*. But you know, this is how I am, like a mule."

Paz tried to recall if his mother had ever apologized to him about anything and came up blank. This was nearly as disturbing as the revelation about his father.

The shop had no name. It was jammed between a pharmacy and a shoe place in a strip mall on West Flagler near the county auditorium, a twelve-foot frontage with one dusty window that announced BOTÁNICA in peeling gilt letters. Be-hind the window stood a row of dark-skinned plaster *santos* lined up like people waiting for a bus back to heaven: St. Lazarus, who was Babaluaye, curer of ills; the Virgen de Caridad, who was Oshun, the Venus of Cuban Africa; St. Pe-ter, who was Ogun, lord of iron and anger; St. Anthony of Padua, who was Eleggua, the trickster, guardian of the ways; and Yemaya, walking on her plaster seas. Above these a slack piece of wire had been draped, from which hung cello-phane packets of herbs and powders.

Inside it was dim and dusty, heavy with oversweet perfume. Only a narrow way led to the counter in the rear, so crowded was the place with statues and crates, and slapdash shelves holding the physical paraphernalia of the religion: strung cowries, toy weapons of cheap metal, fly whisks, framed pictures of the saints; and cans of purifying sprays, glass jars of dried leaves, crucifixes, bolts of heavy cloth for making costumes for the ceremonies, dream books; and *soperas,* the containers used to hold the holy items appropriate to the various spirits, and a pile of concrete cones, each embedded with three cowry shells to make a crude face, the sign of Eleggua.

The woman behind the counter was over seventy, Paz estimated, with a face as dark, slick, and worn as the seat of an old saddle; her head was wrapped in a cloth of pink African print cotton. When she saw who it was, she smiled, showing her four remaining teeth, put aside her newspaper and came from around the counter to greet them. A warm embrace for Mrs. Paz, and a more ritualized one for her son; the woman smelled of some musky spice.

Chairs were swept clean and set out, chatting commenced. Most of it was about the workings of the various Santería congregations in Miami, and most of the people mentioned were strangers to Paz, except for the people who were denizens of the spirit world. Paz knew those, at least. He listened silently, feeling like a fool, feeling about twelve in the presence of adult conversation. He was grateful that sociability did not seem to be required of him, though, because the premises upon which he had based his whole life had just been overthrown and he was not in the mood to chatter.

After a little over half an hour this part of the visit expired. A brief silence, and Mrs. Paz poked him and said, "Give Julia the things from Lola and Amelia." Paz had not mentioned these items to his mother, but of course, she knew that he knew that *enkangue* could not be made without them. He passed the envelopes to Julia, who made some gesture to his mother, and then both women vanished into the back room of the shop.

Mumbles floated out from there, not all in the Spanish

language. Paz gave up eavesdropping and amused himself
with dream books. These were arranged in convenient al-
phabetical order, by subject. If you dreamt of a judge it
meant you would overcome your enemy and also that you'd
hit on a 28, 50, 70 bet at bolita, the Cuban lottery. He looked
up *jaguar* but none of the dream books covered that one. He
grew bored with this and explored the shop. He knew what a
lot of it meant, but there were also any number of substances
and objects he couldn't identify. There was a basket of toy
tools made of pot metal, and a selection of bow-and-arrow
sets, and little plaster animals with arrows stuck in them. He
picked up a bow and drew it. To his surprise, it was a real
bow, made of some dark, oily wood. Pathetic, came the
thought, miserable poor people desperate to change their
luck. Ridiculous, really. What was he doing here, messing
with this crap? He tossed the bow back into its bin.

Irritable now, he checked his watch. Two thirty-five and
he had to be at the school to pick up Amelia at three. He
could be a little late, but then he would have to endure a lecture from Perfect Miss Milliken about being a model of reli-
ability for the children. Sorry, Miss M., he imagined himself
saying, my family is cursed and I had to drop by the
*botánica* for some antihex medicine. She'd be on the phone
to Child Protective Services within minutes. Or to the
mother, thinking of whom brought the recollection that Lola
got off early Mondays. He'd call her, make something up
about the murder case, hot on the trail, he hated to lie, but
still it was, if not really an emergency, a truly unavoidable
delay. Not that he would a thousand times rather explain all
this to Miss Milliken than to Lola.

He pulled out his cell phone and popped a speed-dial button. But the woman at the ER nurses' station said that Dr.
Wise had gone home sick. What was it? She didn't know,
and here he heard a little hesitancy, something not quite
right. Was it serious? This is her husband. Sorry, Mr. Wise,
she had no information on that. He broke the connection and
dialed home. Five rings and Amelia's little voice saying they
couldn't come to the phone right now could you leave a . . .

He called again with the same result and then dialed Lola's cell phone, which he knew was like one of her breasts, always in reach and always warm. He got her answering service. Now in something close to panic, he skirted the counter and went into the back room. The two women were at a table, and both looked up, startled, as he entered. He explained the situation. The two exchanged an unreadable look.

"We're almost done," his mother said. "Go and wait. We'll drive over to the school."

Paz walked out without a word and called Tito Morales, and got another answering service. No one wanted to talk to him today. He was about to call for a cab when Mrs. Paz and Julia emerged, the former holding a small brown paper bag.

"We can go now," she said. "Everything will be all right."

"Let me drive," he said. And he did, with reckless speed.

A melia is up in the tree, in violation of strict orders not to climb higher than Miss Milliken can reach. Normally she is an obedient child, but this thing in the tree seems outside of normal constraints, like being in a dream. As soon as she reaches the hammock, Moie continues the story where he left off, as if she has not been away for more than a minute.

"So when Rain saw that Caiman would eat the whole world, she went to Sky and mated with him and out of her came Jaguar. She said to him, Jaguar, you are chief of all the beasts now. You must stop Caiman before he eats the whole world that our family has made. So Jaguar attacked Caiman and they fought for many hands of years. But Caiman was too strong. With his mighty tail Caiman threw Jaguar high into the air, up to the moon, so that he crashed into it. This is why you still see his face on the moon. When Jaguar fell back to earth he landed on a field of barren rock, with no food to eat. He was starving. Then came the Hninxa, and she said to him, Jaguar, eat my flesh. I will make you strong enough so that you can defeat Caiman, so he will not eat the whole world. So Jaguar ate the Hninxa . . ."

"What's a Hninxa?" asks Amelia.

"No one knows," says Moie. "There are no animals like that anymore. But this is what we call the little girls we give to Jaguar, so that Caiman does not come back and eat the world again. Now, Jaguar was strengthened so much by the flesh of the Hninxa that he defeated Caiman. He broke off Caiman's long legs, so that he could not crawl far from River, and he broke off half of his tail, and from this he made all the fishes. He said: Caiman, you will not run on the land now, but crawl and eat only the fish I have made from your tail. And Caiman went to the water. But his spirit flew out into the world and became many hands of demons. Now, these demons are still alive and still wish to eat the world. And Jaguar thought, I will make First Man, and he and his people will help me rule the beasts, and if Caiman attacks me again I will have strong allies. So he did. Now it is many hands of years after that time, as many hands as the leaves in the forest, and the demons of Caiman's spirit are in the *wai'ichuranan,* and they want to eat the world again. So Jaguar called me and said, Moie, take me to Miami America so I can fight Caiman as I did long ago. So I came. And Jaguar said also, I will send to you a *hninxa* of the *wai'ichuranan* and you will give her to me to eat, and then I will have strength over the *wai'ichuranan* demons. That is why I am in this tree."

"Did Jaguar send you a . . . one of those little girls yet?"

"Yes."

"Who is it?"

"It is you," says Moie, and he smiles, showing his sharpened teeth.

Amelia stares at him, then giggles. "That was a good story," she says. "Would you like to hear a story?"

"Yes, I would."

But before she is more than halfway through *The Little Mermaid* she hears shouting from below, Miss Milliken's voice and her father's voice.

"I have to go," she says.

"Wait," says Moie, and dipping his finger into a small clay pot, he presses a spot of ointment to the back of her neck. It feels warm on her neck for a moment. She scampers down from limb to limb and drops like a warm mango into her father's arms.

After that she has to endure a stern lecture from the teacher, which her father supports. It is dangerous to climb into the tree. Does she want Miss Milliken to keep her indoors while the other children played? She does not. Well, then.

As parent and child walk away, Paz asks, "What were you doing up there, baby?"

"Nothing. Eating Fritos and watching the bugs. Did you have imaginary friends when you were a kid?"

"Probably, but I don't remember."

"I think it's very babyish. I have a friend named Moie who's half imaginary and half not imaginary."

"Really? Like Mary Poppins?"

They have been strolling across the lawn to the parking lot, but now she stops short and looks at him severely, a look he has seen any number of times on her mother's face. But this fades and is replaced by one more confused. "I forgot what I was going to say."

"That happens to me all the time. Was it something about your imaginary friend?"

She shrugs. Then the animation returns to her face and she asks, "If God said you should kill me with a big knife, would you?"

"Why do you ask?"

"We had Bible study. They used to kill little boys and girls. It's a sacrifice. I think Abraham was mean to sacrifice his little boy just 'cause God said."

"But he didn't sacrifice him."

"No, but he was going to. I think God was mean, too."

"It's just a story, honey. Abraham had faith that God wouldn't really make him do anything bad to his little boy."

Again that dreamy expression crosses her face and clears.

"Isaac. There's a Isaac in my class. He brought his Game

Boy to school and Miss Milliken took it away and gave it back later."

After a short pause she asks, "Anyway, would you?"

"No," replies Paz without thought.

"Even if God would be mad at you?"

"Let him be. I still wouldn't."

"People who let themselves get sacrificed are martyrs, did you know that? And they get to be angels and fly around in heaven. Oh, look there's Abuela!"

"*Abuela!*" she cries and runs across to the car and hoists herself through the window into her grandmother's lap. The two chatter happily in Spanish for the whole drive to South Miami while Paz tries several times to get his wife to answer her cell phone, and grows increasingly worried.

A t the house, after Mrs. Paz departed in her Cadillac, Paz and his daughter went around the back, and Paz noted that Lola's bike was not in its place. She must have taken a cab home, which did not bode well at all. He paused before the door and said, "Look, kiddo, your mom's a little sick and I want you to try and be real quiet, okay?"

"Okay. What's wrong with her?"

"I don't know. Probably a little flu or something. Just watch cartoons for now, and later you can help me make our dinner."

"I could make it myself."

"I'm sure," he said and opened the door.

"What's in the bag, Daddy?" the child asked.

"Nothing, just some stuff Abuela gave me."

"*Torticas?*" Hopefully.

"No, just . . . a kind of medicine for Mommy. I'm going to go in now and see how she is. Go change out of your school clothes now."

The child skipped off to her room and Paz entered his own bedroom. His wife was a mound on the bed under a light throw. He sat carefully on the bed, and as he did, he slipped the *enkangue* made with her hair under the mattress. She stirred and groaned.

He tugged the blanket off her face and felt her forehead. It was clammy but without fever. She blinked at him with red and swollen eyes.

"How're you doing, babe? Not so hot?"

"They sent me home," she croaked.

"Well, yeah. You're sick. It's a hospital."

"I'm not sick. I had a . . . a breakdown."

"A what?"

"I . . . they called me in, we had a kid, a drug OD, comatose. There was a traffic accident, a van, half a dozen seniors all hurt and the ER was jammed. And I couldn't think what to do. I was the only spare M.D. and they were all staring at me and I went blank. I couldn't . . . I told them to . . . I made the wrong call, and they all stared at me, the nurses, because they knew it was wrong and I started screaming at them and . . . I can't remember it all, I was . . . hysterical, and they got Kemmelman and he grabbed me and threw me into the doctors' dressing room. And later I went home, I sneaked away and took a cab and I have to sleep, Jimmy, I need to sleep and I can't. I take pills, I can't remember all the pills I took and I'm a doc. I'm a doc but I can't sleep. Why can't I sleep, Jimmy? I'm so tired and I can't sleep."

"You have bad dreams."

"Sixty milligrams of flurazepam and I can't sleep," she said. Her voice had become high and soft, like a little girl's.

"You have to get off those pills, babe. No more pills."

She stiffened and tried to sit up. "Is Amy okay? Where's Amy?"

"Amy's fine," he said. "She's in her room. Listen, you're going to sleep now. I'm going to stay here with you and rub your back and you're going to go to sleep and when you wake up you'll be fine."

"No . . . I have to see Amy." She repeated her daughter's name several times, weeping now, but he held her close and stroked her back and after a while the sobs faded and were replaced with the sighing breaths of deepest slumber.

\* \* \*

Paz awoke with a start out of one of those dreams that are so confused with reality that it takes more than a few seconds to discover which is which. He thought he'd been on a stakeout and fallen asleep and the suspect had slipped away, and he felt shame and despair. But, thank God, just a *regular* bad dream. Lola was still out, inert next to him, softly snoring. He slipped from the bed and went into his daughter's bedroom. There he placed her new *enkangue* on the bedpost and retrieved his own, returning it to its old place around his neck.

His cell phone played its tune. He pulled it out, saw who was calling, and after a brief hesitation, made the connection.

"What's up, Tito?"

"No one says hello anymore," said Morales, "ever since they figured out how to tell you who's calling. I think that's a major cultural change."

"The end of civilization as we know it. How did you make out?"

"Oh, I got the name and address. We're looking for the Forest Planet Alliance, on Ingraham. Where are you now?"

"At my place."

"I could come by. I think we should pay these folks a visit."

"It can't be now, man. I got personal business." A silence on the line, and Paz added, "Lola's sick."

"Oh? Nothing serious, I hope."

"No, just some kind of flu. Look, I'll check in with you in the morning."

"Fine. Look, you ever hear of a guy named Gabriel Hurtado?"

"No. Who is he?"

"A Colombian. Some kind of drug lord. His name came up. Apparently your . . . I mean, Calderón was in communication with him recently. We got it off his phone logs. The feds have expressed an interest. They've been after him for years, two million reward for information leading to."

"The more the merrier," said Paz, sniffing. Someone was

cooking onions. He heard the familiar rattle of implement against pan. "Look, Tito, I got to go. I'll call you."

"Colombian narcos. Usually they don't use mystic panthers."

"Jaguars," said Paz and broke the connection. Then he went into the kitchen and found his daughter, standing on the little wooden stool she had used as a baby, calmly sautéing chicken pieces. On the stove steamed a pot of rice and a pot of black beans. "I'm making arroz con pollo," she said. "I was hungry and I thought if Mommy was sick and you were sleeping I would cook this for all of us. I didn't make a mess."

Paz looked around the kitchen. Well, not much of a mess. He sat on a chair and watched his daughter cook, rendered speechless by the splendor of it.

# Fifteen

They finished setting out the booby traps just before it got dark, leaving the trip wires slack. They were gunpowder/napalm pipe bombs. Cooksey explained that they would rig them just before they went to bed. There were only ten of them, and it would be an easy matter to set them in the event that anyone nasty arrived during the hours of daylight.

"We'll need to have Kevin now, my dear," he said to Jenny while he camouflaged the last one. "He'll have to walk the property with us so that he knows where these little beauties are to be found."

"I'll get him," she said and ran off to the cottage they had once shared. No Kevin, just the lingering smell of his marijuana smoke.

She called his name, checked the bathroom, both without result, but when she came out the door she heard the sound of a VW starter cranking futilely.

Kevin was in the driver's seat of the van, twisting the ignition key and cursing.

"That won't start," she said.

"Oh, you're the fucking expert now," he snarled and tried it again.

"No, but I can take a distributor rotor off." She took it from her pocket and held it up for him to see. "Kevin, there's a car full of gangsters down the road. They're looking for you and me. Could you please just for once *think!*"

He threw open the door of the van. "Give me that!"

"No. What is so important that you have to go this minute?"

"I'll tell you what, bitch! Me and Kearney are going to blow up the S-9 pump station tonight. Give me that fucking rotor!"

"That's crazy, Kevin . . . ," she began, but stopped when she saw the pistol, pointing at her in his shaking hand.

"You're going to *shoot* me?" she asked after a hideous pause.

"Not if you give me the rotor."

As he said this, she could not help but notice that Kevin still had the pistol's safety on and didn't know it. Even in the fading light she could see the red dot wasn't showing. She could also see in his face the flickering terror behind the arrogant asshole mask. It struck her forcefully for the first time that she was the real thing of which Kevin was the counterfeit, and not the other way around. She was tough, and a survivor, and knew her way around the world, and had shot guns, and been in jail. Kevin was a banker's kid with attitude. She wondered why this had never occurred to her before. In fact, Kevin should not be allowed to cross the street alone. But, she thought, he could change, with some help from her. Now that she knew what a real man was, maybe she could nudge him somehow in the right direction. In any case, she couldn't just ditch him, the jerk!

"All right," she said, "but I'm coming with you."

"No fucking way."

"Then pull the trigger." She took the rotor out of her pocket. "And hurry up, because I'm about to fling this thing into the pond." They stood that way for some moments. Then Kevin cursed and shoved the pistol into his waistband. "Okay, okay, let's go, then. Put that thing back in the engine!"

"Give me the keys first," she said. "I'm driving."

\* \* \*

In the dark van Prudencio Rivera Martínez felt his cell phone vibrate. The number showing was that of Garcia, who was crouching behind a tall hibiscus hedge directly opposite the property they were watching.

"That painted van is coming out," he reported. "The girl is driving, and that little blondie *maricón* is with her."

"Which direction?"

"Just a second." A pause. "North."

"I'll have Montoya pick you up," said Martínez. He had stationed two cars in blocking positions, one at each end of the short road called Ingraham Highway. His own van was lodged in a driveway in the approximate center of this road. Now he formulated a plan and mobilized his vehicles. In a few minutes, the VW van rolled by and Martínez's driver, Cristobal Riba, swung behind it. Traffic was moderate.

"Where are we going to lift them?" asked Riba.

"Just ahead. This road goes under some heavy trees. It's like a tunnel, pitch dark. We'll do it there."

"A lot of traffic for a lift," said Riba doubtfully.

"They'll think it's a little accident. Iglesias will jam on his brakes, and you'll run into their ass. We'll get out, they'll get out, we'll show them guns, they'll get in with Iglesias and Rascon, and I'll get in with them and we'll drive to the garage. One two three."

Jenny gave a little cry and jammed on her brakes when the black van shot into the road from a hidden driveway and was thrown against her seat belt by the impact.

"Oh shit!" cried Kevin, and the same again when the following van rammed against the rear bumper. Dark-skinned men emerged from each van and walked toward the VW.

"Move the car, move the car!" Kevin screamed. He popped his seat belt and shifted in his seat, looking frantically to either side of the VW, watching the men approach.

"I can't, we're stuck," she shouted back at him, and then she saw the man just outside her window, a thick man with a round hard face, heavy brows, pockmarked cheeks, black hair worn in a brush cut. He was dressed in tan slacks and a white short-sleeved shirt, untucked at the waist.

"You hit my car," he said in clear but accented English. "You come out now and we show insurance, all right?"

She started to open her door, but Kevin shouted something she didn't catch and heaved himself across her. To her horror he had his gun out and was pointing it at the man. "Move your fucking car, motherfucker, or I'll blow your head off."

Jenny saw surprise register on the man's face. Kevin's pistol was trembling right before her eyes and she saw that the safety was still on. She was about to mention this to Kevin when the pockmarked man reached under his shirt, drew out a semiautomatic pistol with a strangely long barrel and shot Kevin twice in the face, making less sound than the popping of two birthday balloons. Kevin collapsed, his dead head fell right on her thigh, gushing volumes of blood. She looked down at it, at the great obscene bulge of blood-matted hair, bone splinters, and ropes of gray brain, and drew in breath for the scream of her lifetime.

Whether she made a sound or not she never knew, for between that moment and the next she felt the familiar shaft of coldness shoot through her center and the sounds of the uncaring traffic faded and the face of the killer and everything else contracted to a bright dot and she went away into seizure land.

Tuesday morning, Lola Wise was still sound asleep, and her husband forbore to wake her. He called the hospital and had a brief conversation with Dr. Kemmelman, the chief resident, in which he said that his wife was suffering from exhaustion and would be out for some days. The doctor said he understood, that such things happened often in ER work, and not to worry. He asked if Paz wanted to pick up some meds; Paz declined. Paz then prepared his daughter for school, dodged a series of questions about what was wrong with Mommy, and took her to Providence. On his way back, he received a call from Tito Morales.

"Did you hear yet?"

"Hear what?"

"We should've gone over there last night, man. I had a bad feeling about that. I should've gone myself."

"What're you talking about, Tito?"

"Around nine-thirty last night a van belonging to the Forest Planet Alliance—remember them?—was jammed up on Ingraham Highway by a couple of vans. Witnesses thought it was a fender bender. A man named Kevin Voss took two through the head from a silenced nine and his companion, a woman named Jennifer Simpson, aged nineteen, was abducted by persons unknown. How do you like that shit?"

"Not much. I presume you're all over the Forest Planet office by now."

"You could say that. It's based out of a big property on Ingraham south of Prospect, the bay side. Owned by a guy named Rupert Zenger, who's conveniently out of town. Left just the other day, ho-ho. The only residents are a James Scott Burns, some kind of yard man, and a fellow named Nigel Cooksey, he's an adjunct professor at the U. and the organization's scientific guy. A Brit. Nothing on either of them, but this Simpson woman has a sheet, did six months in Cedar Rapids for guess what?"

"Impersonating a large spotted cat?"

A silence on the line. "You need to take this shit more seriously, amigo. She was muling dope, felony weight, but she caught a break as a first offender. And a cooperative witness. Also, we found a nine-millimeter pistol in the van that Voss and Simpson were in, unfired, with Voss's prints on it. We traced it as stolen from a gun shop in Orlando last March."

"So what's the thinking now with all this?"

"Oh, thinking is not the word, my man. Finnegan and the county are having conniption fits that we found this FPA outfit and didn't tell them like immediately. They're moving to pick up a bunch of Colombians been hanging out on Fisher Island with the surviving Consuela guys. Oliphant is ballistic. How come we weren't on them yesterday? And like I said last night, the feds are interested because of this Hurtado character. I hear they're working on a warrant to raid your sister's company."

"Uh-huh. I think she'll be forthcoming. By the way, did you find the Indian?"

"No, but at this point fucking magical invisible Indians are not high on the priority list. Everybody's pretty well focused on Colombian gang war in the Magic City just before the tourist season."

"None of which explains the two funny murders."

"No, but the bosses got the bone in their teeth now. They want some Colombian *pistoleros* in the cells and we'll figure out how they did it later."

"So am I fired from being a funny-murder consultant?"

"Not that I heard. Why don't you come by this Ingraham place and we'll consult. They got a pool with piranhas in it. It's something to see."

"Twenty minutes," said Paz. By this time he was on his own street. He went into the house and checked on his wife. She hadn't moved since the last time he saw her, and he watched her for a considerable time, comforted by her slow, steady breathing. Then he left a note saying "*Mi amor se nutre de tu amor, amada.* Call me when you get up," and left.

Driving north on Coral Way, Paz had a thought and put it into action. He called his half sister's cell number on his own cell phone.

"It's Jimmy," he said when she answered. "The feds are about to raid your company."

To his relief she was not flustered by this news. "What's their interest?"

"Dad, if I may call him that, apparently spent a lot of time on the horn to Cali, Colombia, talking to a fellow named Gabriel Hurtado. He's a drug lord."

"*¡Coño!*" she said, and Paz chuckled. "Yeah, that explains why your books are fucked up."

"I figured out that much myself. What's your advice, *mi hermano*?"

"Total transparency. Fire the old fart accountant, let him and Dad carry the can. Did you have guilty knowledge?"

She laughed. "Are you serious? I have half a dozen witnesses that'll say he reamed my ass for even asking about a load of funny money I spotted on a balance sheet."

"Then you should be all right personally. The company could go down, though."

"I'll work something out. If we fold, maybe someone will let me waitress in the family restaurant."

"A done deal, Sis."

"And thanks for the heads-up. I don't even know you and I love you already."

Paz closed the call feeling better and more comfortably Cuban than he had in a while.

There were police cars and a crime scene van parked at the Zenger property. Paz had to wait for Morales to let him through the gate.

"Anything interesting?" Paz asked, taking in the scene.

"Not much, but we're still tossing the place. The late Voss had a collection of anarchist-type literature and a stash of high-grade marijuana. Also someone had secreted Baggies full of what looks like white bread at various places. They're going to give it the full lab treatment."

"Far more dangerous to the health than pot, if you ask me. Get anything out of the Professor?"

"Not much. The abducted girl was some kind of lost soul according to him. Epileptic, too. He seems like he's a lot more concerned about her than about Voss getting killed."

"What does he have to say about jaguars?"

"I don't know. I was saving all that for you. Want a crack at him?"

"Lead on," said Paz.

They found Cooksey sitting at the table on the patio, looking forlorn. When the two men approached, Cooksey asked, "Have you found her?"

"No, sir, I'm sorry, not yet," said Morales and introduced

Paz as a consultant on the murders of the two Cuban businessmen.

"I don't understand," said Cooksey. "What have they to do with what just happened?"

Paz smiled and pointed to the garden. "We don't know, sir, that's what we're trying to determine. How about you and me take a stroll around the grounds. You could show me around and we could talk about it."

They strolled. Paz asked questions about the pond and the plantings, about the work of the Alliance and Cooksey's own work. Cooksey was formal, constrained, answering the questions but not allowing a natural flow, which Paz thought was a little off. He'd had much to do with experts in various fields (mainly women) and had learned that when experts got going on their chosen fields, it was if anything hard to shut them up. Another thing that was off about Cooksey was the way he moved down a path. He made very little noise when he walked and his head moved slightly from side to side at each step. Perhaps field biologists also learned to walk like that, but the last time Paz had observed such a walk was when he was in the marines. Guys who had been in close combat walked that way.

They were on a shady sun-dappled path under large mango trees when Paz noticed something glinting against a low trunk in a thin bar of sunlight. He knelt to examine it, then stood and asked, "What's that?"

"It's a hook for a booby trap trip wire," said Cooksey.

"Really?"

"Yes. Raccoons come in at night and steal fruit and try to catch our fish. One can often annoy them by stretching wires across the paths rigged to let off flash-bangs."

"Raccoons trip over wires?"

"Not precisely. But they have a fascination with any sort of wires, as you'd know if you'd ever had one in the house as a pet. They pull on them, and the thing goes off and they run away."

"Very interesting. I didn't know that. They tell me you're an expert on tropical animals."

"Mainly wasps, I'm afraid. But I did some general zoology when I was younger."

"Know anything about jaguars?" Paz watched the man's face as he said this, and was surprised to see a faint smile form.

"This is about those two Cuban businessmen, isn't it?"

"As a matter of fact, it is. But I'd be curious to learn how you came to that conclusion."

Cooksey gave him a long look. "I read the papers."

"The papers didn't mention any jaguars."

Now a real smile. "No, sir, you have me there. Speaking of ferocious beasts, and the press, I must feed our piranhas. Would you like to watch?"

Paz made an acquiescent gesture and Cooksey led the way into the kitchen of the main house, where he took from the refrigerator a large plastic bag containing a whole beef liver. They returned to the paths, on a route that took them through thick lily thorn and wild coffee on a mild upward slope toward the sound of rushing water. When they came into sunlight again they were on a hill of coral rock some fifteen feet above the pool, with the waterfall pouring forth below them.

"We always feed them from here. The force of the water sends the meat down to where they tend to gather. It also helps keep the other fish from unfortunate accidents."

The red mass hit the boiling foam and disappeared. Within seconds there appeared another boiling below and the water blushed pink. Paz could make out a churning mass of gray forms near the bottom of the pond.

"Can they really strip the flesh off a cow in three minutes?" Paz asked.

"A shoal of a thousand could. We've only forty-two. Still, I wouldn't want to go for a swim in there with any sort of bleeding wound. I don't say you'd be an instant skeleton, but it would be distinctly unpleasant." Cooksey washed out the meat bag and put it in the pocket of his shorts.

"About that jaguar, Professor . . . ?"

"You're not a policeman, are you?"

"No, I was. Now I'm just consulting."

"On . . . ?"

"Crimes involving uncanny phenomena?"

Cooksey laughed. "Oh, well, then you've come to the right place. Since you're not a policeman, you can join me in a drink. I'd very much like a whiskey just now."

They went to Cooksey's rooms. While Cooksey attended to the drinks, Paz looked around with interest and the policeman's casual disregard for good manners. He noted the ex–laundry room and the sleeping arrangements therein, the neat piles of female clothing and the worn backpack, a framed photograph of an insect fixed to the wall. On what he took to be Cooksey's desk were three other framed photos, one of a pretty woman holding a child of about two, smiling into the sun, another of an elderly couple in safari clothing, and the third was of three men in military gear, floppy hats, and battle dress, holding automatic rifles. Their faces were darkened for combat, but Paz could see that one of them was a younger Cooksey.

Cooksey didn't comment on the poking around. He handed Paz a glass of amber liquid, no ice.

"Cheers," he said and took a swallow. Paz did the same.

"Good stuff."

"Talisker. It tastes of seaweed. An acquired taste, although I seem to have had no trouble acquiring it. I see you're looking at my little gallery."

"Yeah. That picture—you were a soldier?"

"A marine, actually. We were dropping some waffles just then."

"Excuse me?"

"A joke. When Maggie sent us to the Falklands, Labour was somewhat muddled in their response, yielding the newspaper headline, British Left Waffles on Falklands. A famous victory, although those two men didn't happen to survive."

"And the others are your family?"

"Dead, too. All those people are dead but me."

"I'm sorry."

"Quite. And now poor Jenny is gone as well."

"You had a relationship with her. She slept here."

"But alone, I'm afraid. We were friends, and she helped me in my work. I would very much like to see her safely back here."

"Then you should be forthcoming with information."

Cooksey sat down in his swivel chair and took another drink, a deep one. "I will be, Mr. Paz, although I don't see what good it will do. This abduction and murder must have little direct connection with your, let's call them, jaguar murders. Except through stupidity and inadvertence."

Paz sipped lightly from his drink and waited.

"There is an Indian," began Cooksey, and he told the tale, keeping mainly to the truth, but omitting any indication of where the Indian might be found. He refilled his glass twice during the telling. At the conclusion, he regarded Paz closely. "Is that uncanny enough for you?" he asked.

"Yes. By the way, did you tell this story to Detective Morales?"

"An expurgated version. He knows the Indian was here. I didn't take him for someone who would entertain the, let's say, uncanny portions."

"Yeah, that was a good call. Why they have me. So, have you ever actually seen this Indian, ah, change himself into a gigantic jaguar."

"No. I have only indirect evidence. The weight indicated by the footprints, as I mentioned. And his own testimony. And I wouldn't say 'changes himself'; he claims that the jaguar is a kind of god that takes him over and makes the transformation."

"As a scientist, though, don't you find that a stretch?"

"Frankly? I do indeed. Such things don't happen. Although Jenny, who is no mean observer, says she saw him partially change whilst visiting a captive jaguar in the local zoo. It sent her into an epileptic fit. Of course, I'm sure there's a perfectly materialist explanation for the whole affair, even though just at the moment I can't tell you what it is."

Paz finished his drink and stood up. "Do you think he'll come back here?"

"I rather doubt it. Unless he's assured by someone he

trusts that the danger to his homeland has been eliminated, he will massacre the remaining leaders of the Consuela corporation and anyone else who stands in his way."

"By magic."

"We've just agreed that such things cannot be."

"Assuming he can do it—I mean, kill those people: you don't care?"

"These people are responsible for a good deal of slaughter, Mr. Paz. Indirectly, in the good old quasi-legal and industrial way. Forgive me if I withhold my tears."

"You know where he's hiding, don't you?"

"If I did, I would probably decline to reveal that fact, in the interests of saving lives far more innocent, police officers and the like."

Paz was about to question Cooksey further about the Indian, and also explain the Florida statutes compelling cooperation with the police, when the door burst open and Morales appeared, a triumphant expression on his face. "Jimmy, we found something. You got to see this."

Paz followed him out, trailed by Cooksey.

There were police officers and crime-scene technicians standing around the patio table, upon which lay several objects: a heavy four-pronged forged-steel hand cultivator, whose tines had been filed to a bright pinpoint sharpness; a plaster cast of an animal foot; and a clear Baggie with two brown lumps in it.

"We found all this in a plastic grocery bag under a rock out behind the cottage where Voss and the girl lived," said Morales. "There's your mysterious jaguar."

Paz looked at the things. "You're assuming those turds are from a jaguar."

"I sure as shit intend to find out," said Morales boisterously. "So to speak."

"May I?" said Cooksey. He leaned forward and picked up the Baggie, peering closely, then reaching in and breaking a small clump from one of the black masses. He held this to his nose and crumbled it. Several of the cops exchanged discreet eye rolls. "Cat, and the size suggests a large one. That cast is certainly of a jaguar right forepaw. In fact, I believe it's part of my own collection. I didn't know it was missing."

"And there you have it," said Morales, looking at Paz, unable to hide his glee.

"You think?"

"Fuck, yes!" said Morales. "It was Voss and the Indian. They had a fight in Fuentes's office, they got kicked out, and then they did Fuentes. They used the cast to make the deep footprints. One of them stepped on it and the other one jumped up on his back. There you got your mysterious increase in weight. When we find the Indian, you'll see—the weights will match up." He picked up the cultivator. "They did the killings and the claw marks on the doors with that thing. And Calderón the same way."

Paz nodded agreeably and said, "This is the special kind of hand cultivator that enables you to move with lightning speed and leap up walls."

"Hey, it's an Indian. Who the fuck knows what he can do? He probably spent his whole life climbing up trees. And he might've had other weapons, we don't know."

"No, we don't," Paz said. "I guess my work here is done. Way to go, Tito. You solved the great jaguar murder case. Almost. All you need is one little Indian."

"We'll get him," said Morales. He gave Cooksey his cop stare. "I'm sure the professor here will provide us with a usable description."

"I'm sure," said Paz. "Tell me, Professor, do you think he'll be easy to catch?"

"Almost impossible to catch, in my opinion," said Cooksey.

"And why is that?" asked Morales.

"Because he's very good at hiding. He could be behind that hedge right now or in the tops of any of our big trees." Cooksey pointed and everyone looked, and looked nervous doing so. "Now, if you're finished with me, I do still have my own work to do."

He started to go but Paz held up a hand. "Just one more thing, sir. Does this guy have a name?"

"Yes. His name is Moie," said Cooksey.

\* \* \*

Two minutes later, Paz and a protesting Morales were in the latter's unmarked, heading north on Ingraham at an unsafe speed. Paz was cursing in Spanish, mainly at the absent Cooksey, because an instant after hearing the name, he had loosed a barrage of ferocious questions and quickly determined that the scientist had stashed his Indian in the great banyan that shaded his daughter's school; and cursed also himself, for being too slow to understand that Amelia did not have an *imaginary* little friend up in the tree at all.

It was a short drive. When they stopped on the shoulder next to the school lawn, where the upper boughs of the monster overhung the road, Paz popped his door open and was about to get out when Morales grabbed his arm.

"This is mine, Jimmy," he said.

Paz struggled in his grip. "No, I'm going up, man," he said.

"I could cuff you to the wheel, if you want," said the other. "I'm serious, Jimmy. This fucker is a serial killer and you're unarmed, one, and two, a civilian. I should call for backup, except I don't want to make an ass of myself in front of the whole SWAT team if this is another stupid Paz trick."

"If you don't think he's there, why don't you let me take an unofficial look?"

"Don't be a jerk, Paz. Wait here, I'll be right back."

"Don't break your neck."

Both men left the car and approached the tree. Morales stared upward into its mass and let out a low whistle, as for the first time he realized just how big the thing was.

"You're sure, now?" asked Paz. "I'm a lot closer to our African monkey roots than you are."

"Jimmy, if your daughter can climb this fucker, so can I."

"If you're not down in three days, or if I see chunks of mangled flesh wrapped in a cheap suit, I'm going to call for help, okay?"

Morales did not dignify this last with a response but vanished into the shadowed base of the fig. Paz leaned against the police car and lit a short, thick, black cigar. Occasional cracking sounds reached him from the tree, and frequent curses. The cigar was nearly done before he heard slithering sounds from the tree and a worn and filthy cloth suitcase plopped on the ground amid a small scatter of leaf, twig, and fruit. Shortly thereafter, Morales appeared, amid a larger scatter of the same. He was red-faced, sweating, scratched, disheveled, with his shirttails hanging out and his slacks stained with sap.

"What's in the case?" asked Paz. "Dried businessman jerky?"

"No, a black suit, a pair of shoes, a hat, and a hammock. And I found these." He removed a large evidence envelope from his back pocket. In it were three small empty Fritos bags.

"They might have prints."

"I'm sure," said Paz. "Among them mine and my daughter's. But no Indian."

"No, but he might come back. This is his base. I think we should stake it out."

"Well, you're the cop," said Paz. "And Tito? I'm real glad he wasn't there this time. Don't try to take this guy yourself."

"He's just an Indian, Jimmy."

"So was Geronimo. But he's not just an Indian. And our professor is not just a professor."

"Meaning what?"

"A little too cool. The guy was some kind of commando. He's spent a lot of time in Colombia, too. I were you, I'd find out who he's been calling recently."

Morales gave him a look to see if he was kidding, saw that he wasn't, shrugged, and went to his car to call in the latest news to his superiors.

First there was the taste in her mouth, pennies and puke, and then the pain, as if a thick spike covered with grit had been driven across her skull just behind her eyes. A hot spike. She tried to open her mouth to spit and found she could not. It had been taped, and when she tried to take the tape off, she learned that her arms and legs were similarly bound. It took some time for her eyes to register what they were seeing, for the light was dim and the shapes baffling: pipes, oblong objects, wires, hoses, a dim skylight above this tangle. A smell, too, familiar but hard to place—chemical, heavy, a cold sort of smell, and suddenly everything clicked into the gestalt: she was in the repair bay of a garage, looking up at the ceiling. She was taped to one of the hoists, her arms and legs tied to the X-shaped steel beams of the lifting platform, at about table height above the floor. And she was naked.

Heavy footsteps and men's voices. A shape stepped between her spread legs and she heard a laugh and a cruel insinuating voice speaking in Spanish. A rough finger was thrust into her and she squirmed violently. Someone else spoke in angry tones and the man spat out what sounded like a retort, but he moved away. Then a round, pockmarked brown face appeared above her own, one she recognized with horror. The man who had shot Kevin peeled the tape from her mouth.

"You thirsty?" asked the killer.

"Yes."

The man produced a plastic squeeze bottle and pushed its tube between her lips. Orange juice, cool and sweet. She sucked at it for what seemed a long time.

"Thank you," she said, gasping.

The killer said, "Okay, listen, you in lots of trouble, now. You got to tell them everything, *comprende*? Everything about those *Indios* killing those people. I try to keep those guys off you, I don't know, maybe I can't do, you know? So you tell me before the boss come, 'cause he gonna mess with you, and then you tell him, but maybe you lose some pieces."

He reached over to one of the tool tables and held up a short bolt cutter. "The boss gonna cut you with this, start with your toes, then he burn you with a torch so it don't bleed. I seen him do it before. You don' wanna fuck wit' him, you know? So you tell me an' you be all right, yes? Yes?"

"I don't know anything. I don't know what you're talking

about."

He shook his head sadly. "No, *chica,* that's not the way to go. You think about this, yes? Where those *Indios* stay, who sent them, who their boss is, that's what you got to tell him, you don' wanna get chopped up."

Jenny started to cry, and Prudencio Rivera Martínez left her and went back to the garage office, where he found Santiago Iglesias fiddling with a snowy, staticky television set, and Dario Rascon watching.

"I can't get this whore to work for shit," said Iglesias.

"Forget it," said Martínez. "We won't be here that long. And, Rascon, I told you to keep your hands off that girl."

Rascon shrugged and grinned. "I was just getting her warmed up."

"The man said don't touch her until he gets here. You want to explain playing with her to El Silencio when he told you not to, that's fine with me."

"What, you're going to rat me out?"

"No, but once you get started on a girl, you don't stop until she's all messed up."

Iglesias looked up from the TV. "Yeah, when El Silencio gets finished with her, then you can have her. You can keep her in the parts bin, in those little drawers."

"Shut up, *pendejo!*" said Rascon. "I guarantee you she won't last two cuts, she'll be telling her whole life story."

"If she knows," said Iglesias. "But if not, the man's going to have to take her apart to make sure she don't."

"She knows," said Rascon confidently. "She was with that little *merdita* Prudencio shot, and he was with the *Indio.* She'll spit the whole thing out. And then . . ." Rascon leaned back in his chair and massaged his genitals. "You can have her asshole when I'm finished, Iglesias. You like that the best anyway."

Martínez heard his cell phone ring and he snapped off the television. It was a brief conversation, consisting mainly of affirmatives on his part. When it was over, he said, "That was *el jefe.* We got a small problem. The cops raided the houses on Fisher Island and picked up all our people, including El Silencio. They got nothing on them, he says, they're just fucking us around. He figures they'll keep them for a day or two and let them go. Meanwhile, we're supposed to sit tight here and watch the girl, and not go out for any reason."

Rascon cursed vividly and Iglesias switched on the static again. "Then I better get this piece of shit to work," he said.

# Sixteen

Morales left, but Paz waited in the shade of the tree. After a while, a Florida Power and Light van rolled up and parked across the street. Two men in hard hats and harnesses emerged who, despite this apparatus, did not visibly engage themselves in improving the flow of electricity. Paz waved to them and was ignored. Perhaps they would fool a primitive native of the Orinoco, but he doubted it.

He smoked another cigar and wandered over to the water fountain near the school and drank from it. He hoped that no one called any other police; people nowadays so often did when they observed a grown man hanging around an elementary school. Thinking this, his mind moved to the general phenomenon of men behaving monstrously, and thence to the kidnapped girl, Jenny. Why had they taken her? For information, obviously, but he could not figure out what a girl described by Cooksey as somewhat dim could know that would inspire a bunch of Colombian *drogeros* to snatch her from a Miami street, committing a murder in the process. Unless she wasn't that dim; unless Cooksey was lying about that and other things; unless there were connections between all these ongoing crimes that no one had thought of. In any case, the girl was gone, they'd torture the knowledge, if any, out of her and her broken corpse would go into the Glades or the bay. So convenient, Miami, for disposing of the illegally dead; sad about the girl, but only in principle. He didn't know her and was no longer obliged to concern himself with such pathetic victims. He strolled back to the tree, noting the arrival of some school buses and a number of cars in the lot, good parents, eager to collect their offspring, Paz himself happy to be in their number for a change.

A growing din from the school building and the brightly colored mob of children burst forth. Some were ushered by teachers into the waiting buses, some ran to the parental cars, flapping garish infant art (Look what I made in school today!) producing general cooing and the rumble of expensive engines. The remainder, bright Miss Milliken their shepherdess, moved in a pack across the lawn to a bench beneath the tree. Amelia spotted him, and he noted with mixed feelings the expressions that flew across the dear face: first surprised delight and then feigned indifference. His darling had discovered cool, it seemed, and was showing a primitive version of the untaught universal reluctance of the young to acknowledge the existence of the parent while among peers. With a pang Paz experienced the start of his destined slide from demigod to hapless jerk.

Miss Milliken chivvied the children into seated rows, sat on the bench, and opened *Charlie and the Chocolate Factory*. Paz, still something of a detective, noted that his daughter had arranged herself at the extreme end of the seated arc of tots, and that shortly after the revelations at the chocolate factory spilled forth she had slipped off into the shadows of the hanging boughs. He followed her into the heart of the tree.

"He's not there anymore, baby," he said.

"How do you know?"

"I just do. Tito went up there a little while ago. Your friend's gone and I don't think he's coming back."

"Why did he? I mean Tito."

"Because . . . Moie . . . because the police think that Moie may have, I mean he might know something about some crimes and the police want to talk with him real bad. Do you know anywhere else he hangs out?"

"No. What kind of crimes?"

"Bad crimes. Look, we need to talk about this a little bit. What do you say we walk down to El Piave and get some ice cream."

This was disgraceful. The poor child had a jones for ice cream, the mom doled it out like methadone, and so Daddy could always win a point by playing the genial pusher. She brightened immediately and they walked off, threading through the narrow flower-scented streets of the Grove until they arrived at Commodore Plaza. El Piave, which specialized in homemade Italian gelati, was crowded with after-school business, but Paz and daughter had no trouble getting a seat via the freemasonry of the food service business. Paz had a vanilla soda with coffee ice cream and the girl pigged out on two scoops of cherry vanilla with fudge. The counter guy saw who it was and added, gratis, a tower of whipped cream, several maraschino cherries, and topped it with a paper parasol. Amelia—a foodie princess of Miami—accepted this graciously as her due.

Paz waited for the sugar to drug her into a happy stupor and then said, "Look, I know Moie is your pal, but you need to think about what if he's really not."

"He is. He's nice."

"He may seem nice, Amy, but let's face it—you don't know a lot about him. You say he's magic, for example. Okay, I believe you, he's magic. But what kind of magic? You know there's not just the good kind."

No response to this; she was looking away from him now, concentrating on carving away at the mound of ice cream, artfully saving the whipped cream and cherries until the last bites. He tried another tack. "You know about Santería, right?"

"Uh-huh. What Abuela does."

"That's right. There's a world we can't see, and there are spirits that live in that world. Sometimes they help us and sometimes they hurt us, but the thing you have to remember is they're different from us and dangerous. That's why Abuela and her friends try to find out what they want so we don't get caught in their . . . doings, and maybe get stepped on."

"By bad spirits?"

"No, baby, it's not about good and bad. It's just about power. See, it's like a bunch of boys playing football on the grass and a little kitten wanders out there and maybe it gets stepped on and squashed. The boys didn't really mean to do it, but the kitten is still squashed. You had those bad dreams about a jaguar, remember? And I had the same kind of dreams and I think your mom is having those dreams, too, which is why she's been so upset lately, and—"

"You made them stop with that Santería thing."

"Right, the *enkangue,* and I hope Mommy's got stopped, too. But the thing is, I think Moie was sending those dreams, not him really but a kind of spirit he works for, a jaguar spirit, and I think that spirit wants to hurt you, not because it's bad or Moie is bad but because it's doing something that we don't understand and hurting you is part of it."

Amelia looked up from her dish and met his eye. She seemed suddenly older. "This is like *The Lord of the Rings,* isn't it?"

"Just like," said Paz.

"And we're like the hobbits."

"Uh-huh. Except I think Abuela is more like Gandalf."

Amelia nodded at this—obvious. "And what are you like, Daddy?"

"I don't know, baby. This is all pretty new to me."

"I want you to be the king, Aragorn."

Paz laughed. "You do, huh? Well, I think I'm just another hobbit, and not Frodo either. But the main thing is you need to tell me if you see Moie again, all right? That part isn't make-believe. Amelia, look at me! Promise, now."

Amelia looked into her father's eyes. There was something she had to tell him about . . . about a word she couldn't remember, a little girl and a caiman and a jaguar, but it was all mixed up in her head. So instead of that she said, "Okay. I'm going to be Galadriel, and I could make a silver crown, couldn't I?"

When they were on the street again, Paz called the restaurant and asked Yolanda to fall by the Grove and give them a lift home. The lunch rush would be over by now. He rarely exercised his feudal powers in this way, but he felt it was a special circumstance, his daughter being pursued by a . . . whatever, and besides Yolanda was always ready to do *anything* for Jimmy. More shameless manipulation added to Paz's heavy score.

Yolanda arrived in her battered white Toyota pickup truck. They all squeezed into the front seat, and Paz was glad that he had Amelia as flesh insulation between his thigh and Yolanda's lush brown one, bared by her pink shorts. Yolanda was a reformed bad girl, a mélange of the races and the heartthrob of all the younger waiters and staff, although she had eyes only for the unobtainable Jimmy. This often happened in the restaurant business, and many other sorts of business as well; Paz didn't take it personally. He flirted but did not (despite his tales to his wife) actually grab ass. They talked restaurant on the way home, with Amelia uncharacteristically silent. When they reached the house in South Miami, the girl darted from the truck and into the house without a good-bye.

"Something wrong?" asked Yolanda.

Paz shrugged. "Just growing pains. I'll see you at the place later this week, I guess."

"They caught that guy already? I mean the one that . . ."

"They think so," Paz said, and with a wave turned up the walk to his house.

Entering his bedroom, he was relieved to observe signs of life in his spouse. She blinked, rubbed her eyes, her face, stretched, said, "Oh, God. I fell asleep. What time is it?"

"A little past four."

She struggled into a sitting position against the headboard. "I should call the hospital, see if I still have a job."

"You're cool. I talked to Kemmelman. Apparently it happens all the time. I mean people in the ER losing it. It's no biggie."

Her eyes narrowed. "You talked to Kemmelman about *me*? When was this?"

"I don't know—yesterday morning, I think."

"Yesterday morning? Jimmy, what're you talking about?"

"Lola, it's a little past four on *Wednesday*. You've been out for over forty-eight hours."

The suspicion on her face turned to stunned astonishment. "That's impossible."

"But true. Did you have any dreams?"

Her eyes flicked away from his. He moved his head to catch them again. "No," she said, "not that I can recall."

"Good. But you were having dreams before, weren't you?"

"I guess. What does this have to do—"

"No, not 'I guess,' Lola. You were having nightmares every night, just like me and just like Amy. You couldn't sleep at all, and it made you crazy. Now, let me use my magic powers to tell you what your dreams were about. I don't know the details, but they were all about Amelia. A big jaguar was going to eat her, and even though you wanted to stop it, it made sense that she was going to get eaten, you thought it was a good thing. That's what made it so horrible. Same dream every night, night after night."

He watched her closely, her mouth working, her eyes darting around. "Am I right?" he demanded.

A nod. "I thought I was going crazy."

"Not crazy, no," he said and sat on the bed, enfolding her in his arms. "Look, I know you don't buy this stuff, but here it is. These are the observable facts. One: three members of this family were having nightmares on the same subject. Two: a couple of rich Cubans, including my father, have been murdered, and the killer seems to be a very large cat—"

"What? You know this? The police think . . . ?"

"I know it. The police just want it to be a regular revenge killing. Let me finish. Three: there's a South American Indian in town, who claims to be able to turn himself into a jaguar. This Indian has been stalking Amelia. I mean physically. I've observed this myself on one occasion, at the beach, and he's been hanging out in the big tree at her school. She was talking to him and passing him Fritos. Four: at my mother's *ilé,* her *santero* predicted that Amy would be in danger from a big animal of some kind."

"Jimmy, this is crazy—"

"Shh! I know. The last thing is that the jaguar dreams of all three of us have stopped, because I got my mom to crank out some protective charms, *enkangues*. One of them's under Amy's bed, one of them's around my neck, and the other is under here." He patted the bed.

She pulled away from him and stared. She looked like she was about to cry. "I can't believe that. There's some other explanation."

"You keep saying that. I tell you what, in the interests of science, we'll take the *enkangue* away and see if you have the dream again. It's only fair to advise you, though, that Eleggua won't like it when you reject his gift. He's the guardian of the ways between this world and the dream world. So it might not work again. Want to try?"

Now she let out a sigh, as if rationality were a gas leaking from a puncture somewhere deep inside her, and fell away from him down to the pillows. She pulled the light blanket up over her face. "What I want is for this not to be happening," she said.

He tugged the hem of the blanket down so he could see her eyes. "Can't do that, babe. But I think that if we play this right we can get out from under."

"But *why*?" she wailed. "Why is this Indian after Amy? She hasn't done anything to him, she's a *child,* for God's sake."

"Yeah, Amelia and me were discussing that just the other day. Isaac was innocent, too, so why did God want to kill him? Innocents die every day, without any ceremony at all. It's something about the way the world works, patterns of fate we can't understand. That's why we have Santería and the rest of all that. And science, of course. But scientific civilization doesn't seem to be any better at stopping the slaughter of the innocents than voodoo. Probably does worse, when you think about it. There are forces. You can ignore them, pretend they don't exist, try to control them, or appease them, and hope they won't notice you. We're all hobbits, Amelia says. Meanwhile, more to the immediate point, a four-hundred-pound magic jaguar wants to eat our kid."

"Oh, stop it! You're scaring me." She shivered despite herself, despite the coziness of the room.

"Oh, you think *you're* scared? I'm fucking petrified."

"What should we do?" Her voice had gone high, like a child's, and there was a look on her face that he hadn't seen there before. What we look like when the patina of materialism cracks and we behold the immemorial terror; he'd been there himself. He grasped her hand and replied, "I've been thinking about that. Obviously, my mom is the key player. We'll get her Santería people in on this and see what they recommend. Until then, I want to stick close to Amelia, so she's going to have to skip school for a while. The other thing I want to do is talk with Bob Zwick. In fact, I believe I'll invite him out on the boat tomorrow, with Amelia along, too. We'll fish."

"Why Zwick?"

"Because he's smart and because I want to take one last crack at convincing myself this is all bullshit."

Cooksey waited until dark and then, with a small khaki bag on his shoulder, he walked down Ingraham to the Providence School. The moon had not risen and it was perfectly black in the shade of the giant fig. Feeling his way, stumbling over roots, he reached the gray column of the main trunk, and cupping his hands around his mouth, he imitated the vocalizations of the hoatzin. Shortly, he heard the cry repeated from above and then a faint rustling sound. Then Moie was standing in front of him, although quite invisible in the utter darkness.

"That was a very good hoatzin, Cooksey," said Moie. "For a moment, I thought I was dreaming, or that I had flown back to my home."

"Thank you. I thought I might be a little out of practice. I'm happy to see that the police have not caught you yet."

"No. A man climbed this tree today. He found my hammock and Father Tim's bag and took them. I was very close to this man but I made him not look at me. The *wai'ichuranan* are such bad hunters that it's a good thing for them that their food comes from machines. Two of them are approaching the tree right now. I think they will catch you."

"I believe you're right, but that doesn't matter. I doubt that they'll catch *you,* however. Listen, Moie, the *chinitxi* have killed the Monkey Boy and have stolen the Firehair Woman. Can you find them and bring her back to me?"

"I can find them, yes. They are south of here and not far. Perhaps I can free her, too. But where she goes after that, I can't say. She is on her own path, that one."

"That's true. Well, go now and do the best you can. And I thank you."

Cooksey felt the air move against his face and he knew he was alone again in the dark. He removed a flashlight and some equipment from his bag and set to work. Within minutes strong beams of light penetrated the root forest, and Cooksey found himself grabbed, braced against the tree trunk, and frisked by two strong policemen.

"Where's the Indian?" one demanded.

"I didn't see any Indian," said Cooksey, with perfect honesty.

"What are you doing here, then?" the cop asked.

"I am collecting nocturnal insects. This is a fig tree, and I study fig wasps." Cooksey knew he was a bad liar and so tried always to tell nothing but the truth, although quite often not the entire truth.

━━━━━

Moie has a map in his head showing where to go, but it was not an ordinary map, not a picture of the earth's surface seen from above, drawn to scale. This map he had made at night, while he flew through the dreams of the dead people. Its landmarks were dread and desire, lust and hatred, love and harmony, and while it is difficult to do, he can generate within his own being a concordance between this world and the streets and buildings where the *wai'ichuranan* dwell. He trots south at a steady pace along the delightfully smooth rock paths they have in this land. He is naked except for his loincloth, dream pouch, and woven bag. People see him pass down U.S. 1, but when they look to confirm this surprising sight, he is always gone. I thought I saw an Indian running down the highway, they may remark to one another, if there is another, but the second one never saw what the first one had; and if someone alone catches sight of Moie, they tend to forget it very quickly. Every cop in Miami is on the lookout for a lone Indian, but not one of the several officers he passes on his way south pursues him or calls in the sighting.

He finds the building then, with little trouble. Two of the *chinitxi* are inside it and one is standing in front, in the shadows of a doorway, smoking a cigar and looking around. Moie can also feel the girl within the building. He slips around the back to see if there is a way in.

At the back of the building there is a door that will not open. Moie has observed this of the doors in this land. Sometimes they open and sometimes not, and he has wondered why this is so. It may be, he thinks, that the *wai'ichuranan* are as bad at making doors as they are at hunting. Near the door are heaps of useful things that the *wai'ichuranan* have left out for anyone to take: metal, glass, paper, and high stacks of tires. Moie has observed that this was something they like to do: each morning great trucks drive through the streets and the men on them take away bags and baskets of food and other good things, perhaps to give to other people who did not have enough, or perhaps this is how the food gets into their machines. He does not spend much time considering these mysteries, however, but instead scrambles lightly up the stack of tires to the roof. There he walks toward a little house made of glass. He spits on his hand and wipes the dirt away from a pane and sees what he seeks lying below.

———

In the garage office, Dario Rascon awoke from a troubled dream to the sound of breaking glass. He rose lightly from the cracked leather couch on which he had been sleeping, drew

his pistol, and, without bothering to wake the snoring Iglesias, went through the door to the garage bay. After waiting a
few moments in the dark, ears straining at silence, he snapped
on the lights. Of the eight fluorescent tubes in the pair of
hanging fixtures only three came on, but there was enough
light to see the Indian, a small brown man, nearly naked, with
facial tattoos and a bowl haircut. He was standing under the
dark skylight, with sparkling shards of glass all around him.

Rascon pointed his pistol and ordered the man to approach with his hands up, but the Indian, with a movement
too swift for any response, vanished behind a workbench. It
was dark at that end of the garage, but Rascon was not afraid
of Indians. He had shot lots of Indians at home. He moved
forward confidently. The Indian was not behind the workbench. Rascon moved farther into the darkness, pointing his
pistol here and there like a snake striking.

*Ararah. Ararararh.*

He jumped at the sound and whirled. Some kind of motor
starting up, he thought, the little *pendejo* must have tripped a
switch. Then, amazingly, he was on his face on the concrete,
the gun gone skittering across the floor. He felt, as his last
earthly sensation, a hot breath on his neck.

Jenny was positioned in the right place to see the whole
thing. She saw Moie go dark and vague and his form thicken
and grow and then the thing was standing there lashing its
tail. She saw what it did to the man. Then another man appeared in the garage and shouted out something, and she saw
a speckled blur fly through the air and heard a thump, then a
strangled human cry and, after a moment, liquid gnashing
sounds. These stopped. Then came the slighter noise of
claws clicking on concrete and the beast's head was near her
own, inches away. She looked into the golden merciless
eyes. Through chattering teeth she managed to say, "Moie,
don't kill me." Jaguar opened his mouth. She saw the red
blood spattered on its muzzle, the long yellow fangs. A
breath issued from its mouth, smelling of fresh meat, cop-
pery and rank, and of something else, some sweeter scent,
an overwhelming perfume. She gasped and took it into her

body. Then she felt the aura, the familiar cool feeling in her center and slipped, rather gratefully this time, into the seizure.

When she awoke her bonds had been cut. She found a water spigot and took a drink and washed her face and her hands. Urine had dried on her legs, and she washed this off, too. It was perfectly quiet in the garage, save for the usual hum a city makes. She did not look at what was on the floor. A merciful amnesia had descended on her mind, which now resembled a vast dusty warehouse in which only a few motes of thought floated, the chief of which was LEAVE NOW. She obeyed this and walked out of the repair bay quite nude, pausing only to switch off the lights, having been firmly trained from an early age always to switch off the lights when leaving a room.

Even in Miami, a city void of dress codes, it is hard for a naked woman to go far on a major thoroughfare without someone noticing. Within a quarter mile of where she started, Jenny was fortunate enough to meet a couple of social workers coming home from a movie. Both of them were women and both of them had plenty of experience with drug intoxication among teenagers. They grabbed her, wrapped her in a blanket, and took her to the nearest emergency room, which was at South Miami Hospital.

**P**rudencio Rivera Martínez, after finishing his cigar, had walked a block to a taco joint and used the toilet. Returning to the garage office, he was surprised to see his two companions gone. He went into the repair bay and shouted their names several times. Hearing no reply, he took another few steps and slipped on something, landing painfully on his knee and hand. Standing again, he looked at his hand and found it covered with blood. After he turned the light on, he discovered that what he had slipped on was a piece of Santiago Iglesias's liver. The donor of this morsel was lying a few yards away. In the distance, he could just make out a little mound in the center of a large dark pool, and he concluded that this was Rascon. The girl was gone. He took out his cell phone and was about to push the buttons, when a novel thought entered his mind. He placed the cell phone on a tool cabinet and considered his situation: he had several thousand in cash and a new van and a gun and a small personal stash of very pure cocaine. It was more than enough to make a start in New York. Hurtado might come looking for him, or El Silencio, but they would first have to deal with whatever had silently taken out two extremely experienced and tough Colombian gangsters, or three, counting Rafael in Calderón's house, and he thought that they might have a difficult time doing that. In any case, he was himself no longer willing to participate in this *fregada*. He got into the van and, like so many of his countrymen, immigrated to America.

**P**az's boat was a locally made plywood craft, ugly as the devil and painted peeling pink. It had been called *Marta,* but one of the stick-on metallic letters had fallen into the sea and so it was *Mata* now, which Paz had liked as being suitable for a homicide dick and had left it so. It was damp and uncomfortable and ran like blazes on its planing hull in front of twin Mercury Optimax 200s. Just now it was anchored in Florida Bay over a hole Paz had been fishing for years. They had been out since just past dawn and caught two fat snook (Paz) and a small permit (Zwick) and now it was eleven and the fish had stopped biting. The only person still fishing seriously was Amelia, who was methodically feeding live shrimp to the crabs on the bottom with her hook.

The two men were sitting on a padded locker, working on their second six-pack. Zwick had been talking about his work, a subject he was never reluctant to pursue, but Paz had been encouraging. As a result he had learned a good deal about Penrose's theory that consciousness was in some sense a quantum phenomenon lodged in the exquisitely fine microtubules of neurons, and Edelman's theory that the brain is a set of maps, with sheets of neurons having systematic relationships to sheets of receptor cells wired to the whole sensorium. In this theory, sensory experience essentially constructs consciousness. It was Zwick's idea that the real key lay in a concordance of the two theories: Edelman's notion of reentry mapping explained the way the brain built a picture of the world and of the self within it; Penrose explained, as far as Paz could understand the jargon, why minds were not like machines, why human minds could think up new stuff, something no computer had ever done. Paz listened, asked questions, received detailed answers, some of which he even understood, and waited patiently for Zwick to get drunk enough to deal with Paz's less orthodox queries. He thought it was a lot harder absorbing information from Zwick than from a naked woman in bed, which had been for many years Paz's almost exclusive tutelary venue. Did sex make the neural sheets more receptive? Or did the spray of testosterone that Zwick emitted when making a point have the opposite effect? A good doctoral thesis, Paz thought, but one unlikely ever to be written.

"So what about hallucinations, Doctor?" he asked now. "It can't be a mapping thing because by definition it doesn't exist to be picked up by the senses. But it seems real."

Zwick waved his hands dismissively. "It's all bad connections, neurotransmitter imbalances in the midbrain. We can produce any type of hallucination we want by electrical stimulation, magnetic fields, chemicals . . . it's not a particularly interesting field of study."

"Unless you're having them. What about a hallucination that leaves physical evidence behind it?"

"Then by definition it's not a hallucination."

"Unless the evidence is also hallucinatory. Where do you draw the line?"

"Through your dick. What are you talking about, Paz? More spooky shit?"

"Spooky indeed. Are you drunk enough to give me a scientific opinion?"

"Barely. Why isn't this vessel equipped with daiquiris? Isn't that a Coast Guard requirement?"

"Only in international waters. What do you think of

shape-shifting? Speaking as a renowned physicist and drunk?"

"What do you mean, 'shape-shifting'?"

"I mean that it's universally accepted among shamanic peoples that certain highly trained people can turn themselves into animals."

"Oh, that. I thought they only *thought* that the spirit of the great lion, or whatever, was taking them over and they growled and imagined they were chasing zebras."

"Yeah, they have that, but I meant for real, assuming there's such a thing as real. What it is, I was called in recently to consult on a Miami PD case. A couple of citizens got killed, and all the evidence says it was done by a large animal, a cat of some kind. We got footprints, we got claw marks, the wounds are consistent with teeth and claws. They even figured out how much it weighs, a little over four-fifty. Needless to say, no one has reported such an animal in the area. We also have this little Indian running around town, comes from the jungles in South America, got a grudge against the victims, and also claims to be able to change into a jaguar, more or less. We also have some anecdotal evidence this guy has the ability to, let's say, modify his appearance. What do you make of all that?"

"Of that I make horseshit," said Zwick. "Technically, we in science are not allowed to say that anything's impossible, just that some things are so improbable as to be not worth thinking about, and this falls in that category. I mean organic forms do change shape, obviously, but as growth over time, and via evolution over humongous ranges of time. They don't just change shape like in fairy tales, not in real life."

"Okay, but look at it another way. If you were God, and making a world in which something like that *could* happen, how would you do it?"

"Oh, well, that's the way to my heart, letting me play God." Zwick laughed and finished his beer, tossing the can over his shoulder into the bay. "Although among the many improvements I'd make, that one would probably not be high on the list. Let's see now. . . ." Zwick leaned back against the rail and opened another can. His eyes lost focus as he raised his head to the sky, seeming to seek counsel from the current deity. Paz observed him with interest, as a phenomenon of nature. Watching Robert Zwick cogitate was less fascinating than watching Nolan Ryan pitch or Michael Jordan shoot baskets, but it was the same sort of thing, a thing regular people couldn't hope to do.

"Right," said Zwick after several minutes of this. "We all have in us a neural map of our bodies. No one knows how detailed it is, but let's say for the sake of argument that it descends to the molecular level. So your shape-shifter would have to have a duplicate image of the selected animal in there somewhere. How it's instantiated we don't know, but it's not through any strictly biological process. On the other hand, we're constantly discovering biological processes we never suspected, so call that a gimme. We observe in nature the caterpillar turning into a butterfly, a completely different creature, over a fairly short time. Let's say it's the same kind of thing, but faster. Okay, we need energy. Well, there are humongous reserves of energy in the universe, the so-called dark energy for one thing, and ordinarily we have no access to it. But suppose Penrose is correct, that consciousness is partly a quantum phenomenon, and suppose our little guy has solved the dualism problem, don't ask me how . . ."

"Sorry, what problem?"

"We talked about this before, remember? Substance dualism, the idea that consciousness is its own thing and exists independently of the material brain, as Descartes believed. It satisfies all the problems of consciousness by explaining them away—the ghost in the machine, as they call it, or rather all problems except one, and that's the killer: how do you imagine any gearing or connection between the material and the immaterial? How does an immaterial mind cause a material event, say, the firing of neurons in the motor cortex that move your arms? Which is why it's bullshit, and also why there's no God."

"Except you."

"Of course. But never mind that for the moment. Substance dualism implies conscious immaterial beings that are nevertheless capable of influencing matter, so that takes care of a lot of your energy concerns. This putative being moves the molecules into the right place according to the alternate body plan he keeps in his head. Animal flesh is just air and water and a few minerals, easily obtained from ordinary dirt, if you have godlike powers. So that's one solution. Alternatively, we could posit that there are other universes intimately connected with our own, the unseen world of superstition. We think that our four dimensions are generated by vibrations of the strings wrapped up in the Calabi-Yau geometry, but for the math to work there have to be seven other dimensions tangled up in there, of which we know zip and probably never will. Again, the central question is, What is consciousness? Maybe it can get in there and arrange for the passage of mystic beings. Maybe that'd be a simpler solution than assembling your jaguar from molecules on order. The thing just steps through, and the little Indian goes back the other way, like a revolving door. The energy cost would be huge, but who's counting?"

Paz nodded. He had some experience both with beings appearing from nowhere and with uncanny geometries. "I like that one. So you think it's possible."

"Not the right question. Like I said, anything's possible, but almost everything except what we observe is ridiculously improbable. On the other hand, we don't know shit about either consciousness on the fine grain, or about the probability set associated with dimensions other than the familiar ones." He regarded the present beer can, found it empty, flung it away. "There, that solves the physical problem, but it leaves the sociopolitical one, which I think is the most telling."

"Which is what?"

"Which is that if these little guys, these shamans, can do all that subtle moving of energies with their minds, how come they don't rule the world now? How come scientific technology totally destroys any competing worldview? I mean, destroys it physically? The Indians are all on reservations, if you notice, and all the indigenous people, so called, are flocking into cities, dying to sew underwear and get a TV."

"Mozart," said Paz.

"Say what?"

"A woman I once knew, an anthropologist, said that magic was like a creative art. There were geniuses that could do things that no one else could, just like Mozart, but that they couldn't package what they did so that the whole culture could do it, too. But any asshole can use science packaged as technology, so the primitives get killed off everywhere, like you said."

"Hmph. Sounds like something an anthropologist would cook up. Now, do you want to know the real explanation?"

"If you would be so kind."

"You have perfectly ordinary murders by human murderers, who are also charlatans. The so-called evidence is planted and faked. The observers are distracted and/or scared to death, or are believers and autohypnotize themselves."

"Yeah, that's the current police theory. But how come me and my wife and my kid are having the same dream about a jaguar while this is going on?"

"Oh, *dreams*! Now *there's* a body of reliable evidence! Look, the reason science more or less abandoned self-reporting in the study of the human mind is that with the right suggestion people will report fucking *anything*. I mean the whole purpose of the scientific enterprise is to eliminate—"

"Daddy! My hook is stuck!"

Both men looked at Amelia, whose rod was bowed nearly double. Paz realized with a guilty shock that he had nearly forgotten she was on board. The drag on her reel let out a number of clicks. Paz jumped to her side and took the rod from her. He heaved on it and felt the tug of a live weight on the line. Handing it back, he said, "That's not stuck, baby, you have a fish on there. Reel it in!"

As she did, Zwick leaned over the side and observed the line. "I think it's an old tire. It doesn't seem to be doing much running."

"Shut up, Zwick! Don't tell a Cuban about what's a fish. Am I right, Amelia?"

"It's a fish," she cried. "I can feel it moving."

She was correct. After five minutes of steady cranking a large gray shape could be seen moving toward the surface. Paz reached out with a landing net and heaved the thing over the rail, but it was lively still and with a violent gyration it leaped from the net and began to skip and bounce along the deck.

"What is it, Daddy?" the girl shouted.

"It's a hardhead catfish. God, it must be a two-pounder. Wait a second, I'll get the net on it again . . ."

But the fish skittered across to where Zwick was standing. He raised his foot. Paz saw what he was about to do and a negative expostulation formed in his throat. Too late. Zwick stamped down heavily on the catfish's back, and the sharp, thick, venom-coated spine that marine catfish wear in their dorsal fins went right through the bottom of his sneaker and pierced his foot to the bone.

"**D**oes it still hurt?" Paz called out twenty minutes later as the *Mata* skipped over the bay toward Flamingo, going all out.

"Not really. I just amputated my foot with your bait knife."

"Seriously."

"Seriously? It's *agony*! Why the hell didn't you tell me the goddamn thing had a poison spine in its back?"

"Because I thought you knew everything," said Paz. "Who could imagine that the world's smartest man would tromp on a catfish? We're almost at the channel. Do you want me to take you to Jackson?"

"Hell, no!" said Zwick. "I might get touched by one of my students. No, let's go to South Miami, it's closer anyway."

# Seventeen

"I fail to see why everyone sort of turns away and giggles when I tell them what happened to me," said Zwick to Lola Wise. His tone was aggrieved, but she was hard-pressed not to giggle herself.

"It's nothing to be ashamed of," said Lola. "I heard that Sir Francis Crick once stuck his tongue in a light socket."

"You're giggling, too! You'll probably be laughing your ass off when I get permanent brain damage from this operation."

"It's a local, Zwick. They have to clean out the puncture. You don't get permanent brain damage from a local anesthetic. You're a doctor, you know this. I can't believe you're being such a baby."

Lola felt a tug and leaned over to receive a whisper from her daughter. "Amy says you can get Dove bars in the cafeteria. She says she always gets one when she has to get shots and wishes to know if the same will make you stop whining."

"Thanks, Amy," said Zwick. "Throughout this you've been the only person who hasn't made me feel like a jerk. Tell me, Amy, this is something you learn in kindergarten here? The colors, the alphabet, and catfish have poisonous dorsal spines—that's in the curriculum?"

Before Amelia could consider this question, a nurse came in, giggling, and whisked Zwick off on a gurney.

"Where's Daddy?" Lola asked.

"Around. Mommy, is it my fault that Bob got stuck? It was my catfish."

"No, of course not, sugar. It was an accident. He didn't know it was dangerous to step on it."

"But, *technically,* if I hadn't've caught this fish, he wouldn't be hurt."

Lola bent down and gave the girl a hug and a tickle. "Oh, stop it! *Technically,* if I hadn't met your father and got married and had you, you wouldn't be there and wouldn't have caught the fish. You can't string contingencies out that far; you'd go nuts."

"What's contingencies?"

"Stuff that happens because of other stuff. The point is, contingency is morally neutral. Responsibility follows intent. You didn't intend to hurt Bob's foot, did you? No? Then you're off the hook."

"Like the catfish," said Paz, catching this last as he entered. He caressed his daughter and wife simultaneously. "We have a serious *pescadora* here," he said, nuzzling the girl. "She landed that monster all by herself, two pounds three ounces, a major fish."

"Yes," said his wife, "we were just discussing the tangled web of contingency and how while she was responsible for the fish being there she was not responsible for Bob getting stuck."

"True enough, but on the other hand, you might say that Zwick needed to be punctured a little. A lot of people think that what happens was meant to happen."

"It's a point of view," said Lola, in a tone that indicated she did not share it. "Anyway, I have to go check on a patient."

"Busy day? I was surprised to see you working."

"I'm not meant to lounge, as you know. I was going batty in the house and I figured I'd ease back in on a slow shift. This is a strange one, by the way, this patient. A couple of Good Samaritans found her wandering up Dixie Highway, naked. They thought she'd been drugged and assaulted."

"Was she?"

"Hard to say. No drugs in the blood work. Sexually active,

but she hadn't been raped, not recently anyway. On the other hand, she *had* been tied up with tape, hands and feet. I can't get anything out of her—mute and flaccid. And an epileptic. She seized just after she got here."

"Uh-huh. This person's about nineteen, a tallish good-looking redhead?"

Lola stared at him, dumbfounded. "Yes. How did you know?"

"Her name's Jennifer Simpson and the cops are looking for her. She was snatched off the street a couple of nights ago by a Colombian gang. I need to call Tito on this."

"My God! Are you sure it's the right girl?"

"Unless there's another redheaded teenaged epileptic who's recently been tied hand and foot wandering around Miami. The other thing is . . . well, the bad guys are going to be looking for her."

"But nobody but us knows she's here."

"Not at this second, but they'll think of hospitals right away and put some money on the street. Hospitals are full of low-wage Latinos. It won't take long. Let's take a peek at Jennifer now—maybe she'll talk if we show her we know who she is."

They went down the hall to one of the small rooms where they kept ER patients, with Amelia trailing behind them, temporarily unregarded.

The girl was in bed with the covers pulled up high and her red-gold hair spread wide on the pillow, like a dead girl in a Victorian painting. Lola stood over her and said, "Jennifer? Is that your name? Jennifer Simpson?"

Jenny opened her eyes. She saw a pale blond woman in a white lab coat over green scrubs, and a dark man. They were looking at her with concern, and saying a name, which was strange at first, just nonsense syllables, and then the sounds popped the little switches in her empty mind and she knew it was her own. Memories returned, first trickling in, then a flood as she reoccupied herself, *all* the memories, including the recent ones from the garage. Another face appeared, lower down in her field of view, a little girl, dark-haired, with skin colored a tone just halfway between those of the two adults. These people were covered in sparkly lights like sequins. Waves of color burst from their heads and fell with slow grace to the floor, and the cool waves rolled down from the region of her heart to her groin, really quite delicious this time, and she was gone from there.

When she could see again she found herself not in the hospital room but in a gray place with no horizon lit by a cool light that seemed to come from nowhere at all. The only real color came from the bright-feathered cape and head-dress worn by her companion, who was Moie. For some reason none of this surprised her.

"Hey, Moie," she said. "What's up?"

He answered in a language she did not know, yet the meaning of his words was perfectly clear to her. "Jaguar has taken you to the other side of the moon," he said, "where the dead have their being. I mean the real dead, not the *wai'ichuranan*. This is a great thing, because I don't think that he has ever let one of you here. I think it's possible because you have the *unquayuvmaikat,* the falling gift. It's how the god reaches you, even though you have no training at all."

Jenny accepted this as reasonable and wondered for a moment why she had never thought of it before.

"He breathed in my face."

"Yes. This is another thing that has never been done to one of you. I have no idea of what it means."

"Me neither. Maybe I'll be able to turn into a jaguar, too."

"Possibly, but, you know, it's not a turning into. It's hard to explain. You know how animals mark their territory?"

"Like dogs peeing on trees?"

"Yes, and in other ways. So, those who serve Jaguar are his marks in this world. He can smell them as he passes through the *ajampik,* the spirit world, and then he makes a door through and changes places with the *jampiri,* me. Then I am here until he calls me back again."

"Is he going to do that with me now?"

"All things are possible, but it usually takes a lot of training and practice to walk through the worlds, and you have none. I am the last of my people who can do this, and it would be very strange if you could also do it. If we had many hands of seasons, perhaps I could teach you, but we don't. My time in the land of the dead is nearly over."

"Are you going home?"

"I don't think so. Being with so many dead people is harder than I thought it would be. Father Tim was right—you are as many as the leaves on the trees. If one dies, another takes his place. And I feel my *aryu't* draining out, like water from a gourd with the small crack in it. It's hard to remain a human being without real people around me."

"You could go home. I bet Cooksey could get you back. You wouldn't have to paddle your canoe either."

"I know this. And it would make me happy to go home, as Cooksey has told me, in the flying canoe of the *wai'ichuranan*. But now I am part, and Jaguar is part of a . . . a part of a . . . *thing*. I could say the word, but even if you knew what it meant, you wouldn't know, because there is no place to hold it in the minds of the dead people. It is like a place where many, many paths come together, and the choice made there determines what roads we travel and everything that will or won't happen to us after we take that road. And also for some reason Jaguar wishes to take this girl—that's part of the . . . *thing*. Only this one girl. When I first saw you, I thought that you were the one that was necessary, but it's not so. Then I thought perhaps because she is the grandchild of the man that Jaguar took, Calderón, but that's not it, either. I've served Jaguar all my life, or nearly all, and I still have no understanding of his ways. Why should I? He's a god and I'm not. I don't care about that—this is the life I was chosen for. But I'm curious about what he wants with you."

"Me, too," said Jenny, who was not particularly curious. Perhaps that was why Jaguar had chosen her. She had often noticed that most of the people she met had some kind of motor in them or a compass—they knew where they were going or what they wanted, but she thought that she had never had anything like that in her, or not a very strong one, whatever it was. From her first memories she had been an inert being, ready to go along with whatever was happening, learning how to vanish as an individual that anyone else was obliged to consider. She had gone along with the various weirdness or blandness of her foster homes, had been docile at school, had agreed cheerfully with whatever the other kids wanted to do, had participated in sex when it was time for that to happen, had picked up the environmental radical business from Kevin and the science business from Cooksey, although she considered this last to be a little different, because it was a lot closer to having something real, a real talent or desire within her void. Now there was another thing inside her, not at present making any demands, but *there*; and it had something to do with her disease, if it was a disease at all. Moie certainly didn't think so.

She found he was looking at her with interest, as if at a newly discovered plant. He rarely smiled but now he did, as at a silly joke. She observed for the first time that his incisors had been filed to sharp points. She wondered what was so funny and was about to ask him when bright light flooded the dim scene and she found she was in the hospital room again.

That doctor, the blond one, was filling her field of vision and she had a finger on Jenny's eye, as if she had been about to pry an eyelid open. Jenny twisted her face away from the annoyance.

"You're back with us," said the doctor. "Do you know where you are?"

"A hospital."

"Right. South Miami Hospital. Do you know your name?"

"Sure. Jenny Simpson. I had a seizure, right?"

"More than one," Lola Wise said, and asked a number of other questions pertaining to her condition, after which Jenny asked, "Can I go home now?"

"That's not a good idea, Jenny. You could seize again. We'd like to keep you under observation for a while, see what drugs work best for you and—"

"I don't want any drugs. Dilantin makes me sick."

"There are other drugs besides . . ."

"No. I want to go home." She sat up in the bed, clumsy with the residue of the seizure and the dream, if it had been a dream. Things still looked strange, the little speckled lights were still flashing, and the doctor's face looked transparent—no, not exactly transparent, Jenny thought, but like she could see through the mask that she wore in the way that everyone wore a mask, and see her true feelings. The doctor was frightened, she observed, really scared behind the cool veneer. The man and the little girl were absent.

Jenny looked around the small room. "Can I have my clothes?"

"You don't have any clothes. You were brought in here completely naked. You'd apparently been walking up Dixie Highway that way."

"Oh, right. I forgot. Well, could you get me some?" Giving her measurements in a rush. "And some flip-flops? I could pay you back, or somebody . . ."

"You'd be leaving against medical advice. You'd have to sign a form."

"That's cool."

"And the police would like to talk to you," said Lola. She felt a certain satisfaction at the look on the silly girl's face when she said this, and immediately found herself cringing with guilt. It is not pleasant for those in the helping professions to have their help spurned, and more often than is supposed, they get even.

"I'll get some clothes for you," said Lola the Sucker, and bustled out.

In the hall she found Tito Morales talking with her husband. "She's all yours," Lola said and went to the nurses' station to sign out for an hour of personal time.

"You want in on this?" asked Morales.

"Would it help?"

"I guess. I don't know, *mano,* this fucking case . . . did I tell you they had to let all the Colombians go?"

"No. How the hell did *that* happen?"

"Garza and Ibanez. They swore up and down that these bastards were all bona fide Mexican businessmen. They showed good Mexican paper and smiled a lot. Meanwhile the federal judge and the assistant U.S. attorney are both Cubans, Garza and Ibanez are both generous contributors to the party all Cubans love, and the rest is history. We got absolutely nothing to hang a local warrant on, so it's *hasta la vista, mis amigos,* write when you get back to Cali."

"What if they're really businessmen?"

Morales gave him an eye roll. "Oh, right! Listen, you didn't see any of them. You know how you just know when someone's wrong? Well, these *cabrones* were as wrong as it gets. The feds were chewing pencils and running around in little circles."

"What about Hurtado. Don't they know what *he* looks like?"

"Of course, but that's a whole different game. Everyone knows Hurtado is a drug lord, but no one's ever been able to pin anything on him. The reward is for information leading to arrest and conviction, but there's no such info. He's laundered right up to the nipples. Yet another respectable businessman and our Cubans vouch for him, too. Meanwhile, I'm hoping this girl will help us out on the murder-kidnap."

This the girl did, to an extent. She did not recognize the photos she was shown of the men arrested on Fisher Island, and her descriptions of the three men who had killed Kevin Voss and kidnapped her did not match anyone in whom the police had a current interest. But she recalled where she had been held and its approximate location.

"How did you escape?" asked Paz after she had explained how she had been bound.

"It was hot in there and the tape around one of my wrists was loose enough so I could drag my hand out and there were some tools I could reach. I used a utility knife to cut through the rest of the tape."

"What were the kidnappers doing while this was going on?"

"They were . . . they left for a while," she lied. Paz saw

the lie but declined to call her on it. He left then and hung around with Amelia at the nurses' station until Lola returned, with a don't-ask look on her face and a Target shopping bag in her mitt. She vanished into Jenny Simpson's room. Shortly thereafter, Robert Zwick rolled by in a wheelchair, hoisting a cane.

"Still got the foot, I see," said Paz. "Are you comfortably medicated?"

"Barely. Are you going to drive me home?"

"It might be a while. I have to check out something to do with a police case. The mystic jaguar we were talking about."

"Can I come along?"

"You want to? I'll ask."

Morales was talking on his cell phone. Paz called out, "Hey, Tito, Zwick wants to come on this run with us."

"No," said Morales.

"He's the world's smartest man. He could be a big help if there are any subtle clues."

"No," said Morales and continued his conversation into the cell phone.

"That means yes," said Paz.

Morales detailed a couple of Miami cops to keep an eye on the hospital, and on Jenny Simpson, and then he took Paz and Zwick along in his car and they drove down to the place the girl had described, a blocky buff-colored building south of Dixie near Eighty-second Street with a large FOR LET sign in front. The corrugated steel doors that led to the repair bay of the garage were down and locked, but the door of the garage office had been left open, and even from outside they could hear the insistent nasty buzz that signaled woe in South Florida, and caught a whiff of the sweetish heavy odor that went with it. In the office the TV was still crackling out a snowy image, apparently of *Jeopardy!*, and they passed through to the service bay. Morales found the light switch.

It was like looking at the defective television, so thick were the swarming flies feeding on the blood and the red meat strewn on the floor, although they could not actually see the meat very well because of the giant cockroaches that covered the body and its severed lumps. When the light went on, hundreds of these took to the air in a crackle of chitinous wings. The three men crouched and waved their arms instinctively, ridiculously, and Zwick spun and exited at a remarkably fast hobble. They could hear him being sick outside.

"At least he didn't puke up the scene," said Morales sourly. He flicked a giant cockroach casually off his sleeve. People who refuse to have giant flying roaches crawling on them do not long survive as Miami homicide detectives. "Christ, it looks like . . . what is that down there, a chunk out of this one or is it another guy?"

"Another guy, I think. Let's go see."

Morales led the way, waving his hand continuously before his face to ward off the flies, like a band conductor in hell.

Paz said, "Let's see your flashlight, this looks like something . . ."

Morales handed over a powerful miniature Kel-Light and Paz directed it at the floor. "We've seen those footprints before, right, Tito? Your imposters must've had a whole collection of jaguar paws." Paz directed the beam at a scatter of glass on the floor and then up to the dim skylight. "He broke out the pane and dropped through. What is that, a twenty-inch pane, would you say? A small guy could've dropped through there and . . . yeah, here, check this out, barefoot prints in the dust. He dropped down and someone must have spotted him because, following these footprints, he ducked behind this parts cabinet and . . ."

"Shine it over here, will you?" said Morales. He was squatting near a substantial pattern of dried blood-spatter. In the beam that Paz now provided it was clear that an angular object about the size and approximate shape of a carpenter's try square, or a semiautomatic pistol, had lain in that spot when the blood had been squirted on the floor. The negative shape was clear, like the patterns of leaves that kindergarteners make on paper with toothbrushes dipped in water paints.

"The killer picked up the gun," said Morales. "Look, there's the mark of a shoe, a partial heel there."

"So you think the guy who gutted these two boys was being, what, *tidy*?"

"It could've been the weapon used to shoot Kevin Voss. They didn't want the connection made."

"Well, maybe," Paz replied. "But obviously, this is the place they held the girl." He directed the flashlight beam to the car hoist. "The tape is still on that thing from where they tied her up. But the guy who picked up the gun was from the people who hired the hit on Voss and the kidnap, not whoever did these, um, dismemberments. They must've called the guys who were supposed to be watching our girl, got no answer, and came by to check it out. They found this, grabbed up the guns, and split."

"How do you know they didn't kill them? These guys let the girl get away, and the boss had them whacked and chopped up to set an example."

"You believe the girl's story? That she just happened to wriggle loose and escape from at least two armed Colombian desperados?"

"She got lucky," said Morales with a shrug. "Why, what's your theory?"

"I'll show you. With the dust and grease layer on this floor, it's like reading a book. Our little guy gets up on the roof, breaks the skylight, and drops down to the floor, here." Paz pointed with the beam, like a teacher with a red laser gadget in front of a classroom slide. "He gets spotted by the deceased number one and whips around that parts cabinet. You can see the smeared mark where he made his jump . . . hey, Zwick, how're you feeling?"

Zwick had come into the garage. He looked green in the dimness. "I'm fine," he said, fanning away flies. "What's happening?"

"We're reconstructing the crime." Paz reviewed his recent

conversation with Morales and then shone the beam on the floor. "Here's where the barefoot prints end. They go behind the cabinet and stop. Then we have jaguar prints. The jaguar walks around the other side of the cabinet, and here, you can see where the rear claws dug into the cement when it pushed off. Then it zooms through the air and takes the deceased down, from behind probably, because it bit the back of the man's skull right off, then it flips him over, disembowels him, lots of blood on the paws, because you can see it's walking toward the front of the garage. Then deceased *numero dos* comes in, and here you can see, again, the thing digs in, those scratches, and takes off in one bound, there, and he's on the guy, rips his throat out, tears out his belly, snacks on some liver there, and then he walks over to the hoist and has a conversation with our girlfriend Jenny. By the way, she would have been able to see the whole thing. Now, we observe, here, a pair of barefoot prints standing right where the jaguar prints are, and look at that! If you look real close, you can see that one of them is actually on top of the cat paw print, thus subsequent in time. Also note that the tape's been slashed with a very sharp blade, all four tapes treated the same way, meaning our girl was definitely blowing smoke about wriggling free. She was sprung by the little Indian after he wasted the desperados."

A silence ensued, which Morales broke with "So you're saying your Indian gets in, turns into a jaguar, kills the bad guys, turns back into a man again, frees the girl, and disappears." Morales was speaking slowly and with care, as if to a defective or a child, but Paz could imagine the man's mind scuttling around like one of these cockroaches, trying to find a safe hole where his worldview would be safe from the clear evidence that Paz had presented. He wasn't green like Zwick, but he was sweating and twitchy, his hands plucking, scratching at himself. "Um," said Morales, and was saved from a more articulate response by Zwick's loud snort.

"Oh, you *can't* be serious, Paz. That's just stupid."

"Why? That's what the evidence clearly shows."

"Then the evidence is wrong," said Zwick. "Look, guys, if something clearly *can't* happen, and there's evidence that it *has* happened, then one of two things is true: you've mistaken the evidence, or you're being hoaxed."

"I thought science was based on evidence," said Paz.

"To an extent. If you're adding a data point to an established field, the evidence can be modest. If you're upsetting the entire known order of the physical universe, you better have an enormous shitload of solid gold evidence. Which we don't have here."

"So we forget jumping in and out of the seven Calabi-Yau dimensions for now?"

Zwick gave him a frosty look. "Drunken speculation is one thing; believing a proposed explanation for a particular phenomenon is something else."

"So what would make you believe what this evidence suggests?"

"Did you ever see the movie *Close Encounters of the Third Kind*? Yeah? Remember when the mother ship came down? There was a row of cameras rolling, they had every piece of recording apparatus known to man on site. Same thing here. If you want me to believe that an Indian turned himself into a jaguar, I want it to happen in a floodlit room. I want there to be cameras picking up the entire spectrum from infrared to gamma radiation. I want a complete telemetry suite—mass detectors, radiation detectors, electromagnetic chemosensors. I want your Indian wired to the gills, like a guy in intensive care. Then maybe, just maybe, I'll believe it. This shit?" Here he gestured at the footprints. "I could set this up in an hour with some simple tools. If the guy who did it is any good, I bet you'll even find jaguar hairs and DNA traces on the bodies. Fancy, but no sale."

"Why would anyone go to all that trouble?" Paz asked.

"Hey, you're the fucking detectives. Maybe so you'd think it was a mystical beast instead of a couple of slicks with knives and phony footprint makers, like they do at summer camp to scare the girls. When you find the guy who did it, you could ask him. I got to get out of here." He did so, crunching the roaches in his path.

"And there you have it," said Paz. "The world's smartest man hath spoken."

"You believe him?" asked Morales.

"No, *you're* the detective, Tito. I'm just a superstitious Cuban cook." He put an idiotic smile on his face, and after a moment Morales smiled, too. "Yeah, I keep forgetting," he said. "Anyway, we're in the county here, so I'm going to call Finnegan and let him worry about it. I'm sure it'll make his day just like it made mine."

Paz did not wait around for the county detectives to arrive but called a cab. He dropped Zwick off at his apartment in Coral Gables, near the university. Zwick had taken a double dose of Vicodin, dry, and was somnolent on the drive.

"Well, that was a fun day!" he said as he got out of the cab. "Let's go fishing again real soon."

"I'll call you if I see that Indian," said Paz. "See how he feels about telemetry."

"You do that," said Zwick sourly and limped away.

When Paz arrived at his house the smell of grilling meat was rich in the air and he felt a pang of hunger that reached down to his knees. He realized he had not had anything to eat since his predawn breakfast, and that the garage scene had effectively suppressed his appetite until just now. He went to the bathroom, stripped off his clothes, took a quick hot shower. When he left the shower, as he was drying himself, he noticed a rich odor that penetrated the scent of soap and the fainter one of the meat cooking. It came from his clothes; he had forgotten how the stink of a murder scene stuck to clothing. It was worse than cigar smoke, and his cleaning bills as a homicide detective had been astronomical. He deposited the garments in the washing machine, seized a Beck's from the refrigerator and, now dressed in a T-shirt and shorts, went out to the back patio.

There he found his wife in a chaise, taking her ease like a

duchess, while the food was prepared. This was no surprise; the Lola did not cook. What was surprising was that the grill-person was Jenny Simpson, working under the detailed supervision of Amelia Paz. The two of them were having a fine time, chortling away. Jenny looked about twelve in her new clothes, aqua shorts and a short-sleeved cotton shirt covered with blue flowers and bright green leaves.

Paz greeted everyone affably, complimented the two chefs, finished his beer.

"Where've you been?" asked Lola.

"Out. Could I talk to you for a second?" He indicated with a motion of his head where he wished this conversation to take place. The two of them went to the kitchen, where Paz asked, "What's she doing here?"

"I brought her home with me. You said the hospital might be dangerous and I wanted to keep her under observation. And she seemed like such a lost soul."

"Did anyone see you leave with her?"

"I don't think so. We went out the back way and down to the parking garage. Why?"

"Why? Because the kind of people who're looking for her, when they remove people, they don't like to leave witnesses. What're you going to do if they come here? God, Lola, didn't you *think*?"

"Don't yell at me! She's my patient, all right? I was worried about her."

"You had a zillion patients. You never brought one home before."

Lola opened her mouth to say something nasty and aggressive. If she did that, she knew there would be a fight and a frosty dinner, with both of them speaking with unnatural calm to the child and not to each other and she didn't have the emotional energy to endure one of those. So instead of snarling she let the toxic feelings out in a sigh and said what was the simple truth. "I don't know why, Jimmy. It was just something I thought I had to do. And, you know, I thought of Emmylou Dideroff and how we smuggled her out of the hospital that time. She's the same kind of . . . no, not really the same. Emmylou was some sort of genius and this girl, I don't know, she seems mildly impaired, but there's something unworldly and helpless about her. I was going to leave and I stopped in to check on her, and she was sitting there with her hands on her knees looking like she didn't have a friend in the world and I invited her home for dinner and snuck her out. I honestly didn't think about the danger. What it is, I think I'm beyond scared. I hear that people get that way in combat. Or with the cops. Do they?"

Paz felt his voice get thick. "Yes, they do."

She said, "If you want, I could drive her back to her place on Ingraham—"

Paz flung his arms around his wife and hugged her. They stayed that way for a long time, so long that both of them felt a little strange, felt that they had fallen marginally out of ordinary time, and that as long as they stayed this way, nothing could harm them.

A call from the back of the house broke in—their daughter: "Hey you guys, the food is ready."

"Oh, hell, let her stay the night," said Paz, pulling away with some reluctance. There was a damp patch on his cheek where her flesh had rested. "I'll get out my gun."

They ate: sausages and chicken, banana chips and dirty rice. The adults drank California jug red. Paz kept Jenny's glass full, turned on the charm, and without seeming to, got Jenny to tell the story of her life, or at least those parts suitable for a child's ears. Lola was no mean interrogator herself, and she found in this subtle pumping yet another thing to admire and deplore about her husband.

Then it was dark, in the sudden light-switched way of tropical climes. Lola brought out the candles; Paz carried the wiped-out Amelia to bed. The conversation continued as it had but uncensored now, all the horrible tales of the fostered child. Jenny had never been the center of attention in an adult gathering before, no one but Cooksey had ever focused on her in this way, and she did not want it ever to stop, she sucked their attention in, spongelike, tubules long dry expanded, softened. Cooksey's attention had been this intense, but that was about discipline, turning her into an instrument she could use in his service. She mentioned this, half embarrassed, and the conversation turned to Cooksey himself; all that she knew of his background, his tragedies, emerged into the candlelit air.

The wine slowed her speech at last, then stopped it; her head nodded. Lola took her to the daybed in the home office. The girl was instantly asleep. Lola laid a light blanket over her and went back to the patio.

Paz was in a chaise with a glass of wine. She slid in next to him, the wineglass was drained, now a little postmarital necking, too long absent, they both thought.

When breathing resumed, Lola said, "Poor kid! What a miserable life!"

"Yeah, but there's something intact in there. Somehow she learned how to protect herself. I mean, why isn't she a crack whore? She'd at least have an excuse."

"One of the great mysteries, like you and me. I couldn't help noticing you kept steering her back to this Cooksey. Why the interest?"

"Because, aside from our mystical Indian, he's the most interesting character in this whole strange tale."

"How so? The way she described him he seemed like just another sad refugee who washed up in Miami and couldn't get it together to return to civilization. Not unlike myself."

"I beg to differ. Miami is the center of civilization. It's the only place that has Cuban food, cheap cigars, *and* electricity twenty-four hours a day. Anyway, Professor Cooksey. Sad, all right, but not a refugee. He could work anywhere, but he's here, operating out of a minor environmental group-slash-commune, whose other members seem slightly nuts, or at any rate a little low-end. Why?"

"To forget his sad past?"

"No, Cooksey is not a forgetter. He's a rememberer. Look, you're from another planet, you're walking on a deserted beach on a desert island and you find a watch. What does that tell you?"

"The time?"

He punched her gently in the ribs. "No, you know what I

mean. It implies a watchmaker. So put together the story this kid just told us, all the stuff she's picked up from Cooksey and this Moie character, plus the strange events of the last months, the mysterious killings and so on. Somehow a priest in the middle of the jungle knows the names of the people who're behind the Consuela deal. How? Somehow just that priest who knows these names also has a faithful Indian companion, a kind of Stone Age guided missile, who flies to Miami in his little canoe and starts knocking off those very names. And somehow a Colombian *guapo* gangster is also involved in this timber-cutting scheme, and he gets called to Miami and comes, and now his boys are getting knocked off, too. What's so important about chopping down trees that would make a Colombian drug baron leave his safe haven and travel to the U.S.? Okay, he's laundering money through the Consuela company, we know that, but why the personal involvement? It suggests there's something bigger going on than trees and money laundries. And in the middle of all this is the professor, who just happens to have a background in clandestine warfare. Who lost his wife because someone was illegally cutting down rain forests, indirectly, true, but maybe he doesn't see it that way. Maybe, somehow, he *made* all this happen. . . ."

Lola snuggled closer and kissed his neck. She slid her hand under his shirt. "That's another reason why I love you. Your vivid imagination."

"You don't buy it?"

"There's nothing to buy, dear. You're just like Amy and her fish and Bob Zwick. Things happen, and other things happen as a consequence. If you try to find patterns in it you'll go crazy. In fact, that's one sure sign of crazy— finding patterns where there are none."

"I thought that was the basis of scientific discovery."

"The beginning maybe, but not the end. That's why we have statistical models, to distinguish the causal from the merely contingent. I notice that you didn't include your mystic Indian's interest in Amy in your conspiracy theory."

"No. I have no idea how that fits in."

"Maybe it doesn't. Maybe there's no pattern at all, except in your head. Maybe it's all just unconnected events pieced together by a former brilliant detective who's bored stiff with being a cook. In any case, just now I don't want to hear any more about it. It's boring." Now Lola shed her shirt, and her bra, and presented her fine breasts for his attention, which was given, after which more clothing fell to the patio paving. The candles gave their last light.

"This is a good way to shut down my brain," said Paz. "If that's what was intended."

"To an extent," said his wife, and so he let her, and she let him, but in the midst of this mindless exertion, Paz found that he could not stop thinking about Gabriel Hurtado and why he was in Miami. It was nearly as puzzling as the impossible jaguar.

# Eighteen

The next day, Paz stayed late in bed, drifting in and out of a hypnopompic sleep in whose vapors lurked worry and discontent. Awake at last, he lay with his arms behind his head staring at the white ceiling, counting out the reasons why this should be so. Colombian *pistoleros*? Check. Huge magical jaguar after his little girl? Check. Oddly enough, he decided that these worries, however grim they might seem to an ordinary man, did not constitute the basis of his unease. It was deeper than that, existentially deep. Neither he nor his family had been troubled by nightmares since he'd brought back the Santería charms from the little *botánica*. Which, despite the bravado he'd shown in dealing with his wife's disbelief, he knew was impossible. Little bags of whatever should not have had any effect on their dreams, but they had, even though Amelia was a kid and Lola was a total skeptic. He no longer knew what he believed anymore, but he understood that this amphibian life he had been leading with respect to Santería was breaking down; he would have to go in one direction or the other, toward the sunlit uplands of rationality inhabited by Bob Zwick, his wife, and all their pals, or down, into the soup, with Mom.

And since his social world was composed of people who were either believers or skeptics, there was no one who could give him any meaningful advice, or . . . as this thought crossed his mind he recalled that there was at least one other person who'd been in precisely the same bind, who had in fact introduced him to the possibility that there was in fact an unseen world. He reached for the bedside telephone and his address book and dialed an unlisted number with a Long Island area code.

A woman answered.

"Jane?" he said. "This is Jimmy Paz."

A pause on the line. "From Miami?"

"Among your many Jimmy Pazes, I am in fact the one from Miami. How're you doing, Jane? What is it, eight or nine years?"

"About that. Gosh, let me sit down. Well, this is a blast from the past."

Some small talk here, which Paz encouraged, being a little nervous about broaching the point of this call. He learned how she was—daughter Luz, twelve and flourishing, Jane teaching anthropology at Columbia and running her family's foundation. He told her about his own family.

"You're still with the cops, I take it."

"No, I'm running the restaurant with my mom. Why do you take it?"

"Oh, nothing . . . just that we had an intense twenty-four hours eight years ago but not what you could call a relationship, and suddenly you call. I assumed it was police business."

"Actually, I guess you could call it that. Look, I'm in a . . . I don't know what you'd call it, a kind of existential bind . . ."

She laughed, a deep chuckle that sent him back over that span of years. He brought her face up out of memory: Jane Doe, a handsome fine-boned woman with cropped yellow hair and a mad look in her pale eyes. Jane Doe from the famous Voodoo murders, a woman with whom he had shared the single most frightening experience of his life, actual zombies walking the streets of Miami and the gods of Africa breaking through to warp time and matter.

"Those're the worst kind," she said. "What's the problem? More *voudon*?"

"Not really. Do you know anything about shape-shifting?"

"A little. Are we talking imitative, pseudomorphic, or physical?"

"What's the difference?"

"It's complicated."

"If you have the time, I do."

He heard her take a deep breath.

"Well, in general humans tend to be uncomfortable locked in the prison of the self. Our own identification with nations and sports teams is probably a relic of that, and on a higher level there's religion, of course. Traditional peoples often identify with animals, and from this we get imitative magic. The shaman allows the spirit of the totemic animal to occupy his psyche. He becomes the animal, and not in a merely symbolic way. To him and the people participating he *is* the bison, or whatever. They see a bison."

"You mean they hallucinate it."

"No, I don't mean that at all. 'Hallucination' is not a useful term in this kind of anthropology. It's a mistake to assume that the psyches of traditional people are the same as ours. You might just as well say that the particle physicist hallucinates his data in accordance with a ritual called science. Anyway, that's imitative shape-shifting, well established in anthro literature. In pseudomorphic shape-shifts, the shaman creates or summons a spiritual being which then has an observable reality. The observer hears scratching, sees a shape, smells the creature, and so on. Traditional people are mainly substance dualists, of course. The spirit is completely separate from the flesh, and the body it happens to occupy at the moment is not the only body it can occupy. Anthro tends to draw the line here because we don't understand how it's possible to do that, since we're all supposed to be good little materialist monists. I've had personal experience with both types, if that helps."

"What about physical shape-shifting?"

Another chuckle. "Oh, that. Ah, Jimmy, would you care to tell me what this is all about?"

He told her the whole thing: murders, evidence, dreams, the *enkangues,* the Indian, his conversations with Zwick. And the business with Amelia.

"So what do you think, Jane?" he asked at the end of it. "Hoax or what?"

"It sounds like you think it's real."

"I don't know what to think. That's why I'm talking to you."

"Okay, then: physical shifting. I've never seen it, but there's a lot of anecdotal evidence. There's a whole book on it called *Human Animals* by a guy named Hamel. Makes interesting reading. Obviously, if factual, just like your smart friend says, we have no idea of how it's done. Had I not seen what you and I saw that time, I'd be prepared to discount it, too, but having seen it, I conclude that the world is not what it appears to the senses and is wider than what can fit in a lab. Why do you think it's after your kid?"

"I have no idea. It doesn't make any sense."

"Not to you, maybe, but traditional people think on wavelengths that are closed to us high-tech folks. Your mom still around?"

"Yeah, she is. Why?"

"What does she think of all this?"

"I haven't filled her in."

"Why not?"

"I was hoping you'd say I should load with silver bullets and it'd be cool. Or garlic."

"Yeah, well, a being who can manipulate the fabric of space and matter is unlikely to be swattable by a bullet made of any particular element. You're still afraid to take the plunge, aren't you? I recall you were reluctant to go the whole way back then. Your precious ontological cherry."

A nervous laugh from Paz. It was cool in the bedroom, but he felt the sweat start on his forehead and flanks. "Guilty. I'm not designed for this shit. I just want everything to be regular, as my kid says. Why me? I whine."

"Yeah, the great question. You're not religious, are you?"

"Not if I can help it. Why?"

"Because it answers the 'why me' question pretty good. And the religious can pray their way past a lot of this unseen-world stuff. My advice is, talk to your mom."

"Yeah, I'm on that already, as a matter of fact."

"And . . . ?"

"I don't know, Jane. I guess I'm . . . I guess I've been unwilling to totally, you know, accept the reality of . . ."

"You're scared shitless."

He could not restrain a laugh but was successful in keeping it from blossoming into full hysterics. "Yeah, you could put it like that."

"That's good, actually," Jane said. "If you weren't frightened, you'd be fucking doomed. The fear of the Lord is the beginning of wisdom."

"But we're not talking about God here, are we?"

"Aren't we? It's always a mistake to try to put him in a box and say this is holy and this is not. As soon as we worship any good thing that's not ourselves we're worshipping him. You and I are on what they used to call the left-hand path. We have the illusion we know where we're going, and how proud we are of our navigational skills. And then, well, what do you know! We end up in this tight little place with no way out except for one little tiny crack, but we can't pass through it unless we admit we're not God Almighty and in total control. That's when we experience that ripping existential terror. If I were you I would visit the bathroom frequently."

"Oh, thanks, Jane, speaking of tight little places—I feel so much better. Listen, you wouldn't consider coming down here and holding my hand, you being so experienced in this kind of shit?"

She hooted. "Oh, no, thank you! After what happened that time, I think I can say that my zombie jamboree days are over: this rough magic I here abjure. I'm a proper Catholic lady now, I take my kid and my dad to mass every Sunday, and I even have a little hat. Oh, and you'll find this amusing. The church we go to is called Mary Star of the Sea—you remember the way you were chanting that when the witching hour hit . . . ?"

"Yes, despite trying to forget," said Paz quickly.

"Yeah, me, too. Anyway, you can tell your mom that every

week, in a church consecrated to her, I light a candle to Yemaya. And, Jimmy? When the time comes, just let it all go, let it bore right down to the deepest level. Love is magic, too. She's not going to let anything bad happen to you."

"If you say so. Well, Jane, thanks for the advice. Maybe our paths will cross again, in this world or the next."

A low laugh. "I bet we will. And good luck. I'll pray for you."

Paz said good-bye and broke the connection and thought about boring down to the deepest level. Without replacing the receiver he rang his sister at home and had a short and somewhat technical conversation with her, after which he was pretty sure that he knew why Gabriel Hurtado was in Miami. So, one problem solved. He dropped the phone into its cradle and was not extremely surprised when the phone rang ten seconds later and his mother's voice came over the line. She got right to the point.

"It's time for you to be *asiento*," she said. "You have to start tonight."

Paz took in a breath to say no to this proposal. *Asiento,* the ritual that prepared a person to act as a "seat" for a god.

Mrs. Paz said, "It's necessary if you want to protect Amelia. The *santeros* have met, and they all agree. You have to be made to the saints. Soon. Now."

He spoke then and heard his voice expressing consent. This did not surprise him either.

"I'll come by in an hour," she said.

"What should I bring?"

"Nothing," she said. "It's not a vacation."

His wife was the surprised one when he informed her that he would be out of reach for a full week.

They were out on the back patio when he told her, having cleverly delayed the moment until she was about to leave for work. Just beyond them arose squeals of delight and the sound of splashing water. Jenny had set up the inflatable pool and was entertaining Amelia.

"That's crazy," said the wife.

"Are you speaking as a psychiatrist or was that a figure of speech?"

"Jimmy, you don't even believe in that stuff." Here a sharp look. "Or do you?"

"Let's say my beliefs are in flux. I know you've forgotten the way you were a little while ago, and about what stopped it, which is real convenient for you, but I seem to be engaged in something here and I can't let it go so easy."

"And what about Amy? I can't take a week off work so you can 'engage' in some ritual to make your mother happy."

"You won't have to. Jenny will take care of her. See, it's all been mystically arranged." He gave her a big smile, which she did not return.

"Don't be ridiculous! That girl can barely take care of herself. What if she seizes again?"

"I thought we were supposed to hire the handicapped."

"And the Colombians?"

"You're covered there. I'll have Tito put a patrol car out on the street twenty-four/seven while I'm away. And if you're uncomfortable with that, I'm sure my mom would volunteer to move in for the week."

She could not keep the look of horror from her face. "We'll talk about this later," she said and climbed onto her bicycle. As he watched her depart Paz could not help chuckling. Manipulative swine that he was, he understood that Lola would give her daughter to a brain-dead quadriplegic before she'd let Margarita Paz move in for a week. He walked back to where the girls were sporting.

"That looks like fun," he said.

"It is," said Amelia. "Are you going to come in the water with us?" Paz glanced at Jenny, who was wearing an electric-blue thong bikini of Lola's that Lola herself had not dared in years, exhibiting as much youthful scrumptiousness as anyone could desire. For about twelve seconds Paz contemplated what would happen, all unwillingly, should he roll about in the tiny pool in contact with *that*. Not.

"I don't think so, baby," he said. "Maybe later. Jenny, could I talk to you for a second?"

She jumped up, jiggling exquisitely; he led her a few paces away. She was perfectly amenable to the plan, seemed almost to have anticipated the request. She had, of course, a vast experience minding young children, often under difficult circumstances. The money he offered was fine. Her medical condition would not be a problem, she said.

"You're on medication, right?"

"Uh-huh."

This was a lie, he detected, but he let it pass. When Amelia was informed of the arrangement, she howled and leaped for joy.

Paz returned to his lounger on the patio, sipped his cooling coffee and read the newspaper without much interest. The lead story concerned the destruction of the S-9, a pumping station north of Miami, by a powerful bomb. An organization that called itself the Earth People's Army had claimed credit, although this was not entirely accepted by the authorities. An editorial suggested the fell hand of Al Qaeda or even more shadowy groups, striking at American prosperity by flooding prime Florida real estate. In a statement published in the paper, this putative organization threatened to bring down industrial society unless the Everglades was restored to its pristine condition and a host of other environmental cures instantly adopted. Wishing the evil ones the best of luck, he tossed the paper aside and drifted into the Florida room, where he watched a golf tournament, an old sitcom, a shopping show, a county commission meeting, and a tour of the French wine country by balloon, each for around two minutes, after which he muted the sound and put in a call to Tito Morales.

"Is this going to mess you up?" Paz asked after informing the detective that he would be unavailable for a number of days and required round-the-clock security for his family. He did not specify his destination. Morales said, "You're worried about the Indian?"

"Yeah, a little. That's why I need to be away for a while."

"I'm not going to ask where. You think a couple of cops are going to stop him?"

"Not really, but what the fuck can I do? I just have to hope

I'll be able to do what I need to do in time. Meanwhile there's the Colombians. They still might have an interest in the Simpson girl. How's the case against them going?"

"Oh, the *case*. Forget the case, man. The case is officially solved. All units are on the lookout for one homicidal Indian. The county is satisfied, we're satisfied, and we're on to newer and greater adventures. You heard about our terrorist?"

"Just what I read in the paper."

"Oh, well, you can imagine. The feds are no longer interested in Colombian drug lords. Everyone could care less if Cuban *guapos* get their livers eaten, and as far as those two narco thugs in the garage are concerned, they're making a medal, whoever did it. Meanwhile, every swinging dick, fed, county, and local, is now on full terror alert. Leaves canceled, automatic weapons issued—it's a total zoo."

"For a pump?"

"See, you say that because you're not hydrologically aware. Miami is a fucking swamp. These bastards blow a few more pumps, and should we happen to get a couple fucking hurricanes this year, they'll be fishing for marlin on Flagler Street. The major said to thank you for your invaluable help, by the way. They might make you a plaque." Paz heard noises in the background, voices and car engines. "Hey, I got to go, man," Morales said. "Catch you later."

Paz had been about to tell Morales that there was at least one man in town with a connection to the environmental movement who had a professional skill with bombs, but the moment passed. Let them figure it out. Paz had a boat, after all, and he thought it might be kind of cool to fish on the drowned avenues of downtown. Besides, he wanted to talk to Cooksey himself, on this and other matters. But not today. His week was spoken for. He went back to the lounger and let his mind go blank, listening to birdsong and his child's laughter until he heard the sound of his mother's car in the driveway.

Jenny felt a certain relief when the man left. He had a way of looking at her, a sharp look that she associated with street cops, as if he knew stuff about her she didn't want out in the open. Cooksey had a sharp look, too, but that was different, like he was seeing something in her that she didn't know was there and it would be a good thing if she learned about it. She missed Cooksey a little, but her life had rendered her nearly immune to missing anyone very badly. Perhaps she missed the fish a little more.

The child was getting wrinkly from the water, so Jenny got her out of the pool, dried and dressed, contemplating the clothes in her wardrobe with wonder. She supposed all of them had been bought new. She herself had never had new clothes as a child, but such was the sweetness of her nature that she bore the present child no resentment. She felt sorry for her, actually, without quite knowing why. A small puzzle here, nagging.

The day progressed pleasantly enough. She called Cooksey and told him more or less what had transpired since she had left La Casita with Kevin, including her rescue by Moie, but omitting the details. She said she thought she'd stay at the Paz house for a while. They seemed to need her. Cooksey made no objection; he was delighted to learn she was safe.

Then she made lunch for the girl, tuna fish sandwiches, from the can, following the child's instruction so that the sandwich would resemble in every detail those made by her father, the toast just so, the crusts removed, the chocolate milk in the special glass. Jenny followed these diktats amiably, delighting in a child who had confidence enough to order an adult around. She had never seen anything like it while growing up.

After lunch she cleaned the kitchen with quick efficiency and then went through the house with the child in tow, making a game of neatening, dusting, mopping, picking up toys and strewn luxuries. She didn't think much of the mother's housekeeping, but she figured that was to be expected from a doctor. Cooksey was a slob, too. The child informed her that no one was allowed in Mom's office when she wasn't around, and Jenny acquiesced in this.

They watched DVDs, *The Lion King* and *The Little Mermaid,* with the child telling Jenny what was going to happen next and singing along with the songs. The Disney music was not able, however, to drive from her head the song that had been circulating around in there for a whole day now, maybe longer, an ancient Pink Floyd number, "Brain Damage." An older kid in one of her foster homes was always playing it. She hadn't thought about it for years but now could not get it out of her head:

> *You lock the door*
> *And throw away the key*
> *There's someone in my head but it's not me.*

There *was* someone in her head that wasn't her, a presence, unobtrusive, silent, but unquestionably *there,* like someone staring at you in a crowded restaurant, but staring from the inside. She was not afraid, however, and this in itself was startling. After all that had gone down recently—Kevin getting his brains blown out all over her lap, being kidnapped and tied up naked, and what she'd seen in the garage—she should be a nervous wreck. I should be a nervous wreck, she said to herself, but I'm not. I feel fine, like I just smoked a huge spliff of primo dope, just kind of floating in the middle of life, like a fish, or this Little Mermaid on the TV. She thought it might have something to do with visiting the land of the dead with Moie. Maybe she had left all fear there. Anyway, it was cool, in a way, like being an X-man with secret powers. She settled back on the cushions and watched the movie, humming softly to herself.

Amelia dozed off toward the end of the film. Jenny watched the rest of it and then, driven by some unsettling energy, polished all the furniture that would take a polish and cleaned all the windows she could reach, with newspaper and vinegar. Then she began to assemble a meal. Invisible and indispensable, the two wings of her life strategy, her default mode. She slipped into it without thought, like a gecko going leaf-green on a leaf.

Thus when Lola came home (noting as she did so the Miami PD car with two cops in it across the street) she was presented with a working mother's wet dream of a helper: she cleans, she cooks, she's live-in, she's dirt cheap, the child adores her, she's sweet-natured, if a bit blank, she's *not* a guilt-making member of the hitherto exploited races, the opposite really, a guilt-lessening member of the handicapped. True, Jenny might be involved with a murderous Colombian mob, and vicious killers might at that very moment be stalking her family (with her wacko husband off at some voodoo party instead of protecting his dear ones, the rat), but on the other hand, you could actually see through the windows, and the floors did not stick to one's bare feet in that disgusting way, and here prepared from food already in the house a delicious crabmeat salad and actual warm biscuits that *she baked from scratch herself,* this alone worth defying the entire Cali cartel, enough even to forgive her husband.

**W**ho had been given by his mother into the care of three elderly white-gowned *santeras,* one of whom turned out to be Julia from the *botánica*; apparently, she was to be his *yubona,* or sponsor. Julia explained to him that what they were doing was quite irregular, that in old Cuba it might take nine months to prepare the head of a *iyawo,* an initiate, for union with the *orisha,* but that Pedro Ortiz and the other *santeros* and *santeras* had agreed that it was necessary, and also out of respect for his mother. They were in a room at the back of the house where Pedro Ortiz held his *ilé,* a room that must at one time have been a closet or workroom, because it had no windows. It was furnished only with a mat and a large mahogany *canistillero,* a cabinet for ritual objects.

The explanations went on for some time. Paz had a reasonable working knowledge of Lucumi, the African-based language of Santería, but Julia was using words that he didn't know, quoting divinations not only from Ifa but also from the special readings that were part of the *asiento* ceremony itself, that were done not with palm nuts or divining chains but with handfuls of cowrie shells. These *ita* divinations foretold a dark something if something didn't do something to something sometime at some particular place.

*"Mi madrina,"* said Paz, "I don't understand what you're saying."

The old woman shrugged and grinned and exchanged looks with the other two. "Of course not, but when the *orisha* is in your head, then you'll understand it all."

"The other thing I don't get," said Paz, "is I always thought that the *orisha* called the person and then the person prepared to receive that *orisha.* But no *orisha* has called me."

"The *orisha* has been calling you for years," said the *yubona,* "but you stopped your ears against him. He called so loud that everyone else heard it. It was very annoying."

"I'm sorry," said Paz, and as he said the conventional phrase, discovered that he really was. The old woman patted his hand. "Don't worry, my son, we'll make everything all right, although it's going to be hard. You're a stubborn donkey, like your mother, God bless her."

"Really? I thought my mother was always made to the saints, from when she was a young girl."

"If you think that, you don't know much," Julia said, and pressed her hand onto Paz's still-inquiring mouth, saying, "No, this is not the time for you to talk. This is the time for you to listen, and watch and prepare your head for the *orisha.*"

So then it began. Paz was ritually bathed and his head was washed and shaven, and he was dressed in white garments. He was placed on a mat, and the three women attended him as if he were a baby, giving him food and drink by hand, holding the spoon and the cup to his lips. The food was bland, mashed, and pale, the drink was herbal tea of many different kinds. There was a good deal of chanting and incense burning. A man Paz did not recognize came in and sacrificed a black pigeon, draining its blood into a coconut-shell bowl. He used the blood to draw designs on Paz's nude scalp. More tea, more smoke, more singing. Paz lost track of time. He felt himself regressing into infancy, which he gathered was the idea. At length he slept.

And of course dreamed. When he awoke, there was Julia, her dark eyes and black-leather face close to his, asking him what his dream had been. The other two sat in the background quietly observing, like judges at a gymnastic event. He told her the dream. He was in Havana, walking down a forest path with Fidel. He felt that he had impressed Fidel so much that Fidel was going to give up communism and free Cuba. Only one thing stood in the way of this great blessing—Fidel wanted to hold a feast to celebrate the end of communism, and the only thing he wanted at the feast was baby wild pigs. They would need seven of them for the feast. Fidel handed Paz a bow and seven arrows and Paz went into the forest to hunt wild pigs. He found he was a great hunter and soon had seven little pigs in his bag. As he walked back to Fidel's palace, he met his daughter. When he told her what he had in the bag she asked him for one of them. But Paz said no, because it was necessary for something very important, the liberation of Cuba, which Fidel would only do if he came back with the seven piglets. Not even one? Amelia cried. No, not even one, said Paz. It has to be seven. Then Amelia went away, and it started to rain and storm, a regular hurricane. Paz came to the palace all wet and battered by the storm and gave Fidel his sack. But when Fidel took out the piglets there were only six. Fidel was angry and said, "Can't you follow my orders, Paz? I said seven. No freedom for Cuba now!"

So, Paz thought, some wicked person has stolen one of the piglets. So despite the hurricane he went back into the forest and found another herd of pigs and with his bow and arrow shot another one and brought it to Fidel, who was very happy with it. Then Fidel said, "You have done good work, and now do you wish anything for yourself? Ask and it shall be done." And Paz thought about this and answered, "Yes, I want that wicked thief who stole my piglet caught by the police and shot." So Fidel said, Let it be done. But the police brought in little Amelia, and Paz had to watch as they put her in front of the firing squad.

"And was she shot, your daughter?"

"I don't know. I pointed my bow at Fidel and threatened to

shoot him if they didn't let her go; it was kind of a standoff,
I think."

"No, in the dream she dies. You know that this is the
dream of Oshosi?"

"I didn't know. How can you tell?"

"It's the same story, what we call the *apataki,* the life of
the *orishas* while they were still human. But in that story Oshosi hunts quail for Olodumare, the god of gods, and his
mother steals it, and Oshosi catches another one, pleasing
Olodumare, and Oshosi asks that his arrow find the heart of
the thief, and so it did, killing his mother. Also Oshosi's
number is seven, and there were seven arrows and seven
pigs. What were you wearing in the dream?"

"I don't know, some kind of uniform, a green and brown
uniform like they wear in Cuba."

"Yes, green and brown are Oshosi's colors. He is the lord
of the hunt. Now you know who is trying to fill your head.
It's good." She smiled broadly at him, and the other holy
ladies did, too. And it *was* good, Paz thought. Oshosi the
Hunter felt right to him. He had been a hunter himself, a
hunter of men, and even though he was one no longer, he felt
the pull, and so he had let himself become involved in hunting the magic jaguar. He recalled how he'd handled the
small bow at the *botánica,* and also one of the symbols of
Oshosi was a jailhouse, yes, and what was Paz's favorite
fruit—the mango, also Oshosi's. Yes, everything was connected, a sure sign of insanity, his wife might have said, but
his wife was not here. Only the *madrinas* were here, unless
this was another dream, that he was in a small white room
with white-clad women treating him like a baby, in which
case he was doomed, so why think about it?

He watched with interest as they laid out the round stones,
the *fundamentos* of Oshosi in a half circle in front of him.
These contained the *ashe* of the *orisha,* which would be
transmitted into Paz's head. The woman honored the *fundamentos* by bathing them and pouring herbal decoctions on
their smooth surfaces. The same was done to Paz's head.

Five days passed in this way, Paz not being permitted to

walk or talk, being fed by hand. Was he drugged? He didn't know, and after a short while he didn't care. His former life became vague, a distant half-recalled dream. This was the only reality, the slow, chanting, smoky, endless afternoons and nights. And more sacrifices. The *santero* came in at intervals and sacrificed beasts: roosters, pigeons, a small piglet, a black goat. The *santero* fed a portion of the blood of the sacrificed to the stones and arranged their heads and feet in the deep-bellied clay pots, *soperas.* At the end of the five days, Julia announced that a seat for the *orisha* had formed in Paz's head.

Paz felt this, too, a difference subtle but real, like the loss of virginity or how you felt after killing a man. He could talk now, it seemed, and was free to walk around, which he did on tender feet that seemed not to quite touch the floor. The five days of private gestation were over; now was *el dia de la coronación.* Paz was *iyawo,* a bride of the orisha. The *madrinas* dressed him in fresh white garments and freshly shaved his head, renewing the markings on it. He was given a crown of bright green parrot feathers, a cloak of emerald brocade, and the symbols of his *orisha:* a bow, and a leather quiver with seven arrows, and a small wooden model of a jail. Around his shoulders he wore the great embroidered, bead-worked, shell-dangling *collares de mazo,* and thus clothed they led him to the main room of the house, one corner of which had been made into a throne room, with silk hangings of green and brown and a *pilón,* a royal stool of the kind used by the kings of Ifé. There they sat him, and around his feet they lay yams and mangoes in piles, and the air was scented by these and by the cooking for the wedding feast, the roasting and frying of the sacrificial beasts.

People arrived in numbers, singing praise songs and abasing themselves before the throne of Paz-Oshosi. Among these was his mother, and seeing her, Paz understood that his previous relationship with her was over, that the personality of a rather bratty and sarcastic man he'd used to defend himself against her force during the whole of his life was gone, that now they would be demigods together.

The room became more crowded and grew warmer. Paz was given a glass and told to drink it: it was *aguardiente,* Oshosi's drink. The sweat popped out on his upper lip. The drummers arrived, three very black men, and greeted the *santero,* and set up their instruments on a wooden platform built on one side of the room: the *iya,* the great mother drum, the smaller *itotele,* and the little *okonkolo.* As usual, in the casual African way, the thing began. The sharp penetrating crack of the *iya* rang out, and the chatter of the other drums and the gourd rattle in the hands of the *santero,* weaving the ancient and intricate sounds, music as the language of the *santos.* The *ilé* took up the song to Eshu-Eleggua, the guardian of the gates, *ago ago ago ilé ago*: open up, open up.

Paz sat on his throne-stool thinking about his mother and about someone he seemed to have heard of long ago named Jimmy Paz, who had a kid and who was married to a doctor, nice enough guy, something of a wiseass, and wondered if what he was now could ever be fitted back into that container.

People swayed to the rhythm, and an elderly woman made to Eshu danced in front of Paz. The chanting grew louder, more insistent. The people sang for Oshosi to come down to take his new bride. Paz blinked sweat from his eyes; the shapes of people and objects were starting to get weird and shaky. And there was a little inquiring voice in his mind, and Paz had to admit that yes, he'd gone through this somewhat tedious ritual, and he understood the benefits of purification, and he recognized it as a symbol of some kind of coming-of-age, some kind of making peace with the Afro-Cuban part of his background, and yes, it had changed him, he was really a better person for it, and he even imagined himself explaining all of this in a rational voice to his wife. But in the midst of this pleasant notional conversation (itself born of a terror that Paz was yet unwilling to own), Oshosi, Lord of Beasts, stepped through the gate from the unseen world and into Paz's head.

So now Paz understood that there is a virginity much deeper than the sexual one about which people make so

much fuss, the basic bedrock understanding of physical being we bring from earliest childhood that nearly everyone in
the modern world carries intact to their graves: that the
world is as it is represented by our senses; that we sit perma-
nently within our own heads, all alone in there; that belief is
a choice we make with our minds. All this vanished in the
first seconds, as the *orisha* penetrated his body, and here he
understood that calling the person in this situation a bride
was no mere figure of speech; he was being fucked by a god,
not unwillingly it seemed, but undeniably possessed, never
again to be the same.

Paz has seen people ridden by the *orishas* before this and
had supposed that while the *orisha* was in charge the people
were unconscious, but now he finds that this is not so. He is
now outside his body, a disembodied spirit containing nothing but a benign interest in what his body is doing. It is down
there dancing in front of the throne while the drums sing. It
goes on for a long time, this dance; Paz sees his body do
things it cannot normally do.

Then he is back in the flesh, with people helping him to
stand. His legs barely support him, and he is covered with
sweat. There was a warmth in his groin and his joints, as if
he has just made love for hours. They sat him on his throne,
and Julia and the *madrinas* and the *santero* spoke to him
about his new life, and of the *ewos,* the ritual tasks and pro-
hibitions that came with it. Thus passed *el dia de la coronación.* The next day was *el dia del medio,* devoted to
feasting and visits of congratulation by Miami's Santería
world. People prostrated themselves in front of Oshosi as
Paz. Paz found he enjoyed being a god. His mother came by,
and they had a long conversation about this, during which
Paz was able to admit cheerfully that he'd been wrong about
nearly everything, and his mother was able to do the same
about all her mistakes in raising him, and they had a good
laugh about it.

The next day was *el dia del Ita.* A man, the *italero,* very
old and brown and dressed in immaculate white, came in

and threw cowrie shells on a mat and from the fall predicted the remainder of Paz's life, its dangers, failures, and triumphs. Paz was surprised at some of it, but the rest seemed a reasonable projection from his current state.

He asked the *italero* about jaguars and daughters and got the usual oracular answer. Apparently it was all up to Paz, either he'd make the right decision or not. He should depend on his *orisha*. Having now met this entity, Paz thought this was pretty good advice.

# Nineteen

While Paz is becoming a god, Moie appears in the bedroom of Felipe Ibanez, slipping unseen past the guards Ibanez has hired. Moie has prepared for Jaguar to come, but Jaguar does not. In this case it proves unnecessary. Ibanez wakes from his usual nightmare, sees the small Indian, understands what he represents, and recalls what has been done to his colleagues. Wetting himself in terror, the businessman promises to dissolve the Consuela Company, to stop all cutting of trees in the Puxto reserve. He speaks in Spanish, and Moie understands. Moie starts to leave, but the man wants to keep talking. Moie has noticed this about the dead people, that they want to fill the air with words even when everything necessary has been said. Ibanez says that because Consuela will not cut the Puxto, it doesn't mean that others won't. There are many other timber operations. It's Hurtado who is making the whole thing move, Hurtado with the contacts in the Colombian government, Hurtado who bribes the guerrillas and the paramilitaries who fight the guerrillas, Hurtado who wants the Puxto cleared so he can plant coca in the virgin territory and also for another reason that he now tells to Moie. "You have to kill Hurtado," Ibanez shouts as the Indian departs. Then he presses the alarm button. In the ensuing melee one of the hired guards shoots another one, not seriously. No one sees the Indian, and the guards privately agree that the old fart was dreaming. Ibanez is already on the phone to his subsidiary in Cali.

━━━━━━━━

While Paz is becoming a god, Hurtado stays in a mediocre residence hotel in North Miami. When he heard the news that Ibanez had pulled out of the Puxto operation, he summoned El Silencio to his room. "See, you didn't believe me, but this is the proof. He's behind this whole thing, Ibanez, that *chingada,* one of the others must have got to him."

"Are you sure? He was okay on the first shipment. It got to Miami with no problem."

"To put me off my guard! He was very smart, smarter than I thought. Some of these old Cubans . . . this is a good lesson, Ramon, never underestimate the intelligence of your enemies, especially when they're your friends."

El Silencio studied his employer as the man paced back and forth in front of the blaring television. It was unlikely that anyone knew they were staying in this particular shithole, but Hurtado had the TV on whenever he said anything out loud. The boss did not look good. It had been a long time since Hurtado had been on the run, thought El Silencio, and even longer since he was afraid of anything. The arrests and losing those three men had got to him. He kept asking where was Martínez, as if he had the kind of instant information system here that he had back home. Who knew where the *cabrón* had run off to? Clearly he disappeared after the two men were killed and the girl escaped, and that was enough to get Hurtado upset all by itself. People did not run out on Hurtado. It had made the man twitchy.

"Do we know where Ibanez's granddaughter is?"

"Yeah, somebody called and said she's staying at that place with the fish pool, where the other girl was staying."

"Go there. Get her. Cut off her tit and send it to Ibanez. And kill anyone else in that fucking house, all of them."

El Silencio didn't move. Hurtado glared at him. "Well?"

"Boss, you know, maybe this isn't such a great idea. At

home, sure, no problem. But there's something going on here I don't like. I don't like it when I don't understand what I'm up against . . ."

"It's Indians. Ibanez and whoever he's with—Equitos or the Pastorans, or somebody from Medellín—brought down a crew of Indians. You'll see, we grab up his girl and he'll give us the fucking Indians. We should've done it first thing, but how could you figure . . . ?"

"I don't know, boss, I think there's something else . . ."

"Ramon, you're thinking again," said Hurtado sharply. "Stop thinking and go do what I said!"

El Silencio left the room without another word. After almost twenty years of working for Hurtado, he was about as independent as a toaster oven, but he could not entirely suppress the feeling that the organization was out of its depth for the first time. At home, for example, there would be no problem with the police. They owned the police, and the army, and the special incorruptible drug police who worked with the Americans, and should anyone appear on the scene who could not be bought, he could be killed. This was apparently not the case here in America. Also, Hurtado was persisting in his belief that a rival Colombian gang was behind this business, using Ibanez as a tool and Indians as soldiers. El Silencio thought this was unlikely, and he knew more about Indians than Hurtado did, being a quarter Indian himself. He'd heard stories from his grandmother about what some of those up-country Indians could do, and while he was not a particularly superstitious man, the carnage in the garage had given him pause. El Silencio had presided at a number of mutilations and he knew for a fact that the two gunmen had not been slashed by a human being. Nor was Prudencio Martínez a superstitious man. He was (had been) the most efficient crew boss the Hurtados had owned, and if *he* had pulled the plug, then what they faced was *not* just a bunch of Indians.

El Silencio walked down the dim hallway, which stank of chlorine from the pool and frying from the coffee shop, and went into a room. Here were his available troops, six men, all of whom looked up from the card game, the TV, the magazine, when he came in. He didn't know them well, for he was not a crew boss himself and uneasy with command. He almost always worked alone, besides which he would have to leave one person behind to watch over Hurtado. This was even more disturbing.

They were all staring at him. Someone muted the television, which drew El Silencio's attention: someone who could act independently, a little more alert than the others? Or he just didn't care for what was on? The guy was named . . . something Ochoa, a veteran of the paramilitaries that the big *latifundistas* used for protection against the Marxists, a solid shaven-headed man with a scar under his eye. El Silencio gestured to him. *Delegate,* that was one of Hurtado's favorite words. *Delegate* and *hold accountable.* El Silencio had never had a problem with the latter of these, and now he was going to learn about the former. He took Ochoa to his own room for an interview.

**W**hile Paz is becoming a god, Geli Vargos is hiding out in Rupert Zenger's house. The woman had arrived late one night with only the clothes on her back, having fled her grandfather's house in the disturbances following the arrest of Hurtado's men. Cooksey was kind, gave her a drink, questioned her gently.

"Was Hurtado himself arrested?"

"No, he was never there except once. My grandfather was terrified of him. But he mainly stayed at some hotel. There was this other guy carrying whatever orders he had . . . even the thugs were scared of him, but the cops got him, too. Then I heard they got sprung, and that's when I left. I feel like such a coward! What do you think they'll do to my grandfather?"

"Nothing, I imagine," said Cooksey. "He's covering for them, and they need him intact for the Puxto operation to go forward. I expect that they are not the primary threat to Mr.

Ibanez. If he doesn't stop cutting down that rain forest, I'm afraid . . . I mean what happened to his partners could well happen to him."

When Geli understood what he meant she burst into hysterical sobs. Cooksey held her and stroked her back absently. In irregular warfare, he had been taught, there was a time to stir things up and a time to lie low and wait. This was the waiting time.

**P**az returned home on the evening of the Sunday, eight days after he'd left. His mother drove him home.

"You'll be all right," she said when they pulled up to the curb. "You have my prayers and the prayers of everyone in the *ilé*. Keep on the path of the saints." They embraced, clumsily, as one does in the front seat of a car, and also because embracing had not been much practiced between them. Paz watched his mother drive off. He was carrying his bow and arrows and his model jailhouse, and for a moment he felt like a kid being dropped off to play at a friend's house, holding toys, and the thought made him laugh out loud.

There was laughter coming from his house as well, from the patio in the back, and Paz went around the side of the house to join in the fun. Lola was apparently entertaining. Paz stepped into the patio and everyone stared at him as at a ghost. Amelia was the first one to respond. With a shrill "Dadeeeee!" she propelled herself at him and swarmed up him like a monkey. Paz had to put his emblems down on a chair so that he could hug her, which he did until she objected. He put her down and surveyed the party: Lola, Bob Zwick, Beth Morgensen, and an older balding man with a pleasantly ugly face whom Paz recognized as Kemmelman, Lola's boss at the hospital.

Conversation sprang up again; everyone wanted to know all about what had happened. Paz ignored this, leaned over Lola, and kissed her.

"How easily I'm replaced," he whispered. "And a Jewish doctor, too."

"I won't dignify that with a response," she whispered

back, but the dynamics of the group had changed. Kemmel-man seemed to become uncomfortable, and shortly he stood and said he had to get home. When he'd gone, Zwick said, "So, give. Paz. Are you all holy now?"

"I am, as a matter of fact."

"Yeah? Do something holy. What are these objects?" He picked up the bow and twanged it. "Or are they too sacred for me to touch?"

"No, they're just symbols of my status, like your white coat."

"Oh, so they *are* sacred."

The adults laughed, easing some of the tension, but Paz remained wary. There was something wrong with their faces, or maybe he was just seeing with new eyes. It was as if he could penetrate the social masks they displayed to the real person hiding beneath. It was not a pleasant experience: Zwick's intellectual arrogance sheltering the frightened, driven nerd, Beth's fear of loneliness generating a spas-modic seductivity . . . he found it hard to look at his wife. Married people, however intimate, require a reserve of pri-vacy; he felt that he could violate that now, and the ability re-pelled him. Only Amelia seemed true all the way to the core.

There were questions about the ritual he'd just been through, and he found himself dodging these with studied humor, although he admitted to having been possessed by his *orisha,* which Zwick explained away as arising from the effect of entraining rhythms, drugged food, and varying light levels upon the medial temporal lobe of the brain. Appar-ently it was well established in the literature.

Paz found this explanation more exhausting than the ritual itself. "What happened to Jenny?" he asked when Zwick at last ran down.

"She's cooking our dinner," said Amelia. "She's a good cook, Daddy. We're having shrimp. I helped peel."

And here was the girl herself, carrying a steaming wok full of stir-fried shrimp and vegetables. Paz watched her place it on the table, amid applause. She looked up and he met her gaze. A chill flashed up his neck, blossomed out in sweat on his forehead. There was a mask there, too, but behind it was not just Jenny Simpson.

They ate and engaged in the usual chat, in which Paz joined when it would have been rude not to. They seemed like children to him; it was like sitting down at a kids' birthday party, pleasant, unchallenging, slightly tedious. When they were done, he went out into the garden and picked a few ripe mangoes from his tree. He cut them up efficiently at the table and fed his guests the dulcet yellow flesh, together with the coconut ice cream that Jenny fetched from the freezer.

After this dessert was done, Paz said, "Who's up for an expedition?"

"Where to?" Lola asked.

"I think we should go by Jenny's old homestead. We could bring Professor Cooksey a little basket of mangoes."

"They have plenty of mangoes on the property," said Jenny.

"Well, we'll bring a bottle of *aguardiente,* too. We'll sit around and drink *aguardiente* and eat mangoes and talk. They have a big open-air pool with tropical fish in it. We could go skinny-dipping after we get high on *aguardiente.*"

"I'm up for that," said Zwick, and Beth Morgensen produced a naughty laugh.

"Shouldn't we call?" Lola asked.

"Oh, I don't think so," said Paz. "Dr. Cooksey keeps an open house. He's a welcoming kind of guy. Isn't that right, Jenny?"

Who shrugged and said, "I guess."

"We'll want bathing suits, those of us who require them," said Paz.

They all piled into the Volvo and drove to the house on Ingraham. Paz took his bow and arrows along with the fruit and the *aguardiente;* no one asked why. As predicted, Professor Cooksey was home and perfectly gracious, as if he were used to groups of mainly strangers dropping by in the evening. Cooksey arranged them all around the big table in the terrace, and they drank a round from Paz's bottle, chased with beers. Cooksey expatiated in a lively manner about the history and architecture of the house and its gardens, and about the construction and ecological design of the fishpond. Those who had not seen this marvel asked to see it, so Cooksey led the party into the garden. He switched on the underwater lights, and they all gawked.

Taking advantage of this distraction, Cooksey approached Jenny and said in a confidential tone, "I'm very pleased to see you again, my dear. Are you back for good?"

"Sure. I was just helping out over there."

"Are you quite all right? You look different."

"Yeah, well, I'm still a little bent out of shape from what happened."

"Of course. You haven't seen Moie since the, ah . . ."

"No," she said. "Have you?"

"Not as such. But he's certainly about."

At that moment Scotty and Geli Vargos came down one of the paths. The woman stopped short when she saw the new people. She seemed about to retreat the way she had come when Jenny spotted her.

"Oh, there's Geli!" she cried and ran to greet her friend with hugs and Jennyesque babble, at which Geli collapsed into sobs. Jenny led her away to a nearby bench, where the two engaged in what seemed like intense conversation. Zwick, Lola, Beth, and Amelia had missed this byplay and were now splashing in the shallows of the pool.

"I sort of figured you had her stashed here," said a voice at Cooksey's side.

"And why did you think that, Mr. Paz? Although *stashed* is not the word I would have used. Geli seems to be having family difficulties."

"Oh, yeah, you could say that. Difficulties you arranged."

"Again, arranged would not have been my word. I think that what's happening here is something rather outside any concept of arrangement. Or perhaps, having been a copper, you see everything in terms of plots and conspiracies."

"Tell me you don't have anything to do with the guy who's been blowing up pumping stations."

"Oh, that. I suppose I had some purely theoretical discussions about how to make, shape, fuse, and detonate certain charges. Kevin and his friend were interested, and being a professional teacher, it's hard for me to keep from sharing information at my command, especially as the same material can easily be found on the Internet. I suppose I was concerned that they not blow up merely themselves. I explained to them that it would be quite futile to restore the Glades by explosives alone, but, you know, impetuous youth. The terrorist's name is Kearney, by the way. He worked at the zoo, which is where they got the jaguar droppings for the silly game they played at the houses of the Consuela people. He shouldn't be hard to find."

"You didn't try to discourage them or call the cops?"

"No, I didn't, although I just gave him to you. I would feel responsible were he to kill himself or anyone else. I suppose, being a scientist and a beneficiary of western civ, I should be quite against tearing it to pieces. But these children do so much less damage than western civ does to itself that it seems absurd to go bonkers about their pathetic efforts. When it does collapse, that will not be the way."

Paz ignored this and said, "And obviously, you knew that Moie was doing these murders, and you helped him."

Cooksey smiled at this. "Well, he hardly needed help. Moie and his spotted friend are quite capable of doing anything they please. As for going to the police . . . they'd think I was barking mad if I told them the truth. They'd think *you* were as well, as I imagine you know."

"Yeah, you got that right," Paz admitted. "I'm curious about one thing, though. I already figured out that you got the names of the Consuela people from Ms. Vargos there, and that you got them somehow to this priest in the jungle. How did you know that Moie would come?"

Cooksey chuckled and rolled his eyes skyward. It was getting hard for Paz to see his face in the growing dusk, but he saw that. Cooksey said, "Honestly, my dear man, you give me far too much credit. Our Jenny will have told you about the death of my wife, how she exhausted herself trying to rescue some tiny portion of the living information being turned into money during that time, and so met her doom.

What Jenny didn't say, because I didn't tell her, is this. First, the destruction of that particular patch of forest was a Consuela operation, and so all the calamities that followed in my life may be laid at the door of that firm. Second, after she died I went quite insane. I took a *canoa* and traveled upriver until I got to San Pedro Casivare, the last place on the map. I drank pisco. I had enough money to drink myself to death, which was my plan. There was one other fellow there who seemed to have the same thing in mind."

"The priest," said Paz.

"Just so. Father Timothy. Well, not to draw this out, we exchanged sad stories, and after that we drank a little less each day, and fished more. He decided to return to being a priest, to the extent that he resolved to seek holy martyrdom among a tribe of people we'd heard of, who routinely killed anyone who strayed within their borders. He convinced me that I owed it to my daughter to go home and take care of her. So I did; I took care of her by killing her. She was the image of my wife."

Cooksey fell silent here. Paz waited, observing that Cooksey was staring at the group by the pool, and especially, it seemed, at the frolicking Amelia. The adults had removed varying levels of clothing. Zwick and Scotty were in their shorts. Jenny was entirely nude, as was Beth. Lola and Amelia were in suits, Geli in bra and panties. Someone had brought the *aguardiente* bottle out and a bottle of Mount Gay rum to keep it company; little remained in either. The first faint feelings of uneasiness prickled in Paz's belly. There was something a little too exuberant about the scene. Geli Vargos, for example, had been depressed a moment ago; now she was near naked and whooping.

Cooksey began to speak again, distracting him from these thoughts. "The priest went to the Runiya, and I came here. When I found out who Geli was, I encouraged her to discover what Consuela was doing, and I passed the information on to the priest, who used it to achieve his martyrdom, a little late, but better late than never. I imagined that naturalists or environmentalists or whoever would pick up on that information and make a fuss. I assure you I did not expect Moie."

"Why didn't you make a fuss at this end? You had this whole environmental organization here."

"Yes, well, that would have compromised Geli, wouldn't it? She has, let's say, mixed loyalties. She wanted to avoid what eventually happened, Colombian bad boys arriving in force. Also, as soon as we began to make the sort of stink respectable environmentalists can make, Consuela would have vanished in a tangled trail of dummy companies. And the cut would have continued. What I hoped for was that Father Tim would appear on the scene full of wrath, with photos and so forth. But in the event he somehow sent Moie. But you understand, of course, that something much larger is happening here."

"What do you mean, larger?"

"Well, to begin with, why did you suddenly decide to arrive tonight with this group of people? A rather peculiar thing for you to do, yes?"

"I was advised to in the course of a . . . religious ritual," said Paz, and felt stupid at how this sounded.

"Yes, I'd imagined something like that. You know, personally I have virtually no sympathy in that area: nothing to do with belief or disbelief, a matter of temperament, I suppose. Perhaps in reaction to my mother: she was always looking vaguely off and predicting events."

"Did they happen?"

"More or less. Mum was a competent plain witch, and had been trained by several famous shamans. In any case, whatever talent she had didn't pass on to me, although I can usually spot it when I see it in another. You have it—I noticed it when we met earlier—and of course our Jenny is in a class of her own."

Here he gazed to where Jenny was poised on a flat rock at the lip of the waterfall, about to dive into the pool. The pool lamps illuminated her from below, setting red sparks in her hair, and giving to her face and body the appearance of a sculpted figure from a forgotten and terrible cult.

"Ah, magnificent!" Cooksey exclaimed softly when she had vanished in a splash of dark water. "But not entirely human. Do you know, when she arrived, everyone here thought she was mentally deficient, but that's not the case at all. She's perfectly competent at the ordinary tasks of life, and in at least one area, wasp taxonomy, she's nearly brilliant, despite being a practical illiterate. She has what we call a feeling for the organism, very rare indeed. I think her story is that her upbringing was so perfectly dreadful that at an early age she simply drew a magic circle around some inner core of her being and sheltered there, while responding minimally to what was happening to her body. A perfectly empty vessel, perfectly open to . . . whatever. God. Gods. The pulse of nature. Moie thinks she's quite something, and he should know. But back to tonight. Here you are, summoned in some way, and here we are, and why do you suppose that is?"

"I'm not really sure," said Paz, "but it has something to do with my daughter. He wants her."

"Yes, he does. I've tried to think why. Come with me, I believe the drinks table needs refreshing." At that he moved off toward the house, and Paz followed. The night remained warm but not sultry, perfect in fact, and the breeze had dropped to nothing. Every blade and leaf of foliage was still as stone, and the larger trees and shrubs seemed to Paz to have a presence, as if they had personalities. It was very like being at a *bembé,* the slight thickening of the air, the way living objects seemed to be haloed with tiny spirals of neon light. Paz's head felt oddly heavy, as if the stones of his *orisha* were really, rather than figuratively, sitting in his head, and behind him, intimately close, as if someone treaded on his heels, or was wearing his body like a suit of clothes, he felt the loom of his saint.

He didn't follow Cooksey into the house but waited on the patio. For some reason he was reluctant to leave the outdoors, to suffer artificial structure around him. He spent the time (of uncertain duration—there was something wrong with the flow of time as well, he discovered) contemplating a banana tree, its goodness, the modest green beauty of its long leaves, the dense dark redness of its fruits. Then Cooksey emerged bearing a tin tray upon which sat an ice bucket, several bottles of various spirits, and a six-pack of St. Pauli Girl beer.

"And have you come up with any conclusions?" Paz asked as he snagged one of the beers.

"Oh, mere theorizing. I suppose all this comes under the heading of some things man was not meant to know, as in those old horror films, but it seems to me that this is in the nature of a reverse butterfly effect. You're familiar with the term?"

"It's from chaos theory. The butterfly in China makes the tornado in Iowa."

"Just so," said Cooksey, setting the tray down on the poolside table. The swimming party had now wrapped themselves in towels taken from the plywood box and were arranged on lounge chairs and smooth rocks. Only Amelia and Jenny were still playing in the water. There was something very Greek about the gathering now, thought Paz, and it wasn't just the towels. He mentioned this to Cooksey.

"Yes, I was getting to that. It's Pan come again. Real Eros has been drained from the world these many centuries and now it's back in this little garden for the night. But to continue: a reverse butterfly effect would be when something gigantic and complex throws out something tiny and simple, which yet has a significance at some other level of being. I'll tell you a little story." He poured a healthy measure of scotch into a plastic cup and drank from it. "When I was quite a small boy, my mother took me to visit a relative of hers in a village by the sea, in Norfolk. It was late in the war, and when we arrived, we found that an errant German flying bomb had landed nearby and exploded. No one was hurt and there was almost no damage, but a small piece of metal from the blast had flown into this man's garden and struck down an ancient Bourbon rosebush. The old gent was carrying on as if all of the Second World War had been a vast conspiracy to destroy this particular rosebush. Quite dotty really, but it stuck in my mind, the idea that immense enterprises produce these strange little catastrophes, and further, that from some unknowable vantage point these tiny events are significant indicators. On the one hand fifty millions of dead people, on the other a killed rosebush."

"That doesn't make any sense," said Paz. He was trying to concentrate on Amelia and Lola, to fix their location in his mind, so he could move to protect them when whatever was about to happen took place. For something *was* about to happen: the queerness he had been feeling for the last few minutes (and was it really just minutes—surely it had been strange for a longer time) had turned to dread, and he felt something like madness plucking at the edges of his mind. He started to move toward his family. Cooksey drifted in his wake, still talking.

"Yes, it doesn't make *sense,* not from our viewpoint, but perhaps there are others. There may be imperatives of which we know nothing, any more than the fig wasp does when she sacrifices her individual life for the preservation of her species. Studying the social insects gives one a somewhat different perspective about the survival of the individual, you know. In any case, when my family died, or was killed, I devoted a good deal of thought to the subject, descending at least partway into lunacy, as you might understand, being a family man yourself, but one thought did emerge that I rather fancied, which was that *something* is trying to send us a message."

"Something," said Paz. He was now within a few yards of where Amelia and his wife lay, swathed in towels. Lola was rubbing her daughter's hair. Zwick and Beth lay on one of the chaises, Scotty and Geli on the other. Jenny was standing, wrapped in a yellow towel, drying her hair with a green one. She was looking into the dark, dense foliage beyond the reach of the pool lights, as if waiting for something. Everything seemed to be moving too slowly, as it does in a dream. Behind him, Cooksey's voice continued.

"Yes, the planet, for example, or its guardians, or the noetic sphere, however you want to describe it. You see at a certain point we decided that everything was dead, including us, and that it was perfectly all right to turn the entire substance of nature into some imaginary abstraction—power, or some idea of the nation, or race, or just at present it happens to be money. So let's say this *something* has awakened after a long nap, not really long for something that's been alive for four billion years, but long in our terms, and it noticed a little itch, a little raw spot, and it scratches idly, and that was the twentieth century, a hundred million dead from war and famine, but unfortunately we kept on, learning nothing, and now it's a little more interested, because now we're fiddling with the basic balancing mechanisms of the whole shebang. And now it turns out that great Pan wasn't dead after all. Now he wakes up, not among *us,* of course, because we're dead, but among Moie's people, and because of what happened to me I'm impelled, let's say, to provide the impetus to bring him here."

"And what does it all mean?" Paz asked, not because he thought Cooksey really knew, but to keep him talking as if his talking was a preface to whatever was going to happen and it had to wait until he was finished. Paz thought he needed a little more time. He also needed his bow and arrows. This was a new thought, and he felt his body turning away, being pulled back toward the Volvo. He lifted the rear hatch with some difficulty; for his hands seemed to have forgotten how to work the latch, and the whole vehicle seemed unhealthy in some way, hideous, something that should not exist. He walked back to the pool, holding the bow and the quiver of arrows. The last time Paz had actually shot a bow, the arrows had been tipped with suction cups. He had no idea what he was supposed to do with the things, only that it was necessary for him to have them in hand.

No one seemed to have moved; Cooksey seemed not to have finished, seemed to have been talking to the night. ". . . in any case, we could be seeing a new order of things, a nexus of some kind. We see this in evolution occasionally, a time or a place where speciation seems to move at an accelerated pace—we have no idea why. Now we may have a situation where a certain kind of unconscious evil is directly punished, a partial solution to the question of why bad things happen to good people and not the reverse. Someone gives an order and at the other end of a long chain of actors we have murder, destruction, rapine, the world ground to paste to change the registers in certain bank accounts. What would it be like if the hand that gave the order was then bitten off? Would *that* change things, or are we so ungodly stupid that not even *that* would work. Or what if, as now, a child sacrifice were required? Would *that* get our fucking attention?"

Cooksey's voice had risen for this last phrase, but no one seemed to notice. Everyone was looking at Jaguar.

# Twenty

**J**aguar emerged soundlessly from the darkness and now stood full on the paved patio that surrounded the pool. He was a lot bigger than Paz had imagined, nearly the size of an African lion, but leaner and longer, much larger than a real jaguar. It shone as if illuminated from within, like a jack-o'-lantern, its black rosettes seeming to vibrate against their golden ground. Cooksey was now speechless, frozen, his mouth still open holding the shape of his last words. Paz wanted to yell at Lola to take the child and run, but his voice was somehow missing. He felt his hands withdraw an arrow from the quiver and nock it on the bowstring. The arrows were long and fletched with bright green parrot feathers, and tipped with points of milky stone, very sharp.

Jaguar glided across the pool patio to where Lola and Amelia lay. The child's head was bent across her mother's knees. Lola had been untangling Amelia's wet hair with her fingers. Paz could see his daughter look into the topaz lanterns of the god's eyes. She had a soft smile on her face. Lola was looking at the beast with what seemed to Paz to be casual polite interest, as if the girl were about to introduce a new and suitable playmate. Everyone else seemed to be fixed solidly in place, like the background figures in a classical painting, an effect augmented by their draped towels, their languid postures.

Paz decided that he had been wrong and that this was, in fact, a particularly vivid dream, and really, just like the ones he'd had so often in the recent past. There was his girl and there was the jaguar and it would take her as a sacrifice and everything would be better for everyone, the world would be made whole again by it, and he felt an odd stirring of pride that his daughter should be so honored. And here he contemplated the being of the girl herself, the lines of inheritance combined in her, the generations of Jews back to Jerusalem, and Africans back to Ife, and Spaniards back to wherever, Rome, Greece, the Gothic lands, Arabia, all the ancestors, studying in synagogues, serving the gods of Yoruba, serving the masters in the cane fields, conquering the infidels, worshipping Allah, all to produce the particularity of this gleaming child . . .

But now these portentous musings were interrupted by a swift movement near the pool. Jenny Simpson had dashed out of her place in the frieze and was hanging on Jaguar's neck, tugging at the golden head, shouting "No, no. Stop it, leave her alone," which Paz thought was absurd, she was treating him like a naughty puppy, and he felt vaguely annoyed at her for disturbing the stately aesthetics of the scene. Jaguar shuddered like a dog, flinging the young woman aside, casting her down on the paving with an audible thud. Paz heard a sound, a deep growl so low he thought it might be imaginary, like one of the false sounds one hears upon just falling into sleep.

*Ararah. Arararararh.*

As if it were a signal, Paz felt something move inside his head at the sound, felt his limbs moving to the urging of the Other within, felt the tension of the bow in his hands, the feather against his cheek, felt the twang of the release in his shoulder and his spine.

Jaguar opened his jaws above the child just before the arrow struck him behind his foreleg.

Paz tried to keep his eyes open, but an agency deep in his midbrain forced them shut to avoid registering events that evolution did not permit his brain to process. He recorded a

wind and an unidentifiable noise, though, and when he could
see again, he saw chaos on the pool deck. A small brown
man with a bowl haircut was lying in a pool of blood, coughing blood, with Paz's long arrow stuck in his side. Zwick
was kneeling by his side, rallying long-dormant medical instincts. He took a moment to yell, "Jesus, Paz, why the hell
did you do that!"

Lola meanwhile was attending Jenny, who had seized dramatically just as the arrow struck. She frothed at the mouth,
her naked body bent into a paraboloid, with only the crown
of her head and her heels touching the ground. Paz found
himself with an armful of Amelia, who was shrieking and
shaking as if she had absolutely rolled in sand spurs. The
others were standing around the stricken pair, trying to make
themselves useful. Paz carried his girl away to the patio,
where he sat down in a chair and held the small body to him,
kissing her damp hair and murmuring reassurances. The
cries eventually subsided to whooping gasps and then one
last sigh, and she said, sobbing still, "I was scared, Daddy."

"Of course you were. It was very scary. I was scared, too."

"It was going to eat me up, for real!"

"Yes, it was."

"Part of me wanted to get eated up and part of me was so
scared."

"Yes, that was your bad dream, wasn't it? But now it's
over. It can't hurt you anymore."

"And it turned into Moie," she said. "I saw it! Everything
in the air was all *ghizzhy*." She waved her fingers and twisted
them around themselves to illustrate just how *ghizzhy*. "And
Moie got shot with a arrow."

"That's right," said Paz.

"But he won't die because he's good, like Frodo. He got
*wounded,* didn't he?"

"Yes. I hope he'll be all right."

"And Jenny was being weird and shaking. That was really
scary, too. Why was she doing that?"

"She has a sickness that makes her do that. But don't
worry, your mom will take good care of her."

They sat for a while, Paz's mind a perfect blank. Then Amelia said, "Could we look at the parrot? And I want a Coke."

They looked at the parrot. A Coke was found. After some period of innocent fun, which Paz was content to let last for a week, they found a lounger and lay down upon it. All his bones ached. Then Dr. Wise arrived to check on her family. After determining that her daughter was fine, she stood over her husband and said, "You want to tell me what the hell that was all about? Why did you shoot that poor little man?"

"Because what I saw was a very large jaguar just about to bite our daughter's head off. What did you see?"

"What did I . . . ? Jimmy, I saw what was *there*. We were all sitting around, relaxed after swimming, and this guy strolls out from the dark and Jenny goes over and talks to him like she knew him and the next thing I know, I heard the bow and the guy was lying down with an arrow through him."

"How is he, by the way?"

"Oh, he'll probably survive—you seem to have missed the heart. He's got a sucking chest wound. We clipped the arrow, but they'll have to extract it in an OR. The ambulance is on the way. Christ, how the hell are we going to explain what happened?"

"Asshole fooling with bow and arrow accidentally shoots friendly visitor from foreign land," said Paz. "The Miami cops deal with shit like that all the time. I'll plead guilty, suspended sentence. How's the redhead?"

"She's out of seizure and in her bed in the house. I had some Soma in my bag and fed her a couple of caps, and some Xanax. She'll be down for hours."

"Good," said Paz, "and so once again pharmaceuticals solve the problem. You know, Amelia saw the jaguar, too."

She didn't quite roll her eyes. "Jimmy, she's a *child*. What I don't like is that you had a hallucination so strong that you nearly killed a human being. Can you understand that? It means you're not *safe*."

"Sit down, Lola," said Paz gently, and she found herself complying. She placed herself at the foot end of the lounger, not touching him. There was something in his eyes, a kind of presence, that she did not recall seeing there before.

He said, "I've been racking my brains on this. Why did he want Amelia? Why was she the sacrifice? And why did he think a sacrifice was necessary? And what was the meaning of what he did and what I did?"

"Shooting the Indian?"

"No, I mean my whole involvement in this, becoming made to the *orishas,* the whole string of events and coincidences that put me in a particular place at a particular time. And, once again, it wasn't an Indian. It was Jaguar. It was a god or a demigod—a spirit inside an impossible animal. And I see from the look on your face that you've completely forgotten the dreams, how you were weeping like a baby because you couldn't sleep, because Jaguar was in your head telling you stories about how *right* it was to give your daughter to him, and your whole shelf of drugs couldn't help you, but a little bag of magic made by an old Cuban lady fixed you up just fine."

She felt sweat pop out on her forehead and the hair stood stiff on the backs of her arms and on her neck.

"Yeah," he said, searching her eyes, "*now* you remember. If you want, I'll take you into the bushes around the pool and you can see the tracks of a huge cat, fresh tracks, and you'll have to cook up a reasonable explanation for *that,* too."

She said, "So what's *your* explanation? Assuming I buy the story."

"I don't have one. That's my *point*. Look, the difference between us is that you think that at the fucking absolute innermost heart of the universe there's an explanation, a calculation, a formula. I don't. I think that at the fucking absolute innermost heart of the universe there's a mystery. And we just saw, at the pool just now, and in this whole thing with Moie, an edge of it we don't usually see, the stuff we're not usually *allowed* to see. You're going to rationalize it away, which is fine, it's who you are, but I can't do that. I have to treat it with reverence and look at it with awe. All I can say is, it was a good day. The maiden was saved, and the beast was defeated. Another time it might go the wrong way and I'll treat that with reverence and awe, too. So are you sorry you married me now? Speaking of the inexplicable."

"No," she said, "I'm not. But could you be like *in charge* of all that stuff? So I don't have to ever, ever think about it?"

He laughed. "Like taking out the garbage."

"In a manner of speaking."

Sirens ensued then, succeeded by paramedics. They whisked Moie off, attended by Lola. After that, the rest of the party, save Cooksey, who had elected to sit with Jenny, drifted back to the patio, where they all had a round of stiff drinks.

"Well, Paz," said Zwick, "you really know how to throw a party."

Paz looked around the group. "No one noticed anything strange?" he asked. "Everyone just saw me shoot a harmless Indian?"

"What else were we supposed to see?" asked Beth Morgensen.

Paz ignored her. He was looking at Scotty, who had the appearance of a man recently kicked in the groin. He wouldn't meet Paz's gaze. Another one who saw the impossible and wanted to forget it as soon as he could. The other adults had all been scientifically trained to observe only objectively verifiable phenomena.

"Come with me, I want to check on something." He took a four-cell flashlight from the glove compartment of the Volvo and strode rapidly to the path where the being had emerged from the dark. The path was made of coarse oolitic sand, and it did not take long to find a huge paw mark and then another.

"What do you say to that, Doctors?" he asked.

"Oh, for God's sake!" said Zwick. "Tell me you didn't set this all up and shoot that guy with an arrow just to make some stupid point about mystical jaguars!"

Paz looked around the circle of faces, dim in the side glow of the flashlight, and found no support.

"Okay, fine," he said. "I'll take you guys home."

\* \* \*

**W**hen she opened her eyes, there was Cooksey, and she was glad. She was on her pallet in her old alcove in Cooksey's quarters, dressed in one of his worn khaki shirts. Cooksey was wearing a dark tracksuit. His face was smeared with black smudges.

"I seized," she observed.

"You did indeed. How do you feel?"

"Okay. A little sore. Something happened before I went out."

"Yes. Jaguar showed up in his glory and pride. He was going to take that little girl, and you very heroically threw yourself in his way. The sacrifice was not made. God alone knows what it all means. Then Mr. Paz shot it with an arrow, and it turned back into our Moie."

"Is he dead?"

"It appears not. Our party coincidentally included two doctors, or perhaps coincidence is no longer the operative word. In any case, he survived. Do you recall any of that?"

"Sort of. It's kind of like when you remember a dream. And it wasn't really Jimmy. I saw . . . kind of tangled up in him something else, something bigger, a glowing thing, I don't know what it was. But it was good. And . . . but Moie is good, too, isn't he? And Jaguar. He killed those bad guys, and he was only trying to protect his country." She sighed. "I don't understand any of this, Cooksey."

"No, and I'm not sure whether the kinds of good and bad we see in the cinema are useful concepts here. We are in deep waters, my girl, and we poor scientists are out of our depth. And I'm afraid it's not over. Issues less cosmic but just as deadly remain for us to resolve."

"What do you mean?"

"I mean that I expect a visit shortly from the gang that kidnapped you and killed Kevin."

"They're coming here? Because of me?"

"No, because of Geli. They need her to put pressure on her grandfather, because he's crucial to some criminal scheme of theirs."

"But how do they know she's here? She told me she didn't tell anyone where she was, not even her mom."

"Actually, they know because I called her grandfather's house and informed the servant who answered the phone. Of course, all the servants have been suborned or threatened, and so I expect the gang leader knew within minutes. They've been waiting for us to be alone."

"Jesus, Cooksey! Why the hell did you do that?"

"Because I want to kill them, my dear. All of them. That's why you see me in my commando togs and face. I'm afraid I'm rather more like Moie than I revealed. These people are the same people involved in the forest cutting that killed my wife."

"I thought that was a snake."

"Yes, well, I'm sorry to have had to dissimulate there, but a certain security was necessary, and I didn't want to burden you with the truth. In fact, the timber companies hire thugs to clear the people from the forest before they cut, and in our case it was the Hurtado organization that was responsible. Portia had hired a village to catch specimens for her, and while she was there the place was raided by these people, or those hired by them. Everyone was killed. So, only figuratively was she killed by a snake. I've been working toward this evening for a number of years. I hope you'll forgive me."

"Cooksey, this is crazy, just you and Scotty against all those guys . . ."

"Scotty will not be involved. He's been told to look after Geli. They're in his cottage with the doors and windows locked and barred, with instructions to call the police if it goes wrong. And he has his shotgun. Meanwhile, we have to keep you safe during the coming fracas. I can shove my big cabinet in front of the entrance to this alcove. It's not obvious that there's another room within my office, and I doubt that anyone will come searching for you in any case. It's Geli they want. As for your door outside—we'll just have to rely on the lock. It's going to be dark, of course—I intend to pull the fuses from the mains. This will favor the defender, you see."

He rose then and left the little room, returning a moment later brandishing a large black revolver. "My trusty sidearm," he said, showing his long teeth. "Are you comfortable? Is there anything I can get you?"

"No, I'm fine."

He sat on the edge of the pallet. "Then I'm off. In case of the worst, there's a packet with your name on it in the right-hand drawer of my desk. It has some letters of introduction should you wish to pursue a career in wasp entomology. You should work on your reading, of course, but there are a number of people I know who would be happy to have you in their labs. I've made some financial arrangements as well, so you won't be absolutely destitute, I hope you don't mind . . ."

"Cooksey . . ."

"No, no weepies, dear, we haven't the time for it. And may I say what a pleasure it's been knowing you these last months, quite the nicest thing that happened to me in a very bleak time. Oh, and you can have my *Wind in the Willows*."

Before she could say a word to him he was out of the room and pushing the high cabinet into place. She lay back on her pillow, cried briefly, and then exhaustion carried her back into sleep.

El Silencio had prepared for the night's work as best he could, given the short notice. He had located a contact of Hurtado's, a small-time dealer who operated out of a derelict trailer park in the south county, and he had taken his men there to run through the operation. The problem was that although he knew the approximate layout of the property, he had no idea where the woman might be when they arrived. He had decided, therefore, to send teams of two to each of the two small cottages, while he and Ochoa waited at the main house. If the woman was in one of the cottages, they'd bring her out; if she was in the house, then the whole group would surround and assault it from several directions. They rehearsed these evolutions in the trailer park until El

Silencio was satisfied that his people would not actually trip all over themselves during the real thing. He was not really confident, but he had little choice. Besides, he didn't think that a woman and a couple of civilians would give them much trouble.

They arrived at two in the morning, pulling right into the driveway of the property. The gate was not locked, and the place was completely dark and quiet, the only sound being the wind in the foliage and splashing water. El Silencio recalled that there was some kind of pool. The night was clear, with a crescent moon, and with these and the sky glow from the city, there was enough light to walk without stumbling out here, although it would be quite dark on the paths.

He and Ochoa went through the archway that led to the patio and stood in the shadows while their teams set out on the paths leading to the two cottages. From here they could keep watch on the front door of the main house and also keep the exit from the property under watch. They waited without talking.

Then an orange flash lit the undersides of the palm fronds above them and then came the BANG, far louder than a gunshot. They saw the glow of a bright fire. Ochoa cursed and ran out. El Silencio heard a high-pitched shrieking, like that of a pig being stuck, mixed with curses and calls for Momma. In a moment, there was another, louder blast, which rattled the palm tops and the windows.

He heard Ochoa shouting and the sound of footsteps going away. The shrieks died away. Now three loud gunshots, which sounded to El Silencio like .45s. Then silence.

The gangster moved farther into the dark corner of the patio, sinking down behind a large, covered propane grill cart. It was his principle that when things went to shit, the best thing to do was not to race off as Ochoa had just done, but to remain calm and quiet, to see what would develop. He took out his nine-millimeter pistol and listened. Obviously, someone had planted bombs on the paths, and these had taken out his four men. He hadn't thought that these people had the skills to do that, but he had been wrong and that was that. Ochoa had just as obviously stumbled into an ambush, yet another argument for staying calm and quiet. He could probably escape himself, but he was reluctant to do this. He had never failed before, and he thought he could still shoot all the people opposing him and take the Vargos woman. He actually preferred to work alone.

He heard a woman's voice calling out, and then a man speaking. A door slammed shut. He waited for over forty minutes and was about to stand up and change position when he heard footsteps on a sandy path, then the sound of steps on paving. A thin man of around fifty dressed in black clothes walked past into the patio. El Silencio rose from behind the grill and shot him three times in the back.

The bombs had awakened Jenny, and she was looking out the window of the door that led from her alcove to the patio, so she saw Cooksey fall. Without thinking she opened the door and darted out. The man was standing over Cooksey's body. She saw the blood pooling beneath him and let out a cry. The man heard it and turned around, raising his gun. He said something in Spanish and pointed the gun at her. She spun on her heel and ran from the patio.

El Silencio almost shot the girl but checked himself at the last instant. This was clearly the redhead who had escaped from the garage, and he was intensely curious to find out how she had done that. Also, once he had her, he could make her tell him where La Vargos was. He sped off in pursuit.

They were on a dark path. She and El Silencio hurdled the slumped and smoking forms of two of his men and then she cut sharply to the left, down a narrower path that rose slightly and changed from coarse sand to rough stone. The sound of rushing water grew progressively louder. He put on more speed. The girl was not more than three feet from him. Suddenly they burst into the open. His shoes clattered on rock. He reached out to grab at her flowing red hair and then he saw her leap into the air and sink out of sight. His feet splashed through water, he tried to slow down, but his thin city shoes slipped on the slick stones and he felt himself falling through the dark.

It was a fifteen-foot drop to the bottom of the waterfall, and El Silencio fell badly, suffering a compound fracture of his left arm and numerous deep scrapes on his legs and back from the rough coral rock. The force of the falls sent him deep under the water, but he was a competent swimmer and was able to struggle one-armed to the surface. There he rolled onto his back, and keeping his left arm pressed to his chest, he began kicking to move himself to the edge of the pond. He was thinking about what he would do to this girl when he had her.

The first piranha hit at his thigh where it bled from its scrape, ripping out a chunk of meat the size of a shot glass. El Silencio made a sound that would have been a scream in a person with normal vocal machinery but emerged as a long rasping yawp. He flapped both arms and sank, and then the whole school was upon him.

Jenny sat at the shallow end and watched the water churn and churn and grow reddish and then become quiet again. She ran back to the patio. Cooksey was not quite dead yet, but unlike the dying men she had seen in the movies, he did not have any choked last words. She called the police and then sat by him and held his hand while he died. Her tears fell on his face, making clear tracks through the commando paint.

Jimmy Paz slept fitfully that night, although he observed that his wife was perfectly at rest, and after popping in and out of sleep, he decided to get up and start his new life as a maybe demigod with a cup of coffee. He made a pint of Bustelo in the stove-top hourglass pot and warmed an equal amount of milk in a pan, and when the *café con leche* was ready he took it out to the back patio with a plate of Cuban bread toast, butter, and guava jam. He watched the sky go from pink to cerulean blue, dotted with tiny specks of fleece, and then, to his surprise, the front doorbell rang, and it was Tito Morales.

"We need to talk," said the cop. He looked rumpled and frowsy.

"Want some coffee?" Paz asked amiably.

Morales did. They sat at the counter in the kitchen while Paz fixed him the same kind of breakfast he had just enjoyed.

"This is about the Indian, right?" asked Paz as Morales took his first grateful sip.

"What Indian is that?"

"Our Indian. He showed up at Zenger's estate last night and I shot him with my Oshosi bow and arrow."

"Your Oshosi bow and arrow," said Morales in a flat tone. "And why would you do that, Jimmy?"

"Because he was in the form of a giant jaguar and he was about to eat Amelia. Luckily it was a magic arrow and it knocked him out and turned him back into our Indian. He's in South Miami Hospital. I thought that's why you came over."

"No, and I'm going to temporarily forget what you just said, because they dragged me into this out of a sound sleep and I might be hallucinating. What I got is a—what is it, septuple? A septuple homicide situation at the Zenger place. I got four of what look like Colombian *chuteros* blown up by bombs, another one shot dead, and another I don't know what it is, a piece of meat chewed up by those fucking piranhas in that fishpond. No face, no fingers. It could be Jimmy Hoffa."

"That's only six."

"Cooksey's dead, too. Someone shot him, unclear who. The Simpson girl called it in. She told me an interesting story. That's why I'm here, see if you can cast some light."

"What's her story?"

"Well, she says that Cooksey was the mastermind behind it all. These Colombians apparently killed his wife years ago down there in jungle-land, and he set the whole thing up. He knew all about this Consuela deal from Geli Vargos, old Ibanez's granddaughter, and he somehow imported this Indian from South America to do the murders of your dad and Fuentes, which brought Hurtado and his merry band to Miami. The Indian whacked a few of his people and—okay, here's the part she wasn't too clear about—Hurtado had some kind of deal with Ibanez, and Ibanez was getting cold feet on it, so Hurtado wanted to snatch Geli to pressure the old guy. Cooksey set all this up, and he made bombs to take out the bad guys, and he shot one, and pushed the last guy into the pool, but not before getting shot himself. Which is bullshit, but I can't prove it. The girl was wringing wet when we got there, so she was obviously playing in the pool with Señor No-face, who's probably the one who shot Cooksey. I got no idea exactly how it went down, however, not that it matters. We picked up Hurtado, too, by the way."

"Really? I thought he was in the breeze."

"He was, but the girl said Cooksey had tipped off the Ibanez house where Geli was, and that the maid or someone there had tipped Hurtado. We rousted the house, and the maid gave up the number she called him at and we found him in a fleabag in North Miami Beach. I don't know what we'll hold him on. Getting a phone call is no crime, and we have no direct connection between him and the dead people at Zenger's. Now, tell me about this Indian."

Paz smiled. "The Indian's going to walk."

"Fuck he is! He killed four people that we know for sure about. I guarantee you that the naked footprints in that garage and the prints on the gate near your dad's house are both going to match up with him."

"You're probably right. In which case you have two choices. Let me lay them out for you. Plan A is you book the Indian—his name's Moie, incidentally—and you explain to Major Oliphant and the state's attorney all about how a little Indian who can't weigh one-thirty managed to carry off all by himself four murders, including one against a heavily guarded victim and two against armed desperadoes, while leaving jaguar footprints made by something weighing in at nearly five hundred pounds, said murders requiring superhuman strength and agility and leaving the corpses torn by what forensics will tell you could only be the teeth of a large cat. Should you choose Plan A, they will smile sadly and put you on the rubber gun squad for the duration of your career. Plan B is you got a bunch of dead Colombians from a gang noted for its ferocious murders, its gruesome revenges against traitors, a gang that was heavily involved in illegal business deals with said dead Cubans. Obviously, the dead guys did all the killings. Case closed. Oh, and as a bonus, if you pick Plan B, I will give you Hurtado, and you will have the collar of the decade and be the golden boy of the Miami PD and a hero in the Cuban community forever after. And the envelope, please . . ."

Morales stared angrily at Paz for a good thirty seconds and then seemed to deflate. "Ah, fuck this, Jimmy! He killed your father, man! How the hell can you just let him walk?"

"He had nothing to do with killing my father. My father was killed by a supernatural creature as a result of his own crimes, whether you believe it or not. Arresting Moie would be like arresting a Buick for a hit-and-run."

"Okay, man, if that's the way we're going to play it, I give up. I know when I'm over my head. Tell me about Hurtado."

"Good decision, Tito. Okay, Hurtado is a dope lord. He had a nice little laundry set up here with Consuela, but he's still a dope lord, and what I couldn't figure out was what was so important to *him* about cutting down some damn forest in the ass end of Colombia. And just this morning when I was waking up it came to me, something my sister told me about Consuela buying wood-boring equipment down there. And I called her and she described the machinery, what it was for. So I ask you, why would they need a huge wood-boring machine in a timber operation? Now you know that there's a smuggling environment nowadays where the borders are tightening up because of terrorism, they're shooting down planes, they're paying mules to swallow balloons with tiny little amounts of dope. And Hurtado has access to a scheme to import thousands of mahogany logs via a perfectly legitimate and well-established import operation."

"They're shipping dope in hollowed-out logs!"

"*Huge* fucking amounts of dope, with next to no danger that anyone is going to check a warehouse full of logs. I guarantee you that if you go to Ibanez's yard down by the docks with dope-sniffing dogs and some simple tools, you're going to hit the jackpot. I know you're beat, but you should get on this right away. You'll sleep a lot better knowing. Oh,

right, I almost forgot the bonus for making the right choice."
And he told Morales about Kearney the ecoterrorist, too.

In his hospital bed Moie speaks quietly in Spanish to the Fire-hair Woman. The *jampiri,* Paz, translates for them. They have come every day, and this is the last day, Moie thinks. He sees his death clearly now and the bright cords that tie it to his dying body. His wound is healing, yes, but all the *aryu't* has run out of him, and he is hollow, like a fig drilled out by wasps.

He can also see the deaths of the woman and the *jampiri,* so they are not really *wai'ichuranan* any longer, and this is something he had not expected to see. They are marvelous deaths, clearly of great power. Moie did not know that the *wai'ichuranan* could change themselves in this way, or that they had such *jampiri,* which is why he was defeated. Jaguar has left him for that reason, and this is also why he is dying. He tries to tell the woman how to use what she has been given, but the language is too clumsy, and there are words and ideas that can't be expressed in Spanish. He wishes that there was time for her to learn the holy speech. The greatest sadness is that his body will not be handled in the proper way and given to the river. Here in the land of the dead, he has been told, they bury the body under the earth, like a yam, which is disgusting, or else they burn it, as the Runiya do to a witch. The good thing is that the Firehair Woman says that the *chinitxi* are all dead and that the Puxto will survive.

"I would like to go back home," he says after a long silence.

"When you're better, Moie," says the *jampiri.*

"I will not be better. What I mean is, when I am dead and you have burned my body, I would like to have my ash put into our river. We burn witches, but we don't put their ash in the river, of course. Perhaps, if you do this, I will still rise to the moon to be with my ancestors."

"She says she will do this for you," says the *jampiri.* "She promises."

"And take my bag of dreams and my medicine bag back

there, too. Perhaps Jaguar will send another to be *jampiri* to the Runiya."

"She will do that as well," says the *jampiri.*

Moie says to the woman, "You should be careful where your tears fall. An enemy can use them against you."

━━━━━

Jenny Simpson and Jimmy Paz stood in the parking lot of the funeral home in which Moie has just been reduced to a can of ashes. Jenny had secured this can inside her backpack, which also contained some changes of clothing, *The Wind in the Willows,* Hogue's *Latin American Insects and Entomology,* Moie's sorcerous gear, an ultralight tent, a sleeping bag and pad, and twelve hundred dollars of the surprisingly large amount of money left to her by Nigel Cooksey. She was dressed for travel in denim cutoffs, a yellow tube top, and a Dolphins ball cap.

"You're really going to hitch down to Colombia?" said Paz.

"Yep."

"You could fly. You have money now."

"I could, but I guess I want to take a long trip alone, think all this shit through. And I want to save his money, in case I want to get an education. He would've liked that."

"There's a lot of rough country between here and there. A lot of bad guys."

"I'll be fine." She laughed. "All my life nobody ever gave a shit about me, and all of a sudden everyone's looking out for my welfare—Cooksey, you, Lola, Moie."

"Maybe no one saw your virtues before."

She shrugged. "Last night . . . that was real nice, Lola throwing me a going-away party. She thinks I'm crazy to be doing this, doesn't she?"

"Lola thinks a good deal of what people do is crazy. It's her profession."

"Word. And she doesn't buy any of this, does she? What all happened, with Jaguar and stuff."

"No, she's on a different channel."

"How will you, like, handle that?"

"With care. Love makes a lot of allowances. And Amelia knows. That'll help. And my mom."

"God, it's so totally weird all this, all the deaths and how it all worked out. You know, you have a life, and even if it sucks, you think, that's your life and it's not going to change and then, bang! You're a different person with a different life. What's up with that?"

"What's up with that is a ten-hour discussion and a lifetime of contemplation. Meanwhile, if you want to get on the road today, we better get started. I'll drop you at the Bird Road exit on the turnpike. That's probably your best bet going north."

They got in the Volvo and drove west in companionable silence. Paz reflected that both of them were different from what they had been when they first met, both kicked into change by the gods rather more directly than God typically kicked humans into change. He was glad that it had happened, and he prayed fervently that it never had to happen again. Fat chance, he thought, and laughed to himself.

Paz parked near the freeway ramp. She kissed him on the cheek, promised postcards, and left. He waited while she thumbed. Long-legged redheads with knockout bodies do not typically have to wait long for rides, and before too many minutes had passed, an eighteen-wheeler hit its brakes with a great sigh, and she climbed into its cab. Whatever else he now was, Paz was still a dad and a cop, and so he wrote down its license number before it drove away.

Jenny settled herself in the passenger seat and smiled at the driver. He was a fortyish man with long hair, a bad shave, and deeply set, bright blue eyes sporting very small pupils. As he cranked up through his gears he asked, "Where're you going, honey?" He had a Texas accent.

"Colombia."

"In Carolina?"

"No, the country. In South America."

"No lie? Hell, that's a long way for a little girl to go all by her lonesome."

She made no comment on that, so he continued the chatter. She answered when it would have been rude not to, and in response to his probings invented a set of plausible lies. They exchanged names: his was Randy Frye. Randy Frye the Good-Time Guy, as he announced. He liked to talk about himself, and he had lots of stories. By West Palm he was confident enough to make the stories a little raunchy; by Yeehaw Junction, he was probing her sexual history (unsuccessfully) and accentuating his remarks with little touches on her shoulder and arm. By Kissimmee, they were such good pals that he laid his big red hand on her inner thigh, pat pat pat, squeeze.

She turned in her seat and looked him in the face. Randy Frye noticed that her eyes, which had been pale blue, were now lambent yellow with vertical pupils. Out of her throat came a sound that should not have had a home in such a throat.

*Ararah. Ararararh.*

The semi swerved momentarily out of lane, engendering angry honks from a nearly sideswiped van. By the Orlando interchange, Frye had just about managed to forget what he had seen and heard and had invented a story about a cold little bitch, probably a lesbo, wouldn't fuck her with *your* dick . . . After that, without exchanging more than a dozen or so words, he took her all the way to Corpus Christi.

# Runiya Glossary

---

*achaurit*—lit. "the death," but also the visible spirits seen accompanying the living

*ajampik*—the spirit world

*aryu't*—spiritual wholeness, the quality of a real human being

*assua*—*Paullinia sp.*; a stimulant used in rituals

*aysiri*—a witch

*chaikora*—*Cannabis sp.*; a hypnotic

*chinitxi*—demons

*hninxa*—a sacrifice of a female child

*iwai'chinix*—lit. "calling spirits into life"; a kind of dream "therapy" of the Runiya

*jampiri*—animal spirit doctor; pl. *jampirinan*

*Jan'ichupitaolik*—Jesus Christ, lit. "he is dead and alive at the same time"

*layqua*—a spirit-catching box

*mikur-ka'a*—*Petiveria sp.*; guinea hen leaf, a plant used in medicine and magic

*pa'hnixan*—a sacrificial victim

*pacu*—a giant bluegill

*pisco*—cane liquor

Puxto—the region, the native reserve

Runiya—Moie's people, lit. "speakers of language"

*ry'uulu*—mahogany

*ryuxit*—harmony; the life force

*siwix*—disharmonious, taboo

*t'naicu*—amulet

*tayit*—honorific title

*tichiri*—a guardian spirit inhabiting the dream world

*tucunaré*—the peacock bass

*uassinai*—a plant substance of unknown origin used with other hypnotics in ritual

*unancha*—a totem or clan symbol

*unquayuvmaikat*—lit. "the falling-down gift"; epilepsy

*wai'ichuranan*—the dead people, whites; *wai'ichura* (singular)

*yana*—hallucinatory snuff used in ceremonies

# BOOKS BY MICHAEL GRUBER

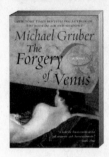

### THE FORGERY OF VENUS
**A Novel**

ISBN 978-0-06-087449-0 (pb) • ISBN 978-0-06-145304-5 (cd)

"A tour-de-force combination of suspense and characterization, as well as a primer on the world of art and art forgery." —*Seattle Times*

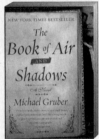

### THE BOOK OF AIR AND SHADOWS
**A Novel**

ISBN 978-0-06-145657-2 (pb)

**A *NEW YORK TIMES* BESTSELLER**

"Breathlessly engaging . . . brilliant . . . unpredictable."
—*USA Today*

## • THE JIMMY PAZ SERIES •

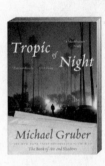

### TROPIC OF NIGHT
**A Novel**

ISBN 978-0-06-165073-4 (pb)

"A blockbuster. As unsettling as it is exciting." —*People*

### VALLEY OF BONES
**A Novel**

ISBN 978-0-06-165074-1 (pb) • ISBN 978-0-06-075930-8 (cd)

"Dazzling, literate, and downright scary."
—*Cleveland Plain Dealer*

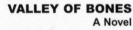

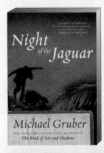

### NIGHT OF THE JAGUAR
**A Novel**

ISBN 978-0-06-165072-7 (paperback)

"An astonishing piece of fiction." —*Washington Post*